omie's Laughs

omie's Laughs

Omerline

To order additional copies of this book, contact:
Xlibris Corporation
1-888-795-4274
www.Xlibris.com
Orders@Xlibris.com
69796

I would like to dedicate this book to my husband Ray. He was so patient hearing my stories over and overr.

Many thanks to

Vic Sokeland
Ruth Cox
Debbie Houdyshell
Cindy Lammers
And all my friends who told me stories.

Contents

Being A Mother

After 21 years of marriage, my wife wanted me to take another woman out to dinner and a move. She said I love you, but I know this other woman loves you and would love to spend some time with you. The other woman that my wife wanted me to visit, was my MOTHER who has been a widow for 19 years but the demands of my work and my three children had made it possible to visit her only occasionally. That night I called to invite her to go out for dinner and a movie. What's wrong are you well she asked? My mother is the type of woman who suspects that a late night call or a surprise invitation is a sign of bad news. I thought that it would be pleasant to spend some time with you, I responded Just the two of us. She thought about it for a moment, and then said I would like that very much. That Friday after work, as I drove over to pick her up I was a bit nervous. When I arrived at her house. I noticed that she too seemed to be nervous about our date. She waited in the door with her coat on. She had curled her hair and was wearing the dress that she had worn to celebrate her last wedding anniversary. She smiled from a face that was as radiant ass an angel's. I told my friends that I was going to go out with my son, and they were impressed, she said as she got into the car. They can't wait to hear about our meeting. We went to a restaurant that, although not elegant, was very nice and cozy. My mother took my arm as if she were the First Lady. After we sat down, I had to read the menu. Her eyes could only read large print. Half way through the entries, I lifted my eyes and saw Mom sitting there staring at me. A nostalgic smile was on her lips. It was I who use to have to read the menu when you were small. She said en it's time that you relax and let me return the favor I responded. During the dinner, we had an agreeable conversation—nothing extraordinary but catching up on recent events of each other's life. We talked so much that we missed the movie. As we arrived at her house later, she said, I'll go out again, but only if you let me invite you. I agreed. How was your dinner date? Asked my wife when I got home. Very nice. Much more so than I could have imagined. I answered. A few days later, my mother died of a massive heart attack. It happened so suddenly that I didn't have a chance to do anything for her. Some time later, I received an envelope with a copy of a restaurant receipt from the same place mother and I had dined. An attached note said I paid this bill in advance. I wasn't sure that I could be there; but nevertheless, I paid for two plates, one for you and the other for your wife. You will never know what that night meant for me. I love you, son. At that moment, I understood the importance of saying in time I LOVE YOU and to give our loved ones the time that they deserve, because these things cannot be put off till some other time. Somebody said it takes about six weeks to get back to normal after you've had a baby . . . somebody doesn't know that once you're a mother, normal is history. Somebody said you learn how to be a mother by instinct . . . somebody never took a three-year old shopping. Somebody said being a mother is boring . . . somebody never rode in a car driven by a teenager with a driver's permit. Somebody said if you're a good mother, your child will turn out good . . . somebody thinks a child comes with directions and a guarantee. Somebody said good mother never raise their voices . . . somebody never came out the back door just in time to see her child hit a golf ball through the neighbor's kitchen window. Somebody said you don't need an education to be a mother . . . somebody never helped a fourth grader with his math. Somebody said you can't love the second child as much as you love the first . . . somebody doesn't have two children. Somebody said a mother can find all the answers to her child-rearing questions in the books . . . somebody never had a child stuff beans up his nose or in his ears. Somebody said the hardest part of being a mother is labor and delivery . . . somebody never watched her "baby" get on the bus for the first day of kindergarten . . . or a plane headed for military "boot camp". Somebody said a mother can do her job with her eyes closed and one hand tied behind her back . . . somebody never organized seven giggling Brownies to sell cookies. Somebody said a mother can stop worrying after her child gets married. somebody doesn't know that marriage adds a new son or daughter-in-law to a mothers heartstrings. Somebody said a mother's job is done when her last child leaves home . . . somebody never had grandchildren. Somebody said your mother knows you love her, so you don't need to tell her . . . somebody isn't a mother. Pass this along to all the "mothers' in your life and to everyone who ever had a mother. It's about appreciating the people in your life while you have them . . . no matter who that person is, People will forget what you said, people will forget what you did, but people will never forget how you made them feel.

Best Prayer I Have Heard in a Long Time

Heavenly Father, Help us remember that the jerk who cut us off in traffic last night is a single mother who worked nine hours that day and is rushing home to cook dinner, help with homework, do the laundry and spend a few precious moments with her children,

Help us to remember that the pierced, tattooed, disinterested young man who can't make change correctly is a worried 19-year-old college student, balancing his apprehension over final exams with his fear of not getting his student loans for next semester.

Remind us, Lord, that the scary looking bum, begging for money in the same spot every day (who really ought to get a job) is a slave to addictions that we can only imagine in our worst nightmares. Help us to remember that the old couple walking annoyingly slow through the store aisles and blocking our shopping progress are savoring this moment, knowing that, based on the biopsy report she got back last week, this will be the last year that they go shopping together.

Heavenly father, remind us each day that, of all the gifts you give us, the greatest gift is love. It is not enough to share that love with those we hold dear. Open our hearts not to just those who are close to us, but to all humanity. Let us be slow to judge and quick to forgive, show patience, empathy and love.

What I Learned from Noah

Everything I need to know, I learned from Noah's Ark.

One: Don't miss the boat.
Two: Remember that we are all in the same boat.
Three: Plan ahead. It wasn't raining when Noah built the Ark.
Four: Stay fit. When you're 60 years old, someone may ask you to do something really big.
Five: Don't listen to critics: just get on with the job that needs to be done.
Six: Build your future on high ground.
Seven: For safety's sake, travel in pairs.
Eight: Speed isn't always an advantage. The snails were on board with the cheetahs.
Nine: When you're stressed, float awhile.
Ten: Remember. The Ark was built by amateurs: the Titanic by professionals.

Two Choices

At a fundraising dinner for a school that serves children with learning disabilities, the father of one of the students delivered a speech that would never be forgotten by all that attended. After extolling the school and its dedicated staff, he offered a question: when not interfered with by outside influences, everything nature does is done with perfection. Yet my son, Shay, cannot learn things as other children do. Where is the natural order of things in my son? The audience was stilled by the query. The father continued, I believe that when a child like Shay, who was mentally and physically disabled, comes into the world, an opportunity to realize true human nature presents itself, and it comes in the way other people treat that child. Then he told the following story.

Shay and I had walked past the park where some boys Shay knew were playing baseball. Shay asked, do you think they'll let me play? I knew that most boys would not want someone like Shay on their team, but as a father I also understood that if my son were allowed to play, it would give him a much-needed sense of belonging and some confidence to be accepted by others in spite of his handicaps. I approached one of the boys on the field and asked (not expecting much) if Shay could play. The boy looked around for guidance and said, We're losing by six runs and the game is in the eighth inning. I guess he can be on our team and we'll try to put him in to bat in the ninth inning.

Shay struggled over to the team's bench and with a broad smile, put on a team shirt. I watched with a small tear in my eye and warmth in my heart. The boys saw my joy at me son being accepted. In the bottom of the eighth inning. Shay's team scored a few runs but was still behind by three.

In the top of the ninth, shay put on a glove and played in the right field. Even though no hits came his way, he was obviously ecstatic, just to be in the game and on the field, grinning from ear to ear as I waved from the stands. In the bottom of the ninth Shay's team scored again. Now with two outs and the bases loaded, the potential winning run was on base and Shay was scheduled to be next at bat. At this juncture, do they let Shay bat and give away their chance to win the game?

Surprisingly, Shay was given the bat. Everyone knew that a hit was all but impossible because Shay didn't even know how to hold the bat properly, much less connect with the ball. However, as Shay stepped up to the plate the pitcher, recognizing that the other team was putting winning aside for this moment in Shay's life, moved in a few steps to lob the ball in softly so Shay could at least make contact. The first pitch came and Shay swung clumsily and missed. The pitcher again took a few steps forward to toss the ball softly towards Shay. As the pitch came in, Shay swung at the ball and hit slow ground ball right back to the pitcher. The game would now be over.

The pitcher picked up the soft grounder and could have easily thrown the ball to the first baseman. Shay would have been out and that would have been the end of the game. Instead, the4 pitcher threw the ball right over the first baseman's head, out of reach of all the team mates.

Everyone from the stands and both teams started yelling, Shay run to first! Run to first. Never in his life had Shay ever run that far, but he made it to first base. He scampered down the baseline, wide-eyed and startled.

Everyone yelled, run to second, run to second! Catching his breath. Shay rounded towards second, gleaming and struggling to make it to the base. By the time Shay rounded towards second base, the right fielder had the ball, the smallest guy on their team who now had his fist chance to be the hero for his team. He could have thrown the ball to the second-baseman for a tag, but he understood the pitcher's intensions so he, too intentionally threw the ball high and over the third baseman's head. Shay ran toward third base deliriously as the runners ahead of him circled the bases toward home. All were screaming Shay, Shay, Shay all the way Shay. Shay reached third base because the opposing shortstop ran to help him by turning him in the direction of third base and shouting Shay, run to third. As Shay rounded third, the boys from both teams and the spectators, were on their feet screaming, Shay, run home! Run home! Shay ran to home, stepped on the plate, and was cheered the hero who hit the grand slam and won the game for his team. That day, said the father with tears rolling down his face, the boys from both teams helped bring a piece of true love and humanity into this world.

Shay didn't make it to another summer. He died that winter, having never forgotten being the hero and making me so happy and coming home and seeing his mother tearfully embrace her little hero of the day!

Crabby old Man

What do you see nurses? What do you see? What are you thinking . . . when you're looking at me? A crabby old man, not very wise, Uncertain of habit . . . with faraway eyes? Who dribbles his food . . . and makes no reply. When you say in a loud voice . . . I do wish you'd try. Who seems not to notice the things that you do. And forever is losing . . . A sock or shoe? Who, resisting of not . . . lets you do as you will. With bathing and feeding . . . The long day to fill? Is that what you're thinking? Is that what you see? Then open your eyes . . . you're not looking at me.

I'll tell you who I am . . . As I sit so still, As I do your bidding . . . as I eat at your will. I'm a small child of Ten . . . with a father and mother, brothers and sisters . . . who love one another. A young boy of Sixteen. With wings on his feet. dreaming that soon now . . . a lover he'll meet. A groom soon at Twenty . . . my heart gives a leap. Remembering the vows . . . that I promised to keep. AT twenty-five, now . . . I have young of my own. Who need me to guide, and a secure happy home. A man of Thirty, My young now grown fast, Bound to each other . . . with ties that should last. Forty, my sons, have grown and are gone. But my woman's beside me . . . to see I don't mourn. At fifty, once more . . . babies play round my knee. Again, we know children . . . My loved one and me.

Dark days are upon me . . . My wife is now dead. I look at the future . . . I shudder and dread. For my young are all rearing . . . young of their own. And I think of the years . . . and the love that I've known. I'm now and old man . . . and nature is cruel. Tis jest to make old age . . . look like a fool. The body, it crumbles . . . grace and vigor, depart. There is now a stone . . . where I once had a heart. But inside this old carcass . . . a young guy still dwells. And now and again . . . my battered heart swells. I remember the joys . . . I, remember the pain. And I'm loving and living . . . life over again. I think of the years . . . all too few . . . gone too fast. And accept the stark fact . . . that nothing can last. So, open your eyes people . . . open and see. Not a crabby old man. LOOK closer . . . see . . . ME!

A Baby's Hug

We were the only family with children in the restaurant. I say Erik in a high chair and noticed everyone was quietly sitting and talking. Suddenly, Erik squealed with glee and said, Hi. He pounded his fat baby hands on the chair tray. His eyes were crinkled in laughter and his mouth was bared in a toothless grin, as he wiggled and giggled with merriment. I looked around and saw the source of his merriment. It was a man whose pants were baggy with a zipper at half-mast and his toes poked out of would be shoes. His whiskers were too short to be called a beard and his nose was so varicose it looked like a road map. We were too far from him to smell anything, but I was sure he smelled. His hands waved and flapped on loose wrists. Hi there, baby: Hi there, big boy. I see ya, buster, the man said to Erik. My husband and I exchanged looks, What do we do? Erik continued to laugh and answer, Hi. Everyone in the restaurant noticed and looked at us and then at the man. The old geezer was creating a nuisance with my beautiful baby. Our meal came and the man began shouting across the room, Do you Patty cake Do you peek-a boo. Nobody thought the old man was cute. He was obviously drunk. My husband and I were embarrassed. We ate in silence; all except Erik, who was running through his repertoire for the admiring skid row bum, who in turn, reciprocated with his cute comments. We finally got through the meal and headed for the door. My husband went to pay the check and told me to meet him in the parking lot. The old man sat poised between me and the door. Lord, just let me out of here before he speaks to me or Erik, I prayed. As I drew closer to the man, I turned my back trying to sidestep him and avoid any air he might be breathing. As I did, Erik leaned over my arm, reaching with both arms in a baby's pick-me-up position. Before I could stop him, Erik had propelled himself from my arms to the man's. Suddenly a very old smelly man and a very young baby consummated their love and kinship . . . Erik in an act of total trust, love, and submission laid his tiny head upon the man's ragged shoulder. The man's eyes closed, and I saw tears hover beneath his lashes. His aged hands full of grime, pain, and hard labor, cradled my baby's bottom and stroked his back. No two beings have ever loved so deeply for so short a time. I stood awestruck. The old man rocked and cradled. Erik in his arms and his eyes opened and set squarely on mine. He said in a firm commanding voice, You take care of this baby. Somehow I managed I will from a throat that contained a stone. He pried Erik from his chest, lovingly and longingly, as though he were in pain. I received my baby, and the man said, God bless you ma'am you've given me my Christmas gift. I said nothing more than a muttered thanks. With Erik in my arms, I ran for the car. My husband was wondering why I was crying and holding Erik so tightly, and why I was saying. My God, my God, forgive me. I had just witnessed Christ's love shown through the innocence of a tiny child who saw no sin, who made no judgment: A child who saw a soul, and a mother who saw a suit of clothes. I was a Christian who was blind, holding a child who was not. I felt it was God asking. Are you willing to share your son for a moment? When He shared His for all eternity. The ragged old man, unwittingly, had reminded me, To enter the Kingdom of God, we must become as little children.

Beatitudes for friends of The Elderly

Blessed are they who understand, My faltering step and palsied hand.
Blessed are they who know my ear must strain what others hear.
Blessed are they who seem to know that my eyes are dim and my wits are slow.
Blessed are they who looked away when my coffee was spilled at the table today.
Blessed are they with a cheery smile who stop to chat for a little while.
Blessed are they who know the ways to bring back memories of yesterdays.
Blessed are they who make it known that I am loved and not alone.
Blessed are they who ease the days on my journey home in loving ways.

Ready for Christmas

Ready for Christmas, she said with a sigh. As she gave a last touch to the gifts piled high.

Then wearily sat for a moment and read till soon, she was nodding her head.

Then quietly spokes a voice in her dream, Ready for Christmas, what do you mean?

Ready for Christmas when only last week you wouldn't acknowledge your friend on the street?

Ready for Christmas while holding a grudge? Perhaps you'd better let God be the judge.

She woke with a start and a cry of despair. There's so little time, and I've still to prepare.

Oh Father, forgive me, I see what you mean! To be ready means more than a house swept clean.

Yes, more than the giving of gifts and a tree. It's the heart swept clean that He wanted of see, A heart that is free from bitterness and sin. So be ready for Christmas—and ready for him.

Jonah Versus The Whale

Now listen, my children, I'll tell you a tale. How old Jonah, the profit, got caught by a whale. The whale caught dear Jonah and bless your dear soul; He not only caught him, but swallowed him whole. A part of this story is awfully sad—How a great big city went bad. When the Lord saw those people with such wicked ways, He said, I can't stand them for more'n forty days. He spoke to Johan and said, Go and cry to those hardhearted people and tell them that I Give them forty days more to get humbled down, And if they don't, I'll tear up their town. Jonah heard the Lord speaking and he said, No, that's against my religion and I won't go. Those Nineveh people ain't nothing to me. And I'm against foreign missions, you see. He went down to Joppa and there, in great haste, He boarded a ship for a different place, The Lord looked down on that ship and said He, Old Jonah is fixing to run off from me. He sent the winds blowing with squeaks and with squeals, And the sea got rowdy and kicked up its heels. Old Jonah confessed it was all for his sin; The crew threw him out and the whale took him in. The whale said, old fellow, don't you forget, I am sent ere to take you out of the wet, You will get punished aright for your sin. So he opened his mouth and poor Jonah went in. On beds of green seaweed that fish tried to rest; He said, I will sleep while my food I digest. But he got mighty restless and sorely afraid, And he rumbled inside as the old profit prayed. The third day that fish rose up from his bed, with his stomach tore up and a pain in his head. He said, I must get to the air mighty quick, For this filthy backslider is making me sick. He winked his big eyes and wiggled his tail. And pulled for the shore to deliver his male. He stopped near the shore and looked all round; And vomited old Jonah right up to the ground. Old Jonah thanked God for his mercy and grace, and turning around to the whale, made a face. He said, After three days I guess you have found, a good man, old fellow, is hard to keep down. He stretched himself out with a yawn and a sigh, and sat down in the sun for his clothing to dry. He thought how much better his preaching would be, since from Whale Seminary he had a degree. When he had rested and dried in the sun, He started for Nineveh most on the run. He thanked his dear Father in Heaven above for his tender mercy and wonderful love.

Thanksgiving

Oh, thank you, thank you, Grandma dear. For this delicious pie! The pumpkin should be thanked, my child, the pumpkin and not I So when I heard my Grandma's words, I thanked the pumpkin vine. You ought to thank the earth it said; The credit hers not mine. Oh, thank you, good old Mother Earth; You're very kind, I know you ought to thank the sun, she said, It's he that makes things grow. Oh, thank you thoughtful Mr. Sun; You shine with might and main See here, he answered with a smile; You ought to thank the rain. Oh thank you, gentle drops of rain, I called up good and loud. You're welcome, but—they pattered back You should ought to thank the cloud. Oh thank you, Mr. cloud, I cried, Then heard this kind reply; We all cooperated, my child to make a pumpkin pie! Your loving Father should be thanked for sun and rain an earth. So gratefully I bowed my head, To say, I thank you, God.

Gold Wrapping Paper

I received this from a friend who had a choice to make. It said that I had a choice to make too. I've chosen. Now it's your turn to choose. The story goes that some time ago a mother punished her five year old daughter for wasting a roll of expensive gold wrapping paper. Money was tight and she became even more upset when the child used the gold paper to decorate a box to put under the Christmas tree. Nevertheless, the little girl brought the gift box to her mother the next morning and then said, 'This is for you, Momma.' The mother was embarrassed by her earlier over reaction, but her anger flared again when she opened the box and found it was empty. She spoke to her daughter in a harsh manner. 'Don't you know, young lady, when you give someone a present there's supposed to be something inside the package?' She had tears in her eyes and said, 'Oh, Momma, it's not empty! I blew kisses into it until it was full.' The mother was crushed. She fell on her knees and put her arms around her little girl, and she begged her forgiveness for her thoughtless anger. An accident took the life of the child only a short time later, and it is told that the mother kept that gold box by her bed for all the years of her life. Whenever she was discouraged or faced difficult problems she would open the box and take out an imaginary kiss and remember the love of the child who had put it there. In a very real sense, each of us, as human beings, have been given a Golden box filled with unconditional love and kisses from our children, family, friends. There is no more precious possession anyone could hold.

In Phoenix, Arizona, a 26 year old mother stared down at her 6 year old son, who was dying of terminal leukemia. Although her heart was filled with sadness, she had a strong feeling of determination. Like any parent, she wanted her son to grow up and fulfill all his dreams. Now that was no longer possible. The leukemia would see to that. But she still wanted her son's dream to come true. She took her son's Hand and asked, Billy did you ever think about what you wanted to be once you grew up? Did you ever dream and wish what you would do with your life? Mommy I always wanted to be a fireman when I grew up Mom smiled back and said, "Lets see if we can make your wish come true. Later that day she went to her local Fire Department in Phoenix, Arizona, she met Fireman Bob, who had a heart as big as Phoenix She explained her son's final wish and asked if it might be possible to give her 6 year old son a ride around the block on a fire engine. Fireman Bob said, Look, we can do better than that. If you'll have your son ready at seven o'clock, Wednesday morning, we'll make him an honorary Fireman for the whole He can come down to the fire station, et with us, go out on all the fire calls, the whole nine yards. And if you'll give us his sizes, we'll get a real fire uniform for him, with a real fire hat—not a toy. One with the emblem of the Phoenix Fire Department on it, a yellow slicker like we wear and rubber boots. They're all manufactured right here in Phoenix, so we can get them fast. Three days later Fireman Bob picked up Billy dressed him in his uniform and escorted him from his hospital bed to the waiting hook and ladder truck. Billy got to sit on the back of the truck and help steer it back to the fire station. He was in heaven There were three fire calls in Phoenix that day and Billy got to go to all three calls. He rode in the different fire engines, the Paramedic's van and even the fire chief's car. He was videotaped for the local news program. Having his dream come true, with all the love and attention that was lavished upon him, so deeply touched Billy, that he lived three months longer than any doctor thought possible One night all of his vital signs began to drop dramatically and the head nurse, who believed in the hospice concept—that no one should die alone, began to call the family members to the hospital. Then she remembered the day Billy had spent as a Fireman, so she called the fire chief and asked if it would be possible to send a fireman in uniform to the hospital to be with Billy as he made his transition. The chief replied, We can do better than that. Will you please do me a favor? When you hear the sirens screaming and see the lights flashing, will you announce over the PA system that there is not a fire? It's the department coming to see one of its finest members one more time. And will you open the window to his room? About five minutes later a hook and ladder truck arrived at the hospital and extended its ladder up to Billy's third floor open window—16 fire fighters climbed up the ladder into Billy's room. With his mother's permission, they hugged him and held him and told him how much they LOVED him.

With his dying breath, Billy looked up at the fire chief and said, Chief, am I really a fireman now? Billy you are, and the Head Chief, Jesus, is holding your hand, the chief said. With these words, Billy smiled and said, I know, he's been holding my hand all day, and the angels have been singing. He closed his eyes one last time.

I Never Found the Time

I knelt to pray but not for long I had to much to do
had to hurry and get to work for bills were overdue
So I knelt and said a hurried prayer, and jumped up off my knees.
My Christian duty was now done. My soul could rest at ease . . .
All day long I had no time to spread a word of cheer.
No time to speak of Christ to friends, They'd laugh at me I'd fear.
No time, no time, too much to do, That was my constant cry,
No time to give to souls in need But at last the time, the time to die.
I went before the Lord, I came, I stood with downcast eyes.
For in his hands God held a book; It was the book of life.
God looked into his book and said "Your name I cannot find."
I once was going to write it down . . . But never found the time.

Why Jesus Is Better than Santa Claus

Santa lives at the North Pole . . . JESUS is everywhere

Santa rides in a sleigh JESUS rides on the wind and walks on the water

Santa comes but once a year. JESUS is an ever present help. Santa fills your stockings with goodies . . . JESUS supplies all your needs.

Santa comes down your chimney uninvited . . . JESUS stands at your door and knocks, and then enters your heart when invited.

You have to wait in line to see Santa . . . JESUS is as close as the mention of His name.

One day a mother died.

And on that clear, cold morning,
in the warmth of her bedroom,
the daughter was struck with
the pain of learning that sometimes
there isn't any more.

No more hugs,
no more lucky moments to celebrate together,
no more phone calls just to chat,
No more 'just one minute'

Sometimes, what we care about the most goes away.
never to return before we can say good-bye,
Say 'I Love You.'

So while we have it . . . it's best we love it . . .
And care for it and fix it when it's broken
and take good care of it when it's sick.

This is true for marriage
and friendships

And children with bad report cards;
And dogs with bad hips;
And aging parents and grandparents
We keep them because they are worth it,
Because we cherish them!

Some things we keep—
like a best friend who moved away
or a classmate we grew up with.
There are just some things that make
us happy, No matter what.

Life is important,
and so are the people we know
And so, we keep them close!

I received this from someone today
who thought I was a 'KEEPER'!

Then I sent It to the people
I Think of in the same way!

Now it's your turn to send this to all those people
who Are 'keepers' in your life!
If you receive this more than once, how wonderful

Look out For The Last Story...
It Will Knock Your Socks off

Author and lecturer Leo Buscaglia once
talked about a contest he was asked to judge.

The purpose of the
contest was to find the most caring child.
The winner was:
A four-year-old child, whose next door
neighbor was an elderly gentleman, who had recently lost his
wife. Upon seeing the man cry, the little boy went into the old
gentleman's yard, climbed onto his lap, and just sat there.
When his mother asked him what he had
said to the neighbor, the little boy just said,
'Nothing, I just helped him cry.'

****

Teacher Debbie Moon's first graders were
discussing a picture of a family. One little boy in the picture
had a different hair color than the other members. One of her
students suggested that he was adopted.
A little girl said, 'I know all about adoption, I was adopted.'
'What does it mean to be adopted?', asked another child.
'It means', said the girl,
'that you grew in your mommy's heart instead of her tummy!'

****

On my way home one day, I stopped to
watch a Little League base ball game that was being played in a
park near my home. As I sat down behind the bench on the
first-base line, I asked one of the boys what the score was
'We're behind 14 to nothing,' he answered with a smile.
'Really,' I said. 'I have to say you don't look very discouraged.'
'Discouraged?,' the boy asked with a puzzled look on his face . . .
'Why should we be discouraged? We haven't been up to bat yet.'

****

Whenever I'm disappointed with my spot in life,
I stop and think about little Jamie Scott.
Jamie was trying out for a part in the school play.
His mother told me that he'd set his heart on being in it,
though she feared he would not be chosen.
On the day the parts were awarded,
I went with her to collect him after school.
Jamie rushed up to her, eyes shining with pride and excitement.
'Guess what, Mom,' he shouted, and then said those words that
will remain a lesson to me . . . 'I've been chosen to clap and cheer.'

****

An eye witness account from New York City,
on a cold day in December, some years ago:
A little boy, about 10-years-old, was standing before a shoe store
on the roadway, barefooted, peering through the window,
and shivering with cold.
A lady approached the young boy and said,
'My, but you're in such deep thought staring in that window!'
'I was asking God to give me a pair of shoes,' was the boy's reply.
The lady took him by the hand, went into the store, and asked the clerk
to get half a dozen pairs of socks for the boy.
She then asked if he could give her a basin of water and a towel.
He quickly brought them to her.

She took the little fellow to the back part of the store and,
removing her gloves, knelt down, washed his little feet,
and dried them with the towel.
By this time, the clerk had returned with the socks.
Placing a pair upon the boy's feet, she purchased him a pair of shoes.
She tied up the remaining pairs of socks and gave them to him.
She patted him on the head and said,
'No doubt, you will be more comfortable now.'
As she turned to go, the astonished kid caught her by the hand,
and looking up into her face, with tears in his eyes, asked her.
'Are you God's wife?'

****

GOD'S WIFE

SEND TO ALL WHO LOVE AND CARE FOR CHILDREN.
Hope this put a smile on your face
it sure did mine.

The Coat Hanger

A woman was at work when she received a phone call that her small daughter was very sick with a fever. She left her work and stopped by the pharmacy to get some medication. She got back to her car and found that she had locked her keys in the car. She didn't know what to do, so she called home and told the baby sitter what had happened.

The baby sitter told her that the fever was getting worse. She said, "You might find a coat hanger and use that to open the door."

The woman looked around and found an old rusty coat hanger that had been left on the ground, possibly by someone else who at some time had locked their keys in their car. She looked at the hanger and said, "I don't know how to use this."

She bowed her head and asked God to send her help. Within five minutes a beat up old motorcycle pulled up, with a dirty, greasy, bearded man who was wearing an old biker skull rag on his head.

The woman thought, "This is what you sent to help me?" But, she was desperate, so she was also very thankful.

The man got off of his cycle and asked if he could help. She said, "Yes, my daughter is very sick. I stopped to get her some medication and I locked my keys in my car. I must get home to her. Please, can you use this hanger to unlock my car?

He said, "Sure." He walked over to the car, and in less than a minute the car was opened.

She hugged the man and through her tears she said, "Thank You So Much! You are a very nice man." The man replied, "Lady, I am not a nice man. I just got out of prison today. I was in prison for car theft and have only been out for about an hour."

The woman hugged the man again and with sobbing tears cried out loud, "Oh, Thank you God! You even sent me a Professional!"

Isn't GOD GOOD!

Somebody's Raising Their Kid Right!

One Nation, "Under God."

One day a 6 year old girl was sitting in a classroom. The teacher was going to explain evolution to the children.

The teacher asked a little boy: Tommy do you see the tree outside?

TOMMY: Yes.
TEACHER: Tommy, do you see the grass outside?
TOMMY: Yes.
TEACHER: Go outside and look up and see if you can see the sky.
TOMMY: Okay. (He returned a few minutes later) Yes, I saw the sky.
TEACHER: Did you see God?
TOMMY: No.
TEACHER: That's my point. We can't see God because he isn't there. He just doesn't exist.

A little girl spoke up and wanted to ask the boy some questions.

The teacher agreed and the little girl asked the boy:

Tommy, do you see the tree outside?

TOMMY: Yes.
LITTLE GIRL: Tommy do you see the grass outside?
TOMMY: Yesssss!
LITTLE GIRL: Did you see the sky?
TOMMY: Yessssss!
LITTLE GIRL: Tommy, do you see the teacher?
TOMMY: Yes
LITTLE GIRL: Do you see her brain?
TOMMY: No
LITTLE GIRL: Then according to what we were taught today in school, she must not have one!

(You Go Girl!)
FOR WE WALK BY FAITH, NOT BY SIGHT" II CORINTHIANS 5:7

Be grateful God doesn't have voice mail . . .

Imagine praying and hearing the following:

Thank you for calling Heaven. Please select one of the following options:

Press 1 for Requests
Press 2 for Thanksgiving
Press 3 for Complaints
Press 4 for all other inquiries

I am sorry, all our angels and saints are busy helping other sinners right now. However, your prayer is important to us and we will answer it in the order it was received. Please stay on the line. If you would like to speak to:

Heavenly Father, press 1
For Jesus, press 2
For the Holy Spirit, press 3

If you would like to hear King David sing a Psalm while you are holding, press 4.

To find a loved one that has been assigned to Heaven, press 5, then enter his or her social security number, followed by the pound sign.
(If you get a negative response, please hang up and try area code 666.)

For reservations at Heaven, please enter J-O-H-N 3-1-6

For answers to nagging questions about dinosaurs, the age of the earth, life on other planets, and where Noah's Ark is, please wait until you arrive.

Our computers show that you have already prayed once today. Please hang up and try again tomorrow.

This office is now closed for the weekend to observe a religious holiday.

Please pray again on Monday after 9:30 am. If you are calling after hours and need emergency assistance, please contact your local bishop or pastor.

Have a nice day!

from the mouths of babes ...

I love kids letters about misinterpreting the Lord's Prayer. "Give us this steak and daily bread, and forgive us our mattresses.

Groton, Mass.
My mother spent her early childhood saying, "Hail Mary, full of grapes."

Missoula, Mont.
My son, who is in nursery school, said, "Our Father, who art in Heaven, how didja know my name?"

Uniontown, Ohio.
I remember thinking this prayer was "Give us this day our jelly bread."

Covina, Calif.
I recall reading something years ago about the Pledge of Allegiance. Some child thought it began, "I led the pigeons to the flag."

Cleveland, Ohio.
When I was little, I often wondered who Richard Stands was. You know: "I pledge allegiance to the flag ... And to the republic for Richard Stands."

Tampa, Fla.
When my husband was 6 years old, he thought a certain Prayer was "He suffered under a bunch of violets." The real words were "under Pontius Pilate," but at that age, he didn't know better. To this day, we still snicker in church whenever that prayer is read.

Oak Harbor, Wash.
When my older brother was very young, he always walked up to the church altar with my mother when she took communion. On one occasion, he tugged at her arm and asked, "What does the priest say when he gives you the bread?"

Mom whispered something in his ear. Imagine his shock many years later when he learned that the priest doesn't say, "Be quiet until you get to your seat."

Grand Junction, Colo.
When I was younger, I believed the line was "Lead a snot into temptation." I thought I was praying for my little sister to get into trouble.

A Little Humor

Cat Humor

A cat died and went to Heaven. An angel met the animal at the Pearly Gates and said, "You have been good all your life; anything you want is yours for the asking." The cat thought and then said, "All my life I lived on a farm and slept on hard, wooden floors. I would like a real fluffy pillow to sleep on." The angel said, "Say no more." Instantly a huge, fluffy pillow appeared for the cat.

A few days later, twelve mice were simultaneously killed in an accident and they all went up to Heaven together The angel met them at the Gates, and made the exact same offer that he made to the cat. The mice said, "Well, we have had to run all of our lives from cats, dogs and people. If we could just have some little roller skates, we would never have to run again." The angel answered, "It is done." All the mice had beautiful little roller skates, and they were very happy.

About a week later, the angel decided to check on the cat. He found her sound asleep on her fluffy pillow. He gently awakened the cat and asked, "Is everything okay? How have you been doing? Are you happy?

The cat replied, "Oh, everything is just wonderful. I've never been so happy in my life! My pillow is always fluffy and those little 'Meals-on-Wheels' that you have been sending over are delicious."

The Road of Life

At first, I saw God as my observer, my judge, keeping track of the things I did wrong, so as to know whether I merited heaven or hell when I die. He was out there sort of like a president. I recognized His picture when I saw it, but I really didn't know Him. But later on when I met Christ, it seemed as though life were rather like a bike ride, but it was a tandem bike, and I noticed that Christ was in the back helping me pedal. I don't know just when it was that He suggested we change places, but life has not been the same since.

When I had control, I knew the way. It was rather boring, but predictable it was the shortest distance between two points. But when He took the lead, He knew delightful long cuts, up mountains, and through rocky places at breakneck speeds. It was all I could do to hang on!

Even though it looked like madness, He said, "Pedal!" I worried and was anxious and asked, "Where are you taking me?" He laughed and didn't answer, and I started to learn to trust. I forgot my boring life and entered into the adventure, and when I'd say, "I'm scared," He'd lean back and touch my hand. I gained love, peace, acceptance and joy; gifts to take on my journey, My Lord's and mine. And we were off again.

He said, "Give the gifts away. They're extra baggage, too much weight." So I did, to the people we met, and I found that in giving I received, and still our burden was light.

I did not trust Him, at first, in control of my life. I thought He'd wreck it; but he knows bike secrets, knows how to make it bend to take sharp corners, knows how to jump to clear high rocks, knows how to fly to shorten, scary passages. And I am learning to shut up and pedal in the strangest places, and I'm beginning to enjoy the view and the cool breeze on my face with my delightful constant companion, Jesus Christ.

And when I'm sure I just can't do it anymore, He just smiles and says . . . "Pedal."

Your Cross

Whatever your cross
Whatever your pain
There will always be sunshine.
After the rain

Perhaps you may stumble
Perhaps even fall
But God's always there
To help you through it all.

A man riding his Harley, was riding along a California beach when suddenly the sky clouded above his head, and in a booming voice the Lord said, "Because you have TRIED to be faithful to me in all ways, I will grant you one wish."

The biker pulled over and said, "Build a bridge to Hawaii, so I can ride over anytime I want."

The Lord said, "Your request is materialistic, think of the enormous challenges for that kind of undertaking; the supports required to reach the bottom of the Pacific and the concrete and steel it would take! It will nearly exhaust several natural resources. I can do it, but it is hard for me to justify your desire for worldly things.

Take a little more time and think of something that could possibly help mankind."

The biker thought about it for a long time. Finally, he said, "Lord, I wish that I, and all men, could understand our wives. I want to know how she feels inside, what she's thinking when she gives me the silent treatment, why she cries, what she means when she says nothing's wrong, and how I can make a woman truly happy".

The Lord replied, "You want two lanes or four on that bridge?"

A Southern Baptist minister decided that a visual demonstration would add emphasis to his Sunday sermon. Four worms were placed into four separate jars.

The first worm was put into a jar of alcohol.
The second worm was put into a jar of cigarette smoke.
The third worm was put into a jar of chocolate syrup.
The fourth worm was put into a jar of good clean soil.

At the conclusion of the Sermon, the Minister reported the following results:

The first worm in alcohol—Dead.
The second worm in cigarette smoke—Dead.
Third worm in chocolate syrup—Dead.
Fourth worm in good clean soil—Alive.

So the Minister asked the congregation—What can you learn from this demonstration?
A little old woman in the back quickly raised her hand and said, "As long as you drink, smoke, and eat chocolate, you won't have worms!"
Don't you just love little old ladies????

- We come to love not by finding a perfect person, but by learning to see an imperfect person perfectly.—Anonymous
- Anyone can be passionate, but it takes real lovers to be silly.—Rose Franken
- Laugh and the world laughs with you. Snore and you sleep alone.—Anthony Burgess
- The most wasted day of all is that in which we have not laughed. —Sebastian Roch Nicolas Chamfort
- Learn to laugh at your troubles and you'll never run out of things to laugh at.—Lyn Karol
- Blessed is he who has learned to laugh at himself, for he shall never cease to be entertained.—John Powell

For those lucky to still be blessed with your Mom this is beautiful.
For those of who aren't, this is even more beautiful.

Mother's Path of Life The young mother set her foot on the path of life. "Is this the long way?" she asked.

And the guide said: "Yes, and the way is hard. And you will be old before you reach the end of it. But the end will be better than the beginning." But the young mother was happy, and she would not believe that anything could be better than these years. So she played with her children, and gathered flowers for them along the way, and bathed them in the clear streams; and the sun shone on them, and the young Mother cried, "Nothing will ever be lovelier than this."

Then the night came, and the storm, and the path was dark, and the children shook with fear and cold, and the mother drew them close and covered them with her mantle, and the children said, "Mother, we are not afraid, for you are near, and no harm can come."

And the morning came, and there was a hill ahead, and the children climbed and grew weary, and the mother was weary. But at all times she said to the children," A little patience and we are there." So the children climbed, and when they reached the top they said, "Mother, we would not have done it without you." And the mother, when she lay down at night looked up at the stars and said, "This is a better day than the last, for my children have learned fortitude in the face of hardness. Yesterday I gave them courage. Today, I have given them strength."

And the next day came strange clouds which darkened the earth, clouds of war and hate and evil, and the children groped and stumbled, and the mother said: "Look up. Lift your eyes to the light." And the children looked and saw above the clouds an everlasting glory, and it guided them beyond the darkness. And that night the Mother said, "This is the best day of all, for I have shown my children God."

And the days went on, and the weeks and the months and the years, and the mother grew old and she was little and bent. But her children were tall and strong, and walked with courage. And when the way was rough, they lifted her, for she was as light as a feather; and at last they came to a hill, and beyond they could see a shining road and golden gates flung wide.

The mother said: "I have reached the end of my journey. And now I know the end is better than the beginning, for my children can walk alone, and their children after them." And the children said, "You will always walk with us, Mother, even when you have gone through the gates."

And they stood and watched her as she went on alone, and the gates closed after her. And they said: "We cannot see her, but she is with us still. A Mother like ours is more than a memory. She is a living presence."

Your Mother is always with you. She's the whisper of the leaves as you walk down the street; she's the smell of bleach in your freshly laundered socks; she's the cool hand on your brow when you're not well. Your Mother lives inside your laughter. And she's crystallized in every tear drop.

She's the place you came from, your first home; and she's the map you follow with every step you take.

She's your first love and your first heartbreak, and nothing on earth can separate you.

Not time, not space . . . not even death!

I Am Thankful

FOR THE WIFE
WHO SAYS IT'S HOT DOGS TONIGHT,
BECAUSE SHE IS HOME WITH ME,
AND NOT OUT WITH SOMEONE ELSE.

FOR THE HUSBAND
WHO IS ON THE SOFA
BEING A COUCH POTATO,
BECAUSE HE IS HOME WITH ME
AND NOT OUT AT THE BARS.

FOR THE TEENAGER
WHO IS COMPLAINING ABOUT DOING DISHES
BECAUSE THAT MEANS SHE IS AT HOME,
NOT ON THE STREETS.

FOR THE TAXES
THAT I PAY
BECAUSE IT MEANS THAT
I AM EMPLOYED.

FOR THE MESS
TO CLEAN AFTER A PARTY
BECAUSE IT MEANS THAT I HAVE
BEEN SURROUNDED BY FRIENDS.

FOR THE CLOTHES
THAT FIT A LITTLE TOO SNUG
BECAUSE IT MEANS
I HAVE ENOUGH TO EAT.

FOR MY SHADOW
THAT WATCHES ME WORK
BECAUSE IT MEANS
I AM OUT IN THE SUNSHINE.

FOR A LAWN
THAT NEEDS MOWING,
WINDOWS THAT NEED CLEANING,
AND GUTTERS THAT NEED FIXING
BECAUSE IT MEANS I HAVE A HOME.

FOR ALL THE COMPLAINING
I HEAR ABOUT THE GOVERNMENT
BECAUSE IT MEANS THAT
WE HAVE FREEDOM OF SPEECH.

FOR THE PARKING SPOT
I FIND AT THE FAR END OF THE PARKING LOT
BECAUSE IT MEANS I AM CAPABLE OF WALKING
AND THAT I HAVE BEEN
BLESSED WITH TRANSPORTATION.

FOR MY HUGE HEATING BILL
BECAUSE IT MEANS
I AM WARM.

FOR THE LADY
BEHIND ME IN CHURCH
THAT SINGS OFF KEY
BECAUSE IT MEANS
THAT I CAN HEAR.

FOR THE PILE
OF LAUNDRY AND IRONING
BECAUSE IT MEANS
I HAVE CLOTHES TO WEAR.

FOR WEARINESS
AND ACHING MUSCLES
AT THE END OF THE DAY
BECAUSE IT MEANS
I HAVE BEEN
CAPABLE OF WORKING HARD.

FOR THE ALARM
THAT GOES OFF
IN THE EARLY MORNING HOURS
BECAUSE IT MEANS THAT I AM ALIVE.

AND FINALLY . . .
FOR TOO MUCH E-MAIL
BECAUSE IT MEANS I HAVE
FRIENDS WHO ARE THINKING OF ME.

My Joke and Funny Story's Book

PROLOG

No matter what else you are doing.
From cradle days through to the end
You are writing your life's secret story—
Each day sees another page penned.
Each month ends a thirty-page chapter,
Each year means the end of a part-
And never an act is misstated
Or even one wish of the heart.
Each day when you wake and the book opens,
Revealing a page clean and white—
What thoughts and what words and what doings
Will cover its pages by night?
God leaves that to you—you're the writer-
And never a word shall grow dim,
Till the day you write the word "Finish"
And give your life's Book back to Him.

Sipping Vodka

This is just too funny—I still have tears in my eyes! Finally, a chain letter that I don't mind forwarding . . .

IT'S FUNNY (DON'T BREAK CHAIN)

A new priest at his first mass was so nervous he could hardly speak.

After mass he asked the monsignor how he had done.

The monsignor replied, "When I am worried about getting nervous on the pulpit, I put a glass of vodka next to the water glass.

If I start to get nervous, I take a sip."

So next Sunday he took the monsignor's advice. At the beginning of the sermon, he got nervous and took a drink. He proceeded to talk up a storm.

Upon his return to his office after mass, he found the following note on the door:

1. Sip the Vodka, don't gulp.
2. There are 10 commandments, not 12.
3. There are 12 disciples, not 10.
4. Jesus was consecrated, not constipated.
5. Jacob wagered his donkey, he did not bet his ass.
6. We do not refer to Jesus Christ as the late J. C.
7. The Father, Son, and Holy Ghost are not referred to as Daddy, Junior and the Spook.
8. *David slew Goliath, he did not kick the shit out of him.*
9. *When David was hit by a rock and was knocked off his donkey, don't say he was stoned off his ass.*
10. *We do not refer to the cross as the "Big T."*

11. *When Jesus broke the bread at the Last Supper he said, "Take this and eat it for it is my body." He did not say "Eat me"*

12. *The Virgin Mary is not called "Mary with the Cherry,"*

A man bought a donkey from a preacher. The preacher told the man that this donkey had been trained in a very unique way, (being the donkey of a preacher).

The only way to make the donkey go, is to say, "Hallelujah!"

The only way to make the donkey stop, is to say, "Amen!"

The man was pleased with his purchase and immediately got on the animal to try out the preacher's instructions.

Hallelujah!" shouted the man. The donkey began to trot.

"Amen!" shouted the man. The donkey stopped immediately.

"This is great!" said the man. With a "Hallelujah", he rode off very proud of his new purchase.

The man traveled for a long time through some mountains. Soon he was heading towards a cliff. He could not remember the word to make the donkey stop.

"Stop," said the man. "Halt!" he cried. The donkey just kept going.

"Oh, no . . . 'Bible . . . Church! . . . Please Stop!!," shouted the man. The donkey just began to trot faster. He was getting closer and closer to the cliff edge.

Finally, in desperation, the man said a prayer . . . "Please, dear Lord. Please make this donkey stop before I go off the end of this mountain, In Jesus name, AMEN."

The donkey came to an abrupt stop just one step from the edge of the cliff.

"HALLELUJAH!", shouted the man.

Windows US sub 10555 Miss Bea, the church organist, was in her eighties and had never been married. She was much admired for her kindness to all.

One early March afternoon the pastor came to call on her. She welcomed him into her Victorian parlor. She asked him to have a seat while she went to make tea. As he waited he noticed her old pump organ sitting in the corner with a beautiful cut glass bowl on top. The bowl was full of water, but to his shock he spotted a condom floating in the water. This was completely unexpected from the very proper Miss Bea.

When Miss Bea returned with the tea and cookies, he tried to make conversation with her. However, his curiosity over the floater in the bowl got the best of him.

"Miss Bea," he said "I wonder if you could explain this," as he pointed to the bowl.

"Oh yes, isn't it wonderful?" she replied. "I was walking downtown last Fall and found this little package on the sidewalk. The directions said to put it on the organ, keep it wet, and it would prevent disease! And you know, I haven't had a cold all winter."

One day, three men were hiking and unexpectedly came upon a large raging, violent river. They needed to get to the other side, but had no idea of how to do so.

The first man prayed to God, saying, "Please God, give me the strength to cross this river." Poof!

God gave him big arms and strong legs, and he was able to swim across the river in about two hours, after almost drowning a couple of times.

Seeing this, the second man prayed to God, saying, "Please God, give me the strength. And the tools to cross this river."

Poof!

God gave him a rowboat and he was able to row across the river in about an hour, after almost capsizing the boat a couple of times. The third man had seen how this worked out for the other two, so he also prayed to God saying "Please God, give me the strength and the tools—and the intelligence—to cross this river."

And poof!

God turned him into a woman. She looked at the map, hiked upstream a couple of hundred yards, then walked across the bridge.

Subject: The Lost Chapter of Genesis . . .

THE LOST CHAPTER OF GENESIS:

Adam was hanging around the garden of Eden feeling very lonely.

So, God asked him, "What's wrong with you?" Adam said he didn't have anyone to talk to. God said that He was going to make Adam a companion and that it would be a woman.

He said, "This pretty lady will gather food for you, she will cook for you, and when you discover clothing, she will wash it for you.

She will always agree with every decision you make and she will not nag you, and will always be the first to admit she was wrong when you've had a disagreement. She will praise you!

She will bear your children.

and never ask you to get up in the middle of the night to take care of them.

"She will NEVER have a headache and will freely give you love and passion whenever you need it."

Adam asked God, "What will a woman like this cost?"

God replied, "An arm and a leg."

Then Adam asked, "What can I get for a rib?"

Of course the rest is history . . .

The Unrealistic Gift

After a few of the usual Sunday evening hymns, the church's pastor slowly stood up, walked over the pulpit, and before he gave his sermon for the evening, briefly introduced a guest minister who was in the service that evening.

In the introduction, the pastor told the congregation that the guest minister was one of his dearest childhood friends and that he wanted him to have a few moments to greet the church and share whatever he felt would be appropriate for the service. With that, and elderly man stepped up to the pulpit and began to speak.

"A father, his son, and a friend of his son were sailing off the Pacific Coast," he began, "when a fast approaching storm blocked any attempt to get back to the shore. The waves were so high, that even though the father was an experienced sailor, he could not keep the boat upright, and the three were swept into the ocean as the boat capsized."

The old man hesitated for a moment, making eye contact with two teenagers who were for the first time since the service began, looking somewhat interested in his story. The aged minister continued with his story, "grabbing a rescue line, the father had to make the most excruciating decision of his life: to which boy would he throw the other end of the life line. He only had seconds to make the decision. The father knew that his son was a Christian, and he also know that his son's friend was not. The agony of his decision could not be matched by the torrent of waves.

As the father yelled out, "I love you, son!" he threw out the lifeline to his son's friend. By the time the father had pulled the friend back to the capsized boat, his son had disappeared beneath the raging swells into the black of night. His body was never recovered.

By this time, the two teenagers were sitting up straight in the pew, anxiously waiting for the next words to come out of the old minister's mouth.

"The father," he continued, "knew his son would step into eternity with Jesus, and he could not bear the thought of his son's friend stepping into an eternity without Jesus. Therefore, he sacrificed his son to save the son's friend. How great is the love of God that he should do the same for us. Our heavenly father sacrificed his only begotten son that we could be saved! I urge you to accept his offer to rescue you and take a hold of the lifeline He is throwing out to you in this service."

With that, the old man turned and sat back down in his chair as silence filled the room. The pastor again walked slowly to the pulpit and delivered a brief sermon with an invitation at the end. However, no one responded to the appeal. Within minutes after the service ended, the two teenagers were at the old man's side.

"That was a nice story," politely stated one of them, "but I don't think it was very realistic for a father to give up his only son's life in hopes that the other boy would become a Christian."

"Well, you've got a point there," the old man replied, glancing down at his worn Bible. A big smile broadened his narrow face. He once again looked up at the boys and said, "It sure isn't very realistic, is it? But I'm standing here today to tell you that story gives me a glimpse of what it must have been like for God to give up his son for me. You see . . . I was that father, and your pastor is my son's friend."

Can Be Told In Church

Attending a wedding for the first time, a little girl whispered to her mother, "Why is the bride dressed in white?" "Because white is the color of happiness, and today is the happiest day of her life." The child thought about this for a moment, then said, "So why is the groom wearing black?"

############

A little girl, dressed in her Sunday best, was running as fast as she could, trying not to be late for Bible class. As she ran she prayed, "Dear Lord, please don't let me be late! Dear Lord, please don't let me be late!" While she was running and praying, she tripped on a curb and fell, getting her clothes dirty and tearing her dress. She got up, brushed herself off, and started running again. As she ran she once again began to pray, "Dear Lord, please don't let me be late . . . But please don't shove me either!"

############

Three boys are in the school yard bragging about their fathers. The first boy says, "My Dad scribbles a few words on a piece of paper, he calls it a poem, they give him $50."

The second boy says, "That's nothing. My Dad scribbles a few words on a piece of paper, he calls it a song, they give him $100."

The third boy says, "I got you both beat. My Dad scribbles a few words on a piece of paper, he calls it a sermon, and it takes eight people to collect all the money!"

############

A police recruit was asked during the exam, "What would you do if you had to arrest your own mother?" He answered "Call for backup."

############

A Sunday School teacher asked her class why Joseph and Mary took Jesus with them to Jerusalem. A small child replied: "They couldn't get a babysitter."

##############

A Sunday school teacher was discussing the Ten Commandments with her five and six year olds. After explaining the commandment to "Honor thy father and thy mother," she asked "Is there a commandment that teaches us how to treat our brothers and sisters?" Without missing a beat one little boy answered, "Thou shall not kill."

#############

At Sunday School they were teaching how God created everything, including human beings. Little Johnny seemed especially intent when they told him how Eve was created out of one of Adam's ribs. Later in the week his mother noticed him lying down as though he were ill, and she said, "Johnny, what is the matter?" Little Johnny responded, "I have pain in my side. I think I'm going to have a wife."

###########

You don't stop laughing because you grow old, You grow old because you stop laughing!

Take heed and pass these along to people who need a laugh

Twas The Night of Thanksgiving,

BUT I JUST COULDN'T SLEEP
I TRIED COUNTING BACKWARDS, I TRIED COUNTING SHEEP.
THE LEFTOVERS BECKONED—THE DARK MEAT AND WHITE
BUT I FOUGHT THE TEMPTATION WITH ALL OF MY MIGHT
TOSSING AND TURNING WITH ANTICIPATION
THE THOUGHT OF A SNACK BECAME INFATUATION.
SO, I RACED TO THE KITCHEN, FLUNG OPEN THE DOOR AND GAZED AT THE FRIDGE,
FULL OF GOODIES GALORE.
I GOBBLED UP TURKEY AND BUTTERED POTATOES, PICKLES AND CARROTS, BEANS
AND TOMATOES.
I FELT MYSELF SWELLING SO PLUMP AND SO ROUND,
'TIL ALL OF A SUDDEN, I ROSE OFF THE GROUND.
I CRASHED THROUGH THE CEILING, FLOATING INTO THE SKY
WITH A MOUTHFUL OF PUDDING AND A HANDFUL OF PIE.
BUT, I MANAGED TO YELL AS I SOARED PAST THE TREES . . .
HAPPY EATING TO ALL—PASS THE CRANBERRIES, PLEASE.

MAY YOUR STUFFING BE TASTY, MAY YOUR TURKEY BE PLUMP.
MAY YOUR POTATOES 'N GRAVY HAVE NARY A LUMP,
MAY YOUR YAMS BE DELICIOUS, MAY YOUR PIES TAKE THE PRIZE,
MAY YOUR THANKSGIVING DINNER STAY OFF OF YOUR THIGHS.

Memo from Santa
Sent: Monday Dec. 2, 2002 6:51 AM
Subject: Memo from Santa

I regret to inform you that, effective immediately, I will no longer serve the States of Georgia, Florida, Virginia, North and South Carolina, Tennessee, Mississippi, Texas, and Arkansas on Christmas Eve. Due to the overwhelming current population of the earth, my contract was renegotiated by North American Fairies and Elves Local 209. As part of the new and better contract I also get longer breaks for milk and cookies so keep that in mind. However, I'm certain that your children will be in good hands with your local replacement, who happens to be my third cousin, Bubba Claus. His side of the family is from the South Pole. He shares my goal of delivering toys to all the good boys and girls; however, there are a few differences between us.

Differences such as:

1. There is no danger of the Grinch stealing your presents from Bubba Claus. He has a gun rack on his sleigh and a bumper sticker that reads: "These toys insured by Smith and Wesson."
2. Instead of milk and cookies, Bubba Claus prefers that children leave an RC cola and pork rinds [or a moon pie] on the fireplace. And Bubba doesn't smoke a pipe. He dips a little snuff though, so please have an empty spit can handy.
3. Bubba Claus' sleigh is pulled by floppy-eared, flyin' coon dogs instead of reindeer. I made the mistake of loaning him a couple of my reindeer one time, and Blitzen's head now overlooks Bubba's fireplace.
4. You won't hear "On Comet, on Cupid, on Donner and Blitzen." When Bubba Claus arrives. Instead, you'll hear, "On Earnhardt, on Andretti, on Elliott and Petty."

5. "Ho, Ho, Ho!" has been replaced by "Yee Haw!" And you also are likely to hear Bubba's elves respond, "I her'd dat!"

6. As required by Southern highway laws, Bubba Claus' sleigh does have a Yosemite Sam safety triangle on the back with the words "Back Off."

7. The usual Christmas movie classics such as "Miracle on 34th Street" and "It's a Wonderful Life" will not be shown in your negotiated viewing area. Instead, you'll see "Boss Hogg Saves Christmas" and "Smokey and the Bandit IV" featuring Burt Reynolds as Bubba Claus and dozens of state patrol cars crashing into each other.

And Finally,

8. Bubba Claus doesn't wear a belt. If I were you, I'd make sure you, the wife, and the kids turn the other way when he bends over to put presents under the tree.

Sincerely Yours,
Santa Claus

Subject: truth

Once upon a time, a perfect man and a perfect woman met. After a perfect courtship, they had a perfect wedding.

Their life together was, of course, perfect.

One snowy, stormy Christmas Eve, this perfect couple was driving their perfect car along a winding road, when they noticed someone at the side of the road in distress. Being the perfect couple, they stopped to help.

There stood Santa Claus with a huge bundle of toys. Not wanting to disappoint any children on the eve of Christmas, the perfect couple loaded Santa and his toys into their vehicle. Soon they were driving along delivering the toys.

Unfortunately, the driving conditions deteriorated and the perfect couple and Santa Claus had an accident. Only one of them survived the accident.

Question: Who was the survivor?

Scroll down for the answer.)

Answer:

The perfect woman survived. She's the only one who really existed in the first place. Everyone knows there is no Santa Claus & there is no such thing as a perfect man.

Women stop reading here, that is the end of the joke.

Men keep scrolling.

So, if there is no perfect man and no Santa Claus, the woman must have been driving. This explains why there was a car accident

Men Keep scrolling

By the way, if you're a woman and you're still reading, this illustrates another point: Women never listen, nor can they follow instructions.

Chili Cook Off

If you can read this whole story without laughing then there's no hope for you. I was crying by the end. Note: Please take time to read this slowly.

(I've read this probably 5 times and it never fails to reduce me to tears of laughter). Hope it does the same for you!!!

If you pay attention to the first two judges, the reaction of the third judge is even better. For those of you who have lived in Texas, you know how true this is. They actually have a Chili Cook Off about the time Halloween comes around. It takes up a major portion of a parking lot at the San Antonio City Park. Judge #3 was an *inexperienced* Chili Taster named Frank, who was visiting from Springfield, IL.

Frank: "Recently, I was honored to be selected as a judge at a chili cook-off. The original person called in sick at the last moment and I happened to be standing there at the judge's table asking for directions to the Coors Light truck, when the call came in. I was assured by the other two judges (Native Texans) that the chili wouldn't be all that spicy and, besides, they told me I could have free beer during the tasting, so I accepted."

Here are the scorecard notes from the event:

□ □

CHILI # 1—MIKE'S MANIAC MONSTER CHILI . . .

Judge # 1—A little too heavy on the tomato. Amusing kick.
Judge # 2—Nice, smooth tomato flavor. Very mild.
Judge # 3 (Frank)—Holy shit, what the hell is this stuff? You could remove dried paint from your driveway. Took me two beers to put the flames out. I hope that's the worst one. These Texans are crazy.

□ □

CHILI # 2—AUSTIN'S AFTERBURNER CHILI . . .

Judge # 1—Smoky, with a hint of pork. Slight jalapeno just like this nuclear waste I'm eating! Is chili an aphrodisiac?

CHILI # 5 LISA'S LEGAL LIP REMOVER . . .

Judge # 1—Meaty, strong chili. Cayenne peppers freshly ground, adding considerable! kick. Very impressive.

Judge # 2—Chili using shredded beef, could use more tomato. Must admit the cayenne peppers make a strong statement.

Judge # 3—My! ears are ringing, sweat is pouring off my forehead and I can no longer focus my eyes. I farted and four people behind me needed paramedics. The contestant seemed offended when I told her that her chili had given me brain damage. Sally saved my tongue from bleeding by pouring beer directly on it from the pitcher. I wonder if I'm burning my lips off. It really pisses me off that the other judges asked me to stop screaming.

CHILI # 6—VERA'S VERY VEGETARIAN VARIETY . . .

Judge # 1—Thin yet bold vegetarian variety chili. Good balance of spices and peppers.

Judge # 2—The best yet. Aggressive use of peppers, onions, and garlic. Superb.

Judge # 3—My intestines are now a straight pipe filled with gaseous, sulfuric flames. I shit on myself when I farted and I'm worried it will eat through the chair. No one seems inclined to stand behind me except that Sally. Can't feel my lips anymore. I need to wipe my ass with a snow cone.

CHILI # 7—SUSAN'S SCREAMING SENSATION CHILI . . .

Judge # 1—A mediocre chili with too much reliance on canned peppers.

Judge # 2—Ho hum, tastes as if the chef literally threw in a can of chili peppers at the last moment. ⬜ ⬜ I should take note that I am worried about Judge # 3. He appears to be in a bit of distress as he is cursing uncontrollably.

Judge # 3—You could put a grenade in my mouth, pull the pin, and I wouldn't feel a thing. I've lost sight in one eye, and the world sounds like it is made of rushing water. My shirt is covered with chili, which slid unnoticed out of my mouth. My pants are full of lava to match my shirt. At least during the autopsy, they'll know what killed me. I've decided to stop breathing it's too painful. Screw it; I'm not getting any oxygen anyway. If I need air, I'll just suck it in through the 4-inch hole in my stomach.

⬜ ⬜

CHILI # 8—BIG TOM'S TOENAIL CURLING CHILI . . .

Judge # 1—The perfect ending, this is a nice blend chili. Not too bold but spicy enough to declare its existence.

Judge # 2—This final entry is a good, balanced chili. Neither mild nor hot. Sorry to see that most of it was lost when Judge #3 farted, passed out, fell over and pulled the chili pot down on top of himself. Not sure if he's going to make it. poor feller, wonder how he'd have reacted to really hot chili?

Judge # 3—No Report

Two sisters, one blonde and one brunette, inherit the family ranch. Unfortunately, after just a few years, they are in financial trouble. In order to keep the bank from repossessing the ranch they need to purchase a bull so that they can breed their own stock. Upon leaving, the brunette tells her sister, "Now, when I get there, if I decide to buy the bull, I'll contact you to drive out after me and haul it home." The brunette arrives at the man's ranch, inspects the bull, and decides she wants to buy it. The man tells her that he will sell it for $599 . . . no less. After paying him, she drives to the nearest town to send her sister a telegram to tell her the news. She walks into the telegraph office, and says, "I want to send a telegram to my sister telling her that I've bought a bull for our ranch. I need her to hitch the trailer to our pickup truck and drive out here so we can haul it home." The telegraph operator explains that he'll be glad to help her, then adds, "It's just 99 cents a word." Well, after paying for the bull, the brunette only has $1 left. She realizes that she'll only be able to send her sister one word. After thinking for a few minutes, she nods, and says, "I want you to send her the word . . . "comfortable". The telegraph operator shakes his head. "How is she ever going to know that you want her to hitch the trailer to your pickup truck and drive out here to haul that bull back to your ranch if you send her the word, 'comfortable'?" The brunette explains, "My sister's a blonde. The word's big. She'll read it slowly . . . ("com-for-da-bul")."

The very first ever Blonde GUY Joke . . . and well worth the wait!

An Irishman, a Mexican and a blonde guy were doing construction work on scaffolding on the 20th floor of a building. They were eating lunch and the Irishman said, "Corned beef and cabbage! If I get corned beef and cabbage one more time for lunch I'm going to jump off this building."

The Mexican opened his lunch box and exclaimed, "Burritos again! If I get burritos one more time I'm going to jump off, too."

The blond opened his lunch and said, "Bologna again. If I get a bologna sandwich one more time, I'm jumping too."

The next day the Irishman opened his lunch box, saw corned beef and cabbage and jumped to his death.

The Mexican opened his lunch, saw a burrito and jumped too.

The blonde guy opened his lunch, saw the bologna and jumped to his death as well.

At the funeral the Irishman's wife was weeping. She said, "If I'd known how really tired he was of corned beef and cabbage, I never would have given it to him again!"

The Mexican's wife also wept and said, "I could have given him tacos or enchiladas!

I didn't realize he hated burritos so much."

Everyone turned and stared at the blonde's wife.

are you ready for it . . .

it's worth the wait

here it comes . . .

"Hey, don't look at me," she said, "He makes his own lunch."

nightnurse

Why I love MoM

Mom and Dad were watching TV when Mom said, "I'm tired, and it's getting late. I think I'll go to bed." She went to the kitchen to make sandwiches for the next day's lunches. Rinsed out the popcorn bowls, took meat out of the freezer for supper the following evening, checked the cereal box levels, filled the sugar container, put spoons and bowls on the table and started the coffee pot for brewing the next morning. She then put some wet clothes in the dryer, put a load of clothes into the washer, ironed a shirt and secured a loose button. She picked up the game pieces left on the table, put the phone back on the charger and put the telephone book into the drawer. She watered the plants, emptied a wastebasket and hung up a towel to dry. She yawned and stretched and headed for the bedroom. She stopped by the desk and wrote a note to the teacher, counted out some cash for the field trip, and pulled a textbook out from hiding under the chair. She signed a birthday card for a friend, addressed and stamped the envelope and wrote a quick note for the grocery store. She put both near her purse. Mom then washed her face with 3 in 1 cleanser, put on her Night Solution & age fighting moisturizer, brushed and flossed her teeth and filed her nails. Dad called out, "I thought you were going to bed." "I'm on my way," she said. She put some water into the dog's dish and put the cat outside, then made sure the doors were locked and the patio light was on. She looked in on each of the kids and turned out their bedside lamps and TV's, hung up a shirt, threw some dirty socks into the hamper, and had a brief conversation with the one up still doing homework. In her own room, she set the alarm; laid out clothing for the next day, straightened up the shoe rack. She added three things to her 6 most important things to do list. She said her prayers, and visualized the accomplishment of her goals. About that time, Dad turned off the TV and announced to no one in particular. "I'm going to bed." And he did . . . without another thought. Anything extraordinary here? Wonder why women live longer . . . ? 'CAUSE WE ARE MADE FOR THE LONG HAUL . . .

Subject: 911 Calls

Dispatcher: Nine-one-one. What is your emergency?
Caller: I heard what sounded like gunshots coming from the brown house on the corner.
Dispatcher: Do you have an address?
Caller: No, I'm wearing a blouse and slacks, . . . why?

Dispatcher: Nine-one-one. What is your emergency?
Caller: Someone broke into my house and took a bite out of my ham and cheese sandwich.
Dispatcher: Excuse me?
Caller: I made a ham and cheese sandwich and left it on a kitchen table and when I came back from the bathroom, someone had taken a bite out of it.

Dispatcher: Nine-one-one.
Caller: Hi, is this the police?
Dispatcher: This is 911. Do you need police assistance?
Caller: Well, I don't know who to call. Can you tell me how to cook a turkey? I've never cooked one before.

Dispatcher: Nine-one-one. Fire or emergency?
Caller: Fire, I guess.
Dispatcher: How can I help you sir?
Caller: I was wondering . . . Does the Fire Dept. put snow chains on their trucks?

Dispatcher: Yes, sir, do you have an emergency?
Caller: Well, I've spent the last 4 hours trying to put these chains on my tires and . . . well . . . Do you think the Fire Dept. could come over and help me?

Dispatcher: Nine-one-one. What is the nature of your emergency?

Caller: I'm trying to reach nine eleven but my phone doesn't have an eleven on it.

Dispatcher: This is nine eleven.

Caller: I thought you just said it was nine-one-one.

Dispatcher: Yes, ma'am nine-one-one and nine-eleven are the same thing.

Caller: Honey, I may be old, but I'm not stupid.

Dispatcher: Nine-one-one. What's the nature of your emergency?

Caller: My wife is pregnant and her contractions are only two minutes apart.

Dispatcher: Is this her first child?

Caller: No, you idiot! This is her husband.

Dispatcher: Nine-one-one.

Caller: Yeah, I'm having trouble breathing. I'm all out of breath. Darn . . . I think I'm going to pass out.

Dispatcher: Sir, where are you calling from?

Caller: I'm at a pay phone. North and Foster. Damn . . .

Dispatcher: Sir, an ambulance is on the way. Are you an asthmatic?

Caller: No

Dispatcher: What where are you doing before you started having trouble breathing?

Caller: I was running from the police

Subject: Three sisters

Three old sisters—92, 94 & 96 years old respectively—all lived together. One day the eldest sister drew a bath. She put one foot in the water, paused, then called downstairs to her sisters, "Am I getting into the tub or out of the tub?" The middle sister started up the stairs to help, then paused and called back downstairs, "Was I going up or coming down the stair?" The youngest sister who was sitting at the kitchen table having tea, said, "I guess I'll have to help. I hope I never get that forgetful!" and knocked on wood. She got up, then paused, and called out, "I'll come up as soon as I see who's at the door!"

-=-=-=-=-=-=-=-=-=-=-=-=-=-

Subject: Snoring

A couple has a dog that snores. Annoyed because she can't sleep, the wife goes to the vet to see if he can help.

The vet tells the woman to tie a ribbon around the dog's testicles and he will stop snoring.

"Yeah, right," she says.

A few minutes after going to bed, the dog begins snoring as usual. The wife tosses and turns, unable to sleep. Muttering to herself, she goes to the closet and grabs a piece of ribbon and ties it carefully around the dog's testicles. Sure enough, the dog stops snoring. The woman is amazed! Later that night, her husband returns home drunk from being out with his buddies. He climbs into bed, falls asleep, and begins snoring loudly. The woman thinks maybe the ribbon will work on him. So she goes to the closet again, grabs a piece of ribbon, and carefully ties it around her husband's testicles. Amazingly, it also works on him!

The woman sleeps soundly. The next morning, the husband wakes up hung over. He stumbles in to the bathroom. As he stands in front of the toilet, he glances in the mirror and sees a blue ribbon attached to his privates. He is very confused, and as he walks back into the bedroom, he sees a red ribbon attached to his dog's testicles. He shakes his head and looks at the dog and says, "Boy, I don't remember where we were or what we did, but, by God, we got first and second place."

News Anchor Dan Rather, NPR Reporter Cokie Roberts, and a U.S. Marine were hiking through the desert one day when they were captured by Iraqis. They were tied up, led to the village and brought before the leader. The leader said, "I am familiar with your western custom of granting the condemned a last wish. Before we kill and dismember you, do you have any last requests?"

Dan Rather said, "Well, I'm a Texan; so I'd like one last bowlful of hot, spicy chili."

The leader nodded to an underling, who left and returned with the chili. Rather ate it all and said, "Now I can die content."

Cokie Roberts said, "I'm a reporter to the end. I want to take out my tape recorder and describe the scene here and what's about to happen. Maybe someday someone will hear it and know that I was on the job til the end."

The leader directed an aide to hand over the tape recorder, and Roberts dictated some comments. She then said, "Now I can die happy."

The leader turned and said, "And now, Mr. U.S. Marine, what is your final wish?"

"Kick me in the ass," said the Marine."

"What?" asked the leader. "Will you mock us in your last hour?"

"No, I'm not kidding. I want you to kick me in the ass," insisted the Marine.

So the leader shoved him into the open, and kicked him in the ass. The Marine went sprawling, but rolled to his knees, pulled a 9mm pistol from inside his cammies, and shot the leader dead. In the resulting confusion, he leapt to his knapsack, pulled out his M4 carbine, and sprayed the Iraqis with gunfire. In a flash, the Iraqis were dead or fleeing for their lives. As the Marine was untying the others, they asked him, "Why didn't you just shoot them? Why did you ask them to kick you in the ass?"

"What!?" said the Marine, "And have you liberal ASSHOLES call ME the aggressor?!?"

Subject: Interesting

AS SMART AS YOU ARE . . . I BET YOU DIDN'T KNOW THIS!! The first couple to be shown in bed together on prime time TV were Fred and Wilma Flintstone.

~~~~~~

Every day more money is printed for Monopoly than the US Treasury.

~~~~~~

Men can read smaller print than women can; women can hear better.

~~~~~~

Coca-Cola was originally green.

~~~~~~

It is impossible to lick your elbow.

~~~~~~

The State with the highest % of people who walk to work: Alaska

~~~~~~

The percentage of Africa that is wilderness: 28% (now get this . . .) The percentage of North America that is wilderness: 38%

~~~~~~

The cost of raising a medium-size dog to the age of eleven: $6,400

~~~~~~

The world's youngest parents were 8 and 9 & lived in China in 1910.

~~~~~~

The youngest pope was 11 years old.

~~~~~~

The first novel ever written on a typewriter: Tom Sawyer.

~~~~~~

San Francisco Cable cars are the only mobile National Monuments.

~~~~~~

Each king in a deck of cards represents a great king from history:
Spades—King David,
Hearts—Charlemagne,
Clubs-Alexander, the Great
Diamonds—Julius Caesar

~~~~~~

$$111,111,111 \times 111,111,111 = 12,345,678,987,654,321$$

~~~~~~

If a statue in the park of a person on a horse has both front legs in the air, the person died in battle. If the horse has one front leg in the air the person died as a result of wounds received in battle. If the horse has all four legs on the ground, the person died of natural causes.

~~~~~~

Only two people signed the Declaration of Independence on July 4th, John Hancock and Charles Thomson. Most of the rest signed on August 2, but the last signature wasn't added until 5 years later.

~~~~~~

"I am" is the shortest complete sentence in the English language.

~~~~~~

Hershey's Kisses are called that because the machine that makes them looks like it's kissing the conveyor belt.

~~~~~~

Q. What occurs more often in December than any other month?
A. Conception.

~~~~~~

Q. Half of all Americans live within 50 miles of what?
A. Their birthplace

~~~~~~

Q. Most boat owners name their boats. What is the most popular boat name requested?
A. Obsession

~~~~~~

Q. If you were to spell out numbers, how far would you have to go until

If you try to kill all your enemies,
You'll never succeed.
But if you kill your anger,
You'll have no enemies.

Shantideva

So, You Think You Know Everything?

A dime has 118 ridges around the edge.

A cat has 32 muscles in each ear.

A crocodile cannot stick out its tongue.

A dragonfly has a life span of 24 hours.

A goldfish has a memory span of three seconds.

A "jiffy" is an actual unit of time for 1/ 100th of a second.

A shark is the only fish that can blink with both eyes.

A snail can sleep for three years.

Al Capone's business card said he was a used furniture dealer.

All 50 states are listed across the top of the Lincoln Memorial on the back of the $5 bill.

Almonds are a member of the peach family.

An ostrich's eye is bigger than its brain.

Babies are born without kneecaps. They don't appear until the child reaches 2 to 6 years of age!

Butterflies taste with their feet.

Cats have over one hundred vocal sounds. Dogs only have about 10.

"Dreamt" is the only English word that ends in the letters "mt".

February 1865 is the only month in recorded history not to have a full moon.

In the last 4,000 years, no new animals have been domesticated.

If the population of China walked past you, in single file, the line would never end because of the rate of reproduction.

If you are an average American, in your whole life, you will spend an average of 6 months waiting at red lights.

It's impossible to sneeze with your eyes open.

Leonardo Da Vinci invented the scissors.

Maine is the only state whose name is just one syllable.

No word in the English language rhymes with month, orange, silver, or purple.

On a Canadian two dollar bill, the flag flying over the Parliament building is an American flag

Our eyes are always the same size from birth, but our nose and ears never stop growing.

Peanuts are one of the ingredients of dynamite.

Rubber bands last longer when refrigerated.

"Stewardesses" is the longest word typed with only the left hand and "lollipop" with your right.

Typewriter is the longest word that can be made using the letters only on one row of the keyboard.

The average person's left hand does 56% of the typing.

The cruise liner, QE2, moves only six inches for each gallon of diesel that it burns.

The microwave was invented after a researcher walked by a radar tube and a chocolate bar melted in his pocket.

The sentence: "The quick brown fox jumps over the lazy dog" uses every letter of the alphabet.

The winter of 1932 was so cold that Niagara Falls froze completely solid.

The words 'racecar,' 'kayak' and 'level' are the same whether they are read left to right or right to left (palindromes).

There are 293 ways to make change for a dollar.

There are more chickens than people in the world.

There are only four words in the English language which end in "dous": tremendous, horrendous, stupendous, and hazardous

There are two words in the English language that have all five vowels in order: "abstemious" and "facetious."

There's no Betty Rubble in the Flintstones Chewables Vitamins.

Tigers have striped skin, not just striped fur.

Winston Churchill was born in a ladies' room during a dance.

Women blink nearly twice as much as men.

Your stomach has to produce a new layer of mucus every two weeks; otherwise, it will digest itself.

. . . Now you know everything

Subject: Chinese Proverbs

Man who run in front of car get tired.

◻ ∿◻ ∿◻ ∿◻ ∿◻ ∿◻ ∿◻ ∿◻ ∿◻

Man who run behind car get exhausted.

◻ ∿◻ ∿◻ ∿◻ ∿◻ ∿◻ ∿◻ ∿◻ ∿◻

Man who walk through airport turnstile sideways going to Bangkok.

◻ ∿◻ ∿◻ ∿◻ ∿◻ ∿◻ ∿◻ ∿◻ ∿◻

Man with one chopstick go hungry.

◻ ∿◻ ∿◻ ∿◻ ∿◻ ∿◻ ∿◻ ∿◻ ∿◻

Man who scratch ass should not bite fingernails.

◻ ∿◻ ∿◻ ∿◻ ∿◻ ∿◻ ∿◻ ∿◻ ∿◻

Man who eat many prunes get good run for money.

◻ ∿◻ ∿◻ ∿◻ ∿◻ ∿◻ ∿◻ ∿◻ ∿◻

Baseball i! s wrong: man with four balls cannot walk.

◻ ∿◻ ∿◻ ∿◻ ∿◻ ∿◻ ∿◻ ∿◻ ∿◻

Panties not best thing on earth! But next to best thing on earth.

◻ ∿◻ ∿◻ ∿◻ ∿◻ ∿◻ ∿◻ ∿◻ ∿◻

War does not determine who is right, war determine who is left.

〰〰〰〰〰〰〰〰〰

! Wife who put husband in doghouse soon find him in cat house.

〰〰〰〰〰〰〰〰〰

Man who fight with wife all day get no piece at night.

〰〰〰〰〰〰〰〰〰

It take many nails to build crib, but one screw to fill it.

〰〰〰〰〰〰〰〰〰

Man who drive like hell, bound to get there.

〰〰〰〰〰〰〰〰〰

Man who stand on toilet is high on pot.

〰〰〰〰〰〰〰〰〰

Man who live in glass house should change clothes in basement.

〰〰〰〰〰〰〰〰〰

Man who fish in other man's well often catch crabs.

〰〰〰〰〰〰〰〰〰

Man who fart in church sit in own pew.

〰〰〰〰〰〰〰〰〰

Crowded elevator smell different to midget.

~~*~*~*~*~*~*~*~*~*

Man who run in front of car get tired.

~~*~*~*~*~*~*~*~*~*

Man who run behind car get exhausted.

~~*~*~*~*~*~*~*~*~*

Man with hand in pocket feel cocky all day.

~~*~*~*~*~*~*~*~*~*

Man who eat many prunes get good run for money.

~~*~*~*~*~*~*~*~*~*

Baseball is wrong: man with four balls cannot walk.

~~*~*~*~*~*~*~*~*~*

War does not determine who is right, war determine who is left.

~~*~*~*~*~*~*~*~*~*

Wife who put husband in doghouse soon find him in cat house.

~~*~*~*~*~*~*~*~*~|*

Man who fight with wife all day get no piece at night.

~~*~*~*~*~*~*~*~*~*

It take many nails to build crib, but one screw to fill it.

~~*~*~*~*~*~*~*~*~*

Man who drive like hell, bound to get there.

~~*~*~*~*~*~*~*~*~*

Man who stand on toilet is high on pot.

~~*~*~*~*~*~*~*~*

Man who live in glass house should change clothes in basement.

~~*~*~*~*~*~*~*~*

Man who fish in other man's well often catch crabs.

~~*~*~*~*~*~*~*~*

Man who fart in church sit in own pew.

~~*~*~*~*~*~*~*

Crowded elevator smell different to midget.

~~*~*~*~*~*~*~*

10 fuNnY tHiNgS to do aT a SuPErMaRkEt

1—in the fruit isle examine all of the fruit carefully and say loudly "eww there's a worm in this apple"

2—get random items and put into other ppl's trolleys

3—ask if you can put your shopping on lay-by

4—take off with someone's trolley and then ditch it near the checkout

5—put 20 bottles of diet coke in your trolley smiling at yourself and say proudly to everyone that walk by "its fat free"

6—when you get to the checkout pretend you've lost your purse and walk off leaving the trolley at the counter

7—run around singing "its raining men" or "i love you, you love me . . ."

8—go to the bulk food isle and fill 2 bag full with sesame seeds

9—lean over peoples trolleys looking at all of the things they have in it

10—knock over all of the canned food and point at the old grannys nearby yelling "come back old granny, you cant get away with this one"

Top 10 Funny Store Signs

1. Outside a muffler shop: "No appointment necessary, we hear you coming."
2. Outside a hotel: "Help! We need inn-experienced people."
3. On a desk in a reception room: "We shoot every 3rd salesman, and the 2nd one just left."
4. In a veterinarians waiting room: "Be back in 5 minutes, Sit! Stay!"
5. At the electric company: "We would be de-lighted if you send in your bill. However, if you don't you will be."
6. On the door of a computer store: "Out for a quick byte."
7. In a restaurant window: "Don't stand there and be hungry, come on in and get fed up."
8. Inside a bowling alley: "Please be quiet, we need to hear a pin drop."
9. In the front yard of a funeral home: "Drive carefully, we'll wait."
10. In a counselors office: "Growing old is mandatory, growing wise is optional.

My
grandpa started walking
five miles a day when he was 60.
Now he's 97 years
old
and we don't know where he is.

I
like long walks,
especially when they are taken
by people who annoy
me.

The
only reason I would take up walking
is so that I could hear heavy breathing
again.

I have to walk early
in the morning,
before my brain figures out what I'm
doing.

· ·

I
joined a health club last year,
spent about 400 bucks.
Haven't lost a
pound.
Apparently you have to go there?

The other day, someone at a store in our town read that a methamphetamine lab had been found in an old farmhouse in the adjoining county, and he asked me a rhetorical question, 'Why didn't we have a drug problem when you and I were growing up?'

I replied: I had a drug problem when I was young: I was drug to church on Sunday morning I was drug to church for weddings and funerals. I was drug to family reunions and community socials no matter the weather.

I was drug by my ears when I was disrespectful to adults. I was also drug to the woodshed when I disobeyed my parents, told a lie, brought home a bad report card, did not speak with respect, spoke ill of the teacher or the preacher, or if I didn't put forth my best effort in everything that was asked of me.

I was drug to the kitchen sink to have my mouth washed out with soap if I uttered a profane four-letter word. I was drug out to pull weeds in mom's garden and flower beds and cockleburs out of dad's fields.

I was drug to the homes of family, friends, and neighbors to help out some poor soul who had no one to mow the yard, repair the clothesline, or chop some firewood; and, if my mother had ever known that I took a single dime as a tip for this kindness, she would have drug me back to the woodshed.

Those drugs are still in my veins; and they affect my behavior in everything I do, say, and think. They are stronger than meth, weed, cocaine, crack, or heroin; and, if today's children had this kind of drug problem, America would be a better place!!!!!!!

~author unknown~

This explains a lot, now I know what my problem is. I know I was going to copy someone else on this e-mail I just can't remember who . . .

Recently, I was diagnosed with A.A.A.D.D.-Age Activated Attention Deficit Disorder. This is how it manifests:

I decided to wash my car. As I start toward the garage, I notice that there is mail on the hall table. I decide to go through the mail before I wash the car. I lay my car keys down on the table, put the junk mail in the trashcan under the table, and notice that the trashcan is full.

So, I decide to put the bills back on the table and take out the trash first. But then I think, since I'm going to be near the mailbox when I take out the trash anyway, I may as well pay the bills first.

I take my checkbook off the table, and see that there is only one check left. My extra checks are in my desk in the study, so I go to my desk where I find the bottle of beer that I had been drinking.

I'm going to look for my checks, but first I need to push the beer aside so that I don't accidentally knock it over. I see that the beer is getting warm, and I decide I should put it in the refrigerator to keep it cold.

As I head toward the kitchen with the beer, a vase of flowers on the counter catches my eye—they need to be watered. I set the beer down on the counter, and I discover my reading glasses that I've been searching for all morning.

I decide I better put them back on my desk, but first I'm going to water the flowers. I set the glasses back down on the counter, fill a container with water and suddenly I spot the TV remote. Someone left it on the kitchen table. I realize that tonight when we go to watch TV, we will be looking for the remote, but nobody will remember that it's on the kitchen table, so I decide to put it back in the den where it belongs, but first I'll water the flowers.

I splash some water on the flowers, but most of it spills on the floor. So, I set the remote back down on the table, get some towels and wipe up the spill.

Then I head down the hall trying to remember what I was planning to do.

At the end of the day: the car isn't washed, the bills aren't paid, there is a warm bottle of beer sitting on the counter, the flowers aren't watered, there is still only one check in my checkbook, I can't find the remote, I can't find my glasses, and I don't remember what I did with the car keys.

Then when I try to figure out why nothing got done today, I'm really baffled because I know I was busy all day long, and I'm really tired. I realize this is a serious problem, and I'll try to get some help for it, but first I'll check my e-mail.

Do me a favor, will you? Forward this message to everyone you know, because I don't remember to whom it has been sent.

Should You Be Institutionalized?

It doesn't hurt to take a hard look at yourself from time to time, and this should help get you started.

During a visit to the mental asylum, a visitor asked the Director what the criterion was which defined whether or not a patient should be institutionalized.

"Well," said the Director, "we fill up a bathtub, then we offer a teaspoon, a teacup and a bucket to the patient and ask him or her to empty the bathtub."

"Oh, I understand," said the visitor. "A normal person would use the bucket because it's bigger than the spoon or the teacup."

"No." said the Director, "A normal person would pull the plug. Do you want a room with or without a view?"

Sorry Guys But This Is Funny!!!

A woman in her fifties is at home, unclothed, happily jumping on her bed and squealing with delight.

Her husband watches her for a while and asks, 'Do you have any idea how ridiculous you look? What's the matter with you?'

The woman continues to bounce on the bed and says, 'I don't care what you think. I just came from having a mammogram and the doctor says that not only am I healthy, but I have the breasts of an 18 year-old. The husband replies, 'What did he say about your 55-year old ass?

'Your name never came up,' she replied.

Blonds

January — Took new scarf back to store because it was too tight.

February — Fired from pharmacy job for failing to print labels . . . "duh" . . . bottles won't fit in typewriter!!!

March — Got excited . . . finished jigsaw puzzle in 6 months . . . box said "2-4 years!"

Apri — Trapped on escalator for hours . . . power went out!!!

May — Tried to make Kool-Aid . . . 8 cups of water won't fit into those little packets!!!

June — Tried to go water skiing . . . couldn't find a lake with a slope.

July — Lost breast stroke swimming competition . . . learned later, other swimmers cheated, they used their arms!!!

August — Got locked out of car in rain storm . . . car swamped, because top was down.

September — The capital of California is "C" . . . isn't it???

October — Hate M &M's . . . they are so hard to peel.

November — Baked turkey for 4 1/2 days . . . instructions said 1 hour per pound and I weigh 108!!!

December — Couldn't call 911 . . . "duh" . . . there's no "eleven" button on the phone!!!

3 Blondes

Three blondes were all vying for the last available position on the California HiWay Patrol. The detective conducting the interview looked at the three of them and said, "So you all want to be a cop, eh?" The blondes all nodded. The detective got up, opened a file drawer and pulled out a file folder. Sitting back down, he opened it up and withdrew a photograph, and said, "To be a detective, you have to be able to DETECT. You must be able to notice things such as distinguishing features and oddities such as scars, etc." So saying, he stuck the photo in the face of the first blonde and withdrew it after about 2 seconds.

"Now, he said, "Did you notice any distinguishing features about this man?" The blonde immediately said, "Yes, I did. He only has one eye!"

The detective shook his head and said, "Of COURSE he only has one eye in this picture! It's a PROFILE of his face! You're dismissed!"

The first blonde hung her head and walked out of the office.

The detective then turned to the second blonde, stuck the photo in her face for two seconds, pulled it back and said, "What about you? Notice anything unusual or outstanding about this man?" The blonde immediately shot back, "Yes! He only has one ear!" The detective put his head in his hand and exclaimed, "Didn't you hear what I just said to the other lady? This is a PROFILE of the man's face! Of COURSE you can see only one ear!! You're excused, too!

The second blonde sheepishly walked out of the office.

The detective turned his attention to the last blonde and said, "This is probably a waste of time, but . . ." He flashed the photo in her face for a couple of seconds and withdrew it, saying, "All right. Did YOU notice anything distinguishing or unusual about this man?" The blonde said, "I did. This man wears contact lenses." The detective frowned, took another look at the picture and began looking at some of the papers in the folder. He looked up at the blonde with a puzzled _expression and said, "You're absolutely right! His bio says he wears contacts! How in the world could tell that by looking at this picture?"

The blonde rolled her eyes and said, "DUH! With only one eye and one ear, he certainly CAN'T WEAR GLASSES!"

Black and White

(Under age 40? You won't understand.)

You could hardly see for all the snow,
Spread the rabbit ears as far as they go.
Pull a chair up to the TV set,
"Good Night, David. Good Night, Chet."

Depending on the channel you tuned,
You got Rob and Laura—or Ward and June.
It felt so good. It felt so right.
Life looked better in black and white.

I Love Lucy, The Real McCoys,
Dennis the Menace, the Cleaver boys,
Rawhide, Gunsmoke, Wagon Train,
Superman, Jimmy and Lois Lane.

Father Knows Best, Patty Duke,
Rin Tin Tin and Lassie too,
Donna Reed on Thursday night!—
Life looked better in black and white.

I wanna go back to black and white.
Everything always turned out right.
Simple people, simple lives . . .
Good guys always won the fights.

Now nothing is the way it seems,
In living color on the TV screen.
Too many murders, too many fights,
I wanna go back to black and white.

In God they trusted, alone in bed, they slept,
A promise made was a promise kept.
They never cussed or broke their vows.
They'd never make the network now.

But if I could, I'd rather be
In a TV town in '53.
It felt so good. It felt so right.
Life looked better in black and white.
I'd trade all the channels on the satellite,
If I could just turn back the clock tonight
To when everybody knew wrong from right.
Life was better in black and white!

Another Goody for The oldtimers

My Mom used to cut chicken, chop eggs and spread mayo on the same cutting board with the same knife and no bleach, but we didn't seem to get food poisoning.

My Mom used to defrost hamburger on the counter AND I used to eat it raw sometimes, too. Our school sandwiches were wrapped in wax paper in a brown paper bag, not in icepack coolers, but I can't remember getting e.coli.

Almost all of us would have rather gone swimming in the lake instead of a pristine pool (talk about boring), no beach closures then.

The term cell phone would have conjured up a phone in a jail cell, and a pager was the school PA system.

We all took gym, not PE . . . and risked permanent injury with a pair of high top Ked's (only worn in gym) instead of having cross-training athletic shoes with air cushion soles and built in light reflectors. I can't recall any injuries but they must have happened because they tell us how much safer we are now.

Flunking gym was not an option . . . even for stupid kids! I guess PE must be much harder than gym.

Speaking of school, we all said prayers and sang the national anthem, and staying in detention after school caught all sorts of negative attention.

We must have had horribly damaged psyches. What an archaic health system we had then. Remember school nurses? Ours wore a hat and everything.

I thought that I was supposed to accomplish something before I was allowed to be proud of myself.

I just can't recall how bored we were without computers, Play Station, Nintendo, X-box or 270 digital TV cable stations

Oh yeah. and where was the Benadryl and sterilization kit when I got that bee sting? I could have been killed!

We played 'king of the hill' on piles of gravel left on vacant construction sites, and when we got hurt, Mom pulled out the 48-cent bottle of Mercurochrome (kids liked it better because it didn't sting like iodine did) and then we got our butt spanked.

Now it's a trip to the emergency room, followed by a 10-day dose of a $49 bottle of antibiotics, and then Mom calls the attorney to sue the contractor for leaving a horribly vicious pile of gravel where it was such a threat.

We didn't act up at the neighbor's house either because if we did, we got our butt spanked there and then we got butt spanked again when we got home.

I recall Donny Reynolds from next door coming over and doing his tricks on the front stoop, just before he fell off. Little did his Mom know that she could have owned our house. Instead, she picked him up and swatted him for being such a goof. It was a neighborhood run amuck.

To top it off, not a single person I knew had ever been told that they were from a dysfunctional family. How could we possibly have known that?

We needed to get into group therapy and anger management classes? We were obviously so duped by so many societal ills, that we didn't even notice that the entire country wasn't taking Prozac! How did we ever survive?

LOVE TO ALL OF US WHO SHARED THIS ERA, AND TO ALL WHO SORRY FOR WHAT YOU MISSED. I WOULDN'T TRADE IT FOR ANYTHING

Pass this to someone (over age 40, of course), and brighten their day by helping them to remember that life's most simple pleasures are very often the best!

Clear Day

The train was quite crowded, so a U.S. Marine walked the entire length looking for a seat, but the only seat left was taken by a well dressed, middle aged, French woman's poodle.

The war weary Marine asked, "Ma'am, may I have that seat?" The French woman just sniffed and said to no one in particular, "Americans are so rude. My little Fifi is using that seat."

The Marine walked the entire train again, but the only seat left was under that dog.

"Please, ma'am. May I sit down? I'm very tired."

She snorted, "Not only are you Americans rude, you are also arrogant!"

This time the Marine didn't say a word; he just picked up the little dog, tossed it out of the window, and sat down.

The French woman shrieked, "Someone must defend my honour! Put this American in his place!"

An English gentleman sitting nearby spoke up, "Sir, you Americans often seem to have a penchant for doing the wrong thing. You hold the fork in the wrong hand. You drive your autos on the wrong side of the road. And now sir, you seem to have thrown the wrong bitch out the window!"

Just some thoughts...

1. I saw a woman wearing a sweat shirt with "Guess" on it. So I said "Implants?" She hit me.
2. How come we choose from just two people to run for president and 50 for Miss America?
3. A good friend will come and bail you out of jail ... but, a true Friend will be sitting next to you saying, "Damn ... that was fun!"
4. I signed up for an exercise class and was told to wear loose-fitting clothing. If I had any loose-fitting clothing, I wouldn't have signed up in the first place!
5. When I was young we used to go "skinny dipping," now I just "chunky Dunk."
6. Don't argue with an idiot; people watching may not be able to tell the difference.
7. Wouldn't it be nice if whenever we messed up our life we could simply press 'Ctrl Alt Delete' and start all over?
8. Why is it that our children can't read a Bible in school, but they can in prison?
9. Wouldn't you know it ... Brain cells come and brain cells go, but FAT cells live forever.
10. Why do I have to swear on the Bible in court when the Ten Commandments cannot be displayed in a federal building?
11. Bumper sticker of the year: "If you can read this, thank a teacher ... and since it's in English, thank a soldier."

Aliens or ???

Clear Day I walked into a Quizno's with a buy-one-get-one-free coupon for a sandwich. I handed it to the girl and she looked over at a little chalkboard that said "buy one-get one free". "They're already buy-one-get-one-free", she said, "so I guess they're both free". She handed me my free sandwiches and I walked out the door. They walk among us, and many work retail.

=====================

One day I was walking down the beach with some friends when one of them shouted, "Look at that dead bird!" Someone looked up at the sky and said, "Where?"

=====================

While looking at a house, my brother asked the real estate agent which direction was north because, he explained, he didn't want the sun waking him up every morning. She asked, "Does the sun rise in the north?" When my brother explained that the sun rises in the east, and has for sometime, she shook her head and said, "Oh, I don't keep up with that stuff."

=====================

I used to work in technical support for a 24/7 call center. One day I got a call from an individual who asked what hours the call center was open. I told him, "The number you dialed is open 24 hours a day, 7 days a week." He responded, "Is that Eastern or Pacific time?" Wanting to end the call quickly, I said,! "Uh, Pacific." They walk among us!

=====================

My sister-in-law has a life-saving tool in her car designed to cut through a seat belt if she gets trapped. She keeps it in the trunk. They walk among us!

=====================

My friends and I were on a beer run and noticed that the cases were discounted 10%. Since it was a big party, we bought 2 cases. The cashier multiplied 2 times 10% and gave us a 20% discount.

=====================

I couldn't find my luggage at the airport baggage area, so I went to the lost luggage office and told the woman there that my bags never showed up. She smiled and told me not to worry because she was a trained professional and I was in good hands. "Now," she asked me, "has your plane arrived yet?"

=====================

While waiting for my order at a pizza parlor, I observed a man ordering a small pizza to go. He appeared to be alone and the cook asked him if he would like it cut into 4 pieces or 6. He thought about it for some time before responding. "Just cut it into 4 pieces; I don't think I'm hungry enough to eat 6 pieces."

==================================

At a McDonald's in Florida, I asked the clerk for a cup of coffee—half regular and half decaf. She asked me which one I wanted on the bottom. She wasn't even blonde. Yep, they walk among us!

Postcard from one Redneck To Another

Dear Cletus—I'm writin' this real slow cause I know you cain't read very fast. We don't live where we did when you left. We read in the paper that most accidents happen within ten miles of home, so we moved.

I won't be able to send you our new address cause the last family that lived here took the house numbers with them so they wouldn't have to change their address.

This place has a washing machine. The first day mama put four shirts in, pulled the chain and we ain't seen them since.

It only rained here twice this week. Three days the first time and five days the second time.

I know it is cold where you are so we're sending you a coat. Mama said it would be to heavy to send in the mail with them buttons on it, so we cut 'em off and put 'em in the pockets.

We got a letter from the funeral home. They said if we don't make the last payment on grandma's funeral bill, up she comes!

My sister had a baby this morning. I ain't heard whether it's a boy or a girl so I don't know if I'm an uncle or an aunt.

Uncle John fell in the big whiskey vat. When they tried to pull him out, he fought them off, so he drowned. We cremated him and he burned for three days.

Three of my friends went off the bridge in a pick-up truck. One was driving, the other two was in the back. The driver got out 'cause he rolled down the window and swam to safety. The other two drowned, they couldn't get the tailgate down.

More next time, nuthin' much is happenin' around here.

older People's Sense of Humor

Bob, a 70-year-old, extremely wealthy widower, shows up at the Country Club with a breathtakingly beautiful and very sexy 25 year—old blonde who knocks everyone's socks off with her youthful sex appeal and charm. She hangs onto Bob's arm and listens intently to his every word. His buddies at the club are all aghast. At the very first chance, they corner him and ask, "Bob, how did you get the trophy girlfriend?" Bob replies, "Girlfriend? She's my wife!" They're amazed, but continue to ask. "So, how did you persuade her to marry you?" "I lied about my age", Bob replies. "What, did you tell her you were only 50?" Bob smiles and says, "No, I told her I was 90."

A group of Americans were traveling by tour bus through Holland. As they stopped at a cheese farm, a young guide led them through the process of cheese making, explaining that goat's milk was used. She showed the group a lively hillside where many goats were grazing. "These" she explained "are the older goats put out to pasture when they no longer produce."; She then asked, "What do you do in America with your old goats?" A spry old gentleman answered, "They send us on bus tours!"

An elderly gentleman of 83 arrived in Paris by plane. At the French customs desk, the man took a few minutes to locate his passport in his carry-on bag. "You have been to France before, monsieur?" the customs officer asked, sarcastically. The elderly gentleman admitted he had been to France previously. "Then you should know enough to have your passport ready." The American said, "The last time I was here, I didn't have to show it." "Impossible. Americans always have to show their passports on arrival in France!" The American senior gave the Frenchman a long hard look. Then he quietly explained. "Well, when I came ashore at Omaha Beach on D-Day in 1944 to help liberate this country, I couldn't find any Frenchmen to show it to."

Doctor was addressing a large audience in Tampa. "The material we put into our stomachs is enough to have killed most of us sitting here, years ago. Red meat is awful. Soft drinks corrode your stomach lining. Chinese food is loaded with MSG. High fat diets can be disastrous, and none of us realizes the long-term harm caused by the germs in our drinking water. But there is one thing that is the most dangerous of all and we all have, or will, eat it. Can anyone here tell me what food it is that causes the most grief and suffering for years after eating it?" After several seconds of quiet, a 75-year-old man in the front row raised his hand, and softly said, "Wedding Cake."

A lady walks into a drug store and tells the pharmacist she needs some cyanide. The pharmacist said, "Why in the world do you need cyanide?" The lady then explained she needed it to poison her husband.

The pharmacist's eyes got big and he said, "Lord have mercy, I can't give you cyanide to kill your husband! That's against the law! I'll lose my license, they'll throw both of us in jail and all kinds of bad things will happen! Absolutely not, you can NOT have any cyanide!"

The lady reached into her purse and pulled out a picture of her husband in bed with the pharmacist's wife. The pharmacist looked at the picture and replied, "Well now, you didn't tell me you had a prescription."

The Cork

Two Arab terrorists are in a locker room taking a shower after their bomb making class, when one notices the other has a huge cork stuck in his butt.

If you do not mind me saying," said the second, "that cork looks very uncomfortable. Why do you not take it out?"

I regret I cannot", lamented the first Arab. "It is permanently stuck in my butt."

"I do not understand," said the other.

The first Arab says, "I was walking along the beach and I tripped over an oil lamp. There was a puff of smoke, and then a huge old man in an American flag attire with a white beard and top hat came boiling out. He said, "I am Uncle Sam, the Genie. I can grant you one wish."

I said, "No shit?"

God Bless America

Aging

A distraught senior citizen phoned her doctor's office. "Is it true," she wanted to know, "that the medication you prescribed has to be taken for the rest of my life?"

"Yes, I'm afraid so," the doctor told her.

There was a moment of silence before the senior lady replied, "I'm wondering, then, just how serious is my condition because this prescription is marked 'NO REFILLS'."

While "flying" down the road yesterday (15 miles over the limit), a woman passed over a bridge only to find a cop with a radar gun on the other side lying in wait.

The cop pulled her over, walked up to the car, and with that classic patronizing smirk we all know and love, asked, "What's your hurry?" To which she replied, "I'm late for work."

"Oh yeah," said the cop, "what do you do?"

"I'm a rectum stretcher," she responded.

The cop stammered, "A what? A rectum stretcher? And just what does a rectum stretcher do?"

"Well," she said, "I start by inserting one finger, then I work my way up to two fingers, then three, then four, then with my whole hand in. I work from side to side until I can get both hands in, and then I slowly but surely stretch, until it's about 6 feet wide."

"And just what the hell do you do with a 6 foot ass hole?" he asked.

"You give him a radar gun and park him behind a bridge . . ."

Traffic Ticket $95.00

Court Costs. $45.00

The Look on Cop's Face . . . PRICELESS.

I bought a new Lexus 350 and returned to the dealer the next day because I couldn't get the radio to work.

The salesman explained that the radio was voice activated.

"Nelson," the salesman said to the radio.

The Radio replied, "Ricky or Willie?"

"Willie!" he continued and "On Te Road Again" came from the speakers.

Then he said, "Ray Charles!", and in an instant "Georgia On My Mind" replaced Willie Nelson.

I drove away happy, and for the next few days, every time I'd say, "Beethoven," I'd get beautiful classical music, and if I said, "Beatles," I'd get one of their awesome songs.

Yesterday, a couple ran a red light and nearly creamed my new car, but I swerved in time to avoid them. I yelled, "Ass Holes!"

Immediately the French National Anthem began to play, sung by Jane Fonda and Barbara Streisand, backed up by Michael Moore and The Dixie Chicks, with John Kerry on guitar, Al Gore on drums, Dan Rather on harmonica, Nancy Pelosi on tambourine, Harry Reid on spoons, Bill Clinton on sax and Ted Kennedy on scotch.

Damn, I LOVE this car!

Philosophy of hypocrisy and ambiguity

For those who love the philosophy of hypocrisy and ambiguity.

1. Don't sweat the petty things and don't pet the sweaty things.
2. One tequila, two tequila, three tequila, floor . . .
3. Atheism is a non-prophet organization.
4. If man evolved from monkeys and apes, why do we still have monkeys and apes?
5. The main reason Santa is so jolly is because he knows where all the bad girls live.
6. I went to a bookstore and asked the saleswoman, "Where's the self-help section?" She said if she told me, it would defeat the purpose.
7. What if there were no hypothetical questions?
8. If a deaf person swears, does his mother wash his hands with soap?
9. If someone with multiple personalities threatens to kill himself, is it considered a hostage situation?
10. Is there another word for synonym?
11. Where do forest rangers go to "get away from it all?"
12. What do you do when you see an endangered animal eating an endangered plant?
13. If a parsley farmer is sued, can they garnish his wages?
14. Would a fly without wings be called a walk?
15. Why do they lock gas station bathrooms? Are they afraid someone will clean them?
16. If a turtle doesn't have a shell, is he homeless or naked?
17. Can vegetarians eat animal crackers?
18. If the police arrest a mime, do they tell him he has the right to remain silent?
19. Why do they put Braille on the drive-through bank machines? (Somebody please explain THIS ONE to me) (I know there's a logical explanation, but it escapes me)
20. How do they get deer to cross the road only at those yellow road signs?
21. What was the best thing before sliced bread?

22. One nice thing about egotists: they don't talk about other people.
23. Does the Little Mermaid wear an algebra?
24. Do infants enjoy infancy as much as adults enjoy adultery?
25. How is it possible to have a civil war? @#&%$!!!#??
26. If one synchronized swimmer drowns, do the rest drown, too?
27. If you ate both pasta and antipasto, would you still be hungry?
28. If you try to fail, and succeed, which have you done?
29. Whose cruel idea was it for the word "Lisp" to have "S" in it?
30. Why are hemorrhoids called "hemorrhoids" instead of assteroids"?
31. Why is it called tourist season if we can't shoot at them?
32. Why is there an expiration date on sour cream?
33. If you spin an oriental man in a circle three times does he become disoriented?
34. Can an atheist get insurance against acts of God?

This has got to be one of the funniest I've heard in a long time. I think this guy should have been promoted, not fired. This is a true story from the Word Perfect Helpline which was transcribed from a recording monitoring the customer care department. Needless to say the Help desk employee was fired; however he/she is currently suing the Word Perfect organization for "Termination without cause."

Actual dialogue of a former Word Perfect Customer Support employee (now I know why they record these conversations!):

"Rich Hall, computer assistance, may I help you?"
"Yes, well, I'm having trouble with Word Perfect."
"What sort of trouble?"
"Well, I was just typing along, and all of a sudden the words went away."

"Went away?"
"They disappeared."
"Hmm. So what does your screen look like now?"
"Nothing."
"Nothing?"
"It's blank, it won't accept anything I type."
"Are you still in Word Perfect, or did you get out?"
"How do I tell?"
"Can you see the C: prompt on the screen?"
"What's a sea-prompt?"
"Never mind, can you move your cursor around the screen?"
"There isn't any cursor; I told you, it won't accept anything I type."

"Does your monitor have a power indicator?"
"What's a monitor?"
"It's the thing with the screen on it that looks like a TV. Does it have a little light that tells you when it's on?"

"I don't know"

"Well, then look on the back of the monitor and find where the power cord goes into it. Can you see the cord?"

"Yes, I think so"

"When you were behind the monitor, did you notice that there were two cables plugged into the back of it?"

"No"

"Well, there are. I need you to look back there again and find the other cable."

"Okay, here it is."

"Follow it for me, and tell me if it's plugged securely into the back of your computer."

"I can't reach."

"Uh huh. Well, can you see if it is?"

"No."

"Even if you maybe put your knee on something and lean way over?"

"Oh, it's not because I don't have the right angle—it's because it's dark."

"Dark?"

"Yes—the office light is off, and the only light I have is coming from the window."

"Well, turn the office light on then."

"I can't."

"No? Why not?"

"Because there's a power failure."

"A power . . . A power failure? Aha, Okay, we've got it licked now. Do you still have the boxes and manuals and packing stuff your computer came in?"

"Well, yes, I keep them in the closet."

"Good. Go and get them, and unplug your system and pack it up just like it was when you got it. Then take it back to the store you bought it from."

"Really? Is it that bad?"

"Yes, I'm afraid it is."

"Well, alright then, I suppose. What do I tell them?"

"Tell them you're too f...g stupid to own a computer."

Two Tough Questions

Question 1:

If you knew a woman who was pregnant, who had 8 kids already, three who were deaf, two who were blind, one mentally retarded, and she had syphilis, would you recommend that she have an abortion?

Read the next question before looking at the answer for this one.

Question 2:

It is time to elect a new world leader, and only your vote counts. Here are the facts about the three leading candidates.

Candidate A—

Associates with crooked politicians, and consults with astrologists. He's had two Mistresses. He also chain smokes and drinks 8 to 10 martinis a day.

Candidate B—

He was kicked out of office twice, sleeps until noon, used opium in college and drinks a quart of whiskey every evening.

Candidate C—

He is a decorated war hero. He's a vegetarian, doesn't smoke, drinks an occasional beer and never cheated on his wife.

Which of these candidates would be your choice? Decide first, no peeking, then turn page for the answer.

————————————

Candidate A is Franklin D. Roosevelt.

Candidate B is Winston Churchill.

Candidate C is Adolph Hitler.

And, by the way, the answer to the abortion question: If you said yes, you just killed Beethoven.

Pretty interesting isn't it? Makes a person think before judging someone.

Never be afraid to try something new. Remember: Amateurs built the ark. Professionals built the Titanic

and in case you never saw this one . . .

Can you imagine working for a company that has a little more than 500 employees and has the following statistics:

* 29 have been accused of spousal abuse
* 7 have been arrested for fraud
* 19 have been accused of writing bad checks
* 117 have directly or indirectly bankrupted at least 2 businesses
* 3 have done time for assault
* 71 cannot get a credit card due to bad credit
* 14 have been arrested on drug-related charges
* 8 have been arrested for shoplifting
* 21 are currently defendants in lawsuits
* 84 have been arrested for drunk driving in the last year

Can you guess which organization this is?

Give up yet?

It's the 535 members of the United States Congress. The same group of idiots that crank out hundreds of new laws each year designed to keep the rest of us in line.

The Year's Best [Actual] Headlines of 2004:

Crack Found on Governor's Daughter imagine that!

Something Went Wrong in Jet Crash, Expert Says no, really?

Police Begin Campaign to Run Down Jaywalkers now that's taking things a bit far!

Is There a Ring of Debris around Uranus? [not if I wipe thoroughly]!

Panda Mating Fails; Veterinarian Takes Over [what a guy]!

Miners Refuse to Work after Death no-good-for-nothin' lazy so-and-sos!

Juvenile Court to Try Shooting Defendant see if that works any better than a fair trial!

War Dims Hope for Peace I can see where it might have that effect!

If Strike Isn't Settled Quickly, It May Last Awhile you think?

Cold Wave Linked to Temperatures who would have thought!

Enfield (London) Couple Slain; Police Suspect Homicide they may be on to something!

Red Tape Holds Up New Bridges you mean there's something stronger than duct tape?

Man Struck By Lightning Faces Battery Charge he probably IS the battery charge!

New Study of Obesity Looks for Larger Test Group weren't they fat enough?

Astronaut Takes Blame for Gas in Spacecraft
That's what he gets for eating those beans!

Kids Make Nutritious Snacks
Taste like chicken?

Local High School Dropouts Cut in Half
Chainsaw Massacre all over again!

Hospitals are Sued by 7 Foot Doctors
Boy, are they tall!

And the winner is . . .

Typhoon Rips Through Cemetery; Hundreds Dead

꜡꜡꜡꜡꜡꜡꜡꜡꜡꜡꜡꜡꜡꜡꜡꜡꜡꜡꜡꜡꜡꜡꜡꜡

Did I read that sign right?

In an office:

TOILET OUT OF ORDER . . . PLEASE USE FLOOR BELOW

In a Laundromat:
AUTOMATIC WASHING MACHINES: PLEASE REMOVE ALL YOUR CLOTHES WHEN
THE LIGHT GOES OUT

In a London department store:
BARGAIN BASEMENT UPSTAIRS

In an office:
WOULD THE PERSON WHO TOOK THE STEP LADDER YESTERDAY PLEASE BRING
IT BACK OR FURTHER STEPS WILL BE TAKEN

In an office:

AFTER TEA BREAK STAFF SHOULD EMPTY THE TEAPOT AND STAND UPSIDE DOWN ON THE DRAINING BOARD

Outside a secondhand shop:
WE EXCHANGE ANYTHING—BICYCLES, WASHING MACHINES, ETC. WHY NOT BRING YOUR WIFE ALONG AND GET A WONDERFUL BARGAIN?

Notice in health food shop window:
CLOSED DUE TO ILLNESS

Spotted in a safari park:
ELEPHANTS PLEASE STAY IN YOUR CAR

Seen during a conference:
FOR ANYONE WHO HAS CHILDREN AND DOESN'T KNOW IT, THERE IS A DAY CARE ON THE 1ST FLOOR

Notice in a farmer's field:
THE FARMER ALLOWS WALKERS TO CROSS THE FIELD FOR FREE, BUT THE BULL CHARGES.

On a repair shop door:
WE CAN REPAIR ANYTHING. (PLEASE KNOCK HARD ON THE DOOR—THE BELL DOESN'T WORK)

Best Lawyer Story

THIS IS THE BEST LAWYER STORY OF THE YEAR, DECADE AND PROBABLY THE CENTURY.

A Charlotte, NC lawyer purchased a box of very rare and expensive cigars, then insured them against fire, among other things. Within a month, having smoked his entire stockpile of these great cigars and without yet having made even his first premium payment on the policy, the lawyer filed claim against the insurance company.

In his claim, the lawyer stated the cigars were lost "in a series of small fires." The insurance company refused to pay, citing the obvious reason that the man had consumed the cigars in the normal fashion.

The lawyer sued . . . and WON! (Stay with me.)

In delivering the ruling, the judge agreed with the insurance company that the claim was frivolous. The judge stated nevertheless, that the lawyer held a policy from the company in which it had warranted that the cigars were insurable and also guaranteed that it would insure them against fire, without defining what is considered to be unacceptable fire" and was obligated to pay the claim. Rather than endure lengthy and costly appeal process, the insurance company accepted the ruling and paid $15,000 to the lawyer for his loss of the rare cigars lost in the "fires".

NOW FOR THE BEST PART . . .

After the lawyer cashed the check, the insurance company had him arrested on 24 counts of ARSON!!! With his own insurance claim and testimony from the previous case being used against him, the lawyer was convicted of intentionally burning his insured property and was sentenced to 24 months in jail and a $24,000 fine.

This is a true story and was the First Place winner in the recent Criminal Lawyers Award Contest.

How the fight got started

I rear-ended another car this morning, on the way to work. I tell you, I knew right then and there, it was going to be a really bad day.

The driver got out of the other car, and wouldn't you know it he was a DWARF!

He looked at me and said, "I am not happy!" So I said "which one are you?" And that's how the fight got started!!

Recently while going through an airport during one of his many trips, President Bush encountered a man with long hair, wearing a white robe and sandals, holding a staff. President Bush went up to the man and said, "Aren't you Moses?"

The man never answered but just kept staring ahead.

Again the President said, "Moses!" in a loud voice.

The man just kept staring ahead, never answering the president. Soon a secret service agent came long and President Bush grabbed him and said, "Doesn't this man look like Moses to you?"

The secret service agent agreed with the President.

"Well," said the President, "every time I say his name, he just keeps staring ahead and refuses to speak. Watch!"

Again, the President yelled, "Moses!" and again the man stared ahead.

The secret service man went up to the man in the white robe and whispered, "You look just like Moses. Are you Moses?"

The man leaned over and whispered, "Yes, I am Moses. However, the last time I talked to a bush I spent 40 years wandering in the desert!"

Subject: Airflight conversation

Thought you might enjoy this one!

A man boarded a plane and took his seat and as he settled in he glanced up and saw a beautiful woman coming down the aisle. He soon realized that she was heading straight toward his seat. As fate would have it she took the seat right beside him. Eager to strike up a conversation, he blurted out,

"Business trip or pleasure?"

She turned, smiled and said, "Business, I'm going to the Annual Nymphomaniacs of America Convention in Chicago."

He swallowed hard. Here was the most gorgeous woman he had ever seen sitting next to him and she was going to a meeting for nymphomaniacs!

Struggling to maintain his composure, he calmly asked, "What's your business role at the convention?"

"Lecture," she responded. "I am the lead lecturer where I use information that I've learned from my own personal experiences to debunk some of the popular myths about sexuality."

He said, "And what kinds of myths are there?"

"Well," she explained, "one popular myth is that African-American men are the most well-endowed of all men, when in fact it is the Native American Indian who is most likely to possess that trait. Another popular myth is that Frenchmen are the best lovers, when actually it is the men of Jewish descent that are the best. I have also discovered that the lover with the absolutely best stamina is the Southern Redneck."

Suddenly the woman became a little uncomfortable and blushed. "I'm sorry," she said, "I sho! uldn't really be discussing all this with you.

I don't even know your name."

"Tonto", the man said. "Tonto Goldstein, but my friends call me Bubba".

Having a bad day

A little guy is sitting at the bar for half an hour staring sadly at his drink when a big trouble-making truck driver walks in and sits next to him, grabs his drink, and gulps it down in one swig. The poor little guy starts crying.

"Come on man, I was just giving you a hard time," says the truck driver, "I'll buy you another drink. I just can't stand to see a man crying."

"This is the worst day of my life," says the little guy between sobs. "I can't do anything right. I overslept. I was late to an important meeting, so my boss fired me. When I went to the parking lot, I found my car was stolen and I have no insurance. I grabbed a cab home but, after the cab left, I discovered my wallet was still in the cab.

I found my wife in bed with the gardener. So I came to this bar trying to work up the courage to put an end to my miserable life, and then you show up and drink the damn poison."

The Good Life

I was walking down the street when I was accosted by a particularly dirty and shabby-looking homeless man who asked me for a couple of dollars for dinner.

I took out my wallet, extracted ten dollars and asked, "If I give you this money, will you buy some beer with it instead?"

"No, I had to stop drinking years ago," the homeless man replied.

"Will you use it to gamble instead of buying food?" I asked.

"No, I don't gamble," the homeless man said. "I need everything I can get just to stay alive."

"Will you spend this on greens fees at a golf course instead of food?" I asked.

"Are you NUTS!" replied the homeless man. "I haven't played golf in 20 years!"

"Will you spend the money on a woman in the red light district instead of food?" I asked.

"What disease would I get for ten lousy bucks?" exclaimed the homeless man.

"Well," I said, "I'm not going to give you the money. Instead, I'm going to take you home for a terrific dinner cooked by my wife Edna."

The homeless man was astounded. "Won't your wife be furious with you for doing that? I know I'm dirty, and I probably smell pretty disgusting."

I replied, "That's okay. I just want her to see what a man looks like who's given up beer, gambling, golf and sex."

I Know Everybody

I told my boss that I knew everyone in the world. He said oh yes I am sure you do ha. So we went to a ballgame and I went down to see Marc McGuire. We stood and talked for a long time. When I came back to my seat he said, you really do know Marc McGuire don't you. We watched the game and went home. A few days later I asked my boss if he wanted to fly to Washington DC with me for a visit with the President. He said Oh Yes and scoffed, we went to the presidents office and his secretary do you want to see Mr. Busch, Omerline? She said well and he is holding a press conference but I will tell him you are here. A few minuets later she said he is in the oval office just go right on in. WE walked right in and the president greeted us with hello, I was holding a press conference but I canceled it to talk to you. My boss was speechless. Sometime later I said to my boss would you like to visit the Pope. He said you don't really know the Pope. We went to Rome and I left my boss standing observing the Mass. I went up on the alter to see the Pope. He stopped the mass and was talking to me when out I the audience We heard a scream. I rushed out into the large congregation gathered listening to the Pope. It was my boss he had fallen down and was laying there. I think I had a heart attack he said, I was watching you and someone came up to me and said, WHO IS THAT MAN TALKING TO OMERLINE?

A recent study found out which days men prefer to have sex. It was found that men preferred to engage in sexual activity on the days that started with the letter "T".

Examples of those days are as follows:

Tuesday
Thursday
Thanksgiving
Today
Tomorrow
Thaturday
Thunday

A recent survey was conducted to discover why men get out of bed in the middle of the night:

5% said it was to get a glass of water
12% said it was go to the toilet
83% said it was to go home

The perfect breakfast . . . as a man sees it . . .
   You're sitting at the table and your son is on the cover of Wheaties, your mistress is on the cover of Playboy, and your wife is on the back of the milk carton.

(Q) What's the best form of birth control after 50?
(A) Nudity

(Q) What's the difference between a girlfriend and a wife?
(A) 45 lbs

(Q) What's the difference between a boyfriend and a husband?
(A) 45 minutes

(Q) What's the fastest way to a man's heart?"
(A) Through his chest with a sharp knife.

(Q) What do you call a smart blonde?
(A) A golden retriever.

(Q) Why did OJ Simpson move to W. Virginia?
(A) Everyone has the same DNA.

(Q) What's the difference between a southern zoo and a northern zoo?
(A) A southern zoo has a description of the animal on the front of the cage along with a recipe.

(Q) What's the difference between a northern fairytale and a southern fairytale?

(A) A northern fairytale begins "Once upon a time". A southern fairytale begins "Y'all ain't gonna believe this shit"

A millionaire lives in a huge mansion with a wife, two children, a butler and a maid.

At the end of the week he went to Sunday brunch with some of his friends. When he returns home, he finds that $25,000 is missing from the drawer in his room. Becoming very upset that someone would steal this from him he asks everyone in the house. He first goes to his children and asks . . .

"Were you playing in my room and took the money?"

and they reply, "no, we have been sick and haven't gotten out of bed."

Then he goes and asks his wife, "Did you go into our room and take the money out of my drawer?"

and she replies, "no I have been taking care of the children while you were out because they are sick."

Then he goes to the butler, "Did you take my money out of my room?"

The butler replies, "no, I just went out and got the mail and sorted it for you."

Then he goes and asks the maid, "did you take the money out of my room?"

and. she replies, "no, I have been making soup for the children and doing the laundry."

With the information he has collected he can figure out who has taken the money out of his room. Who did it??

The butler did it because mail doesn't come on Sunday.

When you have an "I hate my job" day try this:

On your way home from work, stop at your pharmacy and go to the thermometer section. You will need to purchase a rectal thermometer made by "Johnson and Johnson". Be very sure you get this brand. When you get home, lock your doors, draw the drapes, and disconnect the phone so you will not be disturbed during your therapy. Change to very comfortable clothing, such as a sweat suit and lie down on your bed. Open the package and remove the thermometer. Carefully place it on the bedside table so that it will not become chipped or broken. Take out the material that comes with the thermometer and read it. You will notice that in small print there is a statement: "Every rectal thermometer made by Johnson and Johnson is personally tested". Now close your eyes and repeat out loud five times: "I am so glad I do not work for quality control at the Johnson and Johnson Company."

Subject: Trading Places

Interesting story

A man was sick and tired of going to work every day while his wife stayed home. He wanted her to see what he went through so he prayed: "Dear Lord: I go to work every day and put in 8 hours while my wife merely stays at home. I want her to know what I go through, so please allow her body to switch with mine for a day. Amen." God, in his infinite wisdom, granted the man's wish.

The next morning, sure enough, the man awoke as a woman. He arose, cooked breakfast for his mate, awakened the kids, set out their school clothes, fed them breakfast, packed their lunches, drove them to school, came home and picked up the dry cleaning, took it to the cleaners and stopped at the bank to make a deposit, went grocery shopping, then drove home to put away the groceries, paid the bills and balanced the check book. He cleaned the cat's litter box and bathed the dog.

Then it was already 1 P.M. and he hurried to make the beds, do the laundry, vacuum, dust, and sweep and mop the kitchen floor. Ran to the school to pick up the kids and got into an argument with them on the way home. Set out milk and cookies and got the kids organized to do their homework, then set up the ironing board and watched TV while he did the ironing. At 4:30 he began peeling potatoes and washing vegetables for salad, breaded the pork chops and snapped fresh beans for supper.

After supper, he cleaned the kitchen, ran the dishwasher, folded laundry, bathed the kids, and put them to bed. At 9 P.M. he was exhausted, and though his daily chores weren't finished, he went to bed where he was expected to make love which he managed to get through without complaint.

The next morning, he awoke and immediately knelt by the bed and said, "Lord, I don't know what I was thinking. I was so wrong to envy my wife being able to stay home all day. Please, oh please, let us trade back." The Lord, in his infinite wisdom, replied, "My son, I feel you have learned your lesson and I will be happy to change things back to the way they were. You'll just have to wait nine months, though. You got pregnant last night."

This was Voted as Women's Favorite Email of the Year

curtain Rods

She spent the first day packing her belongings into boxes, crates, and suitcases.

On the second day, she had the movers come and collect her things.

On the third day, she sat down for the last time at their beautiful dining room table by candle-light, put on some soft background music, and feasted on a pound of shrimp, a jar of caviar, and a bottle of spring-water.

When she had finished, she went into each and every room and deposited a few half-eaten shrimp shells dipped in caviar into the hollow of the curtain rods.

She then cleaned up the kitchen and left. When the husband returned with his new girlfriend, all was bliss for the first few days.

Then slowly, the house began to smell.

They tried everything; cleaning, mopping, and airing the place out.

Vents were checked for dead rodents and carpets were steam cleaned.

Air fresheners were hung everywhere. Exterminators were brought in to set off gas canisters, during which they had to move out for a few days and in the end they even paid to replace the expensive wool carpeting.

Nothing worked.

People stopped coming over to visit.

Repairmen refused to work in the house.

The maid quit.

Finally, they could not take the stench any longer and decided to move.

A month later, even though they had cut their price in half, they could not find a buyer for their stinky house.

Word got out and eventually even the local realtors refused to return their calls.

Finally, they had to borrow a huge sum of money from the bank to purchase a new place.

The ex-wife called the man and asked how things were going.

He told her the saga of the rotting house. She listened politely and said that she missed her old home terribly and would be willing to reduce her divorce settlement in exchange for getting the house back.

Knowing his ex-wife had no idea how bad the smell was, he agreed on a price that was about 1/10th of what the house had been worth, but only if she were to sign the papers that very day.

She agreed and within the hour his lawyers delivered the paperwork.

A week later the man and his girlfriend stood smiling as they watched the moving company pack everything to take to their new home . . .

And to spite the ex-wife, they even took the curtain rods!!!!!!

I LOVE A HAPPY ENDING, DON'T YOU?

Top 17 Bumper Stickers You Would Like To See

Jesus loves you . . . but everyone else thinks you are an ass.

Impotence . . . Nature's way of saying "No hard feelings,"

The proctologist called . . . they found your head.

Everyone has a photographic memory . . . some just don't have any film.

Save your breath . . . You'll need it to blow up your date.

Your ridiculous little opinion has been noted.

I used to have a handle on life . . . but it broke off.

WANTED: Meaningful overnight relationship.

Guys . . . just because you have one, doesn't mean you have to be one.

Some people just don't know how to drive . . . I call these people "Everybody But Me,"

Heart Attacks . . . God's revenge for eating His animal friends.

Don't like my driving? Then quit watching me.

If you can read this . . . I can slam on my brakes and sue you.

Some people are only alive because it is illegal to shoot them.

Try not to let your mind wander . . . It is too small and fragile to be out by itself.

Hang up and drive!!

And The Number One Bumper Sticker you'd Like To See!!

Welcome to America . . . now speak English

The Most functional word

Well, it's shit . . . That's right, shit!

Shit may just be the most functional word in the English language.

Consider this:
You can be shit faced,
Shit out of luck,
Or have shit for brains.

With a little effort,
you can get your shit together,
find a place for your shit
or decides to shit or get off the pot.

You can smoke shit,
buy shit,
sell shit,
Lose shit,
find shit,
forget shit,
and tell others to eat shit and die.

Some people know their shit,
while others can't tell the difference between shit
and shineolars.

There are lucky shits,
dumb shits,
crazy shits,
and sweet shits.

There is bull shit,
horse shit
and chicken shit.

You can throw shit,
sling shit,
catch shit,
shoot the shit,
or duck when shit hits the fan.

You can give a shit,
or serve shit on a shingle.

You can find yourself in deep shit,
or be happier than a pig in shit.

Some days are colder than shit,
some days are hotter than shit,
and some days are just plain shitty.

Some music sounds like shit,
things can look like shit,
and there are times when you feel like shit.

You can have too much shit,
not enough shit,
the right shit,
the wrong shit,
or a lot of weird shit.

You can carry shit,
have a mountain of shit,
or find yourself up shit creek without a pad!

Sometimes everything you touch turns to shit,
and other times you fall in a bucket of shit and

come out smelling like a rose.

When you stop to consider all the facts,
It's the basic building block of creation.

And remember, once you know your shit,
You don't need to know anything else!

You could pass this along, if you give a shit!

Airline Woes

A lady was flying from San Francisco to Los Angeles. By the time the plane took off, there had been a 45-minute delay and everybody on board was ticked.

Unexpectedly, they stopped in Sacramento on the way. The flight attendant explained that there would be another 45-minute delay, and if the passengers wanted to get off the aircraft, they could reboard in 30 minutes. Everybody got off the plane except one gentleman who was blind.

The lady noticed him as she walked by and could tell he had flown before because his Seeing Eye dog lay quietly underneath the seats in front of him throughout the entire flight.

The lady could also tell he had flown this very flight before because the pilot approached him and, calling him by name, said, "Keith, we're in Sacramento for almost an hour. Would you like to get off and stretch your legs?"

Keith replied, "No thanks, but maybe my dog would like to stretch his legs."

Picture this—All the people in the gate area came to a completely quiet standstill when they looked up and saw the pilot walk off the plane with the Seeing Eye dog! The pilot was even wearing sunglasses. People scattered. They not only tried to change planes, they also were trying to change airlines!

Squeezing Every Last Drop

The local bar was so sure its bartender was the strongest man around that they offered a standing $1000 bet. The bartender would squeeze a lemon until all the juice ran into a glass, and hand the lemon to a patron.

Anyone who could squeeze one more drop of juice out would win the money.

Many people had tried over time, including the professional wrestlers and bodybuilders, but nobody could do it. One day a scrawny little man came in, wearing a tie and a pair of pants hiked up past his belly button.

He said in a squeaky annoying voice, "I'd like to try the bet."

Even the hillbilly chicks burst into laughter.

After the laughter had died down, the bartender said, "Ok," grabbed a lemon, and squeezed away. He then handed the wrinkled remains of the rind to the little man.

But the crowd's laughter turned to total silence as the man clenched his fist around the lemon and six drops fell into the glass. As the crowd cheered, the bartender paid the $1000, and asked the little man, "What did you do for a living? Are you a lumberjack, weight lifter, or what?"

The man replied, "I work for the IRS."

Children . . . This is priceless!

You spend the first 2 years of their life teaching them to walk and talk. Then you spend the next 16 telling them to sit down and shut-up.

Grandchildren are God's reward for not killing your children.

Cleaning your house while your kids are still growing is like clearing the driveway before it has stopped snowing.

There is only one pretty child in the world and every mother has it."
Chinese Proverb.

Mothers of teens know why animals eat their young.

I asked Mom if I was a gifted child . . . she said they certainly wouldn't have paid for me.

Children are natural mimics, who act like their parents despite every effort to teach them good manners.

Children seldom misquote you. In fact, they usually repeat word for word what you shouldn't have said.

The main purpose of holding children's parties is to remind yourself that there are children more awful than your own.

We child proofed our home 3 years ago and they're still getting in!

Be nice to your kids. They'll choose your nursing home.

Doctor Can You Help Me

Don't laugh! Said the patient, Bob. Of course I won't laugh, the doctor said. I'm a professional, in over twenty years I've never laughed at a patient. Okay then, Bob said. And proceeded to drop his trousers, reveling the tiniest "willie" the doctor had ever seen. It couldn't have been bigger than the size of AAA battery. Unable to control himself, the doctor started giggling, then fell laughing to the floor. Ten minutes later he was able to struggle to is feed and regain his composure. I'm so sorry, said the doctor, I really am. I don't know what came over me. On my honor as a doctor and a gentleman. I promise it won't happen again. Now what seems to be the problem? It's swollen Bob replied . . .

A woman walks into an accountant's office and tells him that she needs to file her taxes. The accountant says, "Before we begin, I'll need to ask a few questions. He gets her name, address, social security number, etc., and then asks . . . "What is your occupation?" "I'm a whore" she says. The accountant balks and says, "No, no, no, that will never work. That is much too crass. Let's try to rephrase that."

The woman says, "OK, I'm a high-end call girl". "No, that is still too crude. Try again." They both think for a minute, then the woman states, "I'm an elite chicken farmer." The accountant asks, "What does chicken farming have to do with being a whore or a call girl?"

"Well, I raised over 5,000 little peckers last year!"

Colored Folks? (This was written by a black man in Texas . . . so funny . . . what a great sense of humor and creativity!!!)

When I born, I black, when I grow up, I black, when I go in sun, I black, when I cold, I black, when I scared, I black, when I sick, I black, and when I die, i still black.

You white folks . . . when you born, you pink, when you grow up, you white, when you go in sun, you red, when you cold, you blue, when you scared, you yellow, when you sick, you green, when you bruised, you purple, and when you die, you gray. So who you callin' colored folk's ???

Eternal Truths

1. Once over the hill, you pick up speed.
2. I love cooking with wine. Sometimes I even put it in the food.
3. If it weren't for STRESS I'd have no energy at all.
4. Whatever hits the fan will not be evenly distributed.
5. Everyone has a photographic memory. Some just don't have film.
6. Dogs have owners. Cats have staff.
7. If the shoe fits . . . buy it in every color.
8. If you're too open minded, your brains will fall out.
9. Going to church doesn't make you a Christian any more than standing in a garage makes you a car.
10. If you look like your passport picture, you probably need the trip.
11. Bills travel through the mail at twice the speed of checks.
12. Some days are a total waste of makeup.
13. Men are from Earth. Women are from Earth. Deal with it.
14. A balanced diet is a cookie in each hand.
15. Middle age is when broadness of the mind and narrowness of the waist change places.
16. Opportunities always look bigger going than coming.
17. Junk is something you've kept for years and throw away three weeks before you need it.
18. Experience is a wonderful thing. It enables you to recognize a mistake when you make it again.
19. By the time you can make ends meet, they move the ends.
20. Learn from the mistakes of others. You can't live long enough to make them all yourself.
21. Keep smiling, it makes everyone . . . wonder what you've been up to!

Oh my gosh . . . I'm old as dirt.

I guess this didn't tell me anything I didn't already know.

Hey Dad," one of my kids asked the other day, "What was your fast food when you were growing up?"

"We didn't have fast food when I was growing up," I informed the food was slow."

"C'mon, seriously. Where did you eat?"

"It was a place called 'at home," I explained. "Grandma co??? day and when Grandpa got home from work, we sat down together ??? dining room table, and if I didn't like what she put on my p??? allowed to sit there until I did like it."

By this time, the kid was laughing so hard I was afraid he w??? suffer serious internal damage, so I didn't tell him the pa??? I had to have permission to leave the table.

But here are some other things I would have told him about ??? if I figured his system could have handled it:

Some parents NEVER owned their own house, wore Levis, set fo??? golf course, traveled out of the country or had a credit ca??? later years they had something called a revolving charge ca??? was good only at Sears Roebuck. Or maybe it was Sears AND ??? Either Way, there is no Roebuck anymore. Maybe he died.

My parents never drove me to soccer practice. This was most ??? we never had heard of soccer. I had a bicycle that weighed ??? pounds, and only had one speed, (slow).

We didn't have a television in our house until I was 11, but ??? grandparents had one before that. It was, of course, black ??? they bought a piece of coloured plastic to cover the screen. ??? third was blue, like the sky, and the bottom third was green??? The middle third was red. It was perfect for programs that ??? of fire trucks riding across someone's lawn on a sunny day. ??? had a lens taped to the front of the TV to make the picture ??? larger.

I was 13 before I tasted my first pizza, it was called "pizz??? When I bit into it, I burned the roof of my mouth and the ch??? swung down, plastered itself against my chin and burned tha??? It's still the best pizza I ever had.

We didn't have a car until I was 15. Before that, the only ??? family was my grandfather's Ford. He called it a "machine."

I never had a telephone in my room. The only phone in the ??? the living room and it was on a party line. Before you could ??? had to listen and make sure some people you didn't know were ??? using the line.

Pizzas were not delivered to our home. But milk was. All ne??? were delivered by boys and all boys delivered newspapers. I ??? newspaper, six days a week. It cost 7 cents a paper, of whi??? keep 2 cents. I had to get up at 4 AM every morning. On Sat??? to collect the 42 cents from my customers. My favourite cust??? the ones who gave me 50 cents and told me to keep the change??? favourite customers were the ones who seemed to never be home??? collection day.

Movie stars kissed with their mouths shut. At least, they ??? movies. Touching someone else's tongue with yours was called ??? kissing and they didn't do that in movies. I don't know wha??? French movies. French movies were dirty and we weren't allow??? them.

If you grew up in a generation before there was fast food, ??? want to share some of these memories with your children or ??? Just don't blame me if they bust a gut laughing. Growing up ??? it used to be, is it?

MEMORIES from a friend:

My Dad is cleaning out my grandmother's house (she died in ??? and he brought me an old Royal Crown Cola bottle. In the b??? a stopper with a bunch of holes in it.

I knew immediately what it was, but Kati had no idea. She th??? had tried to make it a salt shaker or something.

I knew it as the bottle that sat on the end of the ironing b??? "sprinkle" clothes with because we didn't have steam irons.

Man, I am old.

How many do you remember?

Head lights dimmer switches on the floor.
Ignition switches on the dashboard.
Heaters mounted on the inside of the fire wall.
Real ice boxes.
Pant leg clips for bicycles without chain guards.
Soldering irons you heat on a gas burner.
Using hand signals for cars without turn signals.

Older Than Dirt Quiz: Count all the ones that you remember ??? you were told about! Ratings at the bottom.

1. Blackjack chewing gum
2. Wax Coke-shaped bottles with coloured sugar water
3. Candy cigarettes
4. Soda pop machines that dispensed bottles
5. Coffee shops with tableside jukeboxes
6. Home milk delivery in glass bottles with cardboard stoppe???
7. Party lines
8. Newsreels before the movie
9. P.F. Flyers
10. Butch wax
11. Telephone numbers with a word prefix (Olive-6933)
12. Peashooters
13. Howdy Doody
14. 45 RPM records
15. S&H Green Stamps
16. Hi-fi's
17. Metal ice trays with lever
18. Mimeograph paper
19. Blue flashbulb
20. Packards
21. Roller skate keys

22. Cork popguns
23. Drive-ins
24. Studebakers
25. Wash tub wringers

If you remembered 0-5 = You're still young
If you remembered 6-10 = You are getting older
If you remembered 11-15 = Don't tell your age,

If you remembered 16-25 = You're older than dirt!

Don't forget to pass this along!!

Especially to all your really OLD friends

Life may not be the party we had hoped for, but while we are ??? might as well dance!

Quote by George Bernad Shaw

Some men see things as they are and say, "Why?" I dream of things that never were and say, "Why not?"

I think we dream so we don't have to be apart so long. If we're in each others dreams, we can be together all the time.

Now for those who made need a laugh, no matter how dumb the joke may be:

Society's Burning Questions

If Fed Ex and UPS were to merge, would they call it Fed UP?

I believe five out of four people have trouble with fractions.

If quitters never win, and winners never quit, what fool came up with, "Quit while you're ahead?"

Do Lipton Tea employees take coffee breaks?

What hair color do they put on the driver's licenses of bald men?

I was thinking that women should put pictures of missing husbands on beer cans.

I was thinking about how people seem to read the Bible a whole lot more as they get older, then it dawned on me . . . they were cramming for their finals.

I thought about how mothers feed their babies with little tiny spoons and forks so I wonder what Chinese mothers use. Perhaps toothpicks?

Why do they put pictures of criminals up in the Post Office?

What are we supposed to do . . . write to these men?

Why don't they just put their pictures on the postage stamps so the mailmen could look for them while they delivered the mail?

Never agree to plastic surgery if the doctor's office is full of portraits by Picasso.

How much deeper would oceans be if sponges didn't live there?

If it's true that we are here to help others, then what exactly are the OTHERS here for?

STRESSED spelled backwards is DESSERTS.

You never really learn to swear until you learn to drive. Clones are people two.

If a man says something in the woods and there are no women there, is he still wrong?

No one ever says "It's only a game," when their team is winning.

If you can't be kind, at least have the decency to be vague.

Ever wonder what the speed of lightning would be if it didn't zigzag?

Nostalgia isn't what it used to be.

Think "honk" if you're telepathic.

Last night I played a blank tape at full blast. The mime next door went nuts.

If a person with multiple personalities threatens suicide, is that considered a hostage situation?

If a cow laughed, would milk come out her nose?

Whatever happened to preparations A through G?

If olive oil comes from olives, where does baby oil come from?

Subject: Martha's way vs. My way

This came today. Thought you'd like a mid-week laugh.

Martha's Way vs. My Way

Martha's way #1: Stuff a miniature marshmallow in the bottom of a sugar cone to prevent ice cream drips.

My way: Just suck the ice cream out of the bottom of the cone, for Pete's sake, you are probably lying on the couch with your feet up eating it anyway.

Martha's way #2: Use a meat baster to "squeeze" your pancake batter onto the hot griddle and you'll get perfectly shaped pancakes every time.

My way: Buy the precooked kind you nuke in the microwave for 30 seconds. The hard part is getting them out of the plastic bag.

Martha's way #3: To keep potatoes from budding, place an apple in the bag with the potatoes.

My way: Buy Hungry Jack mashed potato mix and keep it in the pantry for up to a year.

Martha's way #4: To prevent eggshells from cracking, add a pinch of salt to the water before hard-boiling.

My way: Who cares if they crack, aren't you going to take the shells off anyway?

Martha's way #5: To get the most juice out of fresh lemons, bring them to room temperature and roll them under your palm against the kitchen counter before squeezing.

My way: Sleep with the lemons in between the mattress and box springs.

Martha's way #6:   To easily remove burnt-on food from your skillet, simply
                   add a drop or two of dish soap and enough water to cover
                   bottom of pan, and bring to a boil on stovetop.

My way: Eat at Chili's every night and avoid cooking.

Martha's way #7:   Spray your Tupperware with nonstick cooking spray before
                   pouring in tomato based sauces and there won't be any
                   stains.

My way: Feed your garbage disposal and there won't be any leftovers.

Martha's way #8:   When a cake recipe calls for flouring the baking pan, use a
                   bit of the dry cake mix instead and there won't be any white
                   mess on the outside of the cake.

My way: Go to the bakery. They'll even decorate it for you.

Martha's way #9:   If you accidentally over salt a dish while it's still cooking,
                   drop in a peeled potato and it will absorb the excess salt
                   for an instant "fix me up"

My way: If you over salt a dish while you are cooking, that's too bad.

My motto: I made it and you will eat it and I don't care how bad it tastes.

Martha's way #10: Wrap celery in aluminum foil when putting in the refrigerator
                   and it will keep for weeks.

My way: Celery? Never heard of the stuff.

Martha's way #11: Brush some beaten egg white over piecrust before baking
                   to yield a beautiful glossy finish.

My way: The Mrs. Smith frozen pie directions do not include brushing
                   egg whites over the crust and so I don't do it.

Martha's way #12: Place a slice of apple in hardened brown sugar to soften it.

My Way: Brown sugar is supposed to be "soft"?

Martha's way #13; When boiling corn on the cob, add a pinch of sugar to help
                   bring out the corn's natural sweetness.

My Way: The only kind of corn I buy comes in a can.

Martha's way #14: To determine whether an egg is fresh, immerse it in a pan of cool, salted water. If it sinks, it is fresh, but if it rises to the surface, throw it away.

My way: Eat, cook, or use the egg anyway. If you feel bad later, you will know it wasn't fresh.

Martha's way #15: Cure for headaches: Take a lime, cut it in half and rub it on your forehead. The throbbing will go away.

My way: Martha, dear, the only reason this works is because you can't rub a lime on your forehead without getting lime juice in your eye, and then the problem isn't the headache anymore; the problem is that you are now blind.

Martha's way #16: Don't throw out all that leftover wine. Freeze into ice cubes for future use in casseroles and sauces.

My way: Leftover wine?

Martha's way #17: If you have a problem opening jars: Try using latex dishwashing gloves. They give a non-slip grip that makes opening jars easy.

My way: Go ask the very cute neighbor to do it.

Martha's way #18: Potatoes will take food stains off your fingers. Just slice and rub raw potato on the stains and rinse with water.

My way: Mashed potatoes will now be replacing the anti-bacterial soap in the handy dispenser next to my sink.

Martha's way #19: Now look what you can do with Alka Seltzer. Clean a toilet. Drop in two Alka-Seltzer tablets, wait twenty minutes, brush and flush. The citric acid and effervescent action clean vitreous china. Clean a vase. To remove a stain from the bottom of a glass vase or cruet, fill with water and drop in two Alka-Seltzer tablets. Polish jewelry. Drop two Alka-Seltzer tablets into a glass of water and immerse the jewelry for two minutes. Clean a thermos bottle. Fill the bottle with water, drop in four Alka-Seltzer tablets, and let soak for an hour (or longer, if necessary).

My way: Put your jewelry, vases, and thermos in the toilet. Add some Alka-Seltzer and you have solved a whole bunch of problems at once.

Subject: Kids say the darndest things...

I was driving with my three young children one warm summer evening when a woman in the convertible ahead of us stood up and waved. She was stark naked! As I was reeling from the shock, I heard my five-year-old shout from the back seat, "Mom! That lady isn't wearing a seat belt!"

—

My son Zachary, 4, came screaming out of the bathroom to tell me he'd dropped his toothbrush in the toilet. So I fished it out and threw it in the garbage. Zachary stood there thinking for a moment, then ran to my bathroom and came out with my toothbrush. He held it up and said with a charming little smile, "We better throw this one out too then, 'cause it fell in the toilet a few days ago."

—

On the first day of school, a first grader handed his teacher a note from his mother. The note read, "The opinions expressed by this child are not necessarily those of his parents."

—

A woman was trying hard to get the catsup to come out of the jar. During her struggle the phone rang so she asked her four—year old daughter to answer the phone. "It's the minister, Mommy," the child said to her mother. Then she added, "Mommy can't come to the phone to talk to you right now. She's hitting the bottle."

—

A little boy got lost at the YMCA and found himself in the women's locker room. When he was spotted, the room burst into shrieks, with ladies grabbing towels and running for cover. The little boy watched in amazement and then asked, "What's the matter haven't you ever seen a little boy before?"

===

POLICE # 1

While taking a routine vandalism report at an elementary school, I was interrupted by a little girl about six years old. Looking up and down at my uniform, she asked, "Are you a cop?" "Yes," I answered and continued writing the report. "My mother said if I ever needed help I should ask the police. Is that right?" "Yes, that's right," I told her. "Well, then," she said as she extended her foot toward me, "would you please tie my shoe?"

POLICE # 2

It was the end of the day when I parked my police van in front of the station. As I gathered my equipment, my K-9 partner, Jake, was barking, and I saw a little boy staring in at me. "Is that a dog you got back there?" he asked. "It sure is," I replied. Puzzled, the boy looked at me and then towards the back of the van. Finally he said, "What'd he do?"

ELDERLY

While working for an organization that delivers lunches to elderly shut-ins, I used to take my four-year-old daughter on my afternoon rounds. She was unfailingly intrigued by the various appliances of old age, particularly the canes, walkers and wheelchairs. One day I found her staring at a pair of false teeth soaking in a glass. As I braced myself for the inevitable barrage of questions, she merely turned and whispered, "The tooth fairy will never believe this!"

DRESS~UP

A little girl was watching her parents dress for a party. When she saw her dad donning his tuxedo, she warned, "Daddy, you shouldn't wear that suit."

"And why not, darling?" "You know that it always gives you a headache next morning."

DEATH

While walking along the sidewalk in front of his church, our minister heard the intoning of a prayer that nearly made his collar wilt. Apparently, his five-year-old son and his playmates had found a dead robin. Feeling that proper burial should be performed, they had secured a small box and cotton batting, then dug a hole and made ready for the disposal of the deceased. The minister's son was chosen to say the appropriate prayers and with sonorous dignity intoned his version of what he thought his father always said: "Glory be unto the Faaaather. and unto the Sonnn . . . and into the hole he gooooes."

SCHOOL

A little girl had just finished her first week of school. "I'm just wasting my time," she said to her mother. "I can't read, I can't write and they won't let me talk!"

BIBLE

A little boy opened the big family bible. He was fascinated as he fingered through the old pages. Suddenly, something fell out of the Bible. He picked up the object and looked at it. What he saw was an old leaf that had been pressed in between the pages. "Mama, look what I found", the boy called out. "What have you got there, dear"? With astonishment in the young boy's voice, he answered, "I think it's Adam's underwear!"

My mother taught me TO APPRECIATE A JOB WELL DONE—"If you're going kill each other, do it outside. I just finished cleaning!"

My mother taught me RELIGION—

"You better pray that will come out of the carpet."

My mother taught me about TIME TRAVEL:-

"If you don't straighten up, I'm going to knock you into the middle of next week!"

My mother taught me LOGIC-

"Because I said so, that's why."

My Mother taught me LOGIC . . . #2

"If you fall out of that swing and break your neck, you're not going to the store with me."

My mother taught me FORESIGHT—

"Make sure you wear clean underwear, in case you're in an accident."

My mother taught me IRONY—

"Keep crying and I'll give you something to cry about."

My mother taught me about the science of OSMOSIS—"Shut your mouth and eat your supper!"

My mother taught me about CONTORTIONIST—"Will you "look" at the dirt on the back of your neck!"

My mother taught me about STAMINA—

"You'll sit there 'till all that spinach is finished."

My mother taught me about WEATHER—

"It looks as if a tornado swept through your room."

My mother taught me how to solve PHYSICS PROBLEMS—"If I yelled because I saw a meteor coming toward you; would you listen THEN?"

My mother taught me about HYPOCRISY—

"If I've told you once, I've told you a million times—Don't exaggerate!!!"

My mother taught me THE CIRCLE OF LIFE—"I brought you into this world, and I can take you out."

My mother taught me about BEHAVIOR MODIFICATION—"Stop acting like your father!"

My mother taught me about ENVY—

"There are millions of less fortunate children in this world who don't have wonderful parents like you do!"

My Mother taught me about ANTICIPATION . . . "Just wait until we get home."

My Mother taught me about RECEIVING . . .

"You are going to get it when we get home!"

My Mother taught me MEDICAL SCIENCE . . .

"If you don't stop crossing your eyes, they are going to freeze that way."

My Mother taught me to THINK AHEAD . . .

"If you don't pass your spelling test, you'll never get a good job."

My Mother taught me ESP . . .

"Put your sweater on; don't you think I know when you're cold?"

My Mother taught me HUMOR . . .

"When that lawn mower cuts off your toes, don't come running to me."

My Mother taught me how to BECOME AN ADULT . . . "If you don't eat your vegetables, you'll never grow up."

My Mother taught me about GENETICS . . .

"You're just like your father."

My Mother taught me about my ROOTS . . .

"Do you think you were born in a barn?"

My Mother taught me about WISDOM OF AGE . . . "When you get to be my age, you will understand." And my all time favorite . . . JUSTICE . . .

"One day you'll have kids . . . and I hope they turn out just like you!"

Cat Story:

You don't have to own a cat to appreciate this one . . .

A couple was dressed and ready to go out for the evening. They turned on a night light, turned the answering machine on the phone line, covered their pet parakeet and put the cat in the backyard.

They phoned the local cab company and requested a taxi. The taxi arrived and the couple opened the front door to leave their house. The cat they had put out into the yard scoots back into the house.

They don't want the cat shut in the house because "she" always tries to eat the bird. The wife goes out to the taxi while the husband goes inside to get the cat. The cat runs upstairs, the man in hot pursuit. The wife doesn't want the driver to know the house will be empty. She explains to the taxi driver that her husband will be out soon. "He's just going upstairs to say good-bye to my mother."

A few minutes later, the husband gets into the cab. "Sorry I took so long," he says, as they drive away. "Stupid bitch was hiding under the bed. Had to poke her with a coat hanger to get her to come out! Then I had to wrap her in a blanket to keep her from scratching me. But it worked. I hauled her fat ass downstairs and threw her out into the back yard!"

The cabdriver hit a parked car . . .

Subject: Why Men Are Just Happier People

Why Men Are Just Happier People!

What do you expect from such simple creatures!?
Your last name stays put.
The garage is all yours.
Wedding plans take care of themselves.
Chocolate is just another snack.
You can be president.
You can wear a white T-shirt to a water park.
Car mechanics tell you the truth.
The world is your urinal.
You never have to drive to another gas station because this one's just too icky.
Same work, more pay.
Wrinkles add character.
Wedding dress—$5000; tux rental—$100.
People never stare at your chest when you're talking to them.
The occasional well-rendered belch is practically expected.
New shoes don't cut, blister, or mangle your feet.
One mood, ALL the time.
Phone conversations are over in 30 seconds flat.
You know stuff about tanks.
A five-day vacation requires only one suitcase.
You can open all your own jars.
You get extra credit for the slightest act of thoughtfulness.
If someone forgets to invite you, he or she can still be your friend. Your
    underwear is $8.95 for a three-pack.
Everything on your face stays its original color.
Three pairs of shoes are more than enough.
You don't have to stop and think of which way to turn a nut on a bolt. You
    almost never have strap problems in public
You are unable to see wrinkles in your clothes.

The same hairstyle lasts for years, maybe decades.

You don't have to shave below your neck.

Your belly usually hides your big hips.

One wallet and one pair of shoes, one color, all seasons.

You can "do" your nails with a pocketknife.

You have freedom of choice concerning growing a mustache!!

You can do Christmas shopping for 25 relatives, on December 24, in 45 minutes.

To Be 6 Again

A man was sitting on the edge of the bed, observing his wife turning back and forth, looking at herself in the mirror.

Since her birthday was not far off, he asked what she'd like to have for her Birthday.

I'd like to be six again, she replied, still looking in the mirror.

On the morning of her Birthday, he arose early, made her a nice big bowl of Lucky Charms, and then took her to Six Flags theme park. What a day! He put her on every ride in the park; the Death Slide, the Wall of Fear, the Screaming Monster Roller Coaster . . . everything there was. Five hours later they staggered out of the theme park. Her head was reeling and her stomach felt upside down.

He then took her to a McDonald's where he ordered her a Happy Meal with extra fries and a chocolate shake.

Then it was off to a movie, popcorn, a soda pop, and her favorite candy, M&M's. What a fabulous adventure! Finally she wobbled home with her husband and collapsed into bed exhausted.

He leaned over his wife with a big smile and lovingly asked, "Well Dear, what was it like being six again??"

Her eyes slowly opened and her expression suddenly changed.

; I meant my Dress Size, you dumb ass!!

The moral of the story: Even when a man is listening, he is going to get it wrong.

Marriage (Part I)

A macho man married typical good-looking lady and after the wedding, he laid down the following rules:

"I'll be home when I want, if I want and at what time I want-and I don't expect any hassle from you. I expect a great dinner to be on the table unless tell you that I won't be home for dinner. I'll go hunting, fishing, boozing and card-playing when I want with my old buddies and don't you give me a hard time about it. Those are my rules. Any comments?"

His new bride said, "No, that's fine with me. Just understand that there'll be sex here at seven o'clock every night . . . whether you're here or not."

DAMN SHE'S GOOD!

Marriage (Part II)

Husband and wife had a bitter quarrel on the day of their 40th wedding anniversary.

The husband yells, "When you die, I'm getting you a headstone that reads, 'Here Lies My Wife—Cold As Ever.'"

"Yeah?" she replies. "When you die, I'm getting you a headstone that reads, "Here Lies My Husband—Stiff At Last.'"

HE ASKED FOR IT!

Marriage (Part III)

Husband (a doctor) and his wife are having a fight at the breakfast table. Husband gets up in a rage and says, "And you are no good in bed either," and storms out of the house. After sometime he realizes he was nasty and decides to make amends and rings her up. She comes to the phone after many rings and the irritated husband says, "What took you so long to answer he phone?"

She says, "I was in bed." "In bed this late, doing what?" "Getting a second opinion!"

YUP, HE HAD THAT COMING, TOO!

Marriage (Part IV)

A man has six children and is very proud of his achievement. He is so proud of himself, that he starts calling his wife, "Mother of Six" in spite of her objections. One night, they go to a party. The man decides that it's time to go home and wants to find out if his wife is ready to leave as well. He shouts at the top of his voice, "Shall we go home 'Mother of six?'"

His wife, irritated by her husband's lack of discretion shouts right back, "Anytime you're ready, Father of four"

RIGHT ON, LADY!

I am passing this on to you—It is definitely working for me.

I think I have found inner peace. I read an article that said the way to achieve Inner peace is to finish things I had started.

Today I finished two bags of potato chips, a chocolate pie, a bottle of wine and a small box of chocolate candy. I feel better already.

it could be worse

A father passing by his son's bedroom was astonished to see that his bed was nicely made and everything was picked up.

Then he saw an envelope, propped up prominently on the pillow that was addressed to "Dad." With the worst premonition he opened the envelope with trembling hands and read the letter.

> Dear Dad:
>
> It is with great regret and sorrow that I'm writing you. I had to elope with my new girlfriend because I wanted to avoid a scene with Mom and you. I have been finding real passion with Jane and she is so nice. But I knew you would not approve of her because of all her piercings, tattoos, tight motorcycle clothes and the fact that she is much older than I am. But it's not only the passion . . . Dad she's pregnant. Jane said that we will be very happy. She owns a trailer in the woods and has a stack of firewood for the whole winter. We share a dream of having many more children.
>
> Stacy has opened my eyes to the fact that marijuana doesn't really hurt anyone. We'll be growing it for ourselves and trading it with the other people that live nearby for cocaine and ecstasy. In the meantime we will pray that science will find a cure for AIDS so Jane can get better. She deserves it. Don't worry Dad. I'm 15 and I know how to take care of myself.

Someday I'm sure that we will be back to visit so that you can get to know your grandchildren.

Love,
Your Son John

P.S. Dad, none of the above is true. I'm over at Tommy's house. I just wanted to remind you that there are worse things in life than the report card that's in my center desk drawer.

I love you.
Call me when it's safe to come home.

Snow

December 8: 6:00 pm. It started to snow. The first snow of the season and the wife and I took our cocktails and sat for hours by the window watching the huge soft flakes drift down from heaven. It looked like a Grandma Moses print. So romantic we felt like newlyweds again.

I love snow!

December 9: We woke to a beautiful blanket of crystal white snow covering every inch of the landscape. What a fantastic sight! Can there be a more lovely place in the whole world? Moving here was the best idea I've ever had. Shoveled for the first time in years and felt like a boy again. I did both our driveway and the sidewalk. This afternoon the snow plow came along and covered up the sidewalk and closed in the driveway, so I got to shovel again. What a perfect life!

December 12: The sun has melted all our lovely snow. Such a disappointment. My neighbor tells me not to worry, we'll definitely have a white Christmas. No snow on Christmas would be awful! Bob says we'll have so much snow by the end of winter, that I'll never want to see snow again. I don't think that's possible. Bob is such a nice man. I'm glad he's our neighbor.

December 14: Snow, lovely snow! 8" last night. The temperature dropped to -20. The cold makes everything sparkle so. The wind took my breath away, but I warmed up by shoveling the driveway and sidewalks. This is the life! The snowplow came back this afternoon and buried everything again. I didn't realize I would have to do quite this much shoveling, but I'll certainly get back in shape this way. I wish I wouldn't huff and puff so.

December 15: 20 inches forecast. Sold my van and bought a 4x4 Blazer. Bought snow tires for the wife's car and 2 extra shovels Stocked the freezer. The wife wants a wood stove in case the electricity goes out. I think that's silly. We aren't in Alaska, after all.

December 16: Ice storm this morning. Fell on my ass on the ice in the driveway putting down salt. Hurt like hell! The wife laughed for an hour, which I think was very cruel.

December 17: Still way below freezing. Roads are too icy to go anywhere. Electricity was off for 5 hours. I had to pile the blankets on to stay warm. Nothing to do but stare at the wife and try not to irritate her. Guess I should've bought a wood stove, but won't admit it to her. God, I hate it when she's right. I can't believe I'm freezing to death in my own living room.

December 20: Electricity's back on, but had another 14" of the damn stuff last night. More shoveling. Took all day. Goddamn snowplow came by twice. Tried to find a neighbor kid to shovel, but they said they're too busy playing hockey. I think they're lying. Called the only hardware store around to see about buying a snow blower and they're out. Might have another shipment in March. I think they're lying. Bob says I have to shovel or the city will have it done and bill me. I think he's lying.

December 22: Bob was right about a white Christmas, because 13 more inches of the white shit fell today, and it's so cold it probably won't melt till August. Took me 30 minutes to get all dressed up to go out to shovel and then I had to piss. By the time I got undressed, pissed, and dressed again, I was too tired to shovel. Tried to hire Bob, who has a plow on his truck, for the rest of the winter, but he says he's too busy. I think the asshole is lying.

December 23: Only 2" of snow today. And it warmed up to 0. The wife wanted me to decorate the front of the house this morning. What is she . . . nuts??? Why didn't she tell me to do that a month ago? She says she did but I think she's damn well lying.

December 24: 6". Snow packed so hard by snowplow, I broke the shovel. Thought I was having a heart attack. If I ever catch the son of a bitch who drives that snowplow, I'll drag him through the snow by his balls. I know he hides around the corner and waits for me to finish shoveling, and then he comes down the street at a 100 miles an hour and throws snow all over where I've just been. Tonight the wife wanted me to sing Christmas carols with her and open our presents, but I was busy watching for the goddamn snowplow.

December 25: Merry Christmas. 20 more inches of the !$@#&% slop tonight! Snowed in. The idea of shoveling makes my blood boil. God I hate the snow! Then the snowplow driver came by asking for a donation and I hit him over the head with my shovel. The wife says I have a bad attitude. I think she's an idiot. If I have to watch "It's a Wonderful Life" one more time, I'm going to kill her.

December 26: Still snowed in. Why the hell did I ever move here? It was all HER idea. She's really getting on my nerves.

December 27: Temperature dropped to -30 and the pipes froze!

December 28: Warmed up to above -20. Still snowed in. THE BITCH is driving me crazy!!!

December 29: 10 more inches. Bob says I have to shovel the roof or it could cave in. That's the silliest thing I've ever heard. How dumb does he think I am?

December 30: Roof caved in. The snow plow driver is suing me for a million dollars for the bump on his head. The wife went home to her mother. 9" predicted.

December 31: Set fire to what's left of the house. No more shoveling.

January 8: I feel so good. I just love those little white pills they keep giving me, but I don't like being tied to the bed.

Who's Your Daddy

When someone puts in for Child Support, the proper thing to do is to find out who the father is and see why he is not providing support. The following are all replies that Dallas women have written on Child Support Agency forms in the section for listing father's details. Or putting it another way . . . Who's your Daddy! These are genuine excerpts from the forms. Be sure to check out number 11) it takes the prize and #3 is runner up.

1. Regarding the identity of the father of my twins, child A was fathered by Jim Munson. I am unsure as to the identity of the father of child B, but I believe that he was conceived on the same night.
2. I am unsure as to the identity of the father of my child as I was being sick out of a window when taken unexpectedly from behind. I can provide you with a list of names of men that I think were at the party if this helps.
3. I do not know the name of the father of my little girl. She was conceived at a party at 3600 Grand Avenue where I had unprotected sex with a man I met that night. I do remember that the sex was so good that I fainted. If you do manage to track down the father, can you send me his phone number? Thanks.
4. I don't know the identity of the father of my daughter. He drives a BMW that now has a hole made by my stiletto in one of the door panels. Perhaps you can contact BMW service stations in this area and see if he's had it replaced.
5. I have never had sex with a man. I am still a Virginian. I am awaiting a letter from the Pope confirming that my son's conception was immaculate and that he is Christ risen again.
6. I cannot tell you the name of child A's dad as he informs me that to do so would blow his cover and that would have cataclysmic implications for the economy. I am torn between doing right by you and right by the country. Please advise.
7. I do not know who the father of my child was as all blacks look the same to me.

8. Peter Smith is the father of child A. If you do catch up with him, can you ask him what he did with my AC/DC CDs? Child B who was also borned at the same time . . . well I don't have a clue.

9. From the dates it seems that my daughter was conceived at Disney World; maybe it really is the Magic Kingdom.

10. So much about that night is a blur. The only thing that I remember for sure is Delia Smith did a program about eggs earlier in the evening. If I'd have stayed in and watched more TV rather than going to the party at 146 Miller Drive, mine might have remained unfertilized.

11. I am unsure as to the identity of the father of my baby, after all when you eat a can of beans you can't be sure which one made you fart.

How To Drive Men crazy!

Shrink his underwear in the dryer and when he complains, innocently suggest that he's gained a few pounds.

"Accidentally" fill the gas tank of his new Porsche with diesel.

Have your mother fly in for a month-long visit, totally unannounced.

Insist upon a lot of "meaningful conversations."

Take the batteries out of all the remotes in the house. Hide them well.

Organize his desk, workshop, bedroom, or other special place.

Repeatedly lose his cellular phone in restaurants around town.

Bribe his faithful dog away from him with a steady diet of Ding Dongs.

Misplace the cordless phone, preferably in a different room each time, every other day for three weeks . . .

Reverse his contact lenses in their case.

Loan his precious cellular phone to a pregnant girlfriend who "needs it more than he does."

Snip a small hole in his fishing waders, then follow him with a camera to capture his "sinking" on film.

Stare at his forehead and when he notices, casually ask if there is any history of male pattern baldness on his mother's side.

Superglue the pages of his Little Black Book together.

On the farm lived a chicken and a horse, both of whom loved to play together. One day, the two were playing when the horse fell into a bog and began to sink. Scared for his life, the horse whinnied for the chicken to go get the farmer for help!

Off the chicken ran, back to the farm. Arriving at the farm, he searched and searched for the farmer, but to no avail, for he had gone to town with the only tractor. Running around, the chicken spied the farmer's new Z-3 series BMW. Finding the keys inside, the chicken sped off with a length of rope, hoping he still had time to save his friend's life.

Back at the bog, the horse was surprised, but happy, to see the chicken arrive in the shiny BMW, and he managed to get a hold of the loop of rope the chicken tossed to him. After tying the other end to the rear bumper of the farmer's car, the chicken then drove slowly forward and, with the aid of the powerful car, rescued the horse!

Happy and proud, the chicken drove the BMW back to the farmhouse, and the farmer was none the wiser when he returned. The friendship between the two animals was cemented: best buddies, best pals.

A few weeks later, the chicken fell into a mud pit, and soon, he too, began to sink and cried out to the horse to save his life! The horse thought a moment, walked over, and straddled the large puddle. Looking underneath, he told the chicken to grab his "thing" and he would then lift him out of the pit. The chicken got a good grip, and the horse pulled him up and out, saving his life.

The moral of the story?

When you're hung like a horse, you don't need a BMW to pick up chicks.

Kenny the Rooster

An old farmer has about 200 hens, but no rooster, and he wants chicks.

So he goes down the road to the next farmer and asks if he has a rooster that he would sell.

The other farmer says, "Yeah, I've got this neat rooster named Kenny.

He'll service every chicken you got, no problem."

Well, Kenny the rooster costs a lot of money, but the farmer decides he'd be worth it.

The old farmer buys Kenny. He takes Kenny home and sets him down in the barnyard, first, giving the rooster a pep talk:

"I want you to pace yourself now, Kenny, you've got a lot of chickens to service here, and you cost me a lot of money . . . consequently, I'll need you to do a good job.

So, take your time and have some fun."

Kenny seemed to understand, so the farmer pointed toward the hen house and Kenny took off like a shot.

WHAM!—Kenny nails every hen in the hen house three or four times!

The farmer is shocked.

After that the farmer hears a commotion in the duck pen, sure enough, Kenny is in there.

Later, the farmer sees Kenny after a flock of geese, down by the lake.

Once again WHAM!

He gets all the geese.

By sunset he sees Kenny out in the fields chasing quail and pheasants.

The farmer is distraught and worried that his expensive rooster won't even last 24 hours.

Sure enough, the farmer awakens the next morning only to find Kenny on his back, feet in the air, stone still in the middle of the yard, vultures are circling overhead.

The farmer, saddened by the loss of such a colorful and expensive animal, shakes his head and says, "Oh, Kenny, I told you to pace yourself.

I tried to get you to slow down, now look what you've done to yourself!"

Kenny opens one eye, nods toward the buzzards circling in the sky and says:

"Shhh, they're getting closer."

Jokes

SURGERY

A man is recovering from surgery when the Surgical Nurse appears and asks him how he is feeling. I'm okay. But I didn't like the four—letter word the doctor used in surgery; he answered. What did he say, asked the nurse. OOPS.

GOING SHOPPING

While shopping for vacation clothes, my husband and I passed a display of bathing suits. It had been at least ten years and twenty pounds since I had even considered buying a bathing suit, so I sought my husband's advice. What do you think? I asked. Should I get a bikini or an all-in-one? Better get a bikini, he replied. YOU'D NEVER GET IT ALL IN ONE. HE'S STILL IN INTENSIVE CARE.

OUT THE MOUTH OF BABES

Two little kids are in a hospital, lying on stretchers next to each other outside the operating room the first surgeries of the day. The first kid leans over and asks, What are you in here for?
The second kid says, I'm here to get my tonsils out and I'm a little nervous. The first kid says, You've got nothing to worry about. I had that done when I was four. They put to sleep, and when you wake up they give you lots of Jell-o and ice cream. It's a breeze. The second kid then asks, What are you here for? The first kid says, A circumcision. WHOA! The second kid replies, Good Luck buddy. I had the one when I was born. Couldn't walk for a year.

WHY I MARRIED FOUR TIMES

Joan was married four time the first was to a Banker then to a Circus Ring Leader the third time was a Preacher and the last one was a Funeral Director. Her friend asked her why she had married so many times and to four unusual men. She said Well it was like this. One for the money, two for the show, three to get ready and four to go.

911 CALLS

Dispatcher: 911 What is your emergency?

Caller: I heard what sounded like gunshots coming from the brown house on the corner.

Dispatcher: So you have an address?

Caller: No, I have on a blouse and slacks, why?

Dispatcher: 9-1-1 What is your emergency?

Caller: Someone broke into my house and took a bite out of my ham and cheese sandwich.

Dispatcher: Excuse me?

Caller: I made a ham and cheese sandwich and left it on the kitchen table and when I came back from the bathroom, someone had taken a bite out of it.

Dispatcher: Was anything else taken?

Caller: No, but this has happened to me before and I'm sick of it!

Dispatcher: 9-1-1 What is the nature of your emergency?

Caller: I'm trying to reach nine eleven but my doesn't have an eleven on it.

Dispatcher: this is nine—eleven

Caller: I thought you just said it was nine-one-one.

Dispatcher: yes, ma'mn nine-one-one and nine—eleven are the same thing.

Caller: honey, I may be old, but I'm not stupid.

The Box of Chocolates

For all of us who are married, were married, wish you were married, or wish you weren't married, this is something to smile about the next time you open a box of chocolates:

Sally was driving home from one of her business trips in Northern Arizona when she saw an elderly Navajo woman walking on the side of the road. As the trip was a long and quiet one, she stopped the car and asked the Navajo woman if she would like a ride. With a silent nod of thanks, the woman got into the car.

Resuming the journey, Sally tried in vain to make a bit of small talk with the Navajo woman. The old woman just sat silently, looking intently at everything she saw, studying every little detail, until she noticed a white bag on the seat next to Sally.

"What in bag?" asked the old woman.

Sally looked down at the white bag and said, "It's a box of chocolates. I got it for my husband".

"The Navajo woman was silent for another moment or two. Then speaking with the quiet wisdom of an elder, she said: "Good trade."

Pease put your Private Part back inside your pajamas. But Nurse Tracy he replied I told you yesterday that my Private Part died. Yes you did that but why is it hanging out of your pajamas? WELL HE REPLIED TODAY IS THE VIEWING!!!

THE ANSWER WAS REROUTED

A little boy wanted $50 very badly and prayed for weeks but nothing happened. Finally he decided to write God a letter requesting the $50. When the postal authorities received the letter addressed to God. USA they decided to forward it to the President of the United States. As a joke. The President was so amused that he instructed his secretary to send the little boy $30. The President thought this would appear to be a lot of money to a little boy. The little boy was delighted with the $30 and decided to write a thank you note to God, which reached the President and it read. Dear God, Thank you very much for sending the money. However I noticed that you sent it through the White House in Washington, DC and those donkeys deducted $20.00 for taxes.

THE PECAN TREE

On the outskirts of a small town, there was a big, old pecan tree just inside the cemetery fence. One day, two boys filled up a bucketful of nuts and sat down by the tree, out of sight and began dividing the nuts. One for you one for me. One for you one for me. Said one boy. Several had dropped and rolled down toward the fence. Another boy came riding along the road on his bicycle. As he passed he thought he heard voices from inside the cemetery. He slowed down to investigate. Sure enough he heard, one for you one for me, one for you on for me.

   He just knew what it was. He jumped back on his bike and rode off. Just around the bend he met an old man with a cane, hobbling along. Come here quick. Said the boy you won't believe what I heard!! Satan and the Lord are down at the cemetery dividing up the souls. The man said Beat it kid can't you see it's hard for me to walk. When the Boy insisted though, the man hobbled to the cemetery. Standing by the fence they heard one for you and one for me, one for you and one for me. The old man whispered boy you've been telling me the truth. Let us see if we can see the Lord. Shaking with fear, they peered through the fence yet were still unable to see anything. The old man and the boy gripped the wrought iron bars. Of the fence tighter and tighter as they tried to get a glimpse of the lord At last they heard one for you and one for me. That's all. Now let's go get those nuts by the fence and we'll be done. They say the old man made it back to town a full 5 minutes ahead of the kid on the bike. Smile God loves you.

SHOULD HAVE CALLED AAA

A little girl asked her Mom, Mom may I take the dog for a walk around the block? Mom replies no because she is in heat. What's that mean? Asked the child. Go ask your father, I think he's in the garage. The little girl goes to the garage and says Dad may I take Belle for a walk around the block? I asked Mom but she said the dog was in heat and to come ask you. Dad said Bring Belle over here, He took a rag soaked in gasoline and scrubbed the dog's backside with it to disguise the scent and said OK you can go now, but keep Belle on the leash and only go one time round the block. The little girl left and returned a few minuets later with no dog on the leash. Dad asked where's Belle? The little girl said She ran out of gas about halfway down the block, So another dog is pushing her home

WEATHER FORCAST

An Illinois man left the snow-filled streets of Chicago for a vacation on Florida. His wife was on a business trip and was planning to meet him there the next day. When he reached this hotel, he decided to send his wife a quick e-mail. Unable to find the scrap of paper on which he has written her e-mail address, he did his best to type it in from memory. Unfortunately he missed one letter, and his note was directed instead to an elderly preachers wife whose husband had passed away only the day before. When the grieving widow checked her e-mail, she took one look at the monitor and let out a piercing scream, and fell to the floor in a dead faint. At the sound, the family rushed into the room he following note on the screen. Dearest wife, just checked in. Everything prepared for your arrival here tomorrow. P.S. Sure is hot down here!!!

Looks can fool you

A cabbie picks up a nun. She gets in the cab, and the cab driver won't quit staring at her. She asks him why he is staring. He replies, I have a question to ask you, but I don't want to offend you. She answers, My son you cannot offend me. When you're as old as I am and have been a nun as long as I have there is nothing you could say or ask that I would find offensive. Well I've always had a fantasy to have a nun kiss me. She responds. Well let's see what we can do about that #1 you have to be single and # 2 you must be Catholic. The cab driver is very excited and says, Yes I'm single and I'm a Catholic! OK the nun says Pull into the next alley. The nun fulfils his fantasy with a kiss that would make a hooker blush. But when they got back on the road, the cab driver starts crying. My dear child said the nun, why are you crying? Forgive me, but I've sinned. I lied. I must confess, I'm married and I'm Jewish. The nun says that's OK my name is Kevin and I'm going to a Halloween party.

GET A LAWYER

A Polish man moved to the USA and married an American girl. Although his English was far from perfect, they got along very well until one day he rushed into a lawyer's office and asked him if he could arrange a divorce for him. The lawyer said that getting a divorce could depend on the circumstances and asked him the following questions. Have you grounds? Yes, an acre and half and nice home. No I mean what is the foundation of this case? Its made of concrete. I don't think you understand. Does either of you have a real grudge? No we have a carport, and not need one. I mean, what are your relations like? All my relations still in Poland. Is there any infidelity in your marriage. We have hi-fidelity stereo and good DVD player. Does your wife beat you up? No, I always up before her. Is your wife a nagger? No, she white. Why do you want this divorce? She is going to kill me. What makes you think that? I got proof. What kind of proof? She is going to poison me. She bought a bottle at drugstore and put on shelf in bathroom. I can read and it says "Polish Remover"!!

GOTCHA

Little Old Lady From Chicago A little old lady is walking down the street, dragging two plastic garbage bags with her, one in each hand. There's a hole in one of the bags, and every once in a while a $20 bill is flying out of it onto the pavement. Noticing this, a policeman stops her . . . Ma'am there are $20 bills falling out of that bag . . . Dam says the little old lady . . . I'd better go back and see if I can find some. Thanks for the warning!! Well now, not so fast, says the cop, How did you get all that money? Did you steal it? Oh, no, says the little, old lady. You see, my back yard backs up to the parking lot of Wrigley Field. Each time there's a game, a lot of fans come and pee into the bushes, right into my flower beds! So I go and stand behind the bushes with a big clipper, and each time someone sticks his little thingie through the bushes I say $20 or off it comes.! Hey not a bad ides! Laughs the cop. OK good luck! Bye the way, what's in the other bag? Well says the little old lady Some guys think I'm bluffing!!

WHO'S FISHING

A hillbilly was stopped by a game warden in Tennessee recently with two ice chests of fish. He was leaving a cove well known for its fishing. The game warden asked the man Do you have a license to catch those fish? Naw sir, I ain't got none of them licenses, no. You must understand these here are my pet fish. Pet Fish said the game warden. Ya. Every night I take these here fish down to da lake and let them swim round for a while. Then I whistle and they jump rat back into this her ice chest and I take them home. That's a bunch of hooey! Fish can't do that! says the warden. The hillbilly looked at the game warden for a moment and them said It's the truth Mr. Government man. I'll show you. It really works. Okay said the game warden I've GOT to see this!! The hillbilly poured the fish into the lake and stood and waited. After several minutes, the game warden turned and said. Well? Well what said the hillbilly. The warden said When are you going to call them back? The hillbilly said Call who back? The FISH replied the warden. What fish? answered the hillbilly. (We in Tennessee may not be as smart as some city slickers, but we aren't as dumb as most government employees!)

YOU GET WHAT YOU PRAY FOR

A lady goes to her priest one day and tells him Father, I have a problem. I have two female parrots, but they only know how to say one thing. What do they say? Ask the priest. They say Hi we're hookers! Do you want to have some fun? That's obscene The priest exclaimed, then he thought for a moment. You know, he said I may have solution to your problem. I have two male talking parrots, which I have taught to pray and red the Bible. So he took the female parrots home and put them in where his male parrots were. After a few minutes, the female parrots cried out in unison Hi we're hookers!! Do you want to have some fun? There was stunned silence. Shocked, one of the male parrots looked over at the other male parrot and exclaimed, Put the beads away, Frank Our prayers have been answered.

CHUCK IS MY NAME

A farmer has about 200 hens, but no rooster and he wants chicks. So he goes down to the next farmer and asks if he has a rooster which he would sell. The other farmer says, Yeah I have this great rooster named Chuck. He'll service every chicken you have no problem. Well, Chuck the rooster cost a lot of money, but the farmer decides he'd be worth it. So he buys Chuck. The farmer takes Chuck home and sets him down in the barnyard, first giving the rooster a pep talk. Chuck he says I want you to pace yourself now. You've got a lot hens to service here and you cost me a lot of money. Consequently I want you to do a good job. So, take your time and have some fun, The farmer said with a chuckle. Chuck seemed to understand, the farmer points toward the hen house, and Chuck took off like a shot. WHAM Chuck nails every hen in the hen house. Three or four times, and the farmer is really shocked. After that the farmer hears a commotion in the duck pen, sure enough chuck is in there. Later, the farmer sees Chuck after a flock of geese, down by the lake, Once again WHAM he gets all the geese. By sunset, he sees Chuck out in the fields chasing quail, and pheasants. The farmer is distraught, worried that his expensive rooster won't even last 24 hours. Sure enough, the farmer goes to bed and wakes up the next day to find Chuck dead as a door knob—stone cold in the middle of the yard. Buzzards are circling overhead. The farmer, saddened by the loss of such a studly bird, shakes his head and says Oh Chuck I told you to pace yourself. I tried to get you to slow down. Now look what you've done to yourself. Chuck opens one eye, nods toward the buzzards circling in the sky and says SHHHH they're getting closer . . .

2006 DARWIN AWARDS

Yes again that magical time of the year when the 2006 Darwin awards are bestowed, honoring the least evolved among us. This years glorious Winner is:

1. When his 38-caliber revolver failed to fire at his intended victim during a hold-up in Long Beach California, would-be robber James Elliot did something that can only inspire wonder. He peered down the barrel and tried the trigger. This time it worked.

2. Chef at a hotel in Switzerland lost a finger in a meat-cutting machine and submitted a claim to hi8s insurance company. The company expecting negligence sent out one of its men to have a look for himself. He tried the machine and he also lost a finger. The chef's claim was approved.

3. A man who shoveled snow for an hour to clear a space for his car during a blizzard in Chicago returned with his vehicle to find a woman had taken the space. Understandably he shot her.

4. After stopping for drinks at an illegal bar, a Zimbabwean bus driver found that 20 mental patients he was supposed to be transporting from Harre to Bulawaya had escaped. Not wanting to admit his incompetence, the driver went to a nearby bus stop and offered everyone waiting there a free ride. He then delivered the passengers to the mental hospital telling the staff that the patients were very excitable and prone to bizarre fantasies. The deception wasn't discovered for 3 days.

5. An Texas teenager was in the hospital recovering from serious head wounds rece3ived from an oncoming train. When asked how he received the injuries, the lad told police that he was simply trying to see how close he could get his head to a moving train before he was hit.

6. A man walked into a Louisiana Circle-K, put a $20 bill on the counter, and asked for change. When the clerk opened the cash drawer, the man pulled a gun and asked for all the cash from the clerk and fled, leaving the $20 bill on the counter. The total from the drawer: $15. If someone points a gun at you and gives you money, is a crime committed?)

7. Seems an Arkansas guy wanted some beer pretty badly. He decided that he'd just throw a cinderblock through a liquor store window, grab some booze, and run. So he lifted the cinderblock and heaved it over his head at the window. The cinderblock bounced back and hit the would-be thief on the head., knocking him unconscious. The liquor store window was made of Plexiglas. The whole event was caught on video.

8. As a female shopper exited a New York convenience store, a man grabbed her purse and ran. The clerk called 911 immediately, and the woman was able to give them a detailed description of the snatcher. Within minutes, the police apprehended the snatcher. They put him in the car and drove back to the store. The thief was then taken out of the car and told to stand there for a positive ID. To which he replied, yes, officer, that's her. That's the lady I stole the purse from.

9. The Ann Arbor Michigan News crime column reported that a man walked into a Burger King in Ypsilanti, Michigan, at 5 am, flashed a gun and demanded cash. The clerk turned him down because he said he couldn't open the cash register without a food order. When the man ordered onion rings, the clerk said they weren't available for breakfast. The man frustrated, walked away.

***THE 5-STAR STUPIDITY AWARD WINNER ***

10. When a man attempted to siphon gasoline from a motor home parked on a Seattle street, he got much more than he bargained for. Police arrived at the scene to find a very sick man curled up next to a motor home near spilled sewage. A police spokesman said that the man admitted to trying to steal gasoline and plugged his siphon hose into the motor home's sewage tank by mistake. The owner of the vehicle declined to press charges, saying that it was the best laugh he'd had in a very long time.

WHAT WOULD YOU DO

A farmer named Clyde had a car accident. In court, the trucking company's fancy lawyer was questioning Clyde. Didn't you say, at the scene of the accident, I'm fine? Asked the lawyer. Clyde responded, Well I'll tell you t happened. I had just loaded my favorite mule Bessie, into the, I didn't ask for any details, the lawyer interrupted. Just answer the question. Did you not say, at the scene of the accident? I'm fine!? Clyde said, Well I had just got Bessie into the trailer and I was driving down the road . . . The lawyer interrupted again and said Judge, I am trying to establish the fact that at the scene of the accident, this man told the Highway Patrolman on the scene that he was just fine. Now several weeks after the accident he is trying to sue my client. I believe he is a fraud. Please tell him to simply answer the question. By this time the Judge was fairly interested in Clyde's answer and said to the lawyer, I'd like to hear what he has to say about his favorite mule Bessie. Clyde thanked the judge and proceeded, Well as I was saying, I had just loaded Bessie, my favorite mule, into the trailer and was driving down the highway when this huge semi-truck and trailer ran the stop sign and smacked my truck right in the side. I was thrown into one ditch and Bessie was thrown into the other. I was hurting, real bad and didn't want to move. However I could hear ole Bessie moaning and groaning. I knew she was in terrible shape just by the groans. Shortly after the accident a Highway Patrolman came on the scene. He could hear Bessie moaning and groaning so he went over to her. After he looked at her, he took out is gun and shot her between the eyes. Then the Patrolman came across the road, gun in hand, looked at me and said How are you feeling? Now what would you say?

MY NAME IS KEVIN

As a trucker stops for a red light, a blonde catches up. She jumps out of her car, runs up to his truck and knocks on the door. The trucker lowers the window, and she says Hi, my name is Heather and you are losing some of your load. The trucker ignores her and proceeds down the street. When the truck stops for another red light the girl catches up again. She jumps out of her car, runs up and knocks on the door. Again, the trucker lowers the window. As if they've never spoken, the blonde says brightly, Hi my name is Heather and you are losing some of your load. Shaking his head, the trucker ignores her again and continues down the street. At the third red light, the same thing happens again. All out of breath, the blonde gets out of her car, runs up knocks on the truck door. The trucker rolls down the window, Again she says Hi my name is Heather, and you are losing some of your load. When the light turns green the trucker revs up and races to the next light, When he stops this time, he hurriedly gets out of the truck, and runs back to the blonde. He knocks on her window, and after she lowers it, he says Hi, my name is Kevin, it's winter in Michigan and I'm driving the Salt Truck

DON'T MONKEY WITH A DUMB BLONDE

A blonde motorist was two hours from San Diego when she flagged down by a man whose truck had broken down. The man walked up to the car and asked Are you going to San Diego? Sure answered the blonde Do you need a lift? Not for me. I'll be spending the next three hours fixing my truck. My problem is I've got two chimpanzees in the back which have to be delivered to the San Diego Zoo. They're a bit stressed and I don't want to keep them on the road all day. Could you possibly take them to the zoo for me? I'll give you fifty dollars for your trouble. I'd be happy to said the blonde. So the two chimpanzees were ushered into the backseat of the blonde's car and carefully strapped into their seat belts. Off they went. Five hours later, the truck driver was driving through the heart of San Diego when suddenly he saw something that horrified him! There was the blonde walking down the street and holding hands with two chimps, much to the amusement of the crowd. With a screech of brakes he pulled off the road and ran over to the blonde. What the heck are you doing here? I gave you fifty dollars to take these chimpanzees to the zoo. Yes I know you did said the blonde, but we had money left over so we went to the movies.

LONE RANGER AND TONTO

The Lone Ranger and Tonto went camping in the desert. After they got their tent set up, both men fell sound asleep. Some hours later, Tonto wakes the Lone Ranger and says, Kemo Sabe, look towards sky, what you see? The Lone Ranger replies, I see millions of stars. What that tell you? asked Tonto. The Lone Ranger ponders for a minute then says Astronomically speaking, it tells me there are millions of galaxies and potentially billions of planets. Astrologically, it tells me that Saturn is in Leo. Time wise, it appears to be approximately a quarter past three in the morning. Theologically, its evident the Lord is all-powerful and we are small and insignificant. Meteorologically, it seems we will have a beautiful day tomorrow. What's it tell you Tonto? Tonto is silent for a moment, then says, Kemo Sabe, you dumber than buffalo shit. Someone has stolen tent . . .

WATCH WHAT YOU DO

The power mower was broken and wouldn't run; a lady kept hinting to her husband that he should get it fixed. Finally she thought of a clever way to make her point. When her husband came home one day. He found her seated in the tall grass, busily snipping away with a tiny sewing scissors. He watched silently for a short time and them went into the house. He was gone only for a few moments. When he came out again. He handed her a toothbrush. When you finish cutting the grass, he said you might as well sweep the sidewalks. The doctors say he will probably walk again, but he will always have a limp.

APPLYING FOR THE JOB

An Indian walks into a café with a shotgun in one hand and a bucket of buffalo manure in the other. He says to the waiter, Me want coffee. The waiter says Sure coming up He gets the Indian a tall mug of coffee and the Indian drinks it down in one gulp, picks up the bucket of manure, throws it into the air, blasts it with the shotgun, then walks out. The next morning the Indian returns, He has his shotgun in one hand and a bucket of manure it the other. He walks up to the counter and says to the waiter, Me want coffee. The waiter says Whoa! We're still cleaning up your mess from yesterday. What the hell's up with that anyway? Me in training for Upper Management Position. Come in, drink coffee, shoot shit and disappear for rest of day.

RETIREMENT PLAN

If you purchased $1000.00 of Nortel stock one year ago, it would be worth $49.00 With Enron, you would have $16.50 left of the original $1000.00 With WorldCom, you would have less than %5.00 left. But, if you had purchased $1,000.00 of Beer one year ago, drank all the beer, then turned in the cans for aluminum recycling price, you would have $214.00. Based on the above, our current investment advice is to drink heavily and recycle. It's called the 401-keg Plan

GO GET YOUR MOTHER

An Amish boy and his father were visiting a nearby mall for the first time. They were amazed by almost everything they saw, but was especially by two shiny silver walls that moved apart and back together again by themselves. The lad asked What is this, father? The father (having never seen an elevator) responded, I have no idea what it is. While the boy and his father were watching wide-eyed, an old lady in a wheelchair rolled up to the moving walls and pressed a button. The walls opened and the lady rolled between them into a small room. The walls closed and the boy and his father watched as small circles lit up above the walls. The walls opened up again and a beautiful twenty-four—year old woman stepped out. The father looked at his son anxiously and said Hurry go get your mother.

A LETTER FROM GRANDMA

Dear son, I have become a little older since I saw you last, and a few changes have come into my life since then. Frankly, I have become a frivolous old gal. I am seeing five gentlemen everyday. As soon as I wake up, Will Power helps me get out of bed. Then I go to see John. Then Charlie Horse comes along, and when he is here he takes a lot of my time and attention. When he leaves, Arthur Ritis shows up and stays the rest of the day. He doesn't like to stay in one place very long, so he takes me from joint to joint. After such a busy day with Ben Gay. What a life. Oh yes, I'm also flirting with al Zymer. Love Grandma P.S. The preacher came to call the other day. He said at my age I should be thinking of the hereafter. I told him, Oh I do it all the time. No matter where I am, in the parlor, upstairs in the kitchen or down in the basement, I ask myself, Now, what am I here after?

THE GOOD LIFE

I was walking down the street when I was accosted by a particularly dirty and shabby-looking homeless man who asked me for a couple of dollars for dinner. I took out my wallet, extracted ten dollars and asked, If I give you this money, will buy some beer with it instead? No I had to stop drinking years ago, the homeless man replied. Will you use it to gamble instead of buying food, I asked.

No, I don't gamble. The homeless man said, I need everything I can get to stay alive. Will you spend this on greens fees at a gold course instead of food I asked. Are you nuts replied the homeless man, I haven't played golf in 20 years. Will you spend the money on a woman in the red light district instead of food I asked. What disease would I get for ten bucks? Exclaimed the homeless man. Well I'm not going to give you the money instead I'm going to take you home for a terrific dinner cooked by my wife Edna. The homeless man was astounded Won't your wife be furious with you for doing that? O know I'm dirty, and probably smell pretty disgusting. I replied That's okay, I just her to see what a man looks like who's given up beer, gambling, gold and sex.

THE CORK

Two Arab terrorists are in a locker room taking a shower after their bomb making class, when one notices the other has a huge cork stuck in his butt. I you do not mind me saying said the second, that cork looks very uncomfortable. Why do you not take it out? I regret I cannot lamented the first Arab It is permanently stuck in my butt. I do not understand said the other. The first Arab says I was walking along the beach and I tripped over an oil lamp. There was a puff of smoke, and then a huge old man in an American flag attire with a white beard and top hat came boiling out. He said I am Uncle Sam, the Genie. I can grant you one wish. I said No Shit? God Bless America!

AGING

A distraught senior citizen phoned her doctor's office. Is it true, she wanted to know that the medication you prescribed has to be taken for the rest of my life? Yes, I'm afraid so. The doctor told her. There was a moment of silence before the senior lady replied. I'm wondering, then, just how serious is my condition. Because this prescription is marked NO REFILLS!!

I RECTUM THIS IS A JOKE

While flying down the road yesterday (15 miles over the limit) a woman passed over a bridge only to find a cop with a radar gun on the other side lying in wait. The cop pulled her over, walked up to the car with that classic patronizing smirk we all know and love, asked What's the hurry? To which she replied I'm late for work. Oh yeah said the cop what do you do? I'm a rectum stretcher she responded. The cop stammered A what? A rectum stretcher? And just what does a rectum stretcher do? Well she said, I start by inserting one finger, then I work my way up to two fingers, then three, then four, when my whole hand in. I work from side to side until I can get both my hands in and then I slowly but surely, until it's six foot wide. And just what do you do with a six foot asshole? He asked You give him a radar gun and park him behind a bridge . . . Traffic ticket $95.00 Court costs $45.00 The look on the cops face PRICELESS

GOOD, BETTER, BEST

GOOD: Madison, WI policeman had a perfect spot to watch for speeders, but wasn't getting many. Then he discovered the problem—a 12 year old boy was standing up the road with a hand painted sign which read RADAR TRAP AHEAD. The officer also found the boy had an accomplice who was a bit further down the road with a sign TIPS and a bucket full of money. (And we used to just sell lemonade!)

BETTER A motorist was mailed a picture of his car speeding through an automated radar post in La Crosse, WI. A $40 speeding ticket was included. Being cute, he sent the police department a picture of $40. The police responded with another photo of handcuffs.

BEST A young woman was pulled over speeding. As a Wisconsin State Trooper Officer walked to her car window, flipping open his ticket book, she said I bet you are going to sell a ticket to the State Troupers Ball. He replied, Wisconsin State Troopers don't have balls. There was a moment of silence. He then closed his book, got back in his patrol car and left.

A GOOD PHARMIACIST

A lady walks onto a drug store and tells the pharmacist she need some cyanide. The pharmacist said Why in the world do you need cyanide? The lady then explained she needed it to poison her husband. The pharmacists eyes got big and he said Lord have mercy, I can't give you cyanide to kill your husband! That's against the law! I'll lose my license, they'll throw both of us in jail and all kinds of bad things will happen! Absolutely not, you CAN NOT have any cyanide! The lady reached into her purse and pulled out a picture of her husband in bed with the pharmacist's wife. The pharmacist looked at the picture and replied, Well now, you didn't tell me you had a prescription.

AMAZING

Bill owns a company that manufactures and installs car wash systems. (Magic Wand Car Wash Systems, just in case you want to buy one). Bill's company installed a car wash system in Frederick, Md. Now understand that these are compete systems. Including the money changer and money taking machine. The problem started when the new owner complained to Bill that he was losing significant amounts of money from his coin machines each week. He went as far as to accuse Bill's employees of having a key to the boxes and ripping him off. Bill just couldn't believe that his people would do that, so they setup a camera to catch the thief in action. Well. They did catch him on the changer slot of the machine. The bird had to go down into the machine, and back up inside to get the money! That's three quarters he has in his beak! Another amazing thing is that it was not just one bird—there were several working together. Once they identified the thieves, they found over $400.00 in quarters on the roof of the car wash and more under a nearby tree. And you thought you heard of everything by now!!!

HAVING A BAD DAY

A little guy sitting at the bar for half an hour staring sadly at his drink when a bit trouble making truck driver walks in and sits next to him. Grabs his drink, and gulps it down in one swig. The poor little guy starts crying. Come on man, I was just giving you a hard time, says the truck driver, I'll buy you another drink. I just can't stand to see a man crying. This is the worst day of my life says the little guy between sobs. I can't do anything right. I overslept. I was late to an important meeting, so my boss fired me. When I went to the parking lot, I found my car was stolen and I have no insurance. I grabbed a cab home but, after the cab left, I discovered my wallet was still in the cab. I found my wife in bed with the gardener. So I came to this bar trying to work up the courage to put an end to my miserable life, and you show up and drink the dam poison.

7 REASONS NOT TO MESS WITH A CHILD

A little girl was talking to her teacher about whales. The teacher said it was physically impossible for a whale to swallow a human because even though it was a very large mammal its throat was very small. The little girl stated that Jonah was swallowed by a whale. Irated, the teacher reiterated that a whale could not swallow a human; it was physically impossible. The little girl said When I get to heaven I will ask Jonah. The teacher asked What if Jonah went to hell? The little girl replied Then you ask him.

A Kindergarten teacher was observing her classroom of children while they were drawing. She would occasionally walk around to see each child's work. As she got to one little girl who was working diligently, she asked what the drawing was. The girl replied I'm drawing God. The teacher paused and said But no one knows what God looks like. Without missing a beat, or looking up from her drawing, the girl replied They will in a minute.

A Sunday school teacher was discussing the Ten Commandments with her five and six year olds. After explaining the commandment to honor thy Father and Mother, she asked Is there a commandment that teaches us how to treat our brothers and sisters? Without missing a beat one little boy (the oldest of a family) answered Thou shall not kill.

One day a little girl was sitting and watching her mother do the dishes at the kitchen sink. She suddenly noticed that her mother had several strands of white hair out in contrast on her brunette head. She looked at her mother and inquisitively asked, Why are some of your airs white, Mom? Her mother replied well every time that you do something wrong and make me cry or unhappy, one of my hairs turns white. The little girl thought about this revelation for a while and them said Momma, how come All grandma's hair are white?

The children had all been photographed, and the teacher was trying to persuade them each to buy a copy of the group picture. Just think how nice it will be to look at it when you are all grown up and say, There's Jennifer, she's a lawyer or That's Michael, He's a doctor. A small voice at the back of the room rang out. And there's teacher, She's dead.

A teacher was giving a lesson on the circulation of the blood. Trying to make the matter clearer, she said, Now class if I stood on my head, the blood, as you know, would run into it, and turn red in the face. Yes, the class said, Then why is it that while I am standing upright in the ordinary position the blood doesn't run into my feet? A little fellow shouted, Cause your feet ain't empty.

The children were lined up in the cafeteria of a Catholic elementary school for lunch. At the head of the table was a large pile of apples. The nun made a note and posted on the apple tray. Take only ONE. God is watching. Moving further along the lunch line, at the other end of the table was a large pile of chocolate chip cookies. A child had written a note, Take all you want. God is watching the apples.

LITTLE GREEN MEN

McCullan walked into a bar and ordered martini after martini, each time removing the olives and placing them in a jar. When the jar was filled with olives and all the drinks consumed, the Irishman started to leave. S'cuse me, said a customer, who was puzzled over what McCullan had done, what was that all about? Nothin said the Irishman, my wife just sent me out for a jar of olives.

An Irishman arrived at J.F.K. Airport and wandered around the terminal with tears streaming down his cheeks. An airline employee asked him if he was already homesick. No replied the Irishman, I've lost all my luggage! How'd that happen? The cork fell out! said the Irishman

An Irish priest is driving down to New York and gets stopped for speeding in Connecticut. The state trooper smells alcohol on the priests breath and then sees an empty wine bottle on the floor of the car. He says, sir have you been drinking? Just water, says the priest. The trooper says, Then why do I smell wine? The priest looks at the bottle and says Good Lord! He's done it again!

Two Irishmen were sitting at a pub having beer and watching the brothel across the street. They saw a Baptist minister walk into the brothel, and one of them said. Aye, tis a shame to see a man of the cloth goin bad. Then they saw a rabbi enter the brothel, and the other Irishman says Aye tis a shame to see that the Jews are fallin victim to temptation as well. Then they saw a catholic priest enter the brothel, and one of the Irishmen said, What a terrible pity

Three Irishmen, Paddy, Sean and Seamus, were stumbling home from the pub late one night and found themselves on the road which led past the old graveyard. Come have a look over here, says Paddy, It's Michael O'Grady's grave, God bless his soul. He lived to the ripe old age of 87. That's nothing says Sean, here's one named Patrick O'Toole, it says here that he was 95 when he died! Just then Samus yells out, Good God, here's a fella that got to be 145! What was his name? asks Paddy Seamus stumbles around a bit, awkwardly lights a match to see what else is written on the stone marker, and exclaims, Mile from Dublin

Drunk Ole Mulvihill (From the Northern Irish Clan) staggers into a Catholic Church, enters a confessional box, sits down but says nothing. The Priest coughs a few times to get his attention but Ole just sits there. Finally, the Priest pounds three times on the wall. The drunk mumbles, Ain't no use to knockin, there's no paper on this side either.

Mary Clancy goes up to Father O'Grady's after his Sunday morning service, and she's in tears. He says, So what's bothering you, Mary, my dear? She says, Oh Father, I've got terrible news. My husband passed away last night. The priest says, Oh Mary, that's terrible. Tell me, did he have any last requests? She says, That he did Father . . . The priest says What did he ask, Mary? She says, He said, Please Mary, put down the dam gun!!

HEADLINES and comments

THE BEST HEADLINES OF 2004

Crack Found on Governor's daughter Imagine that!

Something went Wrong in Jet Crash, Expert says no really!

Police Begin Campaign to Run Down Jay Walkers now that's taking things a bit far!

Is There a Ring of Debris Around Uranus? not if I wipe thoroughly!

Panda Mating Fails; Veterinarian Takes Over what a guy

Miners Refuse To Work After Death no-good-for nothing 'lazy so-and so!

Juvenile Court to Try Shooting Defendant see if that works any better than a fair trial!

War Dims Hope For Peace I can see it might have that effect!

If Strike Isn't Settled Quickly, It Might Last Awhile you think!

Cold Wave Linked To Temperature who would have thought!

Enfield (London) Couple Slain; Police Suspect Homicide they might be onto something!

Red Tape Holds Up Bridges you mean there's something stronger than duct tape!

Man Struck By Lightning Faces Battery Charges he probably is the battery charge!

New Study of Obesity Looks for Larger Test Group weren't they fat enough!

Astronaut Takes Blame For Gas in Spacecraft—that's what he gets for eating those beans

Kids Make Nutritious Snacks taster like chicken!

Local High School Dropouts Cut In half chainsaw massacre all over again!

Hospitals Are Sued By 7 Foot Doctors Boy, are they tall!!

And the winner is . . .

Typhoon Rips Through Cemetery Hundreds Dead ***

DID I READ THAT SIGN RIGHT???

In an office TOILET OUT OF ORDER . . . PLEASE USE FLOOR BELOW

In a Laundromat: AUTOMATIC WASHING MACHINES; PLEASE REMOVE ALL YOUR CLOTHES WHEN THE LIGHT GOES OUT

In an office WOULD THE PERSON WHO TOOK THE STEP LADDER YESTERDAY PLEASE BRING IT BACK OR FURTHER STEPS WILL BE TAKEN

In an office AFTER TEA BREAK STAFF SHOULD EMPTY THE TEAPOT AND STAND DOWN ON THE DRAINING BOARD

Outside a second hand shop WE EXCHANGE ANYTHING BICYCLES, WASHING ACHINES, ETC. WHY NOT BRING YOUR WIFE ALONG AND GET A WONDERFUL BARGIN?

Notice in a health store window CLOSED DUE TO ILLINESS

Seen during a conference FOR ANYONE WHO HAS CHILDREN AND DOSEN'T KNOW IT, THERE IS A DAY CARE ON THE FIRST FLOOR.

Notice on a farmer's field THE FARMER ALLOWS WALKERS TO CROSS THE FIELD FOR FREE, BUT THE BULL CHARGES.

On a repair shop door. WE CAN REPAIR ANYTHING (PLEASE KNOCK HARD ON THE DOOR, THE BELL DOESN'T WORK).

LITTLE JOHNNY

Little Johnny's neighbor has a new baby. Unfortunately, the baby was born without ears, When the mother brought the new baby home from the hospital.

Little Johnny's family was invited over to see him. Before they left their house, Little Johnny's dad has a talk with him and explained that the baby had no ears. His dad also told him that if he so much as mentioned anything about the baby's missing ears of even said the word ears, he would get the spanking of his life when they came home. Little Johnny told his dad that he understood completely. When Little Johnny looked into the crib he said "What a beautiful baby." Little Johnny said He has beautiful little feet and beautiful little hands, a cut little nose and really beautiful eyes. Can he see? asked Little Johnny, Yes the mother replied, we are thankful. The doctor said he will have 20/20 vision. That's great said Little Johnny, cuz he'd be shit outta luck if he needed glasses.

LIFE IN THE FAST LANE

A man and his wife were celebrating 50 years together. Their three kids, all very successful, agreed to a Sunday dinner in their honor. Happy anniversary Mom and dad said son number one . . . Sorry I'm running late. I had an emergency at the hospital with a patient, you know how it is and didn't have time to get you a gift. Not to worry said the father, The important thing is that we're all together today. Son number two arrived and announced You and Mom look great Dad I just flew in from Los Angeles between depositions and didn't have time to shop for you. It's nothing said the father, we're glad you were able to come. Just then the daughter arrived, Hello and happy anniversary, I'm sorry but my boss is sending me out of town and I was really busy packing so I didn't have time to get you anything. After they had finished dessert, the father said there's something your mother and I have wanted to tell you for a long time. You see, we were very poor. Despite this, we were able to send each of you to college. Throughout the years your mother and I knew that we loved each other very much, but we just never found the time to get married. The three children gasped and all said, you mean we're bastards? Yep said the father and cheap ones too.

GIRLS NIGHT OUT

Two women who had been friends for years, decided to go for a girls Night out, and were decidedly over-enthusiastic on the cocktails. Incredibly drunk and walking home. They needed to use the bathroom. They were very near a graveyard and one of them suggested they do their business behind a head stone or something. The first woman had nothing to dry herself with so she thought she'd take off her panties, use them and them throw them away. Her friend, however, was wearing a rather expensive underwear set and didn't want to ruin hers, but was lucky to salvage a large ribbon from a wreath that was on one of the graves. O she dried herself with the ribbon. The next day the first woman's husband phoned the other husband and said, This girl's night out thing has got to stop right now. My wife came home last night without her panties. That's nothing said the other husband Mine came home with a card stuck to her butt that said. FROM ALL OF US AT THE FIRE STATION, WE'LL NEVER FORGET YOU!!

COOKING A HAM

A man fell in love and got married. Not long after he saw his wife preparing a ham for baking. She had cut the end off the ham. Why do you do that he asked. I don't know she replied because my mother did. He said do you mind if I ask your mother why she cuts the end off the ham, he asks. No I don't mind she replied. So he called up her mother and asked the same question. I don't know the mother replied, because my mother did. Would you mind if I asked her why she cut the end off the hams he asked. No I don't mind she replied. So he called up the grandmother and asked her why she cut the end off her hams. Because it was to big for the pan she replied.

THE MIRACLE of TOILET PAPER

Fresh from the my shower, I stand in front of the mirror complaining to my husband that my breasts are too small. Instead of characteristically telling me it's not so, he uncharacteristically comes up with a suggestion. If you want your breasts to grow, then every day take a piece of toilet paper and rub it between them for a few seconds. Willing to try anything, I fetch a piece of toilet paper and stand in front of the mirror, rubbing it between my breasts. How long will this take? I asked. They will grow larger over a period of years, my husband replies. I stopped, Do you really think rubbing a piece of toilet paper between my breasts everyday will make my breasts larger over the years? Without missing a beat he says Worked for your backside, didn't it? He's still alive, and with a great deal of therapy, he may even walk again, although he will probably continue to take his meals through a straw.

??? miles away. Nothing was found of the technicians, but the lighter was virtually untouched by the explosion. The technician suspected of causing the blast had never been thought of as "bright" by his peers.

Now, the winner of this year's Darwin Award (awarded, as always, posthumously):

The Arizona Highway Patrol came upon a pile of smoldering metal embedded in the side of a cliff rising above the road at the apex of a curve. The wreckage resembled the site of an airplane crash, but it was a car. The type of car was unidentifiable at the scene. Police investigators finally pieced together the mystery. An amateur rocket scientist . . . had somehow gotten hold of a JATO unit (Jet Assisted Take Off, actually a solid fuel rocket) that is used to give heavy military transport planes an extra 'push' for taking off from short airfields. He had driven his Chevy Impala out into the desert and found a long, straight stretch of road. He attached the JATO unit to the car, jumped in, got up some speed and fired off the JATO! The facts as best as could be determined are that the operator of the 1967 Impala hit the JATO ignition at a distance of approximately 3.0 miles from the crash site. This was established by the scorched and melted asphalt at that location.

The JATO, if operating properly, would have reached maximum thrust within 5 seconds, causing the Chevy to reach speeds well in excess of 350 mph and continuing at full power for an additional 20-25 seconds.

The driver, and soon to be pilot, would have experienced G-forces usually reserved for dog fighting F-14 jocks under full afterburners, causing him to become irrelevant for the remainder of the event.

However, the automobile remained on the straight highway for about 2.5 miles (15-20 seconds) before the driver applied and completely melted the brakes, blowing the tires and leaving thick rubber marks on the road surface, then becoming airborne for an additional 1.4 miles and impacting the cliff face at a height of 125 feet leaving a blackened crater 3 feet deep in the rock. Most of the driver's remains were not recoverable.

However, small fragments of bone, teeth and hair were extracted from the crater, and fingernail and bone shards were removed from a piece of debris believed to be a portion of the steering wheel.

Epilogue: It has been calculated that this moron attained a ground speed of approximately 420-mph, though much of his voyage was not actually on the ground.

You couldn't make this stuff up, could you?

. . . AND PEOPLE JUST LIKE THIS ARE ALL AROUND US, BREEDING & VOTING!!! SCARY THOUGHT, ISN'T IT!

Watch Who You Stop

A blonde woman was speeding down the road in her pink Hummer and was pulled over by a woman police officer who was also a blonde.

The blonde cop asked to see the blonde driver's license. She dug through her purse and was getting progressively more agitated. What does it look like?' she finally asked. The policewoman replied, 'its square and it has your picture on it.' The driver finally found a square mirror in her purse, looked at it and handed it to the policewoman. 'Here it is,' she said,

The blonde officer looked at the mirror, then handed it back saying 'Okay, you can go. I didn't realize you were a cop'.

Lawyers

You should never ask a Mississippi grandma a question if they aren't prepared for the answer.

In a trial, a Southern small-town prosecuting attorney called his first witness, a grandmotherly, elderly woman to the stand. He approached her and asked, 'Mrs. Jones, do you know me?' She responded, 'Why, yes, I do know you, Mr. Williams. I've known you since you were a boy, and frankly, you've been a big disappointment to me. You lie, you cheat on your wife, and you manipulate people and talk about them behind their backs. You think you're a big shot when you haven't the brains to realize you'll never amount to anything more than a two-bit paper pusher. Yes, I know you.'

The lawyer was stunned. Not knowing what else to do, he pointed across the room and asked, 'Mrs. Jones, do you know the defense attorney?'

She again replied, 'Why yes, I do. I've known Mr. Bradley since he was a youngster, too. He's lazy, bigoted, and he has a drinking problem. He can't build a normal relationship with anyone, and his law practice is one of the worst in the entire state. Not to mention he cheated on his wife with three different women. One of them was your wife. Yes, I know him.'

The defense attorney nearly died.

The judge asked both counselors to approach the bench and, in a very quiet voice, said, 'If either of you idiots asks her if she knows me, I'll send you both to the electric chair.'

Number One Idiot of 2008

I am a medical student currently doing a rotation in toxicology at the poison control center. Today, this woman called in very upset because she caught her little daughter eating ants. I quickly reassured her that the ants are not harmful and there would be no need to bring her daughter into the hospital. She calmed down and at the end of the conversation happened to mention that she gave her daughter some ant poison to eat in order to kill the ants. I told her that she better bring her daughter in to the emergency room right away.

Here's your sign, lady. Wear it with pride.

~~~~~~

Number Two Idiot of 2008

Early this year, some Boeing employees on the airfield decided to steal a life raft from one of the 747s. They were successful in getting it out of the plane and home. Shortly after they took it for a float on the river, they noticed a Coast Guard helicopter coming toward them. It turned out that the chopper was homing in on the emergency locater beacon that activated when the raft was inflated. They are no longer employed at Boeing.

Here's your sign, guys. Don't get it wet; the paint might run.

~~~~~~

Number Three Idiot of 2008

A man, wanting to rob a downtown Bank of America, walked into the Branch and wrote this, 'Put all your muny in this bag.' While standing in line, waiting to give his note to the teller, he began to worry that someone had seen him write the note and might call the police before he reached the teller's window. So he left the Bank of America and crossed the street to the Wells Fargo Bank. After waiting a few minutes in line, he handed his note to the Wells Fargo teller. She read it and, surmising from his spelling errors that he wasn't the brightest light in the harbor, told him that she could not accept his stickup note because it was written on a Bank of American deposit slip and that he would either have to fill out a Wells Fargo deposit slip or go back to Bank of America. Looking somewhat defeated, the man said, 'OK' and left. He was arrested a few minutes later, as he was waiting in line back at Bank of America.

Don't bother with this guy's sign. He probably couldn't read it anyway.

~~~~~~

Number Four Idiot of 2008

A guy walked into a little corner store with a shotgun and demanded all of the cash from the cash drawer. After the cashier put the cash in a bag, the robber saw a bottle of Scotch that he wanted behind the counter on the shelf. He told the cashier to put it in the bag as well, but the cashier refused and said, 'Because I don't believe you are over 21.' The robber said he was, but the clerk still refused to give it to him because she didn't believe him. At this point, the robber took his driver's license out of his wallet and gave it to the clerk. The clerk looked it over and agreed that the man was in fact over 21 and she put the Scotch in the bag. The robber then ran from the store with his loot. The cashier promptly called the police and gave the name and address of the robber that he got off the license. They arrested the robber two hours later.

This guy definitely needs a sign.

~~~~~~

Idiot Number Five of 2008

A pair of Michigan robbers entered a record shop nervously waving revolvers. The first one shouted, 'Nobody move!' When his partner moved, the startled first bandit shot him.

This guy doesn't even deserve a sign

~~~~~~

Idiot Number Six of 2008

Arkansas: Seems this guy wanted some beer pretty badly. He decided that he'd just throw a cinder block through a liquor store window, grab some booze, and run. So he lifted the cinder block and heaved it over his head at the window. The cinder block bounced back knocking him unconscious. It seems the liquor store window was made of Plexi-Glass. The whole event was caught on videotape.

~~~~~~

Idiot Number Seven of 2008

I live in a semi-rural area (Weyauwega, Wisconsin). We recently had a new neighbor call the local township administrative office to request the removal of the Deer Crossing sign on our road. The reason: 'Too many deer are being hit by cars out here!—I don't think this is a good place for them to be crossing anymore.'

STAY ALERT! They walk among us . . . and they REPRODUCE . . . !!!

THE CROWD IN WASHINGTON

There were a million and a half of people in Washington to see the inauguration Only 15 of them had to call in for a day off.

1During a visit to the mental hospital,
I asked the Director how do you determine
whether or not a patient should be institutionalized?
'Well,' said the Director,
'we fill up a bathtub, then we offer a teaspoon,
a teacup and a bucket to the patient
and ask him or her to empty the bathtub.'
'Oh, I understand,' I said.

'A normal person would use the bucket
because it's bigger than the spoon or the teacup.'
'No' said the Director,
'A normal person would pull the plug.
Do you want a bed near the window?'

Never Choke in a Restaurant in the South!

Two hill billies walk into a restaurant.
While having a bite to eat, they talk about their moonshine operation.
Suddenly, a woman at a nearby table, who is eating a sandwich, begins to cough.
After a minute or so, it becomes apparent that she is in real distress.
One of the hillbillies looks at her and says, "Kin ya swallar?"
The woman shakes her head, "no." Then he asks, "Kin ya breathe?"
The woman begins to turn blue, and again shakes her head, "no."
The hillbilly walks over to the woman, lifts up her dress, yanks down her drawers
   and quickly gives her right butt cheek a lick with his tongue.
The woman is so shocked that she has a violent spasm and the obstruction
   flies out of her mouth. As she begins to breathe again, the Hillbilly walks
   slowly back to his table.
His partner says, "Ya know, I'd heerd of that there 'Hind Lick Maneuver' but I
   ain't niver seed nobody do it afore!"

Due to the climate of political correctness now pervading America, kentuckianns, tennessans, Okies, Texans, and West Vigrinians will no longer be referred to as hillbillies. You must now refer to them as Applachian—Americans. And furthermore how to speak about women and be politically correct: Bested Women 1. She is not Easy—She is horicontially Accessible. @. mShe is not a dumb Blonde—She is a Light-Haired detour off the Information Superhighway. # She has not Been Around—She is a previously—enjoyed companion. 4. She does not nag you—She becomes Verbally repetitive. % she is not a Two Bit hooker—She is a Low Cost Provider.

HOW TO SPEAK ABOUT MEN AND BE POLITICALLY CORRECT

1. He does not have a Beer Gut—He has developed a Liquid Grain Storage
    Facility.

2. he is not a Bad dancer—He is Overly Caucasian.
3. He does not Get Lost All the time. He Investigates Alternative Destinations.
4. He is not Balding—he is in Follicle Regression.
5. he does not act like a total Ass—He develops a case of Rectal—Cranial Inversion. (Loved this one).
6. it's not his Crack you see hanging out of his pants—it's Rear Cleavage.

Lesson 1:

A man is getting into the shower as his wife is finishing her shower, when the doorbell rings. The wife quickly wraps herself in a towel & runs downstairs. When she opens the door, there stands Bob, the next-door neighbor.

Before she says a word, Bob says, 'I'll give you $800 to drop that towel.'

After thinking for a moment, the woman drops her towel & stands naked. After a few seconds, Bob hands her $800 & leaves.

The woman wraps back up & goes upstairs. Her husband asks, 'Who was that?'

'It was Bob the next door neighbor,' she replies.

'Great,' the husband says, 'did he say anything about the $800 he owes me?'

Moral of the story:
If you share critical info pertaining to credit & risk with your shareholders in time, you may be in a position to prevent avoidable exposure.

Lesson 2:

A priest offered a Nun a lift. She got in & crossed her legs, forcing her gown to reveal a leg. The priest nearly had an accident.

After controlling the car, he stealthily slid his hand up her leg. The nun said, 'Father, remember Psalm 129?'

The priest removed his hand. But, changing gears, he let his hand slide up her leg again. The nun once again said, 'Father, remember Psalm 129?'

The priest apologized 'Sorry sister but the flesh is weak.'

Arriving at the convent, the nun sighed heavily & went on her way.

On his arrival at the church, the priest rushed to look up Psalm 129. It said, 'Go forth and seek, further up, you will find glory.'

Moral of the story:
If you are not well informed in your job, you might miss a great opportunity.

Lesson 3:
A sales rep, an admin clerk & the manager are walking to lunch when they find an antique oil lamp.

They rub it and a Genie comes out.

The Genie says, 'I'll give each of you just one wish.' 'Me first! Me first!' says the admin clerk. 'I want to be in the Bahamas, driving a speedboat, without a care in the world.'

Puff! She's gone.

'Me next! Me next!' says the sales rep. 'I want to be in Hawaii, relaxing on the beach with my personal masseuse, an endless supply of Pina Coladas & the love of my life.'

Puff! He's gone.

'OK, you're up,' the Genie says to the manager. The manager says, 'I want those two back in the office after lunch.'

Moral of the story:
Always let your boss have the first say.

Lesson 4
An eagle was sitting on a tree resting, doing nothing.

A small rabbit saw the eagle and asked him, 'Can I sit like you & do nothing?'

The eagle answered: 'Sure, why not.'

So, the rabbit sat on the ground below the eagle & rested. All of a sudden, a fox appeared, jumped on the rabbit & ate it.

Moral of the story:
To be sitting and doing nothing, you must be sitting very, very high up.
Lesson 5
A turkey was chatting with a bull.

'I would love to be able to get to the top of that tree' sighed the turkey, 'but I haven't got the energy.'

'Well, why don't you nibble on some of my droppings?' replied the bull. 'They're packed with nutrients.'

The turkey pecked at a lump of dung, & found it actually gave him enough strength to reach the lowest branch of the tree.

The next day, after eating some more dung, he reached the second branch.

Finally after a fourth night, the turkey was proudly perched at the top of the tree.

He was promptly spotted by a farmer, who shot him out of the tree.

Moral of the story:
BS may get you to the top, but it won't keep you there.

Lesson 6
A little bird was flying south for the winter. It was so cold the bird froze & fell to the ground into a large field.

While he was lying there, a cow came by & dropped some dung on him.

As the frozen bird lay there in the pile of cow dung, he began to realize how warm he was. The dung was actually thawing him out!

He lay there all warm & happy, & soon began to sing for joy. A passing cat heard the bird singing & came to investigate.

Following the sound, the cat discovered the bird under the pile of cow dung, promptly dug him out & ate him.

Morals of the story:
(1) Not everyone who craps on you is your enemy.
(2) Not everyone who gets you out of crap is your friend.
(3) And when you're in deep crap, it's best to keep your mouth shut!

NIGHT LIGHT

At age 90, George went for his annual physical. All of his tests came back normal results.

Dr. Smith said. George everything looks great physically. How are you doing mentally and emotionally? Are you at peace with yourself, and do you have a good relationship with God?

George replied, God and I are tight. He knows I have poor eyesight, so he's fixed it so that when I get up in the middle of the night to go to the bathroom, poof, the light goes on, when I'm done, poof, the light goes off. Wow, replied Dr. Smith, That's incredible.

A little later in the day Dr Smith called George's wife. Ethel he said George is doing fine. Physically he's great. But I had to call because I'm in awe of his relationship with God. Is it true that he gets up during the night and, poof, the light goes on in the bathroom, and then when he is through, poof, it goes off?

Ethel exclaimed, Oh Dear Lord! He's peeing in the refrigerator again!!

NOW I AM NOT CONFUSED

I became confused when I heard these terms with reference to the word 'service'.

Internal Revenue 'Service'
U.S. Postal 'Service'
Telephone 'Service'
Cable 'Service'
Civil 'Service'
Customer 'Service'
State, City & County Public 'Service'

This is not what I thought 'service' meant.

But today, I overheard two farmers from Calhoun talking, and one of them said he had hired a bull to come 'service' a few cows. BAM!!! It all came into focus. Now I understand what all those 'service' agencies are doing to us.

I hope you are now as enlightened as I am.

THE BEST EVER DUMB BLONDE JOKE

A blonde calls her boyfriend and says, 'Please come over here and help Me. I have a killer jigsaw puzzle, and I can't figure out how to get Started.'

Her boyfriend asks, 'What is it supposed to be when it's finished?'

The blonde says, 'According to the picture on the box, it's a rooster.'

Her boyfriend decides to go over and help with the puzzle.

She lets him in and shows him where she has the puzzle spread all over
The table.

He studies the pieces for a moment, then looks at the box, then turns to
Her and says,

'First of all, no matter what we do, we're not going to be able to Assemble
these pieces into anything resembling a rooster.'

He takes her hand and says, 'Second, I want you to relax. Let's have a Nice
cup of tea, and then . . .' he said with a deep sigh, . . .

Now lets put the KELLOGS CORN FLAKES back in the box

*Jane and Arlene are outside their nursing home, having a drink and a smoke,
when it starts to rain. Jane pulls out a condom, cuts off the end, puts it over
her cigarette, and continues smoking.*

Arlene: What in the hell is that?
Jane: A condom. This way my cigarette doesn't get wet.
Arlene: Where did you get it?
Jane: You can get them at any drugstore.

*The next day, Arlene hobbles herself into the local drugstore and announces to
the pharmacist that she wants a box of condoms.*

*The pharmacist, obviously embarrassed, looks at her kind of strangely
(she is after all, over 80 years of age), but very delicately asks what brand of
condom she prefers.*

'Doesn't matter Sonny, as long as it fits on a Camel.'
The pharmacist fainted.

OLD FOLKS ARE WORTH A FORTUNE

Old folks are worth a fortune: With silver in their hair, gold in their teeth, stones
in their kidneys, lead in their feet and gas in their stomachs.

I have become a lot more social with the passing of the years; some might
even call me a frivolous old gal. I'm seeing five gentlemen every day. As soon as
I wake, Will Power helps me get out of bed. Then I go to see John. Then Charley

Horse comes along, and when he is here he takes a lot of attention. When he leaves, Arthur Ritis shows up and stays the rest of the day. (He doesn't like to stay in one place very long, so he takes e from joint to joint). After such a busy day, I'm glad to go to bed _ with Ben Gay. What a life!

PS The preacher came to call t5he other day. He said that at my age, I should be thinking about the hereafter. I told him I do _ all the time. No matter where I am—in the parlor, upstairs in the kitchen or down in the basement _ I ask myself, Now, what am I here after?

NEW YORK—Idaho resident Kathy Evans brought humiliation to her friends and family Tuesday when she set a new standard for stupidity with her appearance on the popular TV show, 'Who Wants To Be A Millionaire.'

It seems that Evans, a 32-year-old wife and mother of two, got stuck on the first question, and proceeded to make what fans of the show are dubbing 'the absolute worst use of lifelines ever.'

After being introduced to the show's host Meredith Vieira, Evans assured her that she was ready to play, whereupon she was posed with an extremely easy $100 question. The question was: 'Which of the following is the largest?'

A) A Peanut
B) An Elephant
C) The Moon
D) Hey, who you calling large?

Immediately Mrs. Evans was struck with an all consuming panic as she realized that this was a question to which she did not readily know the answer.

'Hmm, oh boy, that's a toughie,' said Evans, as Vieira did her level best to hide her disbelief and disgust. 'I mean, I'm sure I've heard of some of these things before, but I have no idea how large they would be.'

Evans made the decision to use the first of her three lifelines, the 50/50. Answers A and D were removed, leaving her to decide which was bigger, an elephant or the moon. However, faced with an incredibly easy question, Evans still remained unsure.

'Oh! It removed the two I was leaning towards!' exclaimed Evans. 'Darn. I think I better phone a friend.'

Using the second of her two lifelines on the first question, Mrs. Evans asked to be connected with her friend Betsy, who is an office assistant.

'Hi Betsy! How are you? This is Kathy! I'm on TV!' said Evans, wasting the first seven seconds of her call. 'Ok, I got an important question. Which of the following is the largest? B, an elephant, or C, the moon. 15 seconds hun.'

Betsy quickly replied that the answer was C, the moon.

Evans proceeded to argue with her friend for the remaining ten seconds . . . take her friend's advice and pick 'The Moon.'

'I just don't know if I can trust Betsy. She's not all that bright. So I think I'd like to ask the audience,' said Evans.

Asked to vote on the correct answer, the audience returned 98% in favor of answer C, 'The Moon.' Having used up all her lifelines, Evans then made the dumbest choice of her life.

'Wow, seems like everybody is against what I'm thinking,' said the too-stupid-to-live Evans. 'But you know, sometimes you just got to go with your gut. So, let's see. For which is larger, an elephant or the moon, I'm going to have to go with B, an elephant. Final answer.'

Evans sat before the dumbfounded audience, the only one waiting with bated breath, and was told that she was wrong, and that the answer was in fact, C, 'The Moon.'

Caution . . . they walk among us!

This one is actually better! (No comments needed!)

Subject: The Preacher's Paycheck

A pastor's wife was expecting a baby, so he stood before the congregation and asked for a raise. After much discussion, they passed a rule that whenever the preacher's family expanded, so would his paycheck.

After 6 children, this started to get expensive and the congregation decided to hold another meeting to discuss the preacher's expanding salary. A great deal of yelling and inner bickering ensued, as to how much the clergyman's additional children were costing the church, and how much more it could potentially cost.

After listening to them for about an hour, the pastor rose from his chair and spoke, 'Children are a gift from God, and we will take as many gifts as He gives us'.

Silence fell on the congregation.

In the back pew, a little old lady struggled to stand, and finally said in her frail voice, 'Rain is also a gift from God, but when we get too much of it, we wear rubbers.'

The entire congregation said, 'Amen.'

The Box of Chocolates

Sally was driving home from one of her business trips in Northern Arizona when she saw an elderly Navajo woman walking on the side of the road. As the trip was a long and quiet one, she stopped the car and asked the Navajo woman if she would like a ride. With a silent nod of thanks, the woman got into the car. Resuming the journey, Sally tried in vain just to make a bit of small talk with the Navajo woman. The old lady just sat silently, looking intently at everything she saw, studying every little detail, until she noticed a white bag on the seat next to Sally. What in bag? Asked the old woman. Sally looked down at the white bag and said, It's a box of chocolates, I got it for my husband. The Navajo woman was silent for another moment or two. Then speaking with the quiet wisdom of an elder, she said GOOD TRADE.

ALLIENS OR ???

Clear day! Walked into Quizeno's with a buy-one-get-one free coupon for a sandwich. I handed it to the girl and she looked over at a little chalkboard that said buy—one—get-one free. She said so I guess they both free. She handed me my sandwiches and I walked out the door. They walk among us, and many work retail.

One day I was walking down the beach with some friends when one of them shouted

Look at that dead bird! Someone looked up at the sky and said Where??

While looking at a house, my brother asked the real estate agent which direction was north because, he explained, he didn't want the sun waking him up every morning. She asked Does the sun rise in the north? When my brother explained that the sun rises in the east, and has for sometime she shook her head and said, Oh I don't keep up with that stuff.

I used to work in technical support for a 24/7 call center. One day I got a call from an individual who asked what hours the call center was open. I told him The number you dialed is open 24 hours a day, 7 days a week. He responded, Is that eastern or Pacific time? Wanting to end the call quickly I said uh Pacific. They walk among us!

CAN BE TOLD IN CHURCH

Attending a wedding for the first time, a little girl whispered to her mother, Why is the bride dressed in white? Because white is the color of happiness, and today is the happiest day of her life. The child thought about this for awhile then asked So why is the groom wearing black?

A little girl, dressed in her Sunday best, was running as could, trying not to be late for Bible class. As she ran she prayed "Dear Lord, please don't let me be late", Dear Lord please don't let me be late! While she was running and praying, she tripped on a curb and felt, getting her clothes dirty and tearing her dress. She got up, brushed her self off., and be and started to pray again. As she ran once again began to pray. Dear Lord, please don't let me be late . . . But please don't shove me either!!

Three boys are in school yard bragging about their fathers. The first boy says My dad scribbles a few words on a piece of paper, he calls it poem they give him $50. the second boy says that's nothing, My dad scribbles a few words on a piece of paper, he calls it a song, they give him $100. The third boy says, I got you both beat, my dad scribbles a few words on a piece of paper, he calls it a sermon, and it takes eight people to collect all the money.

A police recruit was asked during the exam, What would you do if you had to arrest your own mother? He answered Call for backup.

A Sunday school teacher asked her class why Joseph and Mary took Jesus with them to Jerusalem. A small child replied They couldn't get a baby—sitter.

A Sunday school teacher was discussing the Ten Commandments with her five and six year olds. After explaining the commandment to Honor thy father and thy mother, she asked Is there a commandment that teaches us how to treat out brothers and sisters? Without missing a beat one little boy answered Thou Shall Not Kill!

At Sunday School they were teaching how God created everything, including human beings. Little Johnny seemed especially intent when they told him how Eve was created out of one of Adams ribs. Later in the week his mother noticed him lying down as though he were ill, and she said Johnny, what is the matter? Little Johnny responded, I have pain in my side. I think I'm going to have a wife.

OR ?????

My sister has a life-saving tool in her car designed to cut through a seat-belt if she gets trapped. She keeps it in the trunk. They walk among us!

My friends and I were on a beer run and noticed that the cases were discounted 10%. Since it was a big party, we bought 2 cases. The cashier multiplied 2 times 10% and gave us a 20% discount.

I couldn't find my luggage at the airport baggage area, so I went to the lost luggage office and told the woman there that my bags never showed up. She smiled and told me not to worry because she was a trained professional and I was in good hands. Now she asked me, has your plane arrived yet?

While waiting for my order at a pizza parlor, I observed a man ordering a small pizza to go. He appeared to be alone and the cook asked him if he would like it cut into 4 pieces of 6. He thought about it for some time before responding. Just cut it into 4 pieces: I don't think I'm hungry enough to eat 6 pieces.

At a McDonald's in Florida, I asked the 3 clerk for a cup of coffee—half regular and half decaf. She asked me which one I wanted on the bottom. She wasn't even blonde. Yep they walk among us!!!

RETARDED GRANDPARENTS

After Christmas, a teacher asked her young pupils how they spent their holiday away from school. One child wrote the following: We always used to spend the holidays with Grandma and Grandpa. They used to live in a big brick house but

Grandpa got retarded and they moved to Florida. Now they live in a tin box and have rocks painted green to look like grass. They ride around on their bicycles and wear name tags because they don't know who they are anymore. They go to a building called a wrecked center, but they must have got it fixed because it is all okay now, and do exercises there, but they all jump up and down with hats on. At their gate there is a doll house with a little old man sitting in it. He watches all day so nobody can escape. Sometimes they sneak out. They go cruising in their golf carts. Nobody there cooks, they just eat out. And, they eat the same thing every night: Early birds. Some of the people can't get out past the man in the doll house. The ones who do get out, bring food back to the wrecked center and call it pot luck. My grandma says that Grandpa worked all his life to earn his retardment and says I should work hard so I can be retarded someday too. When I earn my retardment, I want to be the man in the doll house. Then I will let people out so they can visit their grandchildren.

BASEBALL NUNS

Sitting behind a couple of nuns at a baseball game (whose habits partially blocked their view) three men decided to badger the nuns, in an effort to get them to move. In a very loud voice, the first man said, I think I'm going to move to Utah, there are only 100 nuns there. The second guy spoke up and said, I want to go to Montana, there are only 50 nuns living there. The third guy said I want to go to Idaho, there are only 25 nuns living there. One of the nuns turned around, looked at the man and in a very sweet, calm voice said, why don't you go to hell? There aren't any nuns there.

TO BE 6 AGAIN

A man was sitting on the edge of the bed, observing his wife turning back and forth, looking at herself in the mirror. Since her birthday was not far off, he asked what she'd like to have for her birthday. I'd like to bee 6 again, she replied still looking in the mirror, On the morning of her birthday, he arose early, made her a nice big bowl of Lucky Charms, and then took her to six Flags theme park. What a day! He put her on every ride in the park; the Death slide, the Wall of Fear, Screaming Monster roller Coaster . . . everything there was. Five hours later they staggered out of the theme park. Her head was reeling and her stomach felt upside down. He then took her to a McDonald's where he ordered her a Happy Meal with extra fries and a chocolate shake. Then it was off to a movie, popcorn, a soda pop, and her favorite candy, M&M's. What a fabulous adventure! Finally she wobbled home with her husband and collapsed into bed exhausted. He leaned over his wife with a big smile and lovingly asked, Well Dear what was it like being six again? Her eyes slowly opened and her expression suddenly changed. I meant my dress size you dumb ass!! The moral of the story: even when a man is listening, he is going to get it wrong.

AIR FLIGHT CONVERSATION

A man boarded a plane and took his seat and as he settled in he glanced up and saw a beautiful woman coming down the isle. He soon realized that she was heading straight toward his seat. As fate would have it she took the seat right beside him. Eager to strike up a conversation, he blurted out. Business trip or pleasure? She turned, smiled and said, Business, I'm going to the Annual Nymphomaniacs of America Convention in Chicago. He swallowed hard. Here was the most gorgeous woman he had ever seen sitting next to him and she was going to a meeting of nymphomaniacs! Struggling to maintain his composure, he calmly asked, What's your business role at the convention? Lecture, she replied. I am lead lecturer where I use information that I've learned from my own personal experiences to debunk some of the popular myths about sexuality. He said what kind of myths are there? Well she explained one popular myth is that African-American men are the most, well-endowed of all men, when in fact it is the Native American Indian who is most likely to possess that trait. Another popular myth is that Frenchmen are the best lovers, when actually it is the men of Jewish descent that are the best. I have discovered that the lover with the absolutely best stamina is the Southern Redneck. Suddenly the woman became a little uncomfortable and blushed, I'm sorry, she said I shouldn't really be discussing all this with you. I don't even know your name. Tonto, the man said "Tonto Goldstein, but my friends call me Bubba

SNAKES

Never bring plants into the house. Garden grass Snakes can be dangerous. Here is why. A couple in Sweetwater Texas had a lot of potted plants. During a recent cold spell, the wife was bringing a lot of them indoors to protect them from a freeze. It turned out that a little green garden snake was hidden in one of the plants and when it had warmed up, it slithered out and the wife saw it go under the sofa. She let out a scream. The husband (who was taking a shower) ran out into the living room naked to see what the problem was. She told him there was a snake under the sofa He got down on the floor on his hands and knees to look for it. About that time the family dog came and cold-nosed him on the behind. He thought the had bitten him, so he screamed and fell over on the floor. His wife thought he had a heart attack, so she covered him up, told him to lie still and called an ambulance. The attendants rushed in, wouldn't listen to his protests and loaded him on the stretcher and started carrying him out. About that time the snake came out from under the sofa and the Emergency Medical Technician saw it and dropped his end of the stretcher. That's when the man broke his leg and why he is still in the hospital. His wife still had a problem of the snake in the house, so she called on a neighbor man. He volunteered to capture the snake. He armed himself with a rolled-up newspaper and began poking under the couch. Soon he decided it was gone and told the woman, who sat down on the sofa in relief. But while relaxing her hand dangled in between the cushions, where she felt the snake wiggling around. She screamed and fainted, the snake rushed back under the sofa. The neighbor man, seeing her lying there passed out, tried to use CPR to revive her. The neighbors wife, who had just returned from shopping at the grocery store, saw her husbands mouth on the woman's mouth and slammed her husband in the back of the head with a bag off canned goods, knocking him out and cutting his scalp to a point where it needed stitches. The noise woke the woman from her dead faint and she saw her neighbor lying on the floor with his wife bending over him, so she assumed that he had been bitten by the snake.

She went into the kitchen and got a small bottle of whiskey, and began pouring it down the man's throat. By now the police had arrived. They saw the unconscious man, smelled the whiskey, and assumed that a drunken fight occurred. They were about to arrest them all, when the women tried to explain how it all happened over a little garden snake. The police call an ambulance, which took away the neighbor and his sobbing wife. The little snake again crawled out from under the sofa. One of the policemen drew his gun and fired at it. He missed the snake and hit the leg of the end of the table. The table fell over and the lamp on it shattered and as the bulb broke it started a fire in the drapes. The other policeman tried to beat out the flames, and fell through the window into the yard on top of the family dog who, startled, jumped out and raced into the street where an oncoming car swerved to avoid it and smashed into the parked police car. Meanwhile, burning drapes, were seen by the neighbors who called the fire department. The firemen had started raising the fire truck ladder when they were halfway down the street. The rising ladder tore out the overhead wires and put out the electricity and disconnected the telephones in a ten-square city block area (but they did get the house fire out). Time passed. Both men were discharged from the hospital, the house was torn down and the snake crawled back into the garden.

LOUISANA GHOST STORY

This happened about a month ago just outside of Cocodrie, a little town in the bayou country of Louisiana, and while it sounds like an Alfred Hitchcock tale, it's real. This out of state traveler was on the side of the road, hitchhiking on a real dark night in the middle of a thunderstorm. Time passed slowly and no cars went by. It was raining so hard he could hardly see his hand in front of his face. Suddenly he saw a car moving slowly, approaching and appearing ghostlike in the rain. It slowly and silently crept toward him and stopped. Wanting a ride real bad the guy jumped in the car and closed the door: only then did he realize there was nobody behind the wheel, and no sound of an engine to be herd over the rain. Again the car crept slowly forward and the guy was terrified, too scared to think of jumping out and running. The guy saw that the car was approaching a sharp curve and, still too scared to jump out, he started to pray and begging for his life: he was sure the ghost car would go off the road ad in the bayou and he would surely drown. But just before the curve a shadow appeared at the drivers window and a hand reached in and turned the steering wheel, guiding the car safely around the bend. Then just as silently, the hand disappeared through the window and the hitchhiker was alone again! Paralyzed with fear, the guy watched the hand reappear every time the reached a curve. Finally the guy scared to near death, had all he could take and jumped out of the car and ran to town. Wet and in shock, he went into a bar and voice quivering, ordered two shots of whiskey, then told everybody about his supernatural experience. A silence enveloped and everybody got goose bumps. When the realized the guy was telling the truth (and not just some drunk). About half an hour later two guys walked into the bar and one says to the other, Look Boudreaux, dere dat itiot that rode in our car when we wuz pushin it in the rain!!

CHILLI COOK OFF

If you can read this whole story without laughing then there's no hope for you. I was crying by the end. Note: Please take time to read this slowly. (I've read this probably 5 times and it never fails to reduce me to tears of laughter). Hope it does the same for you!!! If you pay attention to the first two judges, the reaction of the third judge is even better. For those of you who have lived in Texas, you know how rue this is. They actually have a Chili Cook Off about the time Halloween comes around. It takes up a major portion of a parking lot at the San Antonio City Park. Judge #3 was an inexperienced Chili Taster named Frank, who was visiting from Springfield, IL. Frank: "Recently, I was honored to be selected as a judge at a chili cook-off. The original person called in sick at the last moment and I happened to be standing there at the judge's table asking for directions to the Coors Light truck, when the call came in. I was assured by the other judges (Native Texans) that the chili wouldn't be all that spicy and, besides, they told me I could have a free beer during the tasting, so I accepted. Here are the scorecard notes from the event.

CHILI # 1 MIKES MANIAC MONSTER CHILI . . . Judge #1 A little too heavy on the tomato. Amusing kick. Judge # 2 Nice, smooth tomato flavor. Very mild. Judge # 3 (Frank) Holy shit, what the hell is this stuff? You could remove dried paint from your driveway. Took me two beers to put the flames out. I hope that's the worst one. These Texans are crazy. CHILI # 2 AUSTIN'S AFTERBURNER CHILI . . . Judge # 1 Smokey, with a hint of pork. Slight jalapeno tang. Judge # 2—exciting BBQ flavor, needs more peppers to be taken seriously. Judge # 3 Keep this out of the reach of children. I'm not sure what I'm supposed to taste besides pain. I had to wave off two people who wanted to give me the Heimlich maneuver. They had to rush in more beer when they saw the look on my face. CHILI # 3 FRED'S FAMOUS BURN DOWN THE BARN CHILI . . . Judge # 1 Excellent firehouse chili. Great kick. Judge # 2—A bit salty, good use of peppers. Judge # 3—Call the EPA. I've located a uranium spill. My nose feels like I have been snorting Drano. Everyone knows the routine by now. Get me more beer before I Ignite.

Barmaid pounded me on the back, now my backbone is in the front part of my chest. I'm getting shit-faced from all of the beer. CHILI # 4—BUBBA'S BLACK MAGIC . . . JUDGE # 1—Black bean chili with almost no spice. Disappointing. Judge # 2—Hint of lime in the black beans. Good side 4 dish for fish or other mild foods not much of a chili. Judge # 3—I felt something scraping across my tongue, but was unable to taste it. Is it possible to burn out taste buds? Sally, the beer maid, was standing behind me with fresh refills. That 300-lb woman is starting to look HOT. Just like this nuclear waste I'm eating! Is chili an aphrodisiac? CHILI # 5 LISA'S LEGAL LIP REMOVER . . . JUDGE # 1—Meaty, strong chili. Cayenne peppers freshly ground adding considerable! kick! Very impressive. JUDGE # 2—CHILI USING SHREDDED BEEF, COULD USE MORE TOMATO. Must admit the cayenne peppers make a strong statement. JUDGE # 3—My! ears are ringing, sweat is pouring off my forehead and I can no longer focus my eyes. I farted and four people behind me needed paramedics. The contestant seemed offended when I told her that her chili had given me brain damage. Sally saved my tongue from bleeding by pouring beer directly on it from the pitcher. I wonder if I'm burning my lips off. It really pisses me off that the other judges asked me to stop screaming. CHILI # 6 VERA'S VERY VEGETARIAN VARIETY . . . JUDGE # 1—Thin yet bold vegetarian variety chili. Good balance of spices and peppers. JUDGE # 2—The best yet. Aggressive use of peppers, onions, and garlic. Superb. JUDGE # 3—My intestines are now a straight pipe filled with gaseous, sulfuric flames. I shit on myself when I farted and I'm worried it will eat through the chair. No one seems inclined to stand behind me except that Sally. Can't feel my lips anymore. I need to wipe my ass with a snow cone. CHILI # 7—SUSAN'S SCREAMING SENSATION CHILI—JUDGE # 1—Hohum, tastes as if the chef literally threw in a can of chili peppers at the last moment. ** I should take note that I am worried about Judge # 3. He appears to be in a bit of distress as he is cursing uncontrollably. JUDGE # 3—You could put a grenade in my mouth, pull the pin, and I wouldn't feel a thing. I've lost sight in one eye, and the world sounds like it is made of rushing water, My shirt is covered with chili, which slid unnoticed out my mouth. My pants are full of lava to match my shirt. At least during the autopsy, they'll know what killed me. I've decided to stop breathing it's too painful. Screw it: I'm not getting any oxygen anyway. If I need air, I'll suck it in through the 4-inch hole in my stomach.

■■

Chili # 8—BIG TOM'S TOENAIL CURLING CHILI . . . JUDGE # 1—The perfect ending, this is a nice blend chili. Not too bold but spicy enough to declare its existence. JUDGE # 2—This final entry is a good, balanced chili. Neither mild nor hot. Sorry to see that most of it was lost when Judge # 3 farted, passed out, fell over and pulled the chili pot down on top of himself. Not sure if he's going to make it, poor feller, wonder how he'd have reacted to really hot chili? JUDGE # 3—No Report

THE COWBOY BOOTS

Did you hear about the Texas teacher who was helping one of her kindergarten students put on his cowboy boots? He asked for help and she could see why. Even with her pulling and him pushing, the little boots still didn't want to go on. By the time they got the second boot on, she had worked up a sweat. She almost cried when the little boy said, Teacher, they're on the wrong feet. She looked and sure enough they were. It wasn't any time she managed to keep her cool as, together they worked to get the boots back on, this time on the right feet. He then announced, These aren't my boots. She bit her tongue, rather than get right in his face and scream, Why didn't you say so? Like she wanted to. Once again back to his feet. No sooner had they gotten the boots off when he said, They're my brother's boots. My mom made me wear them. Now she didn't know if she should laugh or cry. But she mustered up what grace and courage she had left to wrestle the boots on his feet again. Helping him into his coat, she asked, Now where are your mittens? He said I stuffed em in the toes of my boots. She will eligible for parole on three years.

WHO'S YOUR DADDY

When someone puts in for Child Support, the proper thing to do is to find out who the father is and see why he is not providing child support. The following are all replies that Dallas women have written on Child Support Agency forms in the section listing father details. Or putting it another way . . . Who's your daddy! These are genuine excerpts from the forms. Be sure to check out no. 11 it takes the prize and #3 is runner up.

1. Regarding the identity of the father of my twins, child A was fathered by Jim Munson. I am unsure as to the identity as to the identity of the father of child B, but I believe he was conceived on the same night.

2. I am unsure as to the identity of the father of my child as I was being sick out of a window when taken unexpectedly from behind. I can provide you with a list of names of men that I think were at the party if this helps.

3. I do not know the name of the father of my girl. She was conceived at a party at 3600 Grand Ave. where I had unprotected sex with a man I met that night. I do remember that the sex was so good that I fainted. If you do manage to track down the father, can you send me his phone number? Thanks

4. I don't know the identity of the father of my daughter. He drives a BMW that now has a hole made by stiletto in one of the door panels. Perhaps you can contact BMW service stations in this area and see if he's had it replaced.

5. I have never had sex with a man. I am still a Virginian. I am awaiting a letter from the Pope confirming that my son's conception was immaculate and that he is Christ risen again.

6. I cannot tell you the name of child A's dad as he informs me that to do so would blow his cover and that would have cataclysmic implications for the economy. I am torn between doing right by you and right by the country. Please advise.

7. I do not know who the father of my child was as all blacks look the same to me.

8. Peter Smith is the father of child A. If you do catch up with him. Can you ask him what he did with AC/Dc CD's? Child B who was also borned at the same time. well I don't have a clue.

9. From the dates it seems that my daughter was conceived at Disney world; maybe it really is the Magic Kingdom.

10. So much about that night is a blur. The only thing that I remember for sure is Delia Smith did a program about eggs earlier in the evening. If I'd stayed in and watched more TV rather than going to the party at 146 Miller Drive, mine might have remained unfertilized.

11. I am unsure as to the identity of the father of my baby, after all when you eat a can of beans you can't be sure which one made you fart.

BAPTIST CHURCH

A crusty old man walks into the local First Baptist church and says to the secretary, I would like to join your damn church. The astonished woman replies, I beg your pardon, sir. I must have misunderstood you. What did you say? Listen up, damn it. I said I want to join this damn church! I'm sorry sir. But that kind of language is not tolerated in this church. The secretary leaves her desk and goes into the pastor's study to inform him of her situation. The pastor agrees that the secretary does not have to listen to that foul language. They both return to her office and the pastor asks the old geezer, sir what seems to be the problem here? There is no damn problem, the man says. I just won $200 million bucks in the damn lottery and I want to join this damn church to get rid of some of this damn money. I see, said the pastor. And is this bitch giving you a hard time?

SOUTHERN GRANDMA

Lawyers should never ask a Southern grandma a question if they aren't prepared for her answer. In a trial, a Southern small-town prosecuting attorney called his first witness, a grandmotherly, elderly woman to the stand. He approached her and asked, Mrs. Jones, do you know me? She responded, Why, yes, I do know you, Mr. Williams. I've known you since you were a boy, and frankly, you've been a big disappointment to me. You lie, you cheat on your wife, and you manipulate people and talk about them behind their backs. You think you're a big shot when you haven't the brains to realize you'll never amount to anything more than a two-bit paper pusher. Yes, I know you. The lawyer was stunned! Not knowing what else to do, he pointed across the room and asked. Mrs. Jones, do you know the defense attorney? She again replied, Why yes, I do. I've known Mr. Bradley since he was a youngster too. He's lazy, bigoted, and has a drinking problem. He can't build a normal relationship with anyone and his law practice is one of the worst in the entire state. Not to mention he's cheated on his wife with three different women, one of them was your wife. Yes, I know him. The defense attorney almost died. The judge asked both counselors to approach the bench and, in a very quiet voice said, If either of you idiots asks her if she knows me, I'll send you both to the electric chair.

BLONDES

January—took new scarf back to store because it was to tight.

February—Fired from pharmacy job for failing to print labels . . . duh . . . bottles won't fit into typewriter!!!

March . . . Got excited finished jigsaw puzzle in 6 months . . box said 2-4 years.

April . . . Trapped on escalator for hours . . . power went out!!!

May . . . Tried to make Kool-Aid . . . 8 cups of water won't fit into those little packets!!!

July . . . Lost breast stroke swimming competition . . . learned later, other swimmers cheated they used the arms!!!

August—got locked out of car in rain storm . . . car swamped, because top was down.

September . . . The capital of California is "C" . . . isn't it??

October . . . Hate M & M's . . . they are hard to peel.!!!

November . . . Baked turkey for 4 ½ days . . . instructions said 1 hour per pound and I weigh 108!!!

December . . . Couldn't call 911 . . . duh . . . there's no eleven button on the phone. WHAT A YEAR

CHINESE PROVERBS

Man who run in front of car get tired. Man who run behind car get exhausted. Man who walk through airport turnstile sideways going to Bangkok. Man with one chopstick go hungry. Man who scratch ass should not bit fingernails. Man who eat many prunes get good run for money. Baseball it's wrong, man with four balls cannot walk. Panties not best thing on earth! But next to best thing on earth. War does not determine who is right, war determine who is left. Wife who put husband in doghouse soon find him in cat house. Man who fight with wife all day get no piece at night. It take many nails to build crib, but one screw to fill it. Man who drive like hell, bound to get there. Man who stand on toilet is high on pot. Man who live in glass house should change clothes in basement. Man who fish in other man's well often catch crabs. Man who far in church sit n own pew. Crowded elevator smell different to midget.

Snow

December 8 6:00 pm it started to snow. The first snow of the season and the wife and I took our cocktails and sat for hours by the window watching the huge snow flakes drift down from heaven. It looked like a Grandma Moses print. So romantic we felt like newlyweds again I love snow! December 9 we woke to a beautiful blanket of crystal white snow covering every inch of landscape. What a fantastic sight!! Can there be a more lovely place in the world? Moving here was the best idea I've ever had. Shoveled for the first time in years and felt like a boy again. I did both our driveway and the sidewalk. This afternoon the snow plow came along and covered up the sidewalk and closed in the driveway, so I got to shovel again. What a perfect life.! December 12: The sun has melted all our snow. Such a disappointment. My neighbor tells me not to worry, we'll definitely have a white Christmas. No snow on Christmas would be awful! Bob says we'll have so much snow by the end of winter, that I'll never want to see snow again. I don't think that's possible. Bob is such a nice man. I'm sure glad he's our neighbor. December 14: Snow, lovely snow! 8 inches last night. The temperature dropped. To -20. The cold makes everything sparkle so. The wind took my breath away, but I warmed up by shoveling the driveway and sidewalks. This is the life! The snowplow came back this afternoon and buried everything. I didn't realize I would have to quite this much shoveling, but I'll certainly get back in shape this way. I wish I wouldn't huff and puff so. December 15 20 inches forecast. Sold my van and bought a 4x4 Blazer. Bought snow tires for the wife's for the wife's car and 2 extra shovels. Stocked the freezer. The wife wants a wood stove in case the electricity goes out. I think that's silly. We aren't in Alaska, after all. December 16. Ice storm this morning. Fell on my ass on the ice in the driveway, putting down salt. Hurt like hell! The wife laughed for an hour, which I think was very cruel. December 17. Still way below freezing. Roads are too icy to go anywhere. Electricity was off for 5 hours. I had to pile the blankets on to stay warm. Nothing to do but stare at the wife and try not to irate her. Guess I should've bought a wood stove, but won't admit it to her. God, I hate it when she's right. I can't believe I'm freezing to death in my own living room. December 20: electricity's back on, but had another 14 inches of the damn stuff last night. More shoveling. Took all day. goddamn snowplow came by twice. Tried to find neighbor kid to shovel, but they said they're too busy playing hockey. I think they're lying. Called the only hardware store around to see about buying a snow blower and they're out. Might have another shipment in March. I think they're lying bob says I have to shovel or the city will have it done and bill me. I think he's lying. December 22: Bob was right about white Christmas, because 13 more inches of the white shit fell today, and it's so cold it probably won't melt till august: Took me 30 minutes to get all dressed up to go out to shovel and then I had to piss. By the time I got undressed, pissed, and dressed again, I was to tired to shovel. Tried to hire Bob, who has a plow on his truck, for the rest of the winter, but he says he's too busy. I think the ass hole is lying. December 23: only 2" of snow today. And it warmed up to 0. The wife wanted me to decorate the front of the house this morning. What is she . . . nuts??? Why didn't she tell me to do that a month ago? She says she did I think she's lying. December 24 6". Snow packed so hard by snowplow. I broke the shovel. Thought I was having a heart attack. If I ever catch the son of a bitch who drives that snowplow, I'll drag him through the snow by his balls. I know he hides around the corner and waits for me to finish shoveling, and then he comes down the street at a 100 miles an hour. And throws snow all over where I've just been. Tonight the wife wanted me to sing Christmas carols with her and open presents, but I was busy watching for the goddamn snowplow. December 25: Merry Christmas. 20 more inches of the !$@#&% slop tonight! Snowed in. The idea of shoveling makes my blood boil. God I hate the snow!

Then the snowplow driver came by asking for a donation and I hit him over the head with my shovel. The wife says I have a bad attitude. I think she's an idiot. If I have to watch "It's a wonderful life" one more time, I'm going to kill her. December 26: Still snowed in. Why in the hell did I move her? It was all her idea. She's really getting on my nerves. December 27: Temperature dropped to -30 and the pipes froze! December 28: Warmed up to above -20. Still snowed in. The BITCH is driving me crazy!!! December 29: 10 more inches. Bob says I have to shovel the roof or it could cave in. That's the silliest thing I've heard. How dumb does he think I am!? December 30: Roof caved in. The snowplow driver is suing me for a million dollars for the bump on his head. The wife went home to her mother. 9" predicted. December 31: Set fire to what's left of the house. No more shoveling. January 8: I feel so good. I just love those little white pills they keep giving me but don't like being tied to the bed.

MY NEW LEXUS

I bought a new Lexus 350 and returned to the dealer the next day because I couldn't get the radio to work. The salesman explained that the radio was voice activated. Nelson the salesman said to the radio. The radio replied Rickey or Willie? Willie he continued and On the road again came from the speakers. Then he said Ray Charles, and in an instant Georgia On My Mind replaced Willie Nelson. I drove away happy, and for the next few days, every time I'd say Beethoven. I'd get beautiful classical music, and if I said Beatles, I'd get one of their awesome songs. Yesterday a couple ran a red light and nearly creamed my new car, but I swerved in time to avoid them. I yelled, Ass Holes! immediately the French National Anthem began to play, sung by Jane Fonda and Barbara Streisand, backed up by Michael Moore and The Dixie Chicks, with John Kerry on guitar, al Gore on drums Dan rather on harmonica, Nancy Paelosi on tambourine, Harry Reid on spoons, Bill Clinton on sax and Ted Kennedy on scotch. Boy do I love this car!!

THE ATHEIST

An atheist was taking a walk through the woods. What majestic trees! What powerful rivers! what beautiful animals! he said to himself. As he was walking alongside the river he heard a rustling in the bushes behind him. He turned to look. He saw a 7 foot grizzly charge towards him. He ran as fast as he could up the path. He looked over his shoulder and saw that the bear was closing in on him. He looked over his shoulder again and the bear was even closer. He tripped and fell on the ground. He rolled over to pick himself up but saw the bear right on top of him, reaching for him with his left paw and raising his right paw to strike him. At that instant the Atheist cried out Oh my god. Time stopped. The bear froze. The forest was silent. As a bright light shone upon the man, a voice came out of the sky. You deny my existence for all of these years, teach others I don't exist, and even credit creation to a cosmic accident. Do you expect me to help you out of this predicament? Am I to count you as a believer? The atheist looked directly into the light. It would be hypocritical of me to suddenly ask You to treat me as a Christian now, but perhaps could you make the BEAR a Christian? Very well said the voice. The light went out. The sounds of the forest resumed. And then the bear dropped his right paw, brought both paws together and bowed his head and spoke Lord Bless this food, which I am about to receive from thy bounty through Christ Our Lord. Amen

KILLER BISCUITS

Killer Biscuit Wanted for Attempted Murder (actual headline). Lisa Burnett 23, a resident of San Diego was visiting her in-laws and while ther3e went to a nearby supermarket to pick up some groceries. Several people noticed her sitting in her car with the windows rolled up and with her eyes closed, with both hands behind the back of her head. One customer who had been at the store for a while became concerned and walked over to her car. He noticed that Lisa's eyes were now open, and she looked very strange. He asked her if she was okay and Lisa replied that she'd been shot in the back of the head, and had been holding her brains in for over an hour. The man called the paramedics, who broke into the car because the doors were locked and Lisa refused to remove her hands from her head. When they finally got in they found that Lisa had a wad of bread dough on the back of her head. A Phillsbury biscuit canister had exploded from the heat, making a loud noise that sounded like a gunshot and the wad of dough hit her in the back of her head. When she reached back to find out what it was she felt the dough and thought it was her brains. She initially passed out, but quickly recovered and tried to hold her brains in for over an hour until someone noticed and came to her aid.

HOW THE FIGHT GOT STARTED

I rear-ended another car this morning on the way to work. I tell you, I knew right then and there it was going to be a really bad day. The drover got out of the other car and wouldn't you know it he was a DWARF! He looked up at me and said I am not HAPPY! So I said then which one are you? And that's how the fight started.

WOULD YOU BELIEVE THIS

Sister Mary, who worked for a home health agency, was out making her rounds visiting homebound patients when she ran out of gas. As luck would have it a gas station was just a block away. She walked to the station to borrow a gas can and to buy some gas. The attendant told her the only gas can he owned had been loaned out but she could wait until it was returned. Since she was on her way to see a patient, she decided not to wait and she walked back to her car. She looked for something in her car that she could fill with gas and spotted the bedpan she was taking to the patient. Always resourceful she carried the bedpan to the station, filled it with gas, and carried the full bedpan back to the car. As she was pouring the gas into her tank two men watched from across the street. One turned to the other and said, If that car starts, I'm turning Catholic.

FROM THE READERS DIGEST

Purely by coincidence I ran into my husband in our local grocery store on Valentines Day. Tom was carrying a beautiful pink azalea, and I joked "That better be for me". From behind, a women's voice "It is now".

The pharmacist arrives at work to find a frightened looking man leaning against the wall. What's wrong with him, he asks the clerk. He wanted cough medicine but I couldn't find any, so I gave him a laxative. Laxative's won't cure a cough yells the pharmacist. Sure it will. Look at him. He's afraid to cough.

FARMERS ADVICE

A Tennessee Amish farmer walking through his field, notices a man drinking from his pond, within his hand. The Amish man shouts: "Trink das wasser nicht. Die kuhen haben dahin gesheissen. Meaning (Don't drink the water, the cows have shit in it.) The man shouts back "I'm Muslin, I don't understand. Please speak in English."" The Amish man says, "Use two hands. You'll get more."

THE PASTOR'S ASS

The pastor entered his donkey in a race and it won. The pastor was so pleased with his donkey that he entered it in the race again, and it won again. The local paper read: THE PASTOR'S ASS OUT FRONT. The Bishop as so upset with this kind of publicity that he ordered the pastor not to enter the donkey in another race. The next day, the local paper read: BISHOP SCRATXCHES PASTOR'S ASS. This was too much for the bishop, so he ordered the pastor to get rid of the donkey. The pastor decided to give it to a nun in a nearby convent. The local paper, hearing of the news, posted the following headline the next day: NUN HAS BEST ASS IN TOWN. The bishop fainted. He informed the nun that she would have to get rid of the donkey, she sold it to a farmer for $10.00. The next day the paper read NUN SELLS ASS FOR $10.00. This was to much for the bishop, so he ordered the nun to buy back the donkey and lead it to the plains where it could run wild. The next day the headlines read: NUN ANNOUNCES HER ASS IS WILD AND FREE. The bishop was buried the next day. The moral of the story is . . . Being concerned about public opinion can bring You much grief and misery. Even shorten your life. So be yourself and enjoy life. Stop worrying what everyone else's ass And you'll be a lot happier and live longer.

THE RUBBER GLOVES

A dentist noticed his next patient, a little old lady, was Nervous so he decided to tell her a little joke as he put on his gloves. Do you know how these gloves are made? He asked. No I don't she replied. Well he spoofed, there's a building in Canada with a big tank of latex and workers of all hand sizes walk up to the tank, dip their hands, let it dry, then peel off the gloves and throw them into a box of the right size. She didn't crack a smile. Oh well I tried he thought. But five minuets later, during a delicate portion of the procedure, She burst out laughing. What's so funny? He asked. I was just envisioning how condoms are made! Gotta watch these old ladies! Their minds are always working!

THREE LITTLE PIGS

Three little pigs went out to dinner one night. The waiter came and took their order. I would like a sprite said the first little pig. I would like a coke said the second little pig. I want a beer, lots and lots of beer said the third little pig. The drinks were brought out And the waiter took their orders for dinner. I want a steak said the firs piggy. I would like a salad plate said the second piggy. I want beer, lots and lots of beer said the third piggy. The meals were brought out and a while later the waiter approached the table and asked if the piggies would like any dessert. I want a banana split, said the first piggy I want a cheesecake said the second piggy. I want beer lots and lots of beer exclaimed the Third piggy. Pardon me for asking said the waiter to the third piggy. But why have you only ordered beer all evening? The third piggy says "Well somebody has to go Wee. Wee, wee all the way home!

MORE DUMB BLONDE JOKES

Three blondes died and found themselves standing before St Peter and the Pearly Gates. He told them before they could enter the Kingdom, they had to tell him what the meaning of Easter is about.

The first blonde steps up and says, Easter is when we give thanks, eat turkey and watch football!! St Peter mutters Blondes, and sends her hurtling as a flaming bolt down to the gates of Hell. The next blonde steps up and says Easter is when we celebrate Jesus birthday, and exchange gifts. St Peter lifts his staff Next he yells and the blonde explodes in a fiery ball.

The third blonde steps up and says, Easter is a Christian holiday that coincides with the Jewish festival of Passover. Jesus was having a Passover feast with his Disciples when Judas betrayed him, and roman soldiers arrested him. The Romans nailed him to a cross and eventually he died. They buried him in a tomb behind a large boulder. Excellent Said St Peter. Before he could welcome her inside, the blonde continued now every year the Jews roll back the boulder and Jesus comes out. If he sees his shadow, we have six more weeks of basketball. St Peter fainted.

THE NAGGING WIFE

An attorney arrived home late, after a very tough day trying to get a stay of execution for a client who was due to be hanged for murder at midnight. His last minute plea for clemency to the governor had failed and he was feeling worn out and depressed. As soon as he walked through the door at home, his wife started on him about What time of night to be getting home is this? Where have you been? Dinner is cold and I am not reheating it. And on and on and on. To shattered to play his usual role in this familiar ritual, he went and poured himself a shot of whiskey and headed off for a long soak in the bathtub, pursued by the predictable sarcastic remarks as he drug himself up the stairs.

While he was in the bath, the phone rang. The wife answered and was told that her husbands client, James Wright, had been granted a stay of execution after all. Wright would not be hanged tonight. Finally realizing what a terrible day he must have had, she decided to go upstairs and give him the good news. As she opened the bathroom door, she was greeted by the sight of her husband, bent over naked, drying his legs and feet. "They're not hanging Wright tonight", she said to which he whirled around and screamed FOR THE LOVE OF GOD WOMAN, DON'T YOU EVER STOP?

YEARLY PHYSICAL

This couple went to the doctor. He told the man it is time for your yearly physical, I will need a urine sample and a stool sample. The man looked at his wife and said what did he say? She leaned over and shouted in his ear, he wants to see your underwear.

MEN HAVE TROUBLE

Three elderly men were sitting around and the first sat. I sure have trouble, I just can't urinate first thing in the morning. The second man said well I don't have trouble that way but I just can't have a bowel movement in the morning. The third man said Oh I don't have any trouble that way at all. Right at six in the morning I urinate every morning and at 7 I have a bowel movement, every morning right at 7. My trouble is I don't wake up till 8.

BOYCOT ANHEISER BUSCH

Help me boycott Anheiser Busch since they are sell outs. Drop your beer at my house and I will dispose of it. That will teach the bastards.

YOUR CHOICE

A man dies and he went up to Heaven. St Peter meets him at the gates and says. We are doing things different now. You decide where you want to go Heaven or hell, so come in and look around. He stayed there for a couple of days and then went down to Hell. They were having a really good time, baseball, beautiful beaches with lots of pretty women laying around. He thought this is the life. So he went back to St Peter and said I think I prefer to go to hell. When he arrived in Hell for the second time, he was made to shovel coal and it was so hot, it was really bad. He approached the Devil and said what happened? When I was here before it was one big party and everyone was having a good time, The Devil said, before you were a prospect, now you are an Employee.

JESSE JACKSON

One day Jesse Jackson got out of the shower and was drying off when he looked in the mirror and noticed he was white from the neck up to the top of his head, In sheer panic and fearing he really was turning white and might have to start working for a living, he called his doctor and told him of his problem. The doctor advised him to come to his office immediately. After an examination, the doctor mixed a concoction of brown liquid, gave it to Jesse, and told him to drink it all. Jesse did and replied, That tasted like bullshit! The doctor replied, it was Jesse. You were a quart low.

WHAT WOULD IT BE?

Presidential candidates Obama and Hillary, while visiting a primary school class, found themselves in the middle of a discussion related to words and their meanings. The teacher asked if they would like to lead the discussion of the word "tragedy". So the illustrious Obama asks the class for an example of a tragedy. One little boy stood up and offered: If my best friend, who lives on a farm, is playing in the field and a runaway tractor comes along and knocks him dead, that would be a tragedy. No says the Great Obama, that would be an accident. A little girl raised her hand, If a school bus carrying 50 children drove over a cliff, killing everyone inside, that would be a tragedy. I'm afraid not, explains Clinton. That's what we would call a great loss. The room goes silent. No other children volunteered. President hopeful searches the room. Isn't there someone here who can give me an example of a tragedy? Finally at the back of the room little Johnny raises his hand. In a stern voice he says, If a plane carrying hopefuls Obama and Clinton were struck by a missile and blown to smithereens, that would be a tragedy. Fantastic exclaims the hopefuls, That's right. And can you tell me why that would be a tragedy? Well, says little Johnny, because it sure as hell wouldn't be a great loss, and it probably wouldn't be an accident either.

THREE MEN ON A HIKE

Three men were hiking through a forest when they came upon a large raging, violent river. Needing to get to the other side, the first man prayed: got please give me the strength to cross the river. Poof! God gave him bug arms and strong legs and he was able to swim across in about 2 hours, having almost drowned twice. After witnessing that, the second man prayed, God please give me the strength and the tools to cross the river. Poof! God gave him a rowboat and strong arms and strong legs and he was able cross in about an hour after almost capsizing once. The third man after seeing what happened to the first two men, prayed God please give me the strength, the tools and the intelligence to cross the river. Poof He was turned into a woman. She checked the map, hiked one hundred yards up stream and walked across the bridge.

PREGNANT TURKEY

Last year at Thanksgiving my mom went to my sister's house for the traditional feast. Knowing how gullible my sister is, my mom decided to play a trick. She told my sister that she needed something from the store. When my sister left, my mom took the turkey out of the oven, removed the stuffing, stuffed a Cornish hen, and inserted it into the turkey, and re stuffed the turkey. She then placed the bird(s) back in the oven. When it was time for dinner, my sister pulled the turkey out of the oven and proceeded to remove the stuffing. When her serving spoon hit something, she reached in and pulled out a little bird. With a look of total shock on her face, my mother exclaimed, Patricia you've cooked a pregnant bird! At the reality of this news, my sister started to cry. It took the whole family two hours to convince her that turkeys lay eggs! Yep . . . SHE'S A BLONDE!

BUBBA AND HIS ATTORNEY

Down south, Bubba called his attorney and asked, 'Is
It true theys suin them cigarette companies fer causin
People to git cancer?'
'Yes, Bubba, sure is true,' responded the lawyer.

'And now someone is suin them fast food restaurants Fer makin them fat an cloggin their arteries with all Them burgers an fries, is that true, Mista Lawyer?'
'Sure is, Bubba.'
'And that lady sued McDonalds for millions when she Was gave that hot coffee that she ordered?'
'Yep.' 'And that football player sued that university when he
Gradiated and still couldn't read?'
'That's right,' said the lawyer.'
'But why are you asking?'
'Well, I was thinkin . . .
What I want to know is, kin I sue Budweiser fer all
them ugly women I slept with?'

AND THEY ASKED WHY I LIKE RETIREMENT

Question; How many days in a week? Answer; 6 Saturdays, 1 Sunday

Question; When is a retiree's bedtime Answer; Three hours after he falls asleep on the couch.

Question; How many retirees to change a light bulb? Answer; Only one, but it might take all day.

Question; What's the biggest gripe of retirees? Answer; There is not enough time to get everything done.

Question; Why don't retirees mind being called Seniors? Answer; The term comes with a 10% discount.

Question; Among retirees what is considered formal attire? Answer; tied shoes.

Question; Why do retirees count pennies? Answer; They are only ones who have the time.

Question; What is the common term for someone who enjoys work and refuses to retire? Answer; NUTS.

Question; Why are retirees so slow to clean out the basement, attic or garage? Answer; They know that as soon as they do, one of their adult kids will want to store stuff there.

Question; what's the biggest advantage of going back to school as a retiree? Answer; if you cut classes, no one calls your parents.

Question; Why does a retiree often say he doesn't miss work, but misses the people he used to work with? Answer; he is too polite to tell the whole truth.

And the favorite . . .

Question; What do you do all week? Answer; Monday through Friday, NOTHING . . . Saturday and Sunday, I rest.

THE BROTHEL

The madam opened the brothel door and saw a rather dignified, well-dressed, good-looking man in his late forties or early fifties.

'May I help you?' she asked.

'I want to see Valerie,' the man replied.

'Sir, Valerie is one of our most expensive ladies. Perhaps you would prefer someone else,' said the madam.

'No. I must see Valerie,' he replied.

Just then, Valerie appeared and announced to the man that she charged $5,000 a visit. Without hesitation, the man pulled out five thousand dollars and gave them to Valerie, and they went upstairs. After an hour, the man calmly left.

The next night, the same man appeared again, once more demanding to see Valerie.

Valerie explained that no one had ever come back two nights in a row—too expensive—and there were no discounts. The price was still $5,000. Again the man pulled out the money, gave it to Valerie, and they went upstairs. After an hour, he left.

The following night the man was there yet again. Everyone was astounded that he had come for a third consecutive night, but he paid Valerie and they went upstairs.

After their session, Valerie questioned the man. 'No one has ever been with me three nights in a row. Where are you from?' she asked.

The man replied, 'Hendersonville, North Carolina". 'Really' she said. 'I have family in Hendersonville, North Carolina."

'I know,' the man said. 'Your father died, and I am your sister's attorney. She asked me to give you your $15,000 inheritance.' The moral of the story is that three things in life are certain:

1. Death
2. Taxes
3. Being screwed by a lawyer

WHY AM I So TIRED

For a couple years I've been blaming on poor blood, lack of vitamins, dieting and a dozen other maladies. But now I found out the real reason. I'm tired because I'm overworked. The population of this country is 237 million. 104 million are retired. That leaves 133 million to do the work. There are 85 million in school, which leaves 48 million to the work. Of these there are 29 million employed by the federal government. This leaves 19 million to do the work. Four million are in the Armed Forces, which leaves 15 million to do the work. Take from the total the 14,800,000 people who work for State and City Government and that leaves 200,000 to do the work. There are 188,000 in hospitals, so that leaves 12,000 to do the work. Now, there are 11,998 people in prisons. That leaves just two people to do the work. You and me. And you're sitting there reading e mail!!

PEOPLE ARE LIKE PoTAToES

Some people are very bossy and like to tell everyone what to do, but of course they do not wish to soil their hands. You might call that type Dick Taters Some people never seem to be motivated to ever participate. They are content to watch while others do. They are Speck Taters Some people never do anything to help, but they are gifted at finding fault with the way others do things. They might be called Comment Tators. Some people are always looking for ways to cause problems. They look for others to agree with them that it is too hot, are too cold, or too sour, or too sweet. You call the Aggle Tators. Then there are those who always say they will, but somehow ever get around to do anything. They are Hezzle Tators. Some people put on a front and act like they are someone they are not. They are Emma Tators. Still there are those who live what they talk. They are always prepared to stop what they are doing to lend a hand. They bring real sunshine into other's lives. You might call them Sweet Tators.

JONAH VERSUS THE WHALE

Now listen, my children, I'll tell you a tale. How old Jonah, the profit, got caught by a whale. The whale caught dear Jonah and bless your dear soul; He not only caught him, but swallowed him whole. A part of this story is awfully sad—How a great big city went bad. When the Lord saw those people with such wicked ways, He said, I can't stand them for more'n forty days. He spoke to Johan and said, Go and cry to those hardhearted people and tell them that I Give them forty days more to get humbled down, And if they don't, I'll tear up their town. Jonah heard the Lord speaking and he said, No, that's against my religion and I won't go. Those Nineveh people ain't nothing to me. And I'm against foreign missions, you see. He went down to Joppa and there, in great haste, He boarded a ship for a different place, The Lord looked down on that ship and said He, Old Jonah is fixing to run off from me. He sent the winds blowing with squeaks and with squeals, And the sea got rowdy and kicked up its heels. Old Jonah confessed it was all for his sin; The crew threw him out and the whale took him in. The whale said, old fellow, don't you forget, I am sent ere to take you out of the wet, You will get punished aright for your sin. So he opened his mouth and poor Jonah went in. On beds of green seaweed that fish tried to rest; He said, I will sleep while my food I digest. But he got mighty restless and sorely afraid, And he rumbled inside as the old profit prayed. The third day that fish rose up from his bed, with his stomach tore up and a pain in his head. He said, I must get to the air mighty quick, For this filthy backslider is making me sick. He winked his big eyes and wiggled his tail. And pulled for the shore to deliver his male. He stopped near the shore and looked all around; And vomited old Jonah right up to the ground. Old Jonah thanked God for his mercy and grace, and turning around to the whale, made a face. He said, After three days I guess you have found, a good man, old fellow, is hard to keep down. He stretched himself out with a yawn and a sigh, and sat down in the sun for his clothing to dry. He thought how much better his preaching would be, since from Whale Seminary he had a degree. When he had rested and dried in the sun, He started for Nineveh most on the run. He thanked his dear Father in Heaven above for his tender mercy and wonderful love.

MUST APPLY IN PERSON

Lonely widow, age 70 decided that it was time to get married again. So she put an ad in the local newspaper that read wanted husband! must be my age group (70's), must not beat me, must not run around on me, and must still be good in bed! all applicants please apply in person.

On the second day she heard the doorbell. Much to her dismay, she opened the door to see a gray-haired gentleman sitting in a wheel chair. He had no arms or legs.

'You're not really asking me to consider you, are you?' the widow said. 'Just look at you—you have no legs!'

The old gentleman smiled, 'Therefore, I cannot run around on you!'

'You don't have any arms either!' she snorted.

Again, the old man smiled, 'Therefore, I can never beat you!'

She raised an eyebrow and asked intently, 'Are you still good in bed??'

The old man leaned back, beamed a big smile and said, 'I rang he doorbell, didn't I?'

The wedding is scheduled for Saturday

Some of these are priceless, especially the last one. And, remember, these idiots walk among us, procreate and vote! Customer: 'I've been calling 700-1000 for two days and can't get through; Can you help?' Operator: 'Where did you get that number, sir?' Customer: 'It's on the door of your business.' Operator: 'Sir, those are the hours that we are open.'

++

Samsung Electronics
Caller: 'Can you give me the telephone number for Jack?' Operator: 'I'm sorry, sir, I don't understand who you are talking about.' Caller: 'On page 1, section 5, of the user guide it clearly states that I Need to unplug the fax machine from the AC wall socket and Telephone Jack before cleaning. Now, can you give me the Number for Jack?' Operator: 'I think it means the telephone plug on the wall.'—

RAC Motoring Services Caller: 'Does your European Breakdown Policy cover me when I am Traveling in Australia?' Operator: 'Does the product name give you a clue?'—Caller (enquiring about legal requirements while traveling in Europe) 'If I register my car in France, and then take it to England, do I have to change the steering wheel to the other side of the car?'—*Directory Enquiries* Caller: 'I'd like the number of the Argo Fish Bar, please' Operator: 'I'm sorry, there's no listing. Are you sure that the spelling is correct?' Caller: 'Well, it used to be called the Bargo Fish Bar but the 'B' fell off.'—Then there was the caller who asked for a knitwear company in Woven. Operator: 'Woven? Are you sure?' Caller: 'Yes. That's what it says on the label—Woven in Scotland'—On another occasion, a man making heavy breathing sounds from a phone box told a worried operator: 'I haven't got a pen, so I'm steaming up the window to write the number on.'—Tech Support: 'I need you to right-click on the Open Desktop.' Customer: 'OK.' Tech Support: 'Did you get a pop-up menu?' Customer: 'No.' Tech Support: 'OK. Right-Click again. Do you see a pop-up menu?' Customer: 'No.' Tech Support: 'OK, sir. Can you tell me what you have done up until this Point?' Customer: 'Sure. You told me to write 'click' and I wrote 'click'.'—Tech Support: 'OK. At the bottom left hand side of your screen, can You see the 'OK' button displayed?' Customer: 'Wow! How can you see my screen from there?'—Caller: 'I deleted a file from my PC last week and I just realized that

I need it. So, if I turn my system clock back two weeks will I get my file back again?'—This has to be one of the funniest things in a long time. I think this guy should have been promoted, not fired. This is a true story from the WordPerfect Helpline, which was transcribed from a recording monitoring the customer care department. Needless to say the Help Desk employee was fired; however, he/she is currently suing the WordPerfect organization for 'Termination without Cause.' Actual dialogue of a former WordPerfect Customer Support employee. (Now I know why they record these conversations!): Operator: 'Ridge Hall, computer assistance; may I help you?' Caller: 'Yes, well, I'm having trouble with WordPerfect.' Operator: 'What sort of trouble??' Caller: 'Well, I was just typing along, and all of a sudden the words went away.' Operator: 'Went away?' Caller: 'They disappeared' Operator: 'Hmm. So what does your screen look like now?' Caller: 'Nothing.' Operator: 'Nothing??' Caller: 'It's blank; it won't accept anything when I type.' Operator: 'Are you still in WordPerfect, or did you get out?' Caller: 'How do I tell?' Operator: 'Can you see the 'C: prompt' on the screen?' Caller: 'What's a sea-prompt?' Operator: 'Never mind, can you move your cursor around the screen?' Caller: 'There isn't any cursor; I told you, it won't accept anything I type.' Operator: 'Does your monitor have a power indicator??' Caller: 'What's a monitor?' Operator: 'It's the thing with the screen on it that looks like a TV. Does it have a little light that tells you when it's on?' Caller: 'I don't know.' Operator: 'Well, then look on the back of the monitor and find where the power cord goes into it. Can you see that??' Caller: 'Yes, I think so.' Operator: 'Great. Follow the cord to the plug, and tell me if it's plugged into the wall. Caller: 'Yes, it is.' Operator: 'When you were behind the monitor, did you notice that there were two cables plugged into the back of it, not just one?' Caller: 'No.' Operator: 'Well, there are. I need you to look back there again and find the other cable.' Caller: 'Okay, here it is.' Operator: 'Follow it for me, and tell me if it's plugged securely into the back of your computer.' Caller: 'I can't reach.' Operator: 'OK. Well, can you *see* if it is?' Caller: 'No.' Operator: 'Even if you maybe put your knee on something and lean way over?' Caller: 'Well, it's not because I don't have the right angle—it's because it's dark.' Operator: 'Dark?' Caller: 'Yes—the office light is off, and the only light I have is coming in from the window.' Operator: 'Well, turn on the office light then.' Caller: 'I can't.' Operator: 'No? Why not?' Caller: 'Because there's a power failure.' Operator: 'A power . . . A *power failure*? Aha. Okay, we've got it licked now. Do you still have the boxes and manuals and packing stuff that your computer came in?'

Caller: 'Well, yes, I keep them in the closet.' Operator: 'Good. Go get them, and unplug your system and pack it up just like it was when you got it. Then take it back to the store you bought it from.' Caller: 'Really? Is it that bad?' Operator: 'Yes, I'm afraid it is.' Caller: 'Well, all right then, I suppose. What do I tell them?' Operator: 'Tell them you're too stupid to own a computer!'

I took my dad to the mall the other day to buy some new shoes. We decided to grab a bite at the food court. I noticed he was watching a teenager sitting next to him. The teenager had spiked hair in all different colors: green, red orange and blue. My dad kept starring at him. The teenager would look and find him starring every time. When the teenager had enough, he sarcastically asked, What's the matter old man, never done anything wild in your life? Knowing my dad, I quickly swallowed my food so that I would not choke on his response; Knowing he would have a god one. And in classic style he did not bat an eye in his response. Got drunk once and had sex with a peacock. I was just wondering if you were my son.

Redneck Lent

Each Friday night after work, Bubba would fire up his outdoor grill and cook a venison steak. But, all of Bubba's neighbors were Catholic. And since it was Lent, they were forbidden from eating meat on Friday. The delicious aroma from the grilled venison steaks was causing such a problem for the Catholic faithful that they finally talked to their priest. The Priest came to visit Bubba, and suggested that he become a Catholic.

After several classes and much study, Bubba attended Mass . . . and as the priest sprinkled holy water over him, he said, 'You were born a Baptist, and raised a Baptist, but now you are a Catholic.

'Bubba's neighbors were greatly relieved, until Friday night arrived, and the wonderful aroma of grilled venison filled the neighborhood. The Priest was called immediately by the neighbors, and, as he rushed into Bubba's yard, clutching a rosary and prepared to scold him, he stopped and watched in amazement.

There stood Bubba, clutching a small bottle of holy water which he carefully sprinkled over the grilling meat and chanted: You wuz born a deer, you wuz raised a deer, but now you a catfish.

IT PAYS TO BE HYPNOTISED

A woman comes home and tells her husband, Remember those headaches I've been having all these years? well they're gone. No more headaches? What happened? His wife replies, Margie referred me to a hypnotist & he told me to stand in front of a mirror, State at my self and repeat, I do not have a headache. I do not have a headache. I do not have a headache. Well it worked! The headaches are all gone. Well that is wonderful, proclaims the husband. His wife then says, You know, you haven't been exactly a ball of fire in the bedroom these last few years, why don't you go see the hypnotist and see if he can do anything for that? Reluctantly, the husband agrees to try it. Following his appointment, the husband comes home, rips off his clothes, picks up his wife and carries her into the bedroom. He puts her on the bed and says, Don't move, I'll be right back. He goes into the bathroom and comes back a few minutes later and jumps into bed and makes passionate love to his wife like never before. His wife says WOW—that was wonderful The husband says, don't move I will be right back. He goes into the bathroom, comes back and round two was even better than the first time. The wife sits up and her head is spinning, OH MY GOD she proclaims. Her husband again says, Don't move, I'll be right back. With that, he goes back into the bathroom. This time, his wife quietly follows him and there, in the bathroom, she sees him standing at the mirror and saying. She's not my wife. She's not my wife. She's not my wife. The funeral service will be held on Saturday.

GREAT PRODUCTS

I am writing to say what an excellent product you have! I've used it all my married life, as my Mom always told me it was the best. Now that I am in my fifties I find it even better! In fact, about a month ago, I spilled some red wine on my new white blouse. My inconsiderate and uncaring husband started to belittle my about how clumsy I was, and generally started becoming a pain in the neck. One thing led to another and somehow I ended up with his blood on my new white blouse! I grabbed my bottle of Tide with bleach alternative! To my surprise and satisfaction, all of the stains came out so well the detectives who came by yesterday told me that the DNA tests on my blouse were negative and then my attorney called and said that I was no longer considered a Suspect in the disappearance of my husband. What a relief! Going through menopause is bad enough without being a murder suspect! I thank you, once again for having a great product. Well gotta go, have to write to the Hefty bag people.

SHIPWRECKED

A man was washed up on a beach after a terrible shipwreck. Only a sheep and a sheepdog were washed up with him. After looking around, he realized, that they were stranded on a deserted island. After being there awhile, he got into the habit of taking his two animal companions to the beach every evening to watch the sunset. One particular evening, the sky was a fiery red with beautiful cirrus clouds, the breeze was warm and gentle a perfect night for romance. As they sat there, the sheep started looking better and better to the lonely man. Soon, he leaned over to the sheep and put his arm around it. But the sleeping sheepdog, ever protective of the sheep, growled fiercely until the man took his arm from around the sheep. After that, the three of them continued to enjoy the sunsets together, but there was no more cuddling. A few weeks passed by and, lo and behold, there was another shipwreck. The only survivor was Hillary Clinton. That evening, the man brought Hillary to the evening beach ritual. It was another beautiful evening—ed sky, cirrus clouds, a warm and gentle breeze—perfect for romance. Pretty soon, the man started to get "those feeling again. He fought the urges as long as he could but he finally gave in and leaned over to Hillary and told her he and't had sex for months. Hillary batted her eyelashes and asked if there was anything she could do for him. He said, "Would you mind taking the dog for a walk."

So true, so very true . . .

My wife sat down on the couch next to me as I was flipping the channels. She asked, 'What's on TV?'

I said, 'Dust.' And then the fight started . . . My wife was hinting about what she wanted for our upcoming anniversary. She said, 'I want something shiny that goes from 0 to 200 in about 3 seconds.'

I bought her new bath scales . . . And then the fight started . . . When I got home last night, my wife demanded that I take her someplace expensive . . . so, I took her to a filling station . . .

And then the fight started . . .

My wife and I were sitting at a table at my high school reunion, and I kept staring at a drunken lady swigging her drink as she sat alone at a nearby table. My wife asked, 'Do you know her?' 'Yes,' I sighed, 'She's my old girlfriend. I understand she took to drinking right after we split up those many years ago, and I hear she hasn't been sober since.' 'My God!' says my wife, 'who would think a person could go on celebrating that long?' And then the fight started . . .

I hit a car from behind this morning. So, there we were alongside the road and slowly the other driver got out of his car. You know how sometimes you just get soooo stressed and little things just seem funny? Yeah, well I couldn't believe it . . . he was a DWARF!!! He stormed over to my car, looked up at me, and shouted, 'I AM NOT HAPPY!' So, I looked down at him and said, 'Well, then which one are you?'

And then the fight started . . .

HALLOWEEN COSTUME

A bald man with a wooden leg is invited to a Halloween party. He doesn't know what costume to wear to hide his head and his leg so he writes to a costume company to explain his problem. A few days later, he received a parcel with the following note: Dear sir, > Please find enclosed a pirate's outfit. The spotted handkerchief will cover your bald head and, with your leg, you will be just right as a pirate. Yours truly The acme costume co.

The man thinks this is terrible because they have emphasized his wooden leg and so he writes a letter of complaint. A week goes by and he receives another parcel and a note, which says:

Dear Sir: Pleased enclosed a monk's habit. The long robe will cover your wooden leg and, with your bald head, you will look the part. Very truly yours, Acme Costume Co. Now the man is really upset since hey have gone from emphasizing his wooden leg to emphasizing his bald head so again he writes the company another nasty letter of complaint. The next day a small parcel and a note, which reads: Dear Sir, Please find Enclosed a bottle of molasses and a bag of crushed nuts. Pour the molasses over your bald head, pat on the crushed nuts, stick your wooden leg up your ass and go as a carmel apple. Very truly yours, Acme Costume co.

20 WAYS To MINTAIN A HEALTHY LEVEL oF INSANITY

1. At lunch time, sit in your parked car with sunglasses on and point a hair dryer at passing cars. See if it slows them down.
2. Page yourself over the intercom, don't disguise your voice.
3. Every time someone asks you to do something, ask if they want fries with that.
4. Put your garbage can on your deck and label it 'in.
5. PUT Decaf in the coffee maker for 3 weeks. Once everyone has gotten over their caffeine addictions. Switch to espresso.
6. In the memo field of all your checks, Write for smuggling Diamonds.
7. Finish all your sentences with in accordance with the Prophecy.
8. Don't use punctuation.
9. As often as possible, skip rather than walk.
10. Order a diet water whenever you go out to eat, with a serious face.
11. Specify that your drive-through order is To Go.
12. Sing along at the opera.
13. Put mosquito netting around your work area and play tropical sounds all day.
14. Go to poetry recital and ask why the poems don't rhyme.
15. Five days in advanced tell all your friends you can't attend their party you're no in the mood.
16. Have your co-workers address you by your wrestling name Rock Bottom.
17. When money comes out of the ATM machine scream I won I won.
18. When leaving the Zoo, start running towards the parking lot, yelling run for your lives, they're loose!!
19. Tell your children over dinner, Due to the economy, we are going to have to let one of you go,
20. And the final way to keep a healthy level of insanity tell these to all your friends.

IT'S ALL IN WHAT YOU DRINK

In a number of carefully controlled trials scientists have demonstrated that if we drink 1 liter of water each day, at the end of the year we would have absorbed more than 1 kilo of Escherichia coli, (e coli) bacteria found in feces. In other words, we are consuming 1 kilo of Poop. However, we do NOT run that risk when drinking wine (or rum or other liquor) because alcohol has to go through a purification process of boiling, filtering and/or fermenting. Remember: water = poop, wine = health Therefore, it's better to drink wine and talk stupid, than to drink water and be full of shit, There is on need to thank me for this valuable information. I'm doing it as a public service.

JOKES

IF YOU MUST SPEED ON THE HIGHWAY, SING THESE HYMNS LOUDLY

At 45 mph "God Will Take Care of Me"
At 55 mph "Guide Me, O great Jehovah"
At 65 mph "Nearer My god to Thee
At 75 mph "Nearer Still Nearer"
At 85 mph "This World is Not My Home"
At 95 mph "Lord I'm Coming Home"
At 100 mph "Precious Memories"

BEST LAWYER STORY

A Charlotte NC lawyer purchased a box of very rare and expensive cigars, then insured them against fire, among other things. Within a month, having smoked his entire stockpile of these great cigars and without yet having made his first premium payment on the policy, the lawyer filed claim against the insurance company. In his claim, the lawyer stated the cigars were lost in a series of small fires. The insurance company refused to ay, citing the obvious reason that the man had consumed the cigars in the normal fashion. The lawyer sued. and Won!!! (stay with me) In delivering the ruling, the judge agreed with the insurance company that the claim was frivolous. The judge stated nevertheless, that the lawyer held a policy from the company in which it had warranted that the cigars were insurable and also guaranteed that it would insure them against fire, and was obligated to pay the claim. Rather than endure lengthy and costly appeal process, the insurance company accepted the ruling and paid $15,000.00 to the lawyer for his loss of the rare cigars lost in the "fires". NOW HERE IS THE BEST PART After the lawyer cashed the check, the insurance company had him arrested on 24 counts of ARSON!!! With his own insurance claim and testimony from the previous case being used against him, the lawyer was convicted of intentionally burning his insured property and was sentenced to 24 months and a $24,000.00 fine This was the first place winner in the Criminal Lawyer awards Contest.

TALKING DOG FOR SALE

A GUY IS DRIVING AROUND AND SEES A SIGN IN FRONT OF A HOUSE "TALKING Dog For Sale" He rings the bell and the owner tells him the dog is in the backyard. The guy goes into the backyard and sees a Labrador retriever sitting there. You talk? he asks. Yep the Lab replies So what's your story? The Lab looks up and says, Well I discovered that I could talk when I was pretty young and I wanted to help the government, so I told the CIA about my gift, and in no time at all they had me jetting from country to country sitting in rooms with spies and world leaders, because no one figured a dog would be eavesdropping. I was told one of the most valuable spies for eight years running. But the jetting around really tired me out, and I knew I wasn't getting any younger so I wanted to settle down, I signed up for a job at the airport to do some undercover security work, mostly wandering near suspicious characters and listening in. I uncovered some incredible dealings and was awarded a batch of medals. I got married, had a mess of puppies, and now I'm retired. The guy is amazed. He goes back in and asks the owner what he wants for the dog. Ten dollars. The guy says. This dog is amazing. Why on earth are you selling min so cheap? Because he's a liar. He didn't do any of that shit.

Clear day. Are you a Democrat, Republican, or a Redneck? You're walking down the street with your wife and two small children. Suddenly, an Islamic Terrorist with a huge knife come around the corner, locks eyes with you, screams obscenities, praises Allah, raises the knife and charges at you. You are carrying a Glock 40 caliber pistol and you're an expert shot. You have mere seconds before he reaches you, and your family. What do you do? Democrat's Answer: Well, that's not enough information to answer the question! Does the man look poor! Or oppressed? Have I ever done anything to him that would inspire him to attack? Could we run away? What does my wife think? What about the kids? What does the law say about this situation? Why am I carrying a loaded gun anyway, and what kind of message does this send to society and to my children? Does he definitely want to kill me, or would he be content just to wound me? Should I call 9-1-1? Why is this street so deserted? We need to raise taxes, have paint and weed day= making this into a happier. Healthier street that would discourage such behavior?

YOU CAN'T BEAT PUPPY LOVE

A farmer has some puppies he needed to sell. He painted a sign advertising the 4 pups. And set about nailing it to a post on the edge of his yard. As he was driving the last nail into the post, he felt a tug on his overalls. He looked down into the eyes of a little boy. Mister he said I want to buy one of your puppies. Well said the farmer, as he rubbed the sweat off the back of his neck, The puppies come from fine parents and cost a good deal of money. The boy dropped his head for a moment. Then reaching into his pocket, he pulled out a handful of change and held it up to the farmer. I've got 39 cents is that enough to take a look? Sure said the farmer. And with that he let out a whistle. Here Dolly! he called. Out from the doghouse and down the ramp ran Dolly followed by four little balls of fur. The little boy pressed his face against the chain link fence. His eyes danced with delight as the dogs made their way to the fence, the little boy noticed something else stirring inside the doghouse. Slowly another little ball of fur appeared, this one noticeably smaller. Down the ramp it slid. Then in a somewhat awkward manner, the little pup began hobbling toward the others, doing its best to catch up. I want that one said the little boy, pointing at the runt. The farmer knelt down at the boy's side and said Son, you don't want that puppy. He will never be able to run and play like these other dogs would. With that the little boy stepped back from the fence, reached down and began rolling up one leg of his trousers. In doing so he revealed a steel brace running down both sides of his leg attaching itself to a specially made shoe. Looking back up at the farmer, he said You see Sir, I don't run too well myself, and he will need someone who understands. With tears in his eyes, the farmer reached down and picked up the little pup. Holding it carefully he handed it to the little boy. No charge, answered the farmer there's no charge for love. The world is full of people who understand

FAST THINKING

A senior citizen in Florida bought a brand new Corvette convertible. He took off down the road, flooring it at 80 mph and enjoying the wind blowing through what little hair he had left on his head. This is great, he thought as he roared down I-75. He pushed the peddle to the metal even more. Then he looked in his rear view mirror and saw a highway patrol trooper behind him, blue lights flashing and siren blaring. I can get away from him with no problem, thought the man and he tromped it some more and flew down the road at over 100 mph. Then 110, 120 mph. Then he thought what am I doing? I'm too old for this kind of thing. He pulled over to the side of the road and waited for the trooper to catch up with him. The trooper pulled in behind the Corvette and walked up to the man. Sir he said, looking at his watch. My shift ends in 30 minuets and to day is Friday. If you can give me a reason why you were speeding that I've not heard before, I'll let you go. The man looked at the trooper and said, Years ago my wife ran off with a Florida State Trooper, and I thought you were bringing her back. Have a good day Sir said the trooper.

ASS SISE STUDY

There is a new study out about women and how they feel about their asses I thought the results were pretty interesting. 85% of women think their ass is to fat . . . 10% of women think their ass is too skinny . . . The other 5% say that they don't care, they love him, he's a good man, and they would have married him anyway.

HILARIOUS

Clear day A man takes the day off from work to go golfing. He is on the second hole when he notices a frog sitting next too the green. He thinks nothing of it and is about to shoot when he hears, Ribbit 9 Iron. The man looks around and doesn't see anyone. Again, he hears Ribbit 9 Iron. He looks at the frog and decides to prove the frog wrong., puts the club away, and grabs a 9 iron. Boom! He hits it 10 inches from the cup. He is shocked. He says to the frog. Wow that's something amazing. You must be a lucky frog, eh? The frog replies, rabbit lucky frog. The man decides to take the frog with him to the next hole. What do you think frog? The man asks Ribbit 3 wood. The guy takes out a 3 wood and boom, Hole in one. The man is befuddled and doesn't know what to say. By the end of the day, the man golfed the best game of golf in his life and asks the frog, OK where to next? The frog replies Las Vegas. They go to Las Vegas and the guy says Ok frog, now what? The frog says Ribbit Rolette Upon approaching the Rolette table. The man asks What do you think I should bet? The frog replies Ribbit $3000, black 6. Now, this is a million to one shot to win, but after the golf game the man figures what the heck. Boom! Tons of cash comes sliding back across the table. The man takes his winnings and buys the best room in the hotel.! He sits the frog down and says Frog, I don't know how to repay you. You've won me all the money and I am forever grateful. The frog replies Ribbit kiss me. He figures why not, since after all the frog did for him He deserves it, With a kiss, the frog turns into a gorgeous 15 year old girl. And that your honor is how the girl ended up on my room. So help me God. Or my name is not William Jefferson Clinton.

WALMART INTERVIEW

An office manager at Wal-Mart was given the task of hiring an individual to fill a job opening. After sorting through a stack of resumes he found four people who were equally qualified. He decided to call the four in and ask them only one question. Their answer would determine which of them would get the job. The day came and as the four sat around the conference room table the interviewer asked, What is the fastest thing you know of? Acknowledging the first man on his right, the man replied A THOUGHT. It pops into your head. There's no warning that it's on the way, It's just there. A thought is the fastest thing I know. That's very good! Replied the interviewer. And now sir? She asked the second man. Hmmm . . . let me see. A blink! It comes and goes and you don't know that it ever happened. A BLINK is the fastest thing I know of. Excellent! said the interviewer. The blink of an eye, that's a very popular cliché for speed. He then turned to the third man who was contemplating his reply. Well out on my dad's ranch. You step put of the house and on the wall there's a light switch. When you flip that switch, way out across the pasture the light in the barn come on in less than an instant Yep, TURNING ON A LIGHT is the fastest thing I can think of. The interviewer was very impressed with the third answer and thought he had found his man. It's hard to beat the speed of light. He said. Turning to Bubba, the fourth and final man, the interviewer posed the same question. Old Bubba replied, After hearing the three previous answer., It's obvious to me that the fastest thing known is DIARRHEA. WHAT? said the interviewer, stunned by the response. Oh I can explain. Said Old Bubba. You see the other day I wasn't feeling so good, and I ran for the bathroom, but before I could THINK, BLINK OR TURN ON THE LIGHT. I had already shit in my pants. Old Bubba is now the new greeter at a Wal-Mart store near you!!!

SISTER MARY

Sister Mary, who worked for a home health agency, was out making her rounds visiting homebound patients when she ran out of gas. As luck would have it a gas station was just a block away. She walked to the station to borrow a gas can and to buy some gas. The attendant told her the only gas can he owned had been loaned out but she could wait until it was returned. Since the nun was on the way to see a patient, she decided not to wait and she walked back to her car. She looked for something in her car that she could fill with gas and spotted the bedpan she was taking to the patient. Always resourceful she carried the bedpan to the station, filled it with gas, and carried the full bed pan back to her car. As she was pouring the gas into her tank two men watched from across the street. One of them turned to the other and said, If it starts, I'm turning Catholic.

POLICE REPORT

Complainant reported neighbor's dog was left outside for days at a time. Complain ant was concerned for dog's well being. Located dog in question and found it to be a statue.

GENTLE THOUGHTS FOR TODAY

Birds of a feather flock together and crap on your car When I'm feeling down, I like to whistle. It makes the neighbor's dog run to the end of his chain and gag himself. If you can't be kind, at least have the decency to be vague. Don't assume malice for what stupidity can explain. A penny saved is a government oversight. The art of real conversation is not only to say the right thing at the right time, but also to leave unsaid the wrong thing at the tempting moment. The older you get the tougher it is to lose weight, because by then your body and you fat have gotten to be really good friends. The easiest way to find something lost around the house is to buy a replacement. He who hesitates is probably right. If you think there is good in everybody, you haven't met everybody. If you smile when things go wrong, you have someone in mind to blame. The sole purpose of a child's middle name is so he can tell when he is in trouble. There's always a lot to be thankful for if you take time to look for it. For example I am sitting here thinking how nice it is that wrinkles don't hurt.

Did you ever notice: When you put 2 words "the" and "IRS" together it spells Theirs?

Did you ever notice: The Roman Numerals for forty (40) are "XL".

TO MUCH TO DRINK

A man goes to a party and has to much to drink. His friends plead with him to let them take him home. He says no . . . he lives only a mile away. About five blocks from the party, the police pull him over for weaving and ask him to get out of the car and walk the line. Just as he starts, the police radio blares out a notice of a robbery taking place in a house just a block away. The police tell the party animal to stay put, they will be right back. The hop a fence and run down the street to the robbery. The guy waits and waits, but finally decides to drive home, When he gets there, he tells his wife he is going to bed, and to tell anyone who might come looking for him that he has the flu and has been in bed all day. A few hours later the police knock on the door. They ask if Mr.

Joe is there and his wife says yes. They ask to see him and she replies that he has the flu and has been there all day. The police produce his driver's license. They ask to see his car and she asks why. They insist on seeing his car, so she takes them to the garage. She opens the door. There sitting in the garage, is the police car, with the lights still flashing.

RoSEBUDS AND HANGING BASKETS***

A teenage granddaughter comes downstairs for her date with a see-through blouse on and no bra. Her grandmother just pitched a fit, telling her not to dare go out like that!! The teenager tells her, Loosen up Grams. These are modern times. You gotta let your rose buds show! And out she goes. The next day the teenager comes downstairs, and the grandmother is sitting there with no top on. The teenager wants to die. She explains to her grandmother that she has friends coming over and that it is just not appropriate . . . The grandmother says Loosen up Sweetie. If you can show off your rose buds, then I can display my hanging baskets.

IN HONOR oF STUPID PEOPLE

In case you needed further proof that the human race is doomed through stupidity, here are some actual label instructions on consumer goods. ON SEARS HAIRDRYER Do not use while sleeping (damn and that's the only time I have to work on my hair) ON A BAG OF FRITOS you could be a winner! No purchase necessary. Details inside (the shoplifter special) ON A BAR OF DIAL SOAP Directions. Use like regular soap (and that would be how???) ON SOME SWANSON FROZEN DINNERS Serving suggestion defrost (but, its just a suggestion) ON TESCO'S TIRAMISU DESSERT (printed on bottom) do not turn upside down (well duh, a bit late, huh) ON MARKS & SPENCERS BREAD PUDDING product will be hot after heating (and you thought?????) ON PACKAGING FOR A ROWENTA IRON do not iron clothes on body (but wouldn't this save me more time) ON BOOTS CHILDREN COUGH MEDICINE do not drive a car or operate machinery after taking the medication (we could do a lot to reduce the rate of construction accidents if we could just get those 5-year-olds with head-colds off those forklifts) ON NYTOL SLEEP AID warning: may cause drowsiness (and . . . I'm taking this because???) ON MOST BRANDS CHRISTMAS LIGHTS for indoor or outdoor use only (as opposed to . . . what?) ON JAPANENESE FOOD

PROCESSOR not to be used for the other use (now somebody out there, help me on this. I'm a bit curious) ON A SAINSBURY PEANUTS warning contains nuts (talk about a news flash) ON AMERICAN AIRLINES PACKET OF NUTS instructions Open packet, eat nuts (step 3 maybe, uh . . . fly Delta) ON CHILDS SUPERMAN COSTUME wearing of this garment does no enable you to fly (I don't blame the company. I blame parents for this one) ON SWEDISH CHAINSAW do not attempt to stop chain with you hands of genitals (oh my God . . . was there a lot of this happening somewhere?)

JESSIE

Clear day Jessie got out of the shower and was drying off when he looked in the mirror and noticed he was white from the neck up to the top of his head. In sheer panic and fearing he really was turning white and might have to start working for a living, he called his doctor and told him of his problem. The doctor advised him to come to his office immediately. After an examination, the doctor mixed a concoction of brown liquid, gave it to Jessie, and told him to drink it all. Jessie did and replied, That tasted like bullshit!! The doctor replied, It was Jessie. You were a quart low.

BLACK EYE

Jack wakes up at home with a huge hangover he can't believe. He forces himself to open his eyes, and the first thing he sees is a couple of aspirins net to a glass of water on the side table. (and a single red rose). Jack sits down and sees his clothing in front of him, all clean and pressed. Jack looks around the room and sees that it is in perfect order, spotlessly clean. So is the rest of the house. He takes the aspirins, cringes when he sees a huge black eye staring back at him in the bathroom mirror, and notices a note on the table. Honey, breakfast is on the stove, I left early to go shopping. Love you!1 He stumbles to the kitchen and sure enough, there is hot breakfast, and the morning paper. His son is also at the table4 eating. Jack asks, Son . . . what happened last night? Well, you came home after 3AM, drunk and out of your mind. You broke some furniture, puked in the hallway, and got that black eye when you ran into the door. So, why is everything in such perfect order, so clean, I have a rose and breakfast is on the table waiting for me? His son replies OH THAT . . . Mom dragged you to the bedroom, and when she tried to take your pants off, you screamed, Lady leave me alone, I'm married!!

WHY I FIRED MY SECRETARY

Two weeks ago was my 49th Birthday and I wasn't feeling too good that morning. I went to breakfast knowing my wife would be pleasant and say, Happy Birthday, and probably have a present for me. As it turned out, she didn't even say good morning, let alone and happy birthday. I thought well, that's wives for you, the children will remember. The children came to breakfast and didn't say word. So when I left for the office, I was feeling pretty low and despondent. As I walked into my office, my secretary Janet said good morning Boss. Happy Birthday. And I felt a little better that someone had remembered. I worked until noon, then Janet knocked on my door and said, You know it's such a beautiful day outside and it's your birthday, lets go to lunch just you and me. I said By George, that's the greatest thing I've heard all day. Let's go!! we went to lunch. We didn't go where we normally go, instead we went out to a private little place. We had two martinis and enjoyed lunch tremendously. On the way back to the office, she said, You know it's such a beautiful day. We don't need to go back to the office, do we? I said No I guess not. She said Let's go to my apartment. After arriving at her apartment she said, Boss, If you don't mind. I think I'll go into the bedroom and slip into something more comfortable. Sure! I excitedly replied. She went into her bedroom and, in about six minutes, she came our carrying a huge birthday cake—followed by my wife, children, and dozens of our friends, all singing Happy Birthday. And I just sit there—on the couch naked.

SHOULD HAVE DONE THE IRONING

The mother-in law stopped unexpectedly by the recently married couple's house. She rang the doorbell and stepped into the house. She saw her daughter-in-law standing naked by the door. What are you doing? She asked. I'm waiting for my husband to come home from work. The daughter-in-law answered. But, you're naked the mother-in-law exclaimed. This is my love dress the daughter-in-law explained. Love, dress? But you're naked! My husband loves me to wear this dress! It makes him happy and it makes me happy. I would appreciate it if you would leave because he will be home from work any minute. The mother-in-law was tired of all this romantic talk and left. On the way home she thought about the love dress. When she got home she got undressed, showered, put on her best perfume and waited by the front door. Finally her husband came home. He walked in and saw her standing naked by the door. What in the world are you doing? He asked. This is my love dress she replied. Needs ironing! What's for supper?

SQUEEZING EVERY LAST DROP

The local bar was so sure it's bartender was the strongest man around that they offered a standing $1000 bet. The bartender would squeeze a lemon until all the juice ran out into a glass, and hand the lemon to a patron. Anyone who could squeeze one more drop of juice out would win the money. Many people had tried over time, including the professional wrestlers and bodybuilders, but nobody could do it. One day a scrawny little man came in, wearing a tie and a pair of pants hiked up past his belly button. He said in a squeaky annoying voice, I'd like to try the bet. Even the hillbilly chicks burst into laughter. After the laughter had died down, the bartender said OK grabbed a lemon and squeezed away. He then handed the wrinkled remains of the rind to the little old man. But the crowd's laughter turned to total silence as the man clenched his fist around the lemon and six drops fell into the glass. As the crowd cheered the bartender paid the $1000, and asked the little man. What did you do for a living? Are you a lumberjack, weight lifter, or what? The man a replied I work for the IRS!!!

THE MEANING OF LIFE

On the first day god created the dog. God said, sit all day by the door of your house and bark at anyone who comes in or walks past. I will give you a life span of twenty years. The dog said That's to long to be barking. Give me ten years and I'll give you back the other ten. So God agreed. On the second day God created the monkey. God said entertain people. Do monkey tricks, make the laugh. I'll give you a twenty-year life span, The monkey said. How boring, monkey tricks for twenty years? I don't think so. Dog gave you back ten, so that's what I'll do too, okay? And God agreed. On the third day God created the cow. God said You must go to the field with the farmer all day long and suffer under the sun, have calves and give milk to support the farmer. I will give you a life span of sixty years. The cow said That's kind of tough life you want me to live for sixty years. Let me have twenty and I'll give back the other forty. And God agreed again. On the fourth day god created man, God said Eat, sleep, play, marry and enjoy your life. I'll give you twenty years. Man said What? Only twenty! years! Tell you what, I'll take my twenty, add the forty the cow gave back and the ten the monkey gave back and the ten the dog gave back, that makes eighty okay? Okay, said God You've got a deal. So that is why the first twenty we eat sleep, play and enjoy ourselves; for the next forty we slave in the sun to support our family; for the next ten years we do monkey tricks to entertain the grandchildren; and for the last ten we sit on the front porch and bark at everyone. This is the meaning of life

MY INSURANCE PLAN

A man having problems remembering things, went to his doctor. The doctor asked him a lot of questions, among which was do you every have intercourse? The man said I don't remember, let me ask my wife. He goes to the door and opens it into the waiting room which was full of people and shouts at his wife. Honey do we ever have intercourse? His wife says I have told you a lot of times can't you remember anything, we have Blue cross and Blue Shield.

MEXICAN OYSTERS

A big Texan stopped at a local restaurant following a day roaming around in Mexico. While sipping his tequila, he noticed a sizzling, scrumptious looking platter being served at the next table. Not only did it look good, the smell was wonderful. He asked the waiter, what is that you just served? The waiter replied, Ah senior, you have excellent taste! Those are called Conjoins de Toro, bull's testicles from the bull fight this morning. A delicacy! The cowboy said What the heck, bring me an order. The waiter replied, I am so sorry senor. There is only one serving per day because there is only one bullfight each morning. If you come early and place your order, we will be sure to save you this delicacy. The next morning, the cowboy returned, placed his order, and that evening was served the one and only special delicacy of the day. After a few bites, inspecting his platter, he called to the waiter and said, These are delicious, but they are much,

much smaller than the ones I saw you serve yesterday. The waiter shrugged his shoulders and replied, Si Senor. Sometimes the bull wins.

MEXICAN EARTHQUAKE

A big earthquake with the strength of 8.1 on the Richter scale hits Mexico. Two million Mexicans have died and over a million are injured. The country is totally ruined and the government doesn't know where to start and is asking for help to rebuild. The rest of the world is in shock. Canada is sending troopers to help the Mexican army control the riots. Saudi Arabia is sending oil. Other Latin American countries are sending supplies. The European community (except France) is sending food and money. The United States, not to be outdone, is sending two million Mexicans to replace the dead ones. God Bless America!!

FIRST DATE EXPERIENCE

If you didn't see this on the Tonight show, I hope you're sitting down when you read it, this is probably the funniest date story ever, first date or not!! Jay went into the audience to find the most embarrassing first date that a woman ever had There was absolutely no question as to shy her tale took first prize. She said it was midwinter. Snowing and quite cold . . . and the guy had taken her skiing in the mountains outside Salt Lake City, Utah. It was a day trip (no overnight). They were strangers, after all, and truly had never met before. The outing was fun but relatively uneventful until they were headed home late that afternoon. They were driving back down the mountain, when she gradually began to realize that she could not have had that extra latte. They were about an hour away from anywhere with a rest room and in the middle of nowhere! Her companion suggested she try to hold it, which she did for awhile. Unfortunately, because of the heavy snow and slow going, there came a point where she told him that he had better stop and let her pee beside the road or it would be the front seat of his car They stopped and she quickly crawled out beside the car, yanked her pants down and started. In the deep snow she didn't have a good footing so she let her butt rest against the rear fender to steady herself & oops: Her companion stood on the side of the car watching for traffic and indeed was a real gentleman and refrained from peaking. All she could think about was the relief she felt despite the rather embarrassing nature of the situation.

Upon finishing however she soon became aware of another sensation, As she bent to pull up her pants, the young lady discovered the buttocks were firmly glued against the car's fender. Thoughts of tongues frozen to pump handles immediately came to mind as she attempted to disengage her flesh from the icy metal. It was quickly apparent that she had a brand new problem due to the extreme cold. Horrified by her plight and yet aware of the humor of the moment she answered her date's concerns about what is taking so long with a reply that indeed, she was freezing her butt off and in need of some assistance. He came around the car as she tried to cover herself with her sweater and them, as she looked imploringly into his eyes, he burst out laughing. She too got the giggles and when they finally managed to compose themselves, they assessed her dilemma. Obviously, as hysterical as the situation was, they also were faced with a real problem. Both agreed it would take something hot to free her chilly cheeks from the grip of the icy metal!! thinking about what had gotten her into the predicament in the first place, both quickly realized that there was only one way to get her free. So, as she looked the other way, her first-time date proceeded to unzip his pants and pee her butt off the fender. As the audience screamed in laughter, she took the Tonight Show prize hands down., or perhaps that should be "pants down".

THIS IS ONE SMART DOG

A wealthy old lady decides to go on a photo safari in Africa, taking her faithful pet poodle along for company. One day the poodle starts chasing butterflies and before long he discovers that he is lost. Wandering about, he notices a leopard heading rapidly in his direction with the obvious intention of having lunch. The poodle thinks Uh-oh, I'm in deep trouble. Now!! Noticing some bones on the ground close by, he immediately settles down to chew on the bones with his back to the approaching cat. Just as the leopard is about to leap, the poodle exclaims loudly, Boy, that was one delicious leopard. I wonder if there are any more around here. Hearing this, the leopard halts his attack in mid-stride, a look of terror comes over him, and he slinks away into the trees. Whew says the leopard that was close. That poodle nearly had me. Meanwhile, a monkey who had been watching the whole scene from a nearby tree, figures he can put this knowledge to good use and trade it for protection from the leopard so off he goes. But the poodle sees him heading after the leopard with great speed, and figures that something must be up. The monkey soon catches up with the leopard, spills the beans and strikes a deal for himself, with the leopard. The leopard is furious at being made a fool of and says, Here monkey, hop on my back and see what's going to happen to that conniving canine. Now the poodle sees the leopard coming with the monkey on his back and thinks, What am I going to do now? Instead of running, the dog sits down with his back to his attackers, pretending he hasn't seen them yet. And just when they get close enough to hear, the poodle says . . . Where's that dam monkey? I sent him off half an hour ago to bring me another leopard. MORAL SOMETIMES BULLSHIT AND BRILLIANCE ARE THE SAME.

THE POLITICIAN

A priest was being honored at his retirement dinner after 25 years in the parish. A leading politician and member of the congregation was chosen to make the presentation and give a little speech at the dinner. He was delayed so the priest decided to say his own few words while they waited. I got my first impression of the parish from the first confession I heard here. I thought I had been assigned to a terrible place. The very first person who entered my confessional told me he had stolen a television set and, when stopped by the police, he had almost murdered the officer. He had stolen money from his parents, embezzled from his place of business, had an affair with his bosses' wife, taken illegal drugs, and gave VD to his sister. I was appalled. But as the days went on I knew that my people were not all like that and I had, indeed, come to a fine parish full of good and loving people. Just as the priest finished his talk, the politician arrived full of apologies at being late. He immediately began to make the presentation and give his talk. I'll never forget the first day our parish priest arrived, said the politician. In fact, I had the honor of being the first one to go to him in confession.

WHAT MARRIAGE IS ABOUT

He ordered one hamburger, one order of French fries and one drink. The old man unwrapped the plain hamburger and carefully cut it in half. He placed one half in front of his wife. He then carefully counted out the French fries, dividing them into two piles and neatly placed one pile in front of his wife. He took a sip of the drink, his wife took a sip and then set the cup down between them. As he began to eat his few bites of hamburger, the people around them kept looking over and whispering. You could tell they were thinking That poor old couple all they can afford is one meal for the two of them. As the man began to eat his fries a young man came to the table. He politely offered to buy another meal for the old couple. The old man said they were just fine—They were used to sharing everything. The surrounding people noticed the little old lady hadn't eaten a bite. She sat there watching her husband eat and occasionally taking turns sipping the drink. Again the young man came over and begged them to let him buy another meal for them. This time the old woman said No thank you we are use to sharing everything. As the old man finished and was wiping his face neatly with the napkin, the young man again came over to the little old lady who had yet to eat a single bite of food and asked What is it you are waiting for? She answered THE TEETH!!

THEY WALK AMONG US

I live in a semi-rural area. We recently had a new neighbor call the local township administration office to request the removal of the Deer Crossing sign on our road. the reason too many deer are being hit by cars out here! I don't think this is a good place for them to be crossing, anymore. From Kingman, KS IDIOTS IN FOOD SERVICE My daughter went to a local taco bell and ordered a taco. She asked the person behind the counter for Minimal lettuce. He said he was sorry, but they only had iceberg. He was a chef Yep . . . From Kansas City! IDIOT SIGHTING I was at the airport, checking in at the gate when airport employee asked, Has anyone put anything in your baggage without your knowledge? To which I replied if it was without my knowledge, how would I know? He smiled knowingly and nodded that's why we asked Happened in Birmingham, Ala IDIOT SIGHTING the stoplight on the corner buzzes when its safe to cross the street. I was crossing with an intellectually challenged coworker of mine. She asked if knew what the buzzer was for. I explained that it signals blind people when the light is red. Appalled she responded, What on earth blind people are doing driving. She was probation officer in Wichita, KS IDIOT SIGHTING At a good-bye luncheon for an old and dear coworker. She was leaving the company due to "downsizing". Our manager commented cheerfully This is fun. We should do this more often. Not another word was spoken. We just all looked at each other with that deer-in-headlights stare. This was a bunch at Texas Instruments. IDIOT SIGHTING when my husband and I arrived at an automobile dealership to pick up our car, we were told they keys had been locked in it. We went to the service department and found a mechanic working feverishly to unlock the driver's side door. As I watched from the passenger side, I instinctively tried the door handle and discovered it was unlocked. Hey, I announced to the technician, it's open. His reply, I know—I already got that side. This was at the Ford dealership in Canton, Mississippi!

YOU KNOW YOU ARE LIVING IN 2005

WHEN 1. You accidentally enter your password on the microwave 2. You haven't played solitaire with real card in years. 3. You have a list of 15 phone numbers to reach your family of three. 4. You e-mail the person who works at the desk next to you. 5. Your reason for not staying in touch with friends and family is that they don't have e-mail addresses. 6. You pull up in your own driveway and use your cell phone to see if anyone is home to help you carry in the groceries. 7. Every commercial on television has a web site at the bottom of the screen. 8. Leavi8ng the house without your cell phone, which you didn't have the first 20 or 30 (or 60) years of your life, is now a cause for panic and you turn around to go and get it. 10. You get up in the morning and go on line before getting your coffee. 11. You start tilting your head sideways to smile. 12. You're reading this and nodding and laughing. 13. Even worse, you know exactly to whom you are going to forward this message. 14. You are too busy to notice there was no # 9 on this list. 15. You actually scrolled back up to check that there wasn't a # 9 on this list.

Windy day

An 85 year old woman was standing on the deck of a cruise ship. It was very windy and she was holding onto her hat with both hands. Her dress was blowing up and she had no underwear on. A man stopped and remarked to her, Lady your dress is blowing up and people can see you don't have any undines on wouldn't it be better to hold you dress down instead of your hat. She replied what you see down there is 85 years old but I just bought this hat yesterday!!

YOUR HOTEL BILL

Husband and wife are traveling by car from Key West to Boston. After almost twenty-four hours on the road, they're too tired to continue, and they decide to stop for a rest. They stop at a nice hotel and take a room, but they only plan to sleep for four hours and then get back on the road. When they check out four hours later, the desk clerk hands them a bill for $350.00. the man explodes and demands to know why the charge is do high, He tell the clerk although it's a nice hotel, the rooms certainly aren't worth $350.00. When the clerk tells him $350.00 is the standard rate, the man insists on speaking to the Manager. The manager appears, listens to the man, and then explains that the hotel has an Olympic-size pool and a huge conference center that were available for the husband and wife to use. But we didn't use them, the man complains, well they are here, and you could have, explains the manager. He goes on to explain they could have taken in one of the shows for which the hotel is famous. The best entertainers from New York, Hollywood and Las Vegas perform here, the Manager says. But we didn't go to any of those shows, complains the man again. Well we have them and you could have, the manager replies. No matter what amenity the Manager mentions, the man replies, but we didn't use it!! The manager is unmoved, and eventually the man gives up and agrees to pay. He writes a check and gives it to the Manager. The Manager is surprised when he looks at the check, But sir, He says this check is only made out of $50.00. That's correct says the man, I charged you $300.00 for sleeping with my wife. But I didn't exclaims the MANAGER. Well too bad, the man replies, She was here and you could have.

SOMEBODY'S RAISING THEIR KID RIGHT

One day a 6 year old girl was sitting in a classroom, The teacher was going to explain evolution to the children. The teacher asked a little boy: Tommy do you see the tree outside? Tommy said yes. Do you see the grass outside? Yes said Tommy, Teacher Go outside and look up and see if you can see the sky. She said. Okay said Tommy (he returned a few minutes later) Yes, I saw the sky. Did you see God? The teacher asked. No said Tommy Teacher That's my point. We can't see God because he isn't there. He just doesn't exist. A little girl spoke up and wanted to ask the boy some questions. The teacher agreed and the little girl asked the boy: Tommy do you see the tree outside? Tommy

Yessssss! Girl did you see the sky? Tommy Yesssss! Girl did you see the sky? Tommy Yessssss! Little Girl Tommy do you see the teacher? Tommy Yes Little girl do you see her brain? Tommy No! Little girl Then according to what we were taught today in school, she must not have one!!! FOR WE WALK BY FAITH, NOT BY SIGHT II CORINTHIANS 5:7

IT COULD BE WORSE

A father passing by his son's bedroom was astonished to see that his bed was nicely made and everything was picked up. Then he saw an envelope, propped up prominently on the pillow that was addressed to Dad. With the worst premonition he opened the envelope with trembling hands and read the letter. Dear Dad:: It is with great regret and sorrow that I'm writing you. I had to elope with my new girlfriend because I wanted to avoid a scene with Mom and you. I have been finding real passion with Jane and she is so nice. But I knew you would not approve of her because of all her piercing, tattoos, tight motorcycle clothes and the fact that she is much older than I am. But it's not only the passion . . . Dad she's pregnant. Jane said that we will be very happy. She owns a trailer in the woods and she has a stack of firewood for the whole winter. We share a dream of having many more children. Stacy has opened my eyes to the fact that marijuana doesn't really hurt anyone. We'll be growing it for ourselves and trading it with other people that live nearby for cocaine and ecstasy. In the meantime we will pray that science will find a cure for AIDS so Jane can get better. She deserves it. Don't worry dad. I'm 15 and I know how to take care of myself. Someday I'm sure that we will be back to visit so that you can get to know your grandchildren. Love Son John P.S. Dad, none of the above is true. I'm over at Tommy's house. I just wanted to remind you that there are worse things in life than a report card that's in my center desk drawer. I love you. Call me when it's save to come home

THE COAT HANGER

A women was at work when she received a phone call that her small daughter was very sick with a fever. She left work and stopped by the pharmacy to get some medication. She got back to her car and found that she had locked her keys in the car. She didn't know what to do, so she called home and told the baby sitter what had happened. The baby sitter told her that the fever was getting worse. She said You might find a coat hanger and use that to open the door. The women looked around and found an old rusty coat hanger that had been left on the ground, possibly by someone else who at some time had locked their keys in their car. She looked at the hanger and said I don't know how to use this. She bowed her head and asked god to send her help. Within five minuets a beat up old motorcycle pulled up, with a dirty, greasy, bearded man who was wearing an old biker skull rag on his head. The woman thought This is what you sent to help me? But, she was desperate, so she was also very thankful. The man got off of his motorcycle and asked if he could help. She said Yes, my daughter is very sick. I stopped to get her some medication and I locked my keys in my car. I must get home to her. Please, can you use this hanger to unlock my car? He said sure. He walked over to the car, and in less than a minute the car was opened. She hugged the man and through her tears she said. Thank you so much! You are a very nice man. The man replied Lady I am not a nice man. I just got out of prison today. I was in prison for car theft and have only been out about an hour. The woman hugged the man again and with sobbing tears cried out loud. Oh Thank you god! You even sent me a Professional. Isn't God Good!!

HUMOR FOR LESOPHILES (LOVER OF WORDS)

I wonder why the baseball was getting bigger. Then it hit me. Police were called to a Day Care where a three-year-old was resisting a rest. Did you hear about the guy whose whole left side was cut off? He's all right now. The roundest knight in King Arthur's round table was Sir Conference. The butcher backed into the meat grinder and got a little behind in his work. To write with a broken pencil is pointless. When fish are in schools they sometimes take debate. The short fortune teller who escaped from prison was a small medium at large. A thief who stole a calendar got twelve months. A thief fell and broke his leg in wet cement. He became a hardened criminal. Thieves who steal corn from a garden could be charged with stalking. We never run out of math teachers because they always multiply. When the smog lifts in Los Angeles, U.C.L.A. The math professor went crazy with a blackboard. He did a number on it. The professor discovered that her theory of earthquakes was on shaky ground The dead batteries were given out free of charge. If you take a laptop computer for a run you could jog your memory. A bicycle can't stand alone: it is two tired. A will is a dead giveaway. Tine flies like an arrow: fruit flies like a banana. A backward poet writes inverse. In a democracy it's your vote that counts; in feudalism; it's your Count that votes. A chicken crossing the road; poultry in motion. If you don't pay your exorcist you can get repossessed. With her marriage she got a new name and a dress. Show me a piano falling down a mine shaft and I'll show you A-flat miner. When a clock is hungry it goes back four seconds. The guy who fell onto an upholstery machine was fully recovered You are stuck with your debt if you can't budget. He broke into song because he couldn't find the key. A calendar's days are numbered. A lot of money is tainted: Taint yours and taint mine. A boiled egg is hard to beat. Those who get to big for their britches will be exposed in the end.

RED NECKS KNOW HOW TO GET THING DONE

A man named Floyd called the Sheriff's office and complained that his neighbor was hiding marijuana in his shed. The Sheriff sends out a couple of deputies to investigate. They found nothing. The man waited and after several days again called the Sheriffs office complaining about the neighbor. The Sheriff said they went out there and did not find anything suspicious. The man said I told you he was hiding it in his shed. He is hiding it in wood he has stored out there, you are not looking in the wood. The sheriff said he would send some Deputies there and then said Thank you very much for the call sir. The next day, the Sheriff's deputies descended on Virgil's house. They searched the shed where the firewood is kept. Using axes, they bust open every piece of wood, but found no marijuana. They sneer at Virgil and leave. Shortly, the phone rings at Virgil's house. Hey, Virgil! This here's Floyd . . . did the Sheriff come? Yeah! did they chop your firewood? Yep! Happy Birthday Buddy. Red Necks know how to get it done.

I KNOW EVERYBODY

I told my boss that I knew everyone in the world. He said oh yes I am sure you do ha. So we went to a ballgame and I went down to see Marc McGuire. We stood and talked for a long time. When I came back to my seat he said, you really do know Marc McGuire don't you. We watched the game and went home. A few days later I asked my boss if he wanted to fly to Washington DC with me for a visit with the President. He said Oh Yes and scoffed, we went to the president's office and his secretary do you want to see Mr. Busch, Omerline.?

She said well and he is holding a press conference but I will tell him you are here. A few minuets later she said he is in the oval office just go right on in. WE walked right in and the president greeted us with hello, I was holding a press conference but I canceled it to talk to you. My boss was speechless. Sometime later I said to my boss would you like to visit with the Pope. He said you don't really know the Pope. We went to Rome and I left my boss standing observing the Mass. I went up on the alter to see the Pope. He stopped the mass and was talking to me when out I the audience We heard a scream. I rushed out into the large congregation gathered listening to the Pope. It was my boss he had fallen down and was laying there. I think I had a heart attract he said, I was watching you and someone came up to me and said, WHO IS THAT MAN TALKING TO OMERLINE?

THE ITALIAN ELBOW

An Italian grandmother is giving directions to her grown grandson who is coming to visit with his wife. "You comma to de front door of the apartmenta. I am inna apartmenta 301. there issa bigga panel at the front door. With your elbow pusha button 301. I will Buzza you in. Come inside, the elevator is on the right. Get in, and with you elbow pusha 3. When you get out, I'mma on the left. With your elbow, hit my doorbell." "Grandma, that sounds easy. But why am I hitting all these buttons with my elbow? What? . . . You coming empty handed?

MONTANA STATE TROUPER

In most of the United States there is a policy of checking on any stalled vehicle on the highway when the temperature drops to single digits or below. About 3:00 A>M> one very cold morning, Montana State Trouper Allan Nixon # 658 responded to a call there was a car off the shoulder of the road outside Great Falls Montana. He located the car stuck in deep snow and with his emergency lights on, the trooper walked to the driver's door to find an older man passed out behind the wheel with a nearly empty vodka bottle on the seat besides him. The driver came awake when the trooper tapped on the window. Seeing the rotating lights in his rearview mirror, the state trooper standing next to his car, the man panicked. He jerked the gear shift into drive and hit the gas. The car's speedometer was showing 20-30-40 and then 50 MPH, but it was still stuck in the snow, wheels spinning. Trooper Nixon, having a sense of humor, began running in place next to the speeding (but stationary) car. The driver was totally freaked, thinking the trooper was actually keeping up with him. This goes on for about 30 seconds, then the trooper yelled "PULL OVER" The man nodded, turned his wheel and stopped the engine. Needless to say, the man from North Dakota was arrested and is probably still shaking his head over the state trooper in Montana who could run 50 miles per hour. Who says troopers don't have a sense of humor?

WALLY'S WEDDING NIGHT

At 85 years of age. Wally married Lou Anne, a lovely 25 year old. Since her new husband is so old, Lou Anne decides that after their wedding she and Wally should have separate bedrooms, because she is concerned that her new but aged husband may overexert himself if they spend the entire night together. After the wedding festivities Lou Anne prepares herself and the expected knock on the door. Sure enough the knock comes, the door opens and there is Wally, her 85 year old groom, ready for action. They unite as one. All goes well. Wally takes leave of his bride, and she prepares to go to sleep After a few minutes, she hears another knock on her bedroom door, and it's Wally. Again he is ready for more action. Somewhat surprised, she consents for more coupling. When the newlyweds are done, he kisses his bride, bids her goodnight and leaves. She is set to go to sleep again, but aha you guessed it—Wally is back again, rapping on the door, and once again and is fresh as a 25-year old ready for more action. Once again they enjoy each other. But as Wally gets set to leave again, his bride says to him I am thoroughly impressed that at your age you can perform so well and so often. I have been with guys less than a third of your age who were only good once. You are truly a great lover "Wally". Wally somewhat embarrassed, turns to Lou Anne and says . . . You mean I was here already? Moral of this story Senior moments have their advantages.

CAKE OR BED

A husband is at home watching a football game when his wife interrupts
Honey could you fix the light in the hallway? It's been flickering for weeks now.

He looked at her and says angrily. Fix the light Now? Does it look like I have GE written on my forehead? I don't think so. Fine!

Then the wife asks well then could fix the fridge door? It won't close.

To which he replied fix the fridge door? Does it look like I have Westinghouse written on my forehead? I don't think so.

Fine, she says then you could at least fix the steps to the front door? They are about to break.

I'm not a carpenter and I don't want to fix the steps. He says, does it look like I have Ace hardware written on my forehead? I don't think so. I've had enough of you I'm going to the bar!!!

So he goes to the bar and drinks for a couple of hours.

He starts to feel guilty about how he treated his wife, and decides to go home.

As he walks into the house he notices that the steps are already fixed.

As he enters the house, he sees the hall light is working.

As he goes to get a beer he notices the fridge door is fixed.

Honey, he asks how'd all this get fixed? She said, well when you left I sat outside and cried.

Just then a nice young man asked me what was wrong, and I told him.

He offered to do all the repairs, and all I had to do was either go to bed with Him or bake a cake.

He said, So what kind of cake did you bake?

She replied. Hellooooo . . . do you see Betty Crocker written on my forehead? I don't think so!

2 CAR ACCIDENT

On the way here I saw a two car accident. The first car was hit broadside bye the second car coming towards the first car from a side road just down 100 a little way from here. The man in the first car had his arm hanging out the window and when the other car hit it cut his arm right off and it was laying right on the road. There was a police car following the first car and so he was right there and he took the arm and laid it beside the car. He called an ambulance and they were there in a short time. They took the arm and put it one of those carriers that they use to put something like that in. They then went to the man and tied off the arties for the arm. While they were doing this the police were directing traffic and someone stole the arm. The police happened to see who did this and gave chase. They arrested the person. Do you know what they charged him with? Well arm robbery of course.

WATCH OUT FOR THESE OLD WOMEN

This 70 year old women bought a used Mercedes, it was just a couple of years old. Just minuets after she bought it and pulled out of the lot she was hit by a 20 year old boy driving an old van. She was so mad she got out of the car and started screaming at the boy. He got out of the van and was trying to say he was sorry. She just started hitting him and he just started backing around the van away from her. She grabbed the aerial from the van and broke it off. She started hitting the boy with the broken off aerial. He finally got under the van to get away from her. The police came and got the boy from under the van upon which he started throwing up. The police arrested him for Van Ariel Debase

BEST LAWYER STORY

A Charlotte NC lawyer purchased a box of very rare and expensive cigars, then insured them against fire, among other things. Within a month, having smoked his entire stockpile of these great cigars and without yet having made his first premium payment on the policy, the lawyer filed claim against the insurance company. In his claim, the lawyer stated the cigars were lost in a series of small fires. The insurance company refused to ay, citing the obvious reason that the man had consumed the cigars in the normal fashion. The lawyer sued. and Won!!! (stay with me) In delivering the ruling, the judge agreed with the insurance company that the claim was frivolous. The judge stated nevertheless, that the lawyer held a policy from the company in which it had warranted that the cigars were insurable and also guaranteed that it would insure them against fire, and was obligated to pay the claim. Rather than endure lengthy and costly appeal process, the insurance company accepted the ruling and paid $15,000.00 to the lawyer for his loss of the rare cigars lost in the "fires". NOW HERE IS THE BEST PART After the lawyer cashed the check, the insurance company had him arrested on 24 counts of ARSON!!! With his own insurance claim and testimony from the previous case being used against him, the lawyer was convicted of intentionally burning his insured property and was sentenced to 24 months and a $24,000.00 fine This was the first place winner in the Criminal Lawyer awards Contest.

CHILDREN ARE So HONEST

1. NUDITY I was driving with my three young children one warm summer evening when a woman in the convertible ahead of us stood up and waved. She was stark naked! As I was reeling from the shock, I heard my 5-year old shout from the back seat, mom, that lady isn't wearing a seat belt!
2. OPINIONS On the first ay of school, a first-grader handed his teacher a note from his mother. The note read, The opinions expressed by this child are not necessarily those of his parents.
3. KETCHUP A woman was trying hard to get the ketchup out of a jar. During her struggle the phone rang so she asked her 4-year-old daughter to answer the phone, Mommy can't come to the phone to talk to you right now, she's hitting the bottle.
4. MORE NUDITY A little boy got lost at the YMCA and found himself in the women's locker room. When he spotted, the room burst into shrieks, with ladies grabbing towels and running for cover. The little boy watched in amazement and then asked, What's the matter, haven't you ever seen a little boy before?
5. POLICE #1 While taking a routine vandalism report at an elementary school, I was interrupted by a little girl about 6 years old, Looking up and down at my uniform, she asked, Are you a cop? Yes, I answered and continued writing the report. My mother said if I ever needed help I should ask the police. Is that right? Yes, that's right, I told her. Well then, she said as she extended her foot toward me, would you please tie my shoe?
6. POLICE # 2 It was the end of the day when I parked my police van in front of the station. As I gathered my equipment, my K-9 partner, Jake, was barking and I saw a little boy staring in at me. Is that a dog you got back there? He asked It sure is, I replied. Puzzled, the boy looked at me and then towards the back of the van, Finally he said, what did he do?
7. ELDERLY While working for an organization that delivers lunches to elderly shut-ins, I used to take my 4-year-old daughter on my afternoon rounds. She

was unfailingly intrigued by the various appliances of old age, particularly the canes, walkers and wheelchairs. One day I found her staring at a pair of false teeth soaking in a glass. As I braced myself for the inevitable barrage of questions, she merely turned and whispered, The tooth fairy will never believe this.

8. RESS-UP A little girl was watching her parents dress for a party. When she saw her dad donning his tuxedo, she warned, daddy, you shouldn't wear that suit. And why not, darling? You know that it always gives you a headache the next morning.

9. DEATH While walking along the sidewalk in front of his church, our minister heard the intoning of a prayer that nearly made his collar wilt. Apparently, his 5-year-old son and his playmates had found a dead robin. Feeling that proper burial should be performed, they had secured a small box and cotton batting, then dug a hole and made ready for the disposal of the deceased. The minister's son was chosen to say the appropriate prayers and with sonorous dignity intoned his version of what he thought his father always said: Glory be unto the Faaather, and unto the Sonnn, and into the hole he goooes☺I want this line used at my funeral)

10. SCHOOL A little girl had just finished her first week of school. I'm wasting my time, she said to her mother, I can't read, I can't write and they won't let me talk!

11. BIBLE a little boy opened the big family Bible. He was fascinated as he fingered through the old pages. Suddenly, something fell out of the Bible. He picked up the object and looked at it. What he saw was an old leaf that had been pressed in between the pages. Mama, look what I found, the boy called out. What have you got there, dear? With astonishment in the young voice, he answered, I think it's Adam's underwear!

NOW IF THIS DON'T BRIGHTEN YOUR DAY, GO BACK TO BED AND FORGET IT.

SPEEDING IN MISSOURI

1. GOOD A Desoto, mo policeman has a perfect spot to watch for speeders, but wasn't getting many. Then he discovered the problem. A twelve-year-old boy was standing up the road with a hand-painted sign, which read RADAR

TRAP AHEAD, The officer then found a young accomplice down the road with a sign reading TIPPS . . . and a bucket full of money. (and we kids use to sell lemonade).

2.   BETTER A motorist was mailed a picture of his car speeding through an automated radar post in St. Peters, Mo. A $40 speeding ticket was included. Being cute, he sent the police department a picture of $40. The police responded with another photo of handcuffs . . .

3.   BEST A young woman was pulled over for speeding. As the Missouri State Trooper walked to her car window, flipping open his ticket book, she said, I bet you're going to sell me a ticket to the State Troopers Ball. He replied, Missouri State Troupers don't have balls. There was a silence while she smiled, and he realized what he'd said. He then closed his book, got back in his patrol car and left. She was laughing too hard to start her car . . .

THE HELICOPTER RIDE

Morris and his wife Esther went to the state fair every year, and Morris would say, Esther, I'd like to ride in that helicopter. Esther always replied, I know Morris, but that helicopter ride is fifty dollars, and fifty dollars is fifty dollars. One year Esther and Morris went to the fair, and Morris said, Esther, I'm 85 years old, if I don't ride that helicopter, I might never get another chance. To this Esther replied, Morris that helicopter ride is fifty dollars, and fifty dollars is fifty dollars. The overheard the couple and said, Folks I'll make you a deal. I'll take the both of you for a ride. If you can stay quiet for the entire ride and not say a word, I won't charge you! But if you say one word, it's fifty dollars. Morris and Esther agreed and up they went. The pilot did all kinds of fancy maneuvers, but not a word was heard. He did his daredevil tricks over and over again, but still not a word. When they landed, the pilot turned to Morris and said, By golly, I did everything I could to get you to yell out, but you didn't, I'm impressed! Morris replied, Well, to tell the truth, I almost said something when Esther fell out, but you know fifty dollars is fifty dollars.

3 REDNECKS

Three Rednecks were working up on a cell phone tower—Cooter, Pete, and KC As they start their descent Cooter slips, falls off the tower and is killed instantly. As the ambulance takes the body away, Pete says, Well damn, someone should go and tell his wife. KC says, OK I'm good at that sensitive stuff, I'll do it. Two hours later, he comes back carrying a case of Budweiser. Pete says, Where did you get that beer, KC? Cooter's wife gave it to me, KC replies. That's unbelievable, you told the lady her husband was dead and she gave you beer Well not exactly, KC says. When she answered the door, I said to her. You must be Cooter's widow. She said, You must be mistaken, I'm not a widow . . . then I said I'll bet you a case of Budweiser you are. Rednecks are good at Sensitive stuff.

A PRAYER AT 80

TODAY, DEAR Lord, I'm 80 there's so much I haven't done. I hope, dear Lord, You'll let me live until I'm 81.

But then, if I haven't finished all I want to do. Would you let me stay awhile—until I'm 82?

The world is changing very fast, there is so much more in store. I'd like it very much to live until I'm 84.

And if by then, I find I'm still alive, I'd really like to stay until I'm 85.

More change, more change, there I'd really like to stick, and see what happens to the world when I'm 86.

I know, dear Lord, it's much to ask (it must be nice in Heaven) but, really, I would like to stay until I'm 87.

I know by then I won't be fast and sometimes will be late. But it would be so pleasant—to be around at 88.

I will have seen so many things, and have had a wonderful time. So I'm sure that I'll be willing to leave at 89. MAYBE!

LETTER FROM KENTUCKY MOM TO HER SON

I'm writing this slow because I know you can't read fast.

We don't live where we did when you left. Your Dad read in the paper where most accidents happen within 20 miles of home, so we moved. I won't be able to send you the address as the last Kentucky family that lived here took the numbers with them for their next house so they won't have to change their address.

This place has a washing machine. The first day I put four shirts in it, pulled the chain and haven't seen them since. It only rained twice this week—three days the first time and three days the second.

The coat you wanted us to send you, your Aunt Sue said it would be a little heavy, to mail with them heavy buttons. So we cut them off and put them in the pocket.

I got a bill from the funeral home—and if we didn't make the last payment on Grandma's funeral, up she comes.

About your father, he has a lovely new job. He has 500 men under him—he is cutting grass in the cemetery. About your sister—she had a baby this morning and I haven't found out whether it is a boy or a girl, so I don't know if you are an aunt or an uncle. Your Uncle John fell in the whiskey vat. Some men tried to pull him out, but he fought them off playfully, so he drowned. WE cremated him and he burned for three days. Three of your friends went off the bridge in a pick-up truck—one was driving, the other two were in the back. The driver got out okay—he rolled the window down and swam to safety. The other two drowned. They couldn't get the tailgate down.

That's about all the good news for now. Write more often.

Love Mom

PS Was going to send you some money, but the envelope was sealed

SERVICE AGENCIES

SERVICE: the act of doing things for other people or so I thought!

I then heard these terms which reference the word service:

Internal Revenue Service.
Telephone Service.
Cable T.V. Service.
Civil Service.

City and County Public Service.
Customer Service.
And Service Stations

Then I became confused about the word service.

So today I overheard two farmers talking, and one of them said he had hired a bull to "service" a few of his cows.

BAM!!! . . . It all came into perspective. Now I understand what all those "Service" agencies are doing to us. I hope you now are as enlightened as I am.

JOB OPENING AT THE FBI

After all the background checks, interviews and testing were done, there were 3 finalists; two men and a woman. For the final test, the FBI agents took one of the men to a large metal door and handed him a gun. We must know that you will follow your instructions no matter what the circumstances. Inside the room you will find your wife sitting in a chair . . . Kill her! The man said, You can't be serious. I could never shoot my wife. The agent said. Them you're not the right man for this job. Take your wife and go home. The second man was given the same instructions. He took the gun and went into the room. All was quiet for about 5 minutes. The man came out with tears in his eyes, I tried, but I can't kill my wife. The agent said You don't have what it takes. Take your wife and go home. Finally, it was the woman's turn. She was given the same instructions, to kill her husband. She took the gun and went into the room. Shots were heard, one after another. They heard screaming, crashing, banging on the walls. After a few minuets, all was quiet. The door opened slowly and there stood the woman, wiping the sweat from her brow. This gun is loaded with blanks, she said. I had to beat him to death with the chair.

TRU LOVE

An elderly gent was invited to an old friends home for dinner one evening. He was impressed by the way his buddy preceded every request to his wife with endearing terms such as Honey, My Love, Darling, sweetheart, Pumpkin, etc. The couple had been married almost 70 years and, clearly, they were still very much in love. While the wife was in the kitchen, the man leaned over and said to his host, I think it's wonderful that, after all these years, you still call your wife those loving pet names. The old man hung his head. I have to tell you the truth, he said, Her name slipped my mind about 10 years ago and I'm scared to death to ask her what is!!

DEAR ABBY

I am a 60-year-old woman who is married to a man who acts like he hates me. In public, he pretends e loves me and talks about how wonderful I am. But in private, he shakes his finger in my face and calls me the "B" word. He constantly tells me how ugly I am without make-up. I've tried everything, including a face-lift, boxtox treatments, and a chin tuck. I even went on a diet and lost 20 pounds. He quit his job about 7 years ago after having an affair with a women in his office. He hasn't even looked for another job. We haven't slept together since I confronted him about the affair. He denied it, of course, but everybody knew it, It was humiliating. I believe he is still messing around. While we both want to sell this house, we argue constantly about when to put in on the market. The house we want will be available in a few months. My husband wants to put our house on the market now. I think we should wait a while. He has already started collecting boxes and packing up his stuff. Do you think he is planning to leave me?

Signed worried in NY

Dear worried in NY:
I doubt it. He wants to move back into the White House as much as you do.

MYSTERIES oF LIFE

Two guys were discussing popular family trends on sex, marriage, and family values. Stu said, I didn't sleep with my wife before we got married, did you? Leroy replied, I'm not sure, what was her maiden name?

A little boy went up to his father and asked: Dad, where did my intelligence come from?

The father replied, Well, son, you must have got it from your mother, cause I still have mine.

Mr. Clark, I have reviewed this case very carefully, the divorce Court judge said and I've decided to give your wife $775 a week. That's very fair, your honor, the husband said. And every now and then I'll try to send her a few bucks myself.

I AGREE

A doctor examining a woman who had been rushed to the Emergency Room, took the husband aside, and said, I don't like the looks of your wife at all. Me neither doc, said the husband. But she's a great cook and really good with the kids.

THE CURSE

An old man goes to the Wizard to ask him if he can remove a curse he has been living for the last 40 years. The Wizard says, Maybe, but you will have to tell me the exact words that were used to put the curse on you! The old man said without hesitation, I now pronounce you man and wife.

REDNECK MURDER

Two reasons. Why it's so hard to solve a Redneck murder. 1. The DNA all matches. 2. There are no dental records.

CALL THE AIRLINES

A blonde calls Delta Airlines and asks, Can you tell me how long it'll take to fly from San Francisco to New York? The agent replies, Just a minute. Thank you, the blonde says and hangs up.

A PUN

TWO Mexican detectives were investigating the murder of Juan Gonzalez. How was he killed? asked one detective. With a golf gun, the other detective replied. A Golf Gun? What is a Golf Gun? I don't know. But it sure made a hole I Juan.

I BELIEVE

Moe: My wife got me to believe in religion. Joe; Really? Moe Yeah. Until I married her I didn't believe in hell.

The Squirrel Grenade

(EXTREMELY funny article)

I never dreamed slowly cruising through a residential neighborhood could be so incredibly dangerous! Studies have shown that motorcycling requires more decisions per second, and more sheer data processing than nearly any other common activity or sport. The reactions and accurate decision making abilities needed have been likened to the reactions of fighter pilots! The consequences of bad decisions or poor situational awareness are pretty much the same for both groups too.

Occasionally, as a rider I have caught myself starting to make bad or late decisions while riding. In flight training, my instructors called this being "behind the power curve". It is a mark of experience that when this begins to happen, the rider recognizes the situation, and more importantly, does something about it. A short break, a meal, or even a gas stop can set things right again as it gives the brain a chance to catch up.

Good, accurate, and timely decisions are essential when riding a motorcycle at least if you want to remain among the living. In short, the brain needs to keep up with the machine.

I had been banging around the roads of east Texas and as I headed back into Dallas, found myself in very heavy, high-speed traffic on the freeways. Normally, this is not a problem, I commute in these conditions daily, but suddenly I was nearly run down by a cage that decided it needed my lane more than I did. This is not normally a big deal either, as it happens around here often, but usually I can accurately predict which drivers are not paying attention and avoid them before we are even close. This one I missed seeing until it was nearly too late, and as I took evasive action I nearly broadsided another car that I was not even aware was there!

Two bad decisions and insufficient situational awareness. all within seconds. I was behind the power curve. Time to get off the freeway. I hit the next exit, and as I was in an area I knew pretty well, headed through a few big residential neighborhoods as a new route home. As I turned onto the nearly empty streets I opened the visor on my full-face helmet to help get some air. I figured some slow riding through the quiet surface streets would give me time to relax, think, and regain that "edge" so frequently required when riding. Little did I suspect.

As I passed an oncoming car, a brown furry missile shot out from under it and tumbled to a stop immediately in front of me. It was a squirrel, and must have been trying to run across the road when it encountered the car. I really was not going very fast, but there was no time to brake or avoid it-it was that close.

I hate to run over animals. and I really hate it on a motorcycle, but a squirrel should pose no danger to me. I barely had time to brace for the impact.

Animal lovers, never fear. Squirrels can take care of themselves!

Inches before impact, the squirrel flipped to his feet. He was standing on his hind legs and facing the oncoming Valkyrie with steadfast resolve in his little beady eyes. His mouth opened, and at the last possible second, he screamed and leapt! I am pretty sure the scream was squirrel for, "Banzai!" or maybe, "Die you gravy-sucking, heathen scum!" as the leap was spectacular and he flew over the windshield and impacted me squarely in the chest.

Instantly he set upon me. If I did not know better I would have sworn he brought twenty of his little buddies along for the attack. Snarling, hissing, and tearing at my clothes, he was a frenzy of activity. As I was dressed only in a light t-shirt, summer riding gloves, and jeans this was a bit of a cause for concern. This furry little tornado was doing some damage!

Picture a large man on a huge black and chrome cruiser, dressed in jeans, a t-shirt, and leather gloves puttering maybe 25mph down a quiet residential street. and in the fight of his life with a squirrel. And losing.

I grabbed for him with my left hand and managed to snag his tail. With all my strength I flung the evil rodent off the left of the bike, almost running into the right curb as I recoiled from the throw.

That should have done it. The matter should have ended right there. It really should have. The squirrel could have sailed into one of the pristinely kept yards and gone on about his business, and I could have headed home. No one would have been the wiser. But this was no ordinary squirrel. This was not even an ordinary pissed-off squirrel. This was an evil attack squirrel of death!

Somehow he caught my gloved finger with one of his little hands, and with the force of the throw swung around and with a resounding thump and an amazing impact he landed square on my back and resumed his rather anti-social and extremely distracting activities. He also managed to take my left glove with him!

The situation was not improved. Not improved at all. His attacks were continuing, and now I could not reach him. I was startled to say the least. The combination of the force of the throw, only having one hand (the throttle hand) on the handlebars, and my jerking back unfortunately put a healthy twist through my right hand and into the throttle. A healthy twist on the throttle of a Valkyrie can only have one result. Torque. This is what the Valkyrie is made for, and she is very, very good at it. The engine roared as the front wheel left the pavement. The squirrel screamed in anger. The Valkyrie screamed in ecstasy. I screamed in. well. I just plain screamed.

Now picture a large man on a huge black and chrome cruiser, dressed in jeans, a slightly squirrel torn t-shirt, and only one leather glove roaring at maybe 70mph and rapidly accelerating down a quiet residential street. on one wheel and with a demonic squirrel on his back. The man and the squirrel are both screaming bloody murder.

With the sudden acceleration I was forced to put my other hand back on the handlebars and try to get control of the bike. This was leaving the mutant squirrel to his own devices, but I really did not want to crash into somebody's tree, house, or parked car. Also, I had not yet figured out how to release the throttle. my brain was just simply overloaded. I did manage to mash the back brake, but it had little affect against the massive power of the big cruiser.

About this time the squirrel decided that I was not paying sufficient attention to this very serious battle (maybe he is a Scottish attack squirrel of death), and he came around my neck and got IN my full-face helmet with me. As the faceplate closed partway and he began hissing in my face I am quite sure my screaming changed tone and intensity. It seemed to have little affect on the squirrel however. The rpm's on The Dragon maxed out (I was not concerned about shifting at the moment) and her front end started to drop. Now picture the large man on the huge black and chrome cruiser, dressed in jeans, a very ragged torn t-shirt, and wearing one leather glove, roaring at probably 80mph, still on one wheel, with a large puffy squirrel's tail sticking out his mostly closed full-face helmet. By now the screams are probably getting a little hoarse.

Finally I got the upper hand. I managed to grab his tail again, pulled him out of my helmet, and slung him to the left as hard as I could. This time it worked. sort-of. Spectacularly sort-of, so to speak.

Picture the scene. You are a cop. You and your partner have pulled off on a quiet residential street and parked with your windows down to do some paperwork.

Suddenly a large man on a huge black and chrome cruiser, dressed in jeans, a torn t-shirt flapping in the breeze, and wearing one leather glove, moving at probably 80mph on one wheel, and screaming bloody murder roars by and with all his strength throws a live squirrel grenade directly into your police car.

I heard screams. They weren't mine . . .

I managed to get the big motorcycle under directional control and dropped the front wheel to the ground. I then used maximum braking and skidded to a stop in a cloud of tire smoke at the stop sign at a busy cross street.

I would have returned to fess up (and to get my glove back). I really would have. Really. But for two things. First, the cops did not seem interested or the slightest bit concerned about me at the moment. One of them was on his back in the front yard of the house they had been parked in front of and was rapidly crabbing backwards away from the patrol car. The other was standing in the street and was training a riot shotgun on the police cruiser.

So the cops were not interested in me. They often insist to "let the professionals handle it" anyway. That was one thing. The other? Well, I swear I could see the squirrel, standing in the back window of the patrol car among shredded and flying pieces of foam and upholstery, and shaking his little fist at me. I think he was shooting me the finger. That is one dangerous squirrel.

And now he has a patrol car.

I took a deep breath, turned on my turn-signal, made an easy right turn, and sedately left the neighborhood. As for my easy and slow drive home? Screw it. Faced with a choice of 80mph cars and inattentive drivers, or the evil, demonic, attack squirrel of death . . . I'll take my chances with the freeway. Every time. And I'll buy myself a new pair of gloves.

??? ice.

The two men yell, screaming, wave their arms and wonder what to do now. The dog, cheered on, keeps coming. One of the guys grabs the shotgun and shoots the dog. The shotgun is loaded with #8 buckshot, hardly big enough to stop a Black Lab.

The dog stops for a moment, slightly confused, but continues on. Another shot and this time the dog, still standing, becomes really confused and of course terrified, thinking these two geniuses have gone insane. The dog takes off to find cover, under the brand new Navigator truck.

The men continue to yell as they run. The exhaust pipe on the truck is still hot, so the dog yelps and drops the dynamite under the truck, and takes off after his master. Then—BOOM—the truck is blown to bits and sinks to the bottom of the lake in a very large hole, leaving the two idiots standing there with this "I can't believe this happened" look on their faces. The insurance company says that sinking a vehicle in a lake, and illegal use of explosives is NOT COVERED. He still had yet to make the first of those $560.00 a month payments!!!

And you thought your day was not going well . . .

Subject: True story ...

This is from a radio program, a true report of an incident in Wisconsin:

A guy buys a brand new Lincoln Navigator truck for $42,500 and has $560 monthly payments. He and a friend go duck hunting in winter, and of course all the lakes are frozen. These two guys go out on the lake with their guns, a dog, and of course the new Vehicle.

They drive out onto the lake ice and get ready. Now, they want to make some kind of a natural landing area for the ducks, something for the decoys to float on. In order to make a hole large enough to look like something a wandering duck would fly down and land on, it's going to take a little more effort than an ice hole drill.

So, out of the back of the new Navigator truck comes a stick of dynamite with a short, 40-second fuse. Now these two Rocket Scientists do take into consideration that they want to place the stick of dynamite on the ice at a location far from where they are standing (and the new Navigator truck), because they don't want to take the risk of slipping on the ice when they run from the burning fuse and possibly go up in smoke with the resulting blast.

They light the 40-second fuse and throw the dynamite. Remember a couple of paragraphs back when I mentioned the vehicle, the guns, and the dog??

Let's talk about the dog: A highly trained Black Lab used for RETRIEVING. Especially things thrown by the owner. You guessed it, the dog takes off at a high rate of doggy speed on the ice and captures the stick of dynamite with the burning 40-second fuse about the time it hits the ???

This is Amazing

Bill owns a company that manufactures and installs car wash systems. (Magic Wand Car Wash Systems, just in case you want to buy one.) Bill's company installed a car wash system in Frederick, Md. Now understand that these are complete systems, including the money changer and money taking machines. The problem started when the new owner complained to Bill that he was losing significant amounts of money from his coin machines each week.

He went as far as to accuse Bill's employees of having a key to the boxes and ripping him off. Bill just couldn't believe that his people would do that, so they setup a camera to catch the thief in action. Well, they did catch him on film!

That's a bird sitting on the change slot of the machine.

The bird had to go down into the machine, and back up inside to get to the money!

That's three quarters he has in his beak! Another amazing thing is that it was not just one bird—there were several working together. Once they identified the thieves, they found over $4000 in quarters on the roof of the car wash and more under a nearby tree

And you thought you heard of everything by now!!!

Talking Dog

A guy is driving around and he sees a sign in front of a house:

"Talking Dog For Sale."

He rings the bell and the owner tells him the dog is in the backyard.

The guy goes into the backyard and sees a Labrador Retriever sitting there.

"You talk?" he asks.

"Yep," the Lab replies.

"So, what's your story?"

The Lab looks up and says, "Well, I discovered that I could talk when I was pretty young and I wanted to help the government, so I told the CIA about my gift, and in no time at all they had me jetting from country to country, sitting in rooms with spies and world leaders, because no one figured a dog would be eavesdropping.

I was one of their most valuable spies for eight years running.

But the jetting around really tired me out, and I knew I wasn't getting any younger so I wanted to settle down. I signed up for a job at the airport to do some undercover security work, mostly wandering near suspicious characters and listening in. I uncovered some incredible dealings and was awarded a batch of medals.

I got married, had a mess of puppies, and now I'm just retired."

The guy is amazed. He goes back in and asks the owner what he wants for the dog.

"Ten dollars." The guy says,

"This dog is amazing. Why on earth are you selling him so cheap?"

"Because he's a liar. He didn't do any of that shit."

Subject:>>>>This is pretty cute.>>Two robins were sitting in a tree.>>"I'm really hungry," said the first >one. "Let's fly down and find some lunch.>>They flew down to the ground and >found a nice plot of newly plowed ground and was full of worms. >They ate and ate and ate till they could eat no more. >>"I'm so full, I don't think I can >fly back up into the tree," said the first one. >>"Let's just lay back here and bask >in the warm sun," said the second.>>"O K," said the first. >>So they plopped down, basking in the >sun. No sooner than they had fallen asleep, when a big fat tomcat up >and gobbled them up. >>As the cat sat washing his face >after his meal, he thought . . . >>>>>>>>>> (ready??)>>>>>>>>>>>>>>>>>"I JUST LOVE BASKIN ROBINS.">>>>>>>>

A man absolutely hated his wife's cat and decided to get rid of him one day by driving him 20 blocks from his home and leaving him at the park.

As he was getting home, the cat was walking up the driveway.

The next day he decided to drive the cat 40 blocks away. He put the beast out and headed home.

Driving back up his driveway, there was the cat!

He kept taking the cat further and further and the cat would always beat him home. At last he decided to drive a few miles away, turn right, then left, past the bridge, then right again and another right until he reached what he thought was a safe distance from his home and left the cat there.

Hours later the man calls home to his wife: "Jen, is the cat there?"

"Yes", the wife answers, "why do you ask?"

Frustrated, the man answered, "Put that son of a bitch on the phone, I'm lost and need directions!"

Well, Girl Potato and Boy Potato had eyes for each other, and finally they got married, and had a little sweet potato, which they called Yam.

Of course, they wanted the best for Yam. When it was time, they told her about the facts of life. They warned her about going out and getting half-baked, so she wouldn't get accidentally mashed, and get a bad name for herself like 'Hot Potato,' and end up with a bunch of Tater Tots.

Yam said not to worry, no Spud would get her into the sack and make a rotten potato out of her! But on the other hand she wouldn't stay home and become a Couch Potato either. She would get plenty of exercise so as not to be skinny like her Shoestring cousins.

When she went off to Europe, Mr. and Mrs. Potato told Yam to watch out for the hard-boiled guys from Ireland. And the greasy guys from France called the French Fries. And when she went out west, to watch out for the Indians so she wouldn't get scalloped.

Yam said she would stay on the straight and narrow and wouldn't associate with those high class Yukon Golds, or the ones from the other side of the tracks who advertise their trade on all the trucks that say 'Frito Lay.'

Mr. and Mrs. Potato sent Yam to Idaho P.U. (that's Potato University) so that when she graduated she'd really be in the Chips. But in spite of all they did for her, one-day Yam came home and announced she was going to marry Tom Brokaw.

Tom Brokaw! . . . Mr. and Mrs. Potato were very upset. They told Yam she couldn't possibly marry Tom Brokaw because he's just . . . Are you ready for this?

Are you sure?

OK! Here it is!

. . .

A COMMON TATER!!>>

Bob . . .

The Grasshopper and the Ant

CLASSIC VERSION:

Once upon a time the ant worked hard in the withering heat all summer long, building his house and laying up supplies for the winter. The grasshopper thought "What a fool and he laughed and danced and played the summer away. Come winter, the ant was warm and well fed. The grasshopper had no food or shelter so he died out in the cold.

MORAL OF THE STORY: Be responsible for yourself!

MODERN VERSION:

The ant works hard in the withering heat all summer long, building his house and laying up supplies for the winter. The grasshopper thinks he's a fool and laughs and dances and plays the summer away.

Come winter, the shivering grasshopper calls a press conference and demands to know why the ant should be allowed to be warm and well fed while others are cold and starving. CBS, NBC, and ABC show up to provide pictures of the shivering grasshopper next to a video of the ant in his comfortable home with a table filled with food.

America is stunned by the sharp contrast. How can this be, that in a country of such wealth, this poor grasshopper is allowed to suffer so?

Kermit the Frog appears on Oprah with the grasshopper, and everybody cries when they sing "It's Not Easy Being Green."

Jesse Jackson stages a demonstration in front of the ant's house where the news stations film the group singing "We shall overcome". Jesse then has the group kneel down to pray to God for the grasshopper's sake.

Al Gore exclaims in an interview with Peter Jennings that the ant has gotten rich off the back of the grasshopper, and calls for an immediate tax hike on the ant to make him pay his "fair share."

Finally, the EEOC drafts the "Economic Equity and Anti-Grasshopper Act," retroactive to the beginning of the summer.

The ant is fined for failing to hire a proportionate number of green bugs and, having nothing left to pay his retroactive taxes, his home is confiscated by the government.

Hillary gets her old law firm to represent the grasshopper in a defamation suit against the ant, and the case is tried before a panel of federal judges that Bill appointed from a list of single-parent welfare recipients.

Thus, the ant loses the case.

The story ends as we see the grasshopper finishing up the last bits of the ant's food while the government house he is in, which just happens to be the ant's old house, crumbles around him because he doesn't maintain it.

The ant has disappeared in the snow.

The grasshopper is found dead in a drug related incident and the house, now abandoned, is taken over by a gang of spiders who terrorize the once peaceful neighborhood.

MORAL OF THE STORY: Vote Republican

Age and Treachery An oldie but goodie.

The Stud Rooster

A farmer goes out one day and buys a brand new stud rooster for his chicken coop.

The new rooster struts over to the old rooster and says, "OK old fart, time for you to retire."

The old rooster replies, "Come on, surely you cannot handle ALL of these chickens. Look what it has done to me. Can't you just let me have the two old hens over in the corner?"

The young rooster says, "Beat it: You are washed up and I am taking over."

The old rooster says, "I tell you what, young stud. I will race you around the farmhouse. Whoever wins gets the exclusive domain over the entire chicken coop."

The young rooster laughs. "You know you don't stand a chance old man.

So, just to be fair I will give you a head start."

The old rooster takes off running. About 15 seconds later the young rooster takes off running after him. They round the front porch of the farmhouse and the young rooster has closed the gap. He is already about 5 inches behind the old rooster and gaining fast.

The farmer, meanwhile, is sitting in his usual spot on the front porch when he sees the roosters running by. He grabs his shotgun and—BOOM—He blows the young rooster to bits.

The farmer sadly shakes his head and says, "Dammit . . . third gay rooster I bought this month."

Why I am Tired . . .

For a couple years I've been blaming it on lack of sleep, not enough sunshine, too much pressure from my job, earwax buildup, poor blood or anything else I could think of. But now I found out the real reason: I'm tired because I'm overworked.

Here's why:

The population of this country is 273 million. 140 million are retired. That leaves 133 million to do the work.

There are 85 million in school, which leaves 48 million to do the work. Of this, there are 29 million employed by the federal government, leaving 19 million to do the work.

2.8 million are in the armed forces, preoccupied with killing the Taliban. Which leaves 16.2 million to do the work.

Take from the total the 14,800,000 people who work for state and city governments. And that leaves 1.4 million to do the work.

At any given time there are 188,000 people in hospitals, leaving 1,212,000 to do the work.

Now, there are 1,211,998 people in prisons. That leaves just two people to do the work.

You and me.

And there you are sitting on your ass, at your computer, reading jokes.

Nice, real nice . . .

Zebediah was in the fertilized-egg business. He had several hundred young layers, called pullets, and eight or ten roosters, whose job was to fertilize the eggs. Zeb kept records, and any rooster that didn't perform well went into the soup pot and was replaced. That took an awful lot of Zeb's times, so Zeb got a set of tiny bells and attached them to his roosters.

Each bell had a different tone so that Zeb could tell, from a distance, which rooster was performing. Now he could sit on the porch and fill out an efficiency report simply by listening to the bells.

Zeb's favorite rooster was old Brewster, a very fine specimen. But on this particular morning, Zeb noticed that Brewster's bell had not rung at all! Zeb went to investigate. The other roosters were chasing pullets, bells a-ringing! The pullets, hearing the roosters coming, would run for cover.

BUT, to Zeb's amazement, Brewster had his bell in his beak, so it couldn't ring. He'd sneak up on a pullet, do his job, and walk on to the next one.

Zeb was so proud of Brewster that he entered him in the County Fair. Brewster was an overnight sensation. The judges not only awarded him The No Bell Piece Prize, but also the Pullet Surprise.

Subject: Little miss muffets revenge

A father watched his daughter playing in the garden. He smiled as he reflected on how sweet and innocent his little girl was. Suddenly she just stopped and stared at the ground. He went over to her and noticed she was looking at two spiders mating.

"Daddy, what are those two spiders doing?" she asked.

"They're mating," her father replied.

"What do you call the spider on top, Daddy?" she asked.

"That's a Daddy Longlegs." Her father answered.

"So, the other one is a Mommy Longlegs?" the little girl asked.

"No," her father replied. "Both of them are Daddy Longlegs."

The little girl thought for a moment, then took her foot and stomped them flat. "Well, we're not having any of that shit in our garden.

A wealthy old lady decides to go on a photo safari in Africa, taking her faithful pet poodle along for company. One day the poodle starts chasing butterflies and before long he discovers that he is lost. Wandering about, he notices a leopard heading rapidly in his direction with the obvious intention of having lunch. The poodle thinks, "Uh-oh, I'm in deep trouble now!"

Noticing some bones on the ground close by, he immediately settles down to chew on the bones with his back to the approaching cat. Just as the leopard is about to leap, the poodle exclaims loudly, "Boy, that was one delicious leopard. I wonder if there are any more around here."

Hearing this, the leopard halts his attack in mid-stride, a look of terror comes over him, and he slinks away into the trees.

"Whew," says the leopard. "That was close. That poodle nearly had me."

Meanwhile, a monkey who had been watching the whole scene from a nearby tree, figures he can put this knowledge to good use and trade it for protection from the leopard so, off he goes.

But the poodle sees him heading after the leopard with great speed, and figures that something must be up.

The monkey soon catches up with the leopard, spills the beans and strikes a deal for himself with the leopard. The leopard is furious at being made a fool of and says, "Here monkey, hop on my back and see what's going to happen to that conniving canine."

Now the poodle sees the leopard coming with the monkey on his back and thinks, "What am I going to do now?" Instead of running, the dog sits down with his back to his attackers, pretending he hasn't seen them yet and, just when they get close enough to hear, the poodle says . . .

"Where's that damn monkey? I sent him off half an hour ago to bring me another leopard!"

MORAL: SOMETIMES BULLSH*T AND BRILLIANCE ARE THE SAME

Clear Day

Never bring plants into the house.

Garden Grass Snakes (also known as Garter Snakes . . . Thamnophissirtalis) can be dangerous . . . Yes, grass snakes, not rattlesnakes.

Here's why . . .

A couple in Sweetwater, Texas, had a lot of potted plants. During a recent cold spell, the wife was bringing a lot of them indoors to protect them from a possible freeze.

It turned out that a little green garden grass snake was hidden in one of the plants and when it had warmed up, it slithered out and the wife saw it go under the sofa.

She let out a very loud scream.

The husband (who was taking a shower) ran out into the living room naked to see what the problem was. She told him there was a snake under the sofa. He got down on the floor on his hands and knees to look for it. About that time the family dog came and cold-nose him on the behind. He thought the snake had bitten him, so he screamed and fell over on the floor.

His wife thought he had a heart attack, so she covered him up, told him to lie still and called an ambulance.

The attendants rushed in, wouldn't listen to his protests and loaded him on the stretcher and started carrying him out.

About that time the snake came out from under the sofa and the Emergency Medical Technician saw it and dropped his end of the stretcher.

That's when the man broke his leg and why he is still in the hospital.

The wife still had the problem of the snake in the house, so she called on a neighbor man. He volunteered to capture the snake. He armed himself with a rolled-up newspaper and began poking under the couch. Soon he decided it was gone and told the woman, who sat down on the sofa in relief.

But while relaxing, her hand dangled in between the cushions, where she felt the snake wriggling around. She screamed and fainted, the snake rushed back under the sofa.

The neighbor man, seeing her lying there passed out, tried to use CPR to revive her. The neighbor's wife, who had just returned from shopping at the grocery store, saw her husband's mouth on the woman's mouth and slammed her husband in the back of the head with a bag of canned goods, knocking him out and cutting his scalp to a point where it needed stitches.

The noise woke the woman from her dead faint and she saw her neighbor lying on the floor with his wife bending over him, so she assumed that he had been bitten by the snake. She went to the kitchen and got a small bottle of whiskey, and began pouring it down the man's throat.

By now the police had arrived.

The saw the unconscious man, smelled the whiskey, and assumed that a drunken fight had occurred. They were about to arrest them all, when the women tried to explain how it all happened over a little green snake.

The police called an ambulance, which took away the neighbor and his sobbing wife.

The little snake again crawled out from under the sofa.

One of the policemen drew his gun and fired at it.

He missed the snake and hit the leg of the end table. The table fell over and the lamp on it shattered and as the bulb broke it started a fire in the drapes.

The other policeman tried to beat out the flames, and fell through the window into the yard on top of the family dog who, startled, jumped out and raced into the street, where an oncoming car swerved to avoid it and smashed into the parked police car.

Meanwhile, burning drapes, were seen by the neighbors who called the fire department.

The firemen had started raising the fire truck ladder when they were halfway down the street.

The rising ladder tore out the overhead wires and put out the electricity and disconnected the telephones in a ten-square city block area (but they did get the house fire out).

Time passed. Both men were discharged from the hospital, the house was torn down and the snake crawled back into the garden.

DON'T WORRY

There are only two things to worry about. Either you are well or you are sick. If you are well, then there is nothing to worry about. But if you are sick, there are two things to worry about. Either you get well, or you die. If you get well there is nothing to worry about. If you die there are only two things to worry about. Either you go to Heaven or Hell. If you go to Heaven, there is nothing to worry about, but if you go to Hell, you'll be so dam busy shaking hands with friends, you won't have time to worry.

MESSAGE FROM THE BEYOND

An Illinois man left the snow-filled streets of Chicago for a vacation in Florida. His wife was on a business trip and was planning to meet him there next week. When he reached his hotel, he decided to send his wife a quick E-Mail. Unable to find the scrap of paper on which he had written her E-Mail address, he did his best to type it in from memory. Unfortunately he missed one letter, and his note was directed instead to an elderly preacher's wife, whose husband had passed away only the day before. When the grieving widow checked her E-Mail, she took one look at the monitor, let out a piercing scream, and fell to the floor in a dead faint. At the sound, her family rushed into the room and saw the following note on the screen.

> Dearest Wife,
>
> Just got checked in. Everything prepared for your arrival here tomorrow.
>
> P.S. Sure is hot down here!!!!

A little boy went to church with his grandparents. He watched as they passed the communion plate. When it came to him, he looked at the man and said "No thanks I'm going to eat at Grandmas."

WATCH WHAT YOU ASK FOR

The pastor couldn't get the congregation to put enough money in the collection basket. He had a large gold pocket watch and he came up with an idea. He told the ushers to wait until he nodded his head to take up the collection. That Sunday after his sermon he took out the watch and began to swing it slowly as in a quiet voice he talked to the people. He nodded his head and the ushers took up the collection. He had more money than he had ever gotten. He decided to do this again next Sunday. As he swung the watch it hit the top of the pulpit and fell apart, the pastor looked at his watch and said OH CRAP, it took all week to clean up the church.

WATCHA YOU MOUTH

This little old Italian women went to church every day to pray the rosary. This morning she was kneeling and praying her rosary. Up in the balcony were 2 big burley construction workers. The one turned to the other and said, watch me have some fun. He said in a loud voice This is God talking", the lady went on praying. The man said in a louder voice "This is God talking", the lady went on praying. The man looked at his companion and said watch this I'll get her this time. He said in a loud booming voice "THIS IS GOOD TALKING". The little old lady said shutup you mouth, I'm talking to your mother.

WHERE IT COUNTS

What is the difference in praying in church or praying at the casinos? At the casinos you really meant it

COMPOUND INTEREST

There were 3 men, one English, one Irish, and one Jewish. The were all attending a wake for their friend Mike. All 3 were standing by his casket. The Irish man said, poor Mike I am going to miss him a lot. I have to do something for him, he was always so good to me, with that he took out a $50.00, patted Mike and said this is something for the other side, and he left. The English man said I think I can do better than that for poor Mike, so he took the $50.00 and laid a $100.00 bill by Mike, patted his hand and left. The Jewish man said I think I can do better than that for poor Mike, he was always so good. With this said he took the $100.00 bill and put it in his pocket, took a check and wrote it for $1000.00, put it in the casket, patted Mike's hand and left.

IT HAPPENED IN CHURCH

This man belonged to a group of men that met every Monday morning for coffee. This morning he walked in and they all said, what happened to you, your face is all beat up. The man said I got this in church yesterday. All the men said In church what did you do? Well the man said, we all stood up to sing and I noticed the lady in front of me, her dress was stuck in her crack. Well I was sure she didn't want that so I reached up and pulled it out of the crack. Well by the looks she gave me, I knew I had done something she didn't like, so the next time we stood up to sing I TOOK THE SIDE OF MY HAND AND DROVE IT BACK IN THERE.

I WARRNED YOU

A young priest was worried about forgetting his sermon when he got up in the pulpit. The older priest hopping to help him said. Just remember the finish. I repeat the finish and the rest comes back to me. The young priest climbed in to the pulpit and as he feared he forgot what his sermon was. He leaned over and repeated I'm coming down, nothing so he repeated I'm coming down, with this he fell off the pulpit and on top of a lady sitting below. He said I'm very sorry. She said that's alright, you gave me enough warning.

DON'T SHOW OFF

Jesus, Moses and an Old man were playing golf. Mosos hit the ball and it sailed over the water hazard and landed in the sand trap. It took him 2 times to hit out of the sand and onto the green. Jesus hit his ball and it sailed over the water hazard and landed on the edge of the sand trap. It took 1 stroke to put it on the green and close to the hole. The old man hit his ball and it fell in the water hazard. A big fish came by and scoped the ball up and into it's mouth. Along came a Eagle and dove into the water and picked up the fish. It then flew over the sand trap and dropped the fish on the green. It fell near the hole and the ball dropped out of it's mouth and into the hole. Jesus said watch it dad if you keep showing off we're going to send you home.

WHY DIDN'T YOU SAY SO

At a gathering of church Minister's, the Presbyterian Minister came up to the food table and said, I'll take a cup of that punch. The lady serving whispered the punch is Spiked reverend. He said Oh well, I'll take one cup anyway. I don't drink but one small cup. The Methodist Minister came to the table and said I'll take a cup of punch. The lady whispered the punch is Spiked. The Methodist Minister said, it's just a small cup so I'll take one anyway. The Baptist Minister came to the table and said he would take a cup of punch. The lady whispered to him but Reverend the punch is Spiked. The Baptist Minister shouted what are you saying? I would rather commit adultery than drink a cup of Spiked Punch. The other two Ministers came back to the table and dumped their punch back into the punch bowl, saying why didn't you tell us we had a choice.

REASON TO CELEBRATE

Two blondes came into a bar and ordered 2 beers. When the beers arrived the blondes toasted each other and did a high five and drank the beer. They ordered another and did the same thing. The bartender curious asked if they were celebrating something. They said Oh Yes we just finished putting a puzzle together in 90 days and the box said 2-4 years.

IF I COULD DO IT

A pretty blonde was in her convertible riding along the road. Her hair was flying in the wind and she was having a good time. She happened to look out into the field she was passing and saw this blonde in a sail boat in the middle of the field, shouting save me. She pulled her car over and got out and went to the edge of the field. She shouted to the blonde in the sail boat, What are you doing? you are the kind that give all us blondes a bad name. If could swim I would swim out there and beat you up.

CLEAN UP THE PLACE

I had 12 bottles of whiskey in my cellar, and my wife told me to empty the contents of each bottle down the sink or else. So I proceeded with the unpleasant task. I withdrew the cork from the first bottle and poured the contents down the sink except for one glass, which I drank.

I took the cork from the second bottle and did likewise, except I drank one glass. I then took the cork from the third bottle and poured it down the sink except for one glass, which I drank. I pulled the cork from the fourth bottle and poured the bottle down the glass which I drank. I pulled the bottle from the cork of the next and drank one sink out of it and threw the rest down the glass. I pulled the sink out of the next glass bottled the drink and drank the pour. When I had everything emptied I steadied the house with one hand the bottles, corks, glasses and sinks with the other which were twenty-nine and as the house came by I counted them again and finally had all the houses with bottles and corks, glasses, and sinks counted except one house and one bottle which I drank.

DON'T SCREW AROUND

A lady came to her Doctor and wanted a face lift. He told her if she got a regular face lift she would have to come back every 3 or 4 years for another to keep it looking like she wanted it to. He told her there was an alternative to this called a screw insert. With this they attached a screw to the top of your head and it could be tightened up anytime the face needed tightening. She elected to have the screw. After the operation the lady came back in a few weeks complaining of bags under her eyes. The doctor looked closely at her face under a magnifying glass and told her they were not bags but her Boobs and if you don't leave that screw alone you are going to have a beard on your face.

YOU HAVE TO KNOW WHERE TO GO

An attractive blonde lady got on the airplane and sat in the first class section. The attendant told her she did not have a first class seat and she would have to move to back. The lady told her I'm blonde and beautiful and I am not moving to the back of plane. The attendant told the Engineer and he went to the lady and asked her to move. She said I'm blonde and beautiful and I am not going to move to the back of the plane. The Captain came down the isle after hearing the story he leaned over the blonde and whispered into her ear. The blonde got and went to the back of the plane. The attendant asked him how he did get her to move to the back of the plane. He said I just told her the front of the plane was going to Chicago and since she was going to New York she would have to move to the back of the plane because the back of the plane was going to New York.

DON'T GET WET

A pretty blonde was going down the road in her convertible, her hair was blowing and she was singing. She looked over to right and she was a pretty Blonde Girl in the middle if a corn field standing by a sailboat. She was hollering for someone to save her before she drowned. The Blonde in the car stopped and got out of her car and walked to the edge of the field. She said you dumb blonde quit you shouting, it's people like you that gives us blondes a bad name, and if I could swim if would swim out there and give you a punch in the nose.

THEY AREN'T ALL WOMEN

A Blonde young man walked into a lumber yard and said I need some 4X2's. The man waiting on him said you mean 2X4's. The blonde man stands for a minute and walks out of the store. He came back and said Yes, I need 2X4's. the clerk said how many? The man stands for a minute and then walks out of the store. He returned and said 20. The clerk asked how long? The man leaves the store and returns in a little while. Oh we need them for a LONG time, were building a house.

GOTCHA

There was three women working in an office. One was a brunette, one a redhead and one a blonde. Their boss was a women she had the habit of leaving early every afternoon. The other 3 women went on working. One day one said you know she leaves early everyday and we still go one working. She never comes back, so why don't we leave right after she does? They decided to do this, the Blonde goes home thinking she would rest for awhile. She quietly opens her bedroom door and finds her husband and her boss in bed together. She quietly closes the door and leaves the house. The next day the other 2 girls thought this was a good idea and the 3 of them might as well do it again. The blonde says Oh no! I can't do this again, I almost got caught.

So THAT'S WHAT THEY GAVE ME

Two men were walking their dogs down the street when one said I'm thirsty lets go into the bar. The second man said they won't let us in there with our dogs. The first man said sure they will just watch me and do exactly like I do. The first man went up to the big bouncer and started to enter, the bouncer said you can't go in there with that German Shepherd dog. The man said but he is my seeing eye dog. The bouncer said well that's different go ahead in. The second man approached the bouncer and started into the bar. The bouncer stopped him and said you cant go in there with that dog. The second man said but mister I'm blind and this is my seeing eye dog. The bouncer said that's a Chiwawa dog who ever heard of a Chiwawa as a seeing eye dog, the man stopped and said so that is what they gave me. The bouncer let him in.

How To LIVE oN $15.00 DoLLARS A WEEK

Whiskey and Beer	$8.80
Wife's beer	1.65
Meat and Groceries	On Credit
Rent Pay	next week
Mid-week whiskey	2.50
Movies	.60
Coal	Borrow from neighbor
Life Insurance "Wifes"	.50
Hot tips on horses	.50
Tobacco	.45
Poker game	1.65
	————
TOTAL	$16.65

This means going into dept.

. . . SO CUT OUT THE
WIFE'S WHISKEY

IF WE oNLY KNEW

An old gentleman approached an elderly lady in a nursing home and said, I would like to make love to you. The lady said alright, come to my room tonight. The old man came to her room and they proceed to make love. When they were finished he said, If I knew you were a virgin I would have been easier on you. She said If I knew you could really do it, I would have taken off my panty hose.

How IT IS

A Frenchman drinks his native wine. A German drinks his beer. An Englishman drinks his "Ale" or "Alf" because it brings good cheer. The Scotchman drinks his whiskey straight because it brings on dizziness. An American has no choice at all he drinks the whole dam business.

A salesman was driving down this country road, by this one farm he passed, they had a rooster. The rooster had on bib overalls. Every day he saw this rooster and it finally got the best of curious nature, so he drove up and knocked on the door. The farmer answered and the salesman said that rooster in bib overalls he looks funny I just had to stop and ask about him. The farmers wife said that rooster got to close to a fire and got his feathers burned so he was ashamed and wouldn't chase the hens, so she made him the bib overalls now he chases the hens all over the yard, and if you think he looks funny now you should see him try to hold a hen with one foot while trying to get those bib overalls down with the other.

MA BROWNS HOUSE

A salesman was driving down interstate 70, when he saw this big billboard on the side of the road. It said MA BROWNS WHORE HOUSE 5 MILES. He thought that sure funny, I've never saw anything like that on a highway. A few miles later he again saw a big sign saying MA BROWNS WHORE HOUSE 2 MILES, his curiosity got him going so when he saw a smaller sigh with an arrow pointing to a side road and the sign saying MA BROWNS 1 MILE he pulled off and said to himself I just have to see this. So he drove up this real rutty road and at the end of it he saw this house with the porch sagging the windows all black and the house in need of painting. He got out of his car and walked to the door. A real old lady in a dirty print dress and long un combed hair answered. He said in this Ma Browns? She said yes do you want to come in? He said yes so she said it will cost you $10.00. He paid and went in, she said, see that door? You just go through there. When he went through the door he found himself on the outside of house. As he turned to reenter the door he saw above it a sign that read YOU HAVE JUST BEEN SCREWED BY MA BROWN.

RoPING

Two young people, both virgins, got married. while driving to their honeymoon they passed two cows doing it in the field, she asked honey what are they doing? He replied their roping. They went on and came by two horses doing it in the field. She asked honey what are they doing? He replied they are roping. They got to where they were to stay and that evening they undressed and started to get aquatinted with each others body. she felt him down below and asked what is this? He replied that is my rope. she felt a little further down and asked honey what is this called? He said that is my knots for my rope. After that they had sex and he asked her how she liked it. She replied on honey it was good but I think you should untie those knots and give me a little more rope.

COMPUTERS

Men think computers should be referred to as females, just like ships because; 1. No one but the Creator understands their internal logic. 2. The language they use to communicate with other computers is incomprehensible to everyone else. 3. The message "Bad Command or file name" is about as informative as "if you don't know why I'm mad at you, I'm certainly not going to tell you." 4. Your smallest mistakes are stored in long term memory for later retrieval. 5. As soon as you make a commitment to one, you find yourself spending half your paycheck on accessories for it.

Women think computers should be referred to as male. Here's why. 1. They have a lot of data, but they are still clueless. 2. They are suppose to help you solve problems, but half of the time, they ARE the problem. 3. As soon as you commit to one, you realize if you has waited a little longer, you could have obtained a better model. 4. In order to get their attention, you have to turn them on. 5. A big power surge will knock them out for the rest of the night.

WRONG NUMBER

Two rednecks went to a gas station that was holding a chance to win free sex when you filled your tank. They pumped their gas and went to pay the attendant. "I'm thinking of a number between one and ten", he said. "If you guess right, you win free sex. "Okay", agreed one of the rednecks, "I guess seven". "Sorry I was thinking of eight." replied the attendant. The next week they tried again. When they went to pay, the attendant told them to pick a number, "Two" said the second redneck. "Sorry it's three this time". "Come back and try again". As they walked out to their car one redneck said to the other. "I think this contest is rigged." "No way," said his buddy, "My wife won twice last week.

HOME COMING

A bunch of Union Troups were returning home after the war. The men were tired cold and hungry. The leader decided he would try to find shelter for his men. He stopped at the first house and asked can you take some of my men for the night, they are tired and hungry. The people said they could take two. He said Jones and Green you stay here. He went to the next house and asked again. They said they could take one. So he Said Peters you stay here. He went and the next place he stopped happen to be a house of ilrepute. He asked the same question. the madam said we can't take them all, how many are there? Well the leader said we have 87 without Peters. The madam said In that case we'll take them all.

SADLEY MISSED

During WW2, two sailors were marooned on a island. They waited several days and finally decided they weren't going to be rescued. They decided to explore the island. On the other side of the island they found a WAC. the 3 of them decided one week she would be with one of the Silors and the next with the other. They were all 3 happy with the arrangement until one day the WAC died. The first week she died was really hard for the sailors. The second week was harder still. The 3rd week was devastating. The 4th week they finally buried her.

GOVERNMENT

DEFINITION OF POLITICS SON: Dad I have to do a special report for school. can I ask you a question? DAD: Sure son, what's the question? Son: What is politics? DAD: Well, lets take our family for example. I am the wage earner, let's call me management. Your mother is the administrator of the money, so we'll call her government. We take care of your needs so let's call you the people. We'll call the maid the working class, and your little brother the future. Do you understand?

Son: I'm not really sure. Dad, I'll have to think about it. That night, awakened by his baby brother's crying, the boy went to see what was wrong. Discovering that the baby had seriously soiled his diaper, the son went to his parents room and found his mother asleep. He then went to the maids room where, peeking through the key hole, he saw his father in bed with the maid. the boy's knocking went totally unheard by his father and the maid. So the boy returned to his room and went back to sleep. The next morning . . . SON: Now I think I understand politics. DAD: That's great son. Explain it to me in your own words. SON Well Dad, while management is screwing the working class, the government is sound asleep, the people are being completely ignored, and the future is full of shit.

ITS A DOG'S WORLD

A UNION MAN'S DOG Four workers were discussing how smart their dogs were. The first was an engineer who said his dog could perform drafting functions. His dog was named T-square, and he told him to get some paper and draw a square, a circle and a triangle, which the dog did with no problem. The accountant said that he thought his dog was better. His dog was named Slide Rule. He told him to fetch a dozen cookies, bring them back, and divide them into piles of three, which he easily accomplished. The chemist said that was pretty good but his dog was even better. His dog Measure, was told to get a quart of milk and pour seven ounces into a ten ounce glass. The dog did this with no problem. All three men agreed that this was very good and that their dogs were equally smart. They all turned to the union member and said, "What can your dog do?" His dog, Coffee Break, went over and ate the cookies, drank the mild, shit on the paper, screwed the other three dogs, and claimed he hurt his back while doing so, filed a grievance for unsafe working conditions, applied for Workers Compensation, and left for home on sick leave!

POSTCARD FROM ONE REDNECK TO ANOTHER

Dear cletus—I'm writing this real slow cause I know you can't read very fast. We don't live where we did when you left. We read in the paper that most accidents happen within ten mile of home so we moved.

I won't be able to send you our new address cause the family that lived here took the house numbers with them so they wouldn't have to change their address.

This place has a washing machine. The first day mama put four shirts in, pulled the chain and we ain't seen them since.

It only rained here twice this week. Three days the first time and five days the second.

I know it's cold where you are so we're sending you a coat. Mama said it would be to heave to send in the mail with the buttons on it, so we cut 'em off and put 'em in the pockets.

We got a letter from the funeral home. They said if we don't make the last payment on grandma's funeral up she comes.

My sister had a baby this morning. I ain't heard whether it's a boy or a girl so I don't know if I'm an uncle or an aunt.

Uncle John fell in the big whiskey vat, when they tried to pull him out, he fought them off, so he drowned, We cremated him and he burned for three days.

Three of my friends went off the bridge in a pick-up truck. One was driving, the other two was in back. The driver got out cause he rolled down the window and swam to safety. The other two drowned, they couldn't get the tail gate down.

MORE NEXT TIME, NUTHIN MUCH HAPPIN' AROUND HERE.

A man was driving down the interstate when his cellular phone rang. He answered it and it was his wife. She said honey please be careful, I just heard on the radio that a car was driving the wrong way on the interstate. He said, what do you mean 1 car? There are hundreds.

LABOR OF LOVE

A couple came to the hospital to have their baby. The Doctor said to them, we have a new machine I would like to try on you, if you agree. This machine hooks up to the father and when turned on it takes 10% of the mothers pain in delivery and gives it to the father. This way it is easier for the mother. They both said yes we can do that. So when the mother started into delivery they hooked the machine to the father. The mother was feeling a little better and the father said he felt nothing. The Doctor said to the father you are taking you are taking this real well how going 50%? The man said O.K. and they increased the machine. The mother was feeling real good about this and her pain was just half of what it was. The father said he was really feeling good and not hurting at all. The Doctor said in that case they could increase the machine to 100%, the father agreed and the mother jelt just swell, no pain at all. The went ahead and delivered the baby and the father was really proud of what he had done and told the doctor he had felt no pain and his wife had no pain either. After seeing the baby and kissing his wife he went home. On the porch he found the Postman laying dead.

COMPLIMENTS

A man came into a bar and ordered a bear. the bartender gave him his beer and a small dish of peanuts. The man drank his beer and then he heard a voice that said "I LIKE YOUR TIE!" The man looked around and the only one he saw was the bartender at the other end of the bar. He again took a drink of beer and some peanuts and then he heard this voice say "I LIKE THE WAY YOU HAVE YOUR HAIR STYLED!" he again looked around and saw no one but the bartender. He said to him, "WHAT'SGOING ON I KEEP HEARING THESE COMPLIMENTS AND THERE IS NO ONE HERE BUT YOU AND ME!" The bartender said on well it's the peanuts. The man said "The peanuts!" The bartender said yes, they are complementary peanuts.

CALL ME BOB

A grasshopper hopped into the bar and the bartender said hi! I'm glad to see you. We have a drink named after you. Oh yes said the grasshopper I never head of a drink named "BOB".

MOM WAS HUNGRY

A little preschooler came to school on day and he was so happy. The teacher told him. "You are so happy today would you like to tell me what you are so happy about today? The little boy said yes we are going to have a little sister or brother. That night when he came home his mother decided to let him feel the new baby. She put his hand on her tummy and let him feel the baby moving. The next day the little boy again came to school but this day he was really sad. The teacher said you were so happy yesterday, has something happened to your little baby sister or brother? The little boy cried out and said yes, I think my mother ate it.

HIDDEN TALENT

A man came into a bar and ordered a drink of Crown Royal. He drank it down and ordered another one. After the second one the bartender said I sorry but that is an expensive drink and I need you to pay for the ones you had before I sell you anymore. The man said I have a frog her that is really talented. He pulled the frog from his pocket and the frog hopped over to the piano and started playing. The bartender was real impressed so he gave the man another drink. AS the man ordered another he was told the bartender said I'm empressed with your frog would you sell him to me for another drink. The man said if I showed you my bird would you give me more drinks? I would have to see him first. So the man pulled out the bird and as the frog played the bird sang songs of the 50's. The bartender was impressed and offered to buy them both. After the deal someone told the man didn't he sell the pair pretty cheap. The man said no because the frog was a ventriloquist.

A man had a bad leg and after doctoring it for a long time. The doctor told him there wasn't much more he could do. The leg had to come off. The decision was made to take it off. The man went into the hospital and was prepped for the operation. The time came to go to surgery and his regular doctor had a heart attack. They came and told the man that he had several choices. One to have another doctor operate. two go home and wait for his doctor to get better, in this case he would have to pay all the bill made up to this time as the insurance co. would not pay twice for an operations that had not been done. The man talked it over with his wife and decided to go ahead. The surgeon came in and the instructions were not clear to him. So he ended up taking off the good leg. After several days the man's regular doctor came back and found the mistake. He said well we have to still take off the bad leg. After it was all over the man was really up set and decided to sue the Dr. He got a lawyer and told him the whole case. the lawyer said he could not take the case. When asked why he told the man he didn't have a leg to stand on.

FROM THE MOUTH OF BIRDS

This lady went to a pet shop and wanted to buy a Parrott. There was one on aperch in the corner. The lady said this is a pretty bird. The store owner said I don't think you would want this one. the lady asked why not. He said theis bird has been in a house of ill repute. The lady listened to the parrott and didn't see anything wrong with him. So she took him home and left the cover over him for awhile. Her 2 daughters came home and lifted the cover and the bird said. Look at these 2 foxey chicks. The girls went on and the husband came home and took the cover off the parrott and he said hi! Mike!

THIS IS A GAS

A man is in the hospital sitting on his bed. He leans to the left and a nurse puts a pillow under him. He leans to the right and another nurse puts a pillow under him. His friend come to see him and asks how he like the hospital. He says it's o.k. but they won't let you pass a fart.

COP ON THE BEAT

In this nursing home a lady in a wheelchair come racing down the hall and a man steps out of his room and says. You can't race down the halls like that I'll have to give you a warning. He takes out a gum wrapper and writes her a warning. The next morning she again goes racing down the hall in her wheelchair. The same man steps out of his room and says I told you yesterday you could not race in the halls, I'm going to write you a ticket. He takes a Kleenex and writes her a ticket. The next morning the same thing this time when the man comes out of his room he is naked and has an errection. The lady looks at him and says Oh no you mean this time I have to take a breath-a-liser?

ONE FOR THE ROAD

This old man was laying in his bed. He had been crabby old man all his life. He was on his bed. He smelled Chocolate Chip Cookies and this was his favorite cookie. He said I am going to have a cookie if it's the last thing I do before I die. he pulled himself up and dropped to the floor. He crawled on the floor through the rooms to get to the kitchen. He reached the kitchen and reached up to the table where the cookies were. His wife hit his hand with a big spoon. He said what did you do that for? I just want a cookie. She said, get out of the cookies they are for the funeral.

GOOD FOR THE GOOSE

A young lady came to live with her grandmother. She was dressing to go out on a date one night. She put on a see through blouse. Her grandmother said you can't wear that out in public. The lady said to her grandmother "Oh grams I'm just showing off my tulips". The next day the young lady came home from work and her grandmother was sitting on the front porch with her see through blouse on. She said "Oh grams you can't sit out her in that. Grams replied "Oh that's alright I'm just showing off my hanging plants".

MIS INTURPETATION

A lady came into a employment office and said I need a job, I need a job any kind of job I'll take, I just need a job. The person at the desk said let me see your resume. She looked at the resume and said Oh you are over qualified for anything we have. The lady said I'll take anything. The person at the desk said well all we have is an assembly line at a Tikle Me Elmo plant. The lady said I'll take it. After the first day the plant called the employment office and said you have to get this person out of her. She has the line shut down and the Elmo's are piled up everywhere. They came over to see what was the problem. The lady was sitting there sewing two little furry round balls on each Elmo. They said "Oh you did not understand, we told you to do two test tickles".

FAST THINKING

It was the first day of school and the teacher of the first grade told the students, you are now in first grade and you are growing up, so there will be no more baby talk, I want you to learn to talk like a young lady and gentleman. She started by asking the question, what did you do this summer? She asked a little girl and she answered my mommie and daddy went of twip. The teacher said I told you no more baby talk. She then asked a little boy he said my brover and me the teacher said I said no more baby talk. The next little boy sat in deep thought. The teacher asked what he did and he slowly said I read a book. The teacher said that's fine what book. He thought some more and finally said Winney the Shit.

There were several Nuns being driven in a car when they had a flat tire. The driver said Suns A Bitch. The Nuns said you would not say that, you should say Lord Have Mercy. The driver put the spare tire on the car and with that, the tire blew. The driver says Lord Have Mercy, the Nuns said Suns A bitch.

The Communicator And The Receiver Must Agree on Terms

An English school teacher was looking for rooms in Switzerland. She called upon the local schoolmaster to help her find an apartment that would be suitable. Such rooms were found, and she returned to London for her belongings. She remembered that she had not noticed a bathroom, or as she called it "a water closet." She wrote to the schoolmaster and asked if there was a "W.C." in or near the apartment.

The schoolmaster, not knowing the English expression, was puzzled by the "W.C." never dreaming that she was talking about a bathroom. He finally sought advice from the parish priest. They concluded that she must mean a Wayside Chapel. The lady received the following letter a few days later:

Dear Madam:

The W.C. is located 9 miles from the house, in the heart of a beautiful grove of trees. It will seat 150 people at one time, and is open on Tuesdays, Thursdays, and Sundays.

Some people bring their lunch and make a day of it. On Thursdays there is an organ accompaniment. The acoustics are very good. The slightest sound can be heard by everyone. It may interest you to know that my daughter met her husband at the W.C. We are now in the process of taking donations to purchase plush seats. We feel that this is a long felt need, as the present seats have holes in them.

My wife, being rather delicate, hasn't been able to attend regularly. It has been six months since she last went. Naturally, it pains her not to be able to go more often.

I will close now with the desire to accommodate you in every way possible, and will be happy to save you a seat either down front or near the door, as you prefer.

Subject: You know you're from Missouri when ...

1. You've never met any celebrities.
2. Everyone you know has been on a "Float Trip"
3. "Vacation" means driving to Silver Dollar City, Worlds of Fun or Six Flags.
4. You've seen all the biggest bands ten years AFTER they were popular.
5. You measure distance in minutes rather than miles.
6. Down South to you means Arkansas.
7. The phrase "I'm going to the Lake this weekend" only means one thing
8. You know several people who have hit a deer.
9. You think Missouri is spelled with an "ah" at the end.
10. Your school classes were canceled because of cold.
11. You know what "Party Cove" is.
12. our school classes were canceled because of heat.
13. You instinctively ask someone you've just met, "What High School did you go to?"
14. You've had to switch from "heat" to "A/C" the same day.
15. You think ethanol makes your truck "run a lot better."
16. You know what's knee-high by the Fourth of July.
17. You see people wear bib overalls at funerals.
18. You see a car running in the parking lot at the store with no one in it, no matter what time of the year.
19. You know in your heart that Mizzou can beat Nebraska in football.
20. You end your sentences with an unnecessary preposition. Example: "Where's my coat at?"
21. All the festivals across the state are named after a fruit, vegetable, or grain.
22. You install security lights on your house and garage and leave both unlocked.
23. You think of the major four food groups as beef, pork, beer, and jello salad with marshmallows.
24. You carry jumper cables in your car and know that everyone else should.

25. You went to skating parties as a kid.
26. You only own three spices: salt, pepper, and ketchup.
27. You design your kid's Halloween costume to fit over a snowsuit.
28. You think sexy lingerie is tube socks and a flannel nightie.
29. The local paper covers national and international headlines on one page, but requires six pages for sports.
30. You think I-44 is spelled and pronounced "farty-far." (St. Louis only)
31. You'll pay for your kids to go to college unless they want to go to KU.
32. You think that deer season is a national holiday.
33. You know that Concordia is halfway between Kansas City and Columbia, and Columbia is halfway between St. Louis and Kansas City, and the Warrenton outlet mall is halfway between Columbia and St. Louis.
34. You can't think of anything better than sitting on the porch in the middle of the summer during a thunderstorm.
35. You know which leaves make good toilet paper.
36. You've said, "It's not the heat, it's the humidity."
37. You know all four seasons: Almost Summer, Summer, Still Summer and Football.
38. You know if another Missourian is from the Bootheel, Ozarks, Eastern, Middle or Western Missouri soon as they open their mouth.
39. You know that Harry S. Truman, Walt Disney and Mark Twain are all from Missouri.
40. You failed world geography in school because you thought Cuba, Versailles, California, Nevada, Houston, Cabool, Louisiana, Springfield, and Mexico were cities in Missouri. (And they are!)
41. You think a traffic jam is ten cars waiting to pass a tractor.
42. You know what "HOME OF THE THROWED ROLL" means!!!
43. You actually get this and forward it to all your Missouri friends!!

4/5/03

Subject: your hotel bil

Clear DayNext time you think your hotel bill is too high you might want to consider this . . .

Husband and wife are traveling by car from Key West to Boston.

After almost twenty-four hours on the road, they're too tired to continue, and they decide to stop for a rest. They stop at a nice hotel and take a room, but they only plan to sleep for four hours and then get back on the road.

When they check out four hours later, the desk clerk hands them a bill for $350.00.

The man explodes and demands to know why the charge is so high. He tells the clerk although it's a nice hotel, the rooms certainly aren't worth $350.00! When the clerk tells him $350.00 is the standard rate, the man insists on speaking to the Manager.

The Manager appears, listens to the man, and then explains that the hotel has an Olympic-sized pool and a huge conference center that were available for the husband and wife to use.

"But we didn't use them," the man complains. "Well, they are here, and you could have," explains the Manager.

He goes on to explain they could have taken in one of the shows for which the hotel is famous. "The best entertainers from New York, Hollywood, and Las Vegas perform here," the Manager says. "But we didn't go to any of those shows," complains the man again.

"Well, we have them, and you could have," the Manager replies.

No matter what amenity the Manager mentions, the man replies, "But we didn't use it!"

The Manager is unmoved, and eventually the man gives up and agrees to pay. He writes a check and gives it to the Manager.

The Manager is surprised when he looks at the check. "But sir," he says, this check is only made out of $50.00."

"That's correct," says the man. "I charged you $300.00 for sleeping with my wife."

"But I didn't!" exclaims the Manager.

"Well too bad," the man replies. "She was here and you could have."

Texas Wisdom:

1. Never slap a man who's chewin' tobacco.
2. Good judgment comes from experience, and a lot of that comes from bad judgment.
3. Lettin' the cat outta the bag is a whole lot easier 'n puttin' it back in.
4. If you're ridin' ahead of the herd, take a look back every now and then to make sure it's still there.
5. If you get to thinkin' you're a person of some influence, try orderin' somebody else's dog around.
6. Never kick a cow chip on a hot day.
7. There's two theories to arguin' with a woman. Neither one works.
8. If you find yourself in a hole, the first thing to do is stop diggin'.
9. Don't squat with your spurs on.
10. It don't take a genius to spot a goat in a flock of sheep.
11. Always drink upstream from the herd.
12. Never miss a good chance to shut up.
13. There are three kinds of people: The ones that learn by reading, The few who learn by observation, and the rest of them who have to touch the fire to see for themselves if it's really hot.

You Know You're From Nebraska If ...

1. During a storm, you check the cattle before the kids.
2. You are related to more than half the community.
3. Your quarterback is hurt and you are hoping an update on his condition is the first thing on the six o'clock news, and it is.
4. You see your life savings to go to the Nebraska-Colorado game.
5. You can wear red and white overalls in public and not feel stupid.
6. There's a tornado warning & everyone is outside watching for the tornado.
7. You think Abraham Lincoln was named for the capital of Nebraska.
10. You go to the State Fair for your ONLY vacation.
11. You are on a first name basis with the county sheriff.
12. When little smokies are something you serve only for special occasions.
13. You go to the lake because you think it is like going to the ocean.
14. You have the number to the Co-op feed store on special dial.
15. You know what the "sea of red & white" is.
16. You think that using the elevator involves a truck.
17. Your mayor is also the doctor, barber, and/or dentist.
18. You listen to the weather forecast before picking out an outfit.
19. You call the wrong number by mistake & talk to the person for an hour anyway.
20. You know cow pies are not made of beef.
21. Your excuse for getting the kids out of school is that the cows got out.
22. Your early Morning Prayer covers rain, cattle, and Frank Solich.
23. You consider a romantic evening to include driving through McDonald's and renting a hunting instruction video.
    (Assuming that there is even a McDonald's in your county.) (MY COUNTY DOESN'T HAVE ONE!)
24. You want to buy manure.
25. You listen to "Paul Harvey" every day at noon.
26. Your nearest neighbor is in the next area code.
27. You know the difference between field corn and sweet corn, when they are still on the stalk.

28. You pick up all the free stuff at the State Fair.
29. Football schedules are checked before wedding dates are set
30. You can eat an ear of corn with no utensils in less than 20 seconds.
31. You wear your irrigation boots to church.
32. You know enough to get your driving done early on Sundays (before the Sunday drivers come out.)
33. It takes 3 minutes to reach your destination and it's clear across town.
34. You can tell the smell of a skunk and the smell of a feedlot apart.
35. True love means you'll ride on a tractor with him.
36. You consider a building to be a "mall" if it's bigger than the local Alco. (WE DON'T EVEN HAVE ONE OF THOSE IN MY COUNTY!!)
37. You call lunch "dinner" and dinner "supper."
38. You complain about interstate construction.
39. You think it's normal to get a side of spaghetti at a steakhouse.
40. You avoid Omaha because you're afraid of getting mugged.

1/12/01

Subject: They Walk Among Us

IDIOTS IN THE NEIGHBORHOOD:
I live in a semi-rural area. We recently had a new neighbor call the local
township administrative office to request the removal of the Deer Crossing
sign on our road.
The reason:
"Too many deer are being hit by cars out here!
I don't think this is a good place for them to be crossing anymore."
From Kingman, KS.

IDIOTS IN FOOD SERVICE:
My daughter went to a local Taco Bell and ordered a taco. She asked the
person behind the counter for "minimal lettuce." He said he was sorry, but
they only had iceberg.

He was a Chef
Yep . . . From Kansas City!

IDIOT SIGHTING:
I was at the airport, checking in at the gate when airport employee asked,
"Has anyone put anything in your baggage without your knowledge?
To which I replied, "If it was without my knowledge, how would I know?"
He smiled knowingly and nodded, "That's why we ask."
Happened in Birmingham, Ala

IDIOT SIGHTING:

The stoplight on the corner buzzes when its safe to cross the street.

I was crossing with an intellectually challenged coworker of mine.

She asked if I knew what the buzzer was for.

I explained that it signals blind people when the light is red.

Appalled, she responded, "What on earth blind people are doing driving?!"

She was probation officer in Wichita, KS

IDIOT SIGHTING:

At a good-bye luncheon for an old and dear coworker.

She was leaving the company due to "downsizing."

Our manager commented cheerfully, "This is fun. We should do this more often."

Not another word was spoken.

We just all looked at each other with that deer-in-headlights stare.

This was a bunch at Texas Instruments.

IDIOT SIGHTING:

I work with an individual who plugged her power strip back into itself and for the sake of her own life, couldn't understand why her system would not turn on.

A deputy with the Dallas County Sheriffs office no less.

IDIOT SIGHTING:

When my husband and I arrived at an automobile dealership to pick up our car, we were told they keys had been locked in it. We went to the service department and found a mechanic working feverishly to unlock the drivers side door. As I watched from the passenger side, I instinctively tried the door handle and discovered it was unlocked. "Hey," I announced to the technician, "it's open!"

His reply, "I know—I already got that side."

This was at the Ford dealership in Canton, Mississippi!

old Man In A Diner

A grizzled old man was eating in a truck stop when three Hell's Angels bikes walked in. The first walked up to the old man, pushed his cigarette into the old man's pie and then took a seat at the counter. The second walked up to the old man, spit into the old man's milk and then he took a seat at the counter. The third walked up to the old man, turned over the old man's plate, and then he took a seat at the counter. Without a word of protest, the old man quietly left the diner. Shortly thereafter, one of the bikers said to the waitress, "Humph, not much of a man, was he?" The waitress replied, "Not much of a truck driver either. He just backed his truck over three motorcycles."

He Said . . . She Said:

She said . . . Want a quickie?
He said . . . As opposed to what?

He said . . . I don't know why you wear a bra; you've got nothing to put in it.
   She said . . . You wear briefs, don't you?

She said . . . Do you love me just because my father left me a fortune?
He said . . . Not at all honey, I would love you no matter who left you the
   money.

He said . . . "This coffee isn't fit for a pig!"
She said . . . "No problem, I'll get you some that is."

She said . . . What do you mean by coming home half drunk?
He said . . . It's not my fault . . . I ran out of money.

He said . . . Since I first laid eyes on you, I've wanted to make love to you in the
   worst way. She said . . . Well, you succeeded.

He said . . . What have you been doing with all the grocery money I gave you?
She said . . . Turn sideways and look in the mirror.

He said . . . Why don't you tell me when you have an orgasm?
She said . . . I would, but you're never there.

She said . . . Let's go out and have some fun tonight.
He said . . . Okay, but if you get home before I do, leave the hallway light on.

Double Dose Disaster ...

A man went to the doctor's office to get a double dose of viagra. The doctor told him that he couldn't allow him a double dose. "Why not?" asked the man. "Because it's not safe," replied the doctor. "But I need it really bad," said the man.

"Well, why do you need it so badly?" asked the doctor ... The man said, "My girlfriend is coming into town on Friday; my ex-wife will be here on Saturday; and my wife is coming home on Sunday. I must have a double dose."

The doctor finally relented saying, "Okay, I'll give it to you, but you have to come in on Monday morning so that I can check you to see if there are any side effects."

Mon Monday, the man dragged himself in; his arm in a sling. The doctor asked, "What happened to you?"

Subject: The Perks of being over 40 :)

1. Kidnappers are not very interested in you.
2. In a hostage situation you are likely to be released first.
3. No one expects you to run—anywhere
4. People call at 9 PM and ask, "Did I wake you?"
5. People no longer view you as a hypochondriac.
6. There is noting left to learn the hard way.
7. Things you buy now won't wear out.
8. You can eat dinner at 4 P.M.
9. You can live without sex but not without glasses.
10. You enjoy hearing about other peoples operations.
11. You get into heated arguments about pension plans.
12. You have a party and the neighbors don't even realize it.
13. You no longer think of speed limits as a challenge.
14. You quit trying to hold your stomach in, no matter who walks into the room.
15. You sing along with elevator music.
16. Your eyes won't get much worse.
17. Your investment in health! Insurance is finally beginning to pay off.
18. Your joints are more accurate meteorologists than the national weather service.
19. Your secrets are safe with your friends because they can't

"OLD" IS WHEN . . . Your friends compliment you on your new alligator shoes and you're barefoot.

"OLD" IS WHEN . . . A sexy babe catches your fancy and your pacemaker opens the garage door.

"OLD" IS WHEN . . . Going bra-less pulls all the wrinkles out of your face.

"OLD" IS WHEN . . . You don't care where your spouse goes, just as long as you don't have to go along.

"OLD" IS WHEN . . . You are cautioned to slow down by the doctor instead of by the police.

"OLD" IS WHEN . . . "Getting a little action" means I don't need to take any fiber today.

"OLD" IS WHEN . . . "Getting lucky" means you find your car in the parking lot.

"OLD" IS WHEN . . . An *"all-nighter"* means not getting up to pee.

Subj: What marriage is about . . .

What marriage is about . . .

He ordered one hamburger, one order of French fries and one drink. The old man unwrapped the plain hamburger and carefully cut it in half.

He placed one half in front of his wife.

He then carefully counted out the French fries, dividing them into two piles and neatly placed one pile in front of his wife.

He took a sip of the drink, his wife took a sip and then set the cup down between them. As he began to eat his few bites of hamburger, the people around them kept looking over and whispering.

You could tell they were thinking, "That poor old couple—all they can afford is one meal for the two of them."

As the man began to eat his fries a young man came to the table. He politely offered to buy another meal for the old couple. The old man said they were just fine—They were used to sharing everything.

The surrounding people noticed the little old lady hadn't eaten a bite. She sat there watching her husband eat and occasionally taking turns sipping the drink.

Again the young man came over and begged them to let him buy another meal for them. This time the old woman said "No, thank you, we are used to sharing everything."

As the old man finished and was wiping his face neatly with the napkin, the young man again came over to the little old lady who had yet to eat a single bite of food and asked "What is it you are waiting for?"

She answered

(This is great)

"THE TEETH."

Having Mom over for Dinner

You don't even have to be a mother to enjoy this one . . . but it helps!

Brian Hester invited his mother over for dinner.

During the course of the meal, Brian's mother couldn't help but keep noticing how beautiful Brian's roommate, Stephanie, was. Mrs. Hester had long been suspicious of a relationship between Brian and Stephanie, and this had only made her more curious. Over the course of the evening, while watching the two react, Mrs. Hester started to wonder if there was more between Brian and Stephanie than met the eye.

Reading his mom's thoughts, Brian volunteered, "I know what you must be thinking, but I assure you Stephanie and I are just roommates."

About a week later, Stephanie came to Brian saying, "Ever since your mother came to dinner, I've been unable to find the beautiful silver gravy ladle. You don't suppose she took it, do you?"

Brian said, "Well, I doubt it, but I'll send her an e-mail just to be sure."

So he sat down and wrote:

Dear Mother:

I'm not saying that you "did" take the gravy ladle from the house, I'm not saying that you "did not" take the gravy ladle. But the fact remains that one has been missing ever since you were here for dinner.

Love, Brian

Several days later, Brian received a letter from his mother that read:

Dear Son:

I'm not saying that you "do" sleep with Stephanie, and I'm not saying that you "do not" sleep with Stephanie. But the fact remains that if she was sleeping in her own bed, she would have found the gravy ladle by now.

Love, Mom

LESSON OF THE DAY . . . NEVER LIE TO YOUR MOTHER!

Why Men Are Never Depressed:

Men Are Just Happier People—What do you expect from such simple creatures? Your last name stays put. The garage is all yours. Wedding plans take care of themselves. Chocolate is just another snack. You can be President. You can never be pregnant. You can wear a white T-shirt to a water park. You can wear NO shirt to a water park. Car mechanics tell you the truth. The world is your urinal. You never have to drive to another gas station restroom because this one is just too icky. You don't have to stop and think of which way to turn a nut on a bolt. Same work, more pay. Wrinkles add character. Wedding dress $5000. Tux rental-$100. People never stare at your chest when you're talking to them. The occasional well-rendered belch is practically expected. New shoes don't cut, blister, or mangle your feet. One mood all the time.!

Phone conversations are over in 30 seconds flat. You know stuff about tanks. A five-day vacation requires only one suitcase. You can open all your own jars. You get extra credit for the slightest act of thoughtfulness. If someone forgets to invite you, he or she can still be your friend.

Your underwear is $8.95 for a three-pack. Three pairs of shoes are more than enough. You almost never have strap problems in public. You are unable to see wrinkles in your clothes. Everything on your face stays its original color. The same hairstyle lasts for years, maybe decades. You only have to shave your face and neck.

You can play with toys all your life. Your belly usually hides your big hips. One wallet and one pair of shoes—one color for all seasons. You can wear shorts no matter how your legs look. You can "do" your nails with a pocket knife. You have freedom of choice concerning growing a mustache.

You can do Christmas shopping for 25 relatives on December 24 in 25 minutes.

No wonder men are happier.

Clear Day

Proud to be your Friend
Make sure you read all the way down to the last sentence, and don't skip ahead.

I've learned . . .
That life is like a roll of toilet paper. The closer it gets to the end, the faster it goes.

I've learned . . .
That we should be glad God doesn't give us everything we ask for.

I've learned . . .
That money doesn't buy class.

I've learned . . .
That it's those small daily happenings that make life so spectacular.

I've learned . . .
That under everyone's hard shell is someone who wants to be appreciated and loved.

I've learned . . .
That the Lord didn't do it all in one day. What makes me think I can?

I've learned . . .
That to ignore the facts does not change the facts.

I've learned . . .
That when you plan to get even with someone, you are only letting that person continue to hurt you.

I've learned . . .
That love, not time heals all wounds.

I've learned . . .
That the easiest way for me to grow as a person is to surround myself with people smarter than I am.

I've learned . . .
That everyone you meet deserves to be greeted with a smile.

I've learned . . .
That there's nothing sweeter than sleeping with your babies and feeling their breath on your cheeks.

I've learned . . .
That no one is perfect until you fall in love with them.

I've learned . . .
That life is tough, but I'm tougher.

I've learned . . .
That opportunities are never lost; someone will take the ones you miss.

I've learned . . .
That when you harbor bitterness, happiness will dock elsewhere.

I've learned . . .
That I wish I could have told my Dad that I love him one more time before he passed away.

I've learned . . .
That one should keep his words both soft and tender, because tomorrow he may have to eat them.

I've learned . . .
That a smile is an inexpensive way to improve your looks.

I've learned . . .
That I can't choose how I feel, but I can choose what I do about it.

I've learned . . .
That when your newly born child holds your little finger in his little fist, that you're hooked for life.

I've learned . . .
That everyone wants to live on top of the mountain, but all the happiness and growth occurs while you're climbing it.

I've learned . . .
That it is best to give advice in only two circumstances; when it is requested and when it is a life threatening situation.

I've learned . . .
That the less time I have to work with, the more things I get done.

6/18/03

A man and his wife were celebrating 50 years together. Their three kids, all very successful, agreed to a Sunday dinner in their honor.

"Happy Anniversary Mom and Dad," gushed son number one . . .

"Sorry I'm running late. I had an emergency at the hospital with a patient, you know how it is, and didn't have time to get you a gift."

"Not to worry," said the father. "The important thing is that we're all together today."

Son number two arrived and announced, "You and Mom look great, Dad I just flew in from Los Angeles between depositions and didn't have time to shop for you."

"It's nothing," said the father, "We're glad you were able to come."

Just then the daughter arrived, "Hello and happy anniversary! I'm sorry, but my boss is sending me out of town and I was really busy packing so I didn't have time to get you anything."

After they had finished dessert, the father said, "There's something your mother and I have wanted to tell you for a long time. You see, we were very poor. Despite this, we were able to send each of you to college. Throughout the years your mother and I knew that we loved each other very much, but we just never found the time to get married."

The three children gasped and all said, "You mean we're bastards?"

"Yep," said the father. "And cheap ones too."

Senior Moments!

Two elderly women were eating breakfast in a restaurant one morning.

Ethel noticed something funny about Mabel's ear and she said, "Mabel, did you know you've got a suppository in your left ear?"

Mabel answered, "I have a suppository?" She pulled it out and stared at it.

Then she said, "Ethel, I'm glad you saw this thing. Now I think I know where my hearing aid is."

When the husband finally died his wife put the usual death notice in the paper, but added that he died of gonorrhea.

No sooner were the papers delivered when a friend of the family phoned and omplained bitterly,

"You know very well that he died of diarrhea, not gonorrhea."

Replied the widow, "I nursed him night and day so of course I know he died of diarrhea, but I thought it would be better for posterity to remember him as a great lover rather than the big shit he always was."

An elderly couple were on a cruise and it was really stormy.

They were standing on the back of the boat, watching the moon, when a wave came up and washed the old woman overboard.

They searched for days and couldn't find her, so the captain sent the old man back to shore with the promise that he would notify him as soon as they found something.

Three weeks went by and finally the old man got a fax from the boat.

It read: "Sir, sorry to inform you, we found your wife dead at the bottom of the ocean.

We hauled her up to the deck and attached to her butt was an oyster and in it was a pearl worth $50,000, please advise."

The old man faxed back: "Send me the pearl and re-bait the trap."

A funeral service is being held for a woman who has just passed away.

At the end of the service, the pall bearers are carrying the casket out when they accidently bump into a wall, jarring the casket.

They hear a faint moan. They open the casket and find that the woman is actually alive!

She lives for ten more years, and then dies. Once again, a ceremony is held, and at the end of it, the pall bearers are again carrying out the casket.

As they carry the casket towards the door, the husband cries out: "Watch the wall!"

When I went to lunch today, I noticed an old lady sitting on a park bench sobbing her eyes out.

I stopped and asked her what was wrong. She said, "I have a 22 year old husband at home.

He makes love to me every morning and then gets up and makes me pancakes, sausage, fresh fruit and freshly ground coffee."

I said, "Well, then why are you crying?"

She said, "He makes me homemade soup for lunch and my favorite brownies and then makes love to me for half the afternoon."

I said, "Well, why are you crying?"

She said, "For dinner he makes me a gourmet meal with wine and my favorite dessert and then makes love to me until 2:00 a.m."

I said, "Well, why in the world would you be crying?"

She said, "I can't remember where I live!"

Two elderly ladies had been friends for many decades. Over the years they had shared all kinds of activities and adventures. Lately, their activities had been limited to meeting a few times a week to play cards.

One day they were playing cards when one looked at the other and said,

Now don't get mad at me . . . I know we've been friend for a long time . . . but I just can't think of your name! I've thought and thought, but I can't remember it. Please tell me what your name is."

Her friend glared at her. For at least three minutes she just stared and glared at her.

Finally she said "How soon do you need to know?"

The Senility Prayer

Grant me the senility to forget the people I never liked anyway, the good fortune to run into the ones I do, and the eyesight to tell the difference.

1/29/04

This is priceless!

RETARDED GRANDPARENTS
(this was actually reported by a teacher).

After Christmas, a teacher asked her young pupils how they spent their holiday away from school. One child wrote the following:

We always used to spend the holidays with Grandma and Grandpa. They used to live in a big brick house but Grandpa got retarded and they moved to Florida. Now they live a tin box and have rocks painted green to look like grass. They ride around on their bicycles and wear name tags because they don't know who they are anymore. They go to a building called a wrecked center, but they must have got it fixed because it is all okay now, and do exercises there, but they don't do them very well. There is a swimming pool too, but in it, they all jump up and down with hats on.

At their gate, there is a doll house with a little old man sitting in it.

He watches all day so nobody can escape.

Sometimes they sneak out.

They go cruising in their golf carts. Nobody there cooks, they just eat out. And, they eat the same thing every night: Early Birds.

Some of the people can't get out past the man in the doll house. The ones who do get out, bring food back to the wrecked center and call it pot luck.

My Grandma says that Grandpa worked all his life to earn his retardment and says I should work hard so I can be retarded someday too. When I earn my retardment, I want to be the man in the doll house. Then I will let people out so they can visit their grandchildren.

School Field Trip

A group of Kentucky second, third, and fourth graders, accompanied by two female teachers, went on a field trip to Churchill Downs, the famous Louisville race track, to see and learn about thoroughbred horses. When it was time to take the children to the bathroom, it was decided that the girls would go with one teacher and the boys would go with the other. The teacher assigned to the boys was waiting outside the men's room when one of the boys came out and told her that none of them could reach the urinal. Having no choice, she went inside, helped the boys with their pants, and began hoisting the boys up, one by one, holding onto their "wee-wees" to direct the flow away from their clothes. As she lifted one, she couldn't help but notice that he was unusually well endowed. Trying not to show that she was staring, the teacher said, "You must be in the fourth grade." "No, ma'am," he replied. "I'm riding Silver Arrow in the seventh race today."

only In America

1. Only in America . . . can a pizza get to your house faster than an ambulance.

2. Only in America . . . are there handicap parking places in front of a skating rink.

3. Only in America . . . do drugstores make the sick walk all the way to the back of the store to get their prescriptions while healthy people can buy cigarettes at the front.

4. Only in America . . . do people order double cheeseburgers, large fries, and a diet coke.

5. Only in America . . . do banks leave both doors open and then chain the pens to the counters.

6. Only in America . . . do we leave cars worth thousands of dollars in the driveway and put our useless junk in the garage.

7. Only in America . . . do we use answering machines to screen calls and then have call waiting so we won't miss a call from someone we didn't want to talk to in the first place.

8. Only in America . . . do we buy hot dogs in pancakes of ten and buns in packages of eight.

9. Only in America . . . do we use the word 'politics' to describe the process so well 'Poli' in Latin meaning 'many' and 'tics' meaning 'bloodsucking creatures'.

10. Only in America . . . do they have drive-up ATM machines with Braille lettering.

Ever Wonder

Why the sun lightens our hair, but darkens our skin?

Why women can't put on mascara with their mouth closed?

Why don't you ever see the headline "Psychic Wins Lottery"?

Why is "abbreviated" such a long word?

Why is it that doctors call what they do "practice"?

Why is that to stop Windows 98, you have to click on "Start"?

Why is lemon juice made with artificial flavor, and dishwashing liquid made with real lemons?

Why is the man who invests all your money called a broker?

Why is the time of day with the slowest traffic called rush hou?

Why isn't there mouse-flavored cat food?

When dog food is new and improved tasting, who tests it?

Why didn't Noah swat those two mosquitoes?

Why do they sterilize the needle for lethal injections?

You know that indestructible black box that is used on airplanes? Why don't they make the whole plane out of that stuff?!

Why don't sheep shrink when it rains?

Why are they called apartments when they are all stuck together?

If con is the opposite of pro, is Congress the opposite of progress?

If flying is so safe, why do they call the airport the terminal?

It was the first day of school and a new student named Martinez, the son of a Mexican restauranteur, entered the fourth grade.

The teacher said, "Let's begin by reviewing some American history. Who said "Give me Liberty, or give me Death?"

She saw a sea of blank faces, except for Martinez, who had his hand up.

"Patrick Henry, 1775."

"Very good! Who said 'Government of the people, by the people, for the people, shall not perish from the earth"?

Again, no response except from Martinez: "Abraham Lincoln, 1863.", said Martinez.

The teacher snapped at the class, "Class, you should be ashamed. Martinez, who is new to our country, knows more about its history than you do."

She heard a loud whisper: "Screw the Mexicans." "Who said that?" she demanded.

Martinez put his hand up. "Jim Bowie, 1836."

At that point, a student in the back said, "I'm gonna puke."

The teacher glares and asks "All right! Now, who said that?"

Again, Martinez says, "George Bush to the Japanese Prime Minister, 1991."

Now furious, another student yells, "Oh yeah? Suck this!"

Martinez jumps out of his chair waving his hand and shouts to the teacher,

"Bill Clinton, to Monica Lewinsky, 1997!"

Now with almost a mob hysteria someone said, "You little shit. If you say anything else, I'll kill you."

Martinez frantically yells at the top of his voice, "Gary Condit to Chandra Levy 2001."

The teacher fainted. And as the class gathered around the teacher on the floor, someone said, "Oh shit, we're in BIG trouble!"

Martinez said, "Saddam Hussein 2003."

Have you noticed anything fishy about the inspection teams who have arrived in Iraq?

They're all men!

How in the name of the United Nations does anyone expect men to find Saddam's stash? We all know that men have a blind spot when it comes to finding things. For crying' out loud! Men can't find the dirty clothes hamper. Men can't find the jar of jelly until it falls out of the cupboard and splatters on the floor . . . and these are the people we have sent into Iraq to search for hidden weapons of mass destruction?

I keep wondering why groups of mothers weren't sent in. Mothers can sniff out secrets quicker than a drug dog can find a gram of dope. Mothers can find gin bottles that dads have stashed in the attic beneath the rafters. They can sniff out a diary two rooms and one floor away. They can tell when the lid of a cookie jar has been disturbed and notice when a quarter inch slice has been shaved off a chocolate cake. A mother can smell alcohol on your breath before you get your key in the front door and can smell cigarette smoke from a block away. By examining laundry, a mother knows more about her kids than Sherlock Holmes. And if a mother wants an answer to question, she can read an offender's eyes quicker than a homicide detective. So . . . considering the value a mother could bring to an inspection team, why are we sending a bunch of old men who will rely on electronic equipment to scout out hidden threats?

My mother would walk in with a wooden soup spoon in one hand, grab Saddam by the ear, give it a good twist and snap, "Young man, do you have any weapons of mass destruction?" And God help him if he tried to lie to her. She'd march him down the street to some secret bunker and shove his nose into a nuclear weapon and say, "Uh, huh, and what do you call this, mister?" Whap! Thump! Whap! Whap! Whap! And she'd lay some stripes across his bare bottom with that soup spoon, then march him home in front of the whole of Baghdad. He'd not only come clean and apologize for lying about it, he'd cut every lawn in Baghdad for free for the whole summer.

Inspectors . . . You want the job done? Call my mother.

Hello! I have found a list of laws from every state that are just down right DUMB! Most of them are funny. I am not making these up.
ENJOY!!!

Alabama: Can not tie an Alligator to a Fire Hydrant

Alaska:

- Moose may not be viewed from an airplane.
- While it is legal to shoot bears, waking a sleeping bear for the purpose of taking a photograph is prohibited.
- It is considered an offense to push a live moose out of a moving airplane. A person may only carry a concealed slingshot if that person has received the appropriate license.

Arizona:

- Any misdemeanor committed while wearing a red mask is considered a felony.
- There is a possible 25 years in prison for cutting down a cactus
- Donkeys cannot sleep in bathtubs.
- When being attacked by a criminal or burglar, you may only protect yourself with the same weapon that the other person possesses.

Glendale
Cars may not be driven in reverse.

Mesa
It is illegal to smoke cigarettes within 15 feet of a public place unless you have a Class 12 liqueur license.

Tombstone
It is illegal for men and women over the age of 18 to have less than one missing tooth visible when smiling.

9/4/03

- Arkansas

- A man can legally beat his wife, but not more than once a month.
- Oral sex is considered to be sodomy.
- Alligators may not be kept in bathtubs

California

- It is a misdemeanor to shoot at any kind of game from a moving vehicle, unless the target is a whale.
- Women may not drive in a house coat.
- Males may not dress as a female unless a special permit is obtained from the sheriff.
- It is illegal to wipe one's car with used underwear.
- Persons classified as "ugly" may not walk down any street.
- Zoot suits are prohibited

Colorado

To own a dog over three months of age, one must obtain a lic

It is permissible to wear a holstered six-gun within city limits, except on Sunday, Election Day, or holidays.

Pueblo

- It is illegal to let a dandelion grow within the city limits.
- Sterling
- Cats may not run loose without having been fit with a taillight.

Connecticut

It is illegal to dispose of used razor blades.

Hartford

- You aren't allowed to cross a street while walking on your hands.
- You may not educate dogs.
- It is illegal for a man to kiss his wife on Sunday

New Britain

- It is illegal for fire trucks to exceed 25mph, even when going to a fire

This is to be Continued at a later time!

A Florida couple, both well into their 80s, go to a sex therapist's office. The doctor asks, "What can I do for you?"

The man says, "Will you watch us have sexual intercourse?"

The doctor raises both eyebrows, but he is so amazed that such an elderly couple is asking for sexual advice that he agrees.

When the couple finishes, the doctor says, "There's absolutely nothing wrong with the way you have intercourse." He thanks them for coming, he wishes them good luck, he charges them $50 and he says goodbye.

The next week, however, the couple returns and asks the sex therapist to watch again. The sex therapist is a bit puzzled, but agrees.

This happens several weeks in a row. The couple makes an appointment, has intercourse with no problems, pays the doctor, then leave.

Finally, after 5 or 6 weeks of this routine, the doctor says, "I'm sorry, but I have to ask. Just what are you trying to find out?"

The old man says, "We're not trying to find out anything. She's married and we can't go to her house. I'm married and we can't go to my house. The Holiday Inn charges $98. The Hilton charges $139. We do it here for $50, and I get $43 back from Medicare."

The cowboy Boots

(Anyone who has ever dressed a child will love this: parents and teachers alike)

Did you hear about the Texas teacher who was helping one of her kindergarten students put on his cowboy boots? He asked for help and she could see why. Even with her pulling and him pushing, the little boots still didn't want to go on. By the time they got the second boot on, she had worked up a sweat.

She almost cried when the little boy said, "Teacher, they're on the wrong feet." She looked, and sure enough, they were. It wasn't any easier pulling the boots off than it was putting them on. She managed to keep her cool as, together, they worked to get the boots back on, this time on the right feet.

He then announced, "These aren't my boots." She bit her tongue, rather than get right in his face and scream, "Why didn't you say so?", like she wanted to. Once again she struggled to help him pull the ill-fitting boots off his little feet. No sooner had they gotten the boots off when he said, "They're my brother's boots. My Mom made me wear 'em."

Now she didn't know if she should laugh or cry. But she mustered up what grace and courage she had left to wrestle the boots on his feet again.

Helping him into his coat, she asked, "Now, where are your mittens?" He said, "I stuffed 'em in the toes of my boots." She will be eligible for parole in three years.

Cowboy

A cowboy was herding his cows in a remote pasture when suddenly a brand-new BMW advanced out of a dust cloud towards him. The driver, a young man in a Brioni suit, Gucci shoes, Ray Ban sunglasses and YSL tie, leans out the window and asks the cowboy,

"If I tell you exactly how many cows and calves you have in your herd, will you give me a calf?"

The cowboy looks at the man, obviously a yuppie, then looks at his peacefully grazing herd and calmly answers,

"Sure, Why not?"

The yuppie parks his car, whips out his Dell notebook computer, connects it to his Cingular RAZR V3 cell phone, and surfs to a NASA page on the Internet, where he calls up a GPS satellite navigation system to get an exact fix on his location which he then feeds to another NASA satellite that scans the area in an ultra-high-resolution photo. The young man then opens the digital photo in Adobe Photoshop and exports it to an image processing facility in Hamburg, Germany.

Within seconds, he receives an email on his Palm Pilot that the image has been processed and the data stored.

He then accesses a MS-SQL database through an ODBC connected Excel spreadsheet with email on his Blackberry and, after a few minutes, receives a response.

Finally, he prints out a full-color, 150-page report on his hi-tech, miniaturized HP Laser Jet printer and finally turns to the cowboy and says,

"You have exactly 1,586 cows and calves."

"That's right. Well, I guess you can take one of my calves," says the cowboy.

He watches the young man select one of the animals and looks on amused as the young man stuffs it into the trunk of his car.

Then the cowboy says to the young man,

"Hey, if I can tell you exactly what your business is, will you give me back my calf?"

The young man thinks about it for a second and then says,

"Okay, why not?"

You're a Congressman for the U.S. Government", says the cowboy.

"Wow! That's correct," says the yuppie, "but how did you guess that?"

"No guessing required." answered the cowboy.

"You showed up here even though nobody called you; you want to get paid for an answer I already knew, to a question I never asked. You tried to show me how much smarter than me you are; and you don't know a thing about cows . . .

Now give me back my dog!

Clear Day

A big Texan stopped at a local restaurant following a day roaming around in Mexico. While sipping his tequila, he noticed a sizzling, scrumptious looking platter being served at the next table.

Not only did it look good, the smell was wonderful. He asked the waiter, "What is that you just served?" The waiter replied, "Ah senior, you have excellent taste! Those are called Cojones de Toro, bull's testicles from the bullfight this morning. A delicacy!"

The cowboy said, "What the heck, bring me an order." The waiter replied, "I am so sorry senor. There is only one serving per day because there is only one bullfight each morning. If you come early and place your order, we will be sure to save you this delicacy."

The next morning, the cowboy returned, placed his order, and that evening was served the one and only special delicacy of the day. After a few bites, inspecting his platter, he called to the waiter and said, "These are delicious, but they are much, much smaller than the ones I saw you serve yesterday."

The waiter shrugged his shoulders and replied, "Si Senor. Sometimes the bull wins.

Subject: good, better, best

GOOD

Madison, WI policeman had a perfect spot to watch for speeders, but wasn't getting many. Then he discovered the problem—a 12-year-old boy was standing up the road with a hand painted sign, which read "RADAR TRAP AHEAD". The officer also found the boy had an accomplice who was a bit further down the road with a sign reading "TIPS" and a bucket full of money. (And we used to just sell lemonade!)

BETTER

A motorist was mailed a picture of his car speeding through an automated radar post in La Crosse, WI. A $40 speeding ticket was included. Being cute, he sent the police department a picture of $40. The police responded with another mailed photo of handcuffs.

BEST

A young woman was pulled over for speeding. As a Wisconsin State Trooper Officer walked to her car window, flipping open his ticket book, she said, "I bet you are going to sell me a ticket to the State Troopers Ball." He replied, "Wisconsin State Troopers don't have balls." There was a moment of silence. He then closed his book, got back in his patrol car and left.

A first grade teacher in Northern Illinois explains to her class that she is a Cubs fan. She asks her students to raise their hands if they, too, are cubs fan everyone in the class raises their hand except one little girl.

The teacher looks at the girl with surprise and says, "Janie, why didn't raise your hand?"

"Because I'm not a Cubs fan," she replied.

The teacher, still shocked, asked, "Well, if you are not a Cubs fan, then who are you a fan of?"

"I am a Cardinal fan and proud of it," Janie replied.

The teacher could not believe her ears. "Janie, why pray tell are You a Cardinal fan?"

"Because my Mom is a Cardinal fan, and my dad is a Cardinal fan, So I'm a Cardinal fan too!"

"Well," said the teacher in an obviously annoyed tone, "that is no reason for you to be a Cardinal fan. You don't have to be just like your parents all of the time. What if your Mom were a moron and your dad were a moron, what would you be then?"

"Then," Janie smiled, "I'd be a Cubs fan."

A Cardinals fan and a Cubs fan are driving, at night, on a twisty, dark road. Both are driving too fast for the conditions and collide on a sharp bend in the road. To the amazement of both, they are unscratched, though their cars are both destroyed. In celebration of their luck, both agree to put aside their dislike for the other from that moment on. At this point, the Cardinals fan goes to the trunk and gets a 12 year old bottle of Whiskey. He hands the bottle to the Cubs fan, who exclaims, "may the Cubs and Cardinals live together forever, in peace, and harmony." The Cubs fan then tips the bottle and gulps half of the bottle down. Still flabbergasted over the whole thing, he goes to hand the bottle back to the Cardinals fan, who replies: "no thanks, I'll just wait till the Police get here."